HOME ON

HUCKLEBERRY HILL

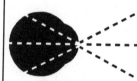

THE MATCHMAKERS OF
HUCKLEBERRY HILL

HOME ON
HUCKLEBERRY HILL

JENNIFER BECKSTRAND

KENNEBEC LARGE PRINT
A part of Gale, a Cengage Company

GALE
A Cengage Company

Farmington Hills, Mich • San Francisco • New York • Waterville, Maine
Meriden, Conn • Mason, Ohio • Chicago

Kennebec Large Print® Superior Collection.
The text of this Large Print edition is unabridged.
Other aspects of the book may vary from the original edition.
Set in 16 pt. Plantin.

LIBRARY OF CONGRESS CIP DATA ON FILE.
CATALOGUING IN PUBLICATION FOR THIS BOOK
IS AVAILABLE FROM THE LIBRARY OF CONGRESS

ISBN-13: 978-1-4328-5547-5 (softcover)

Published in 2018 by arrangement with Zebra Books, an imprint of
Kensington Publishing Corp.

Printed in Mexico
1 2 3 4 5 6 7 22 21 20 19 18

HOME ON HUCKLEBERRY HILL

CHAPTER ONE

Anna Helmuth picked up a tub of colorful mint drops from the shelf and shook the plastic container to see what they sounded like. You could always tell how fresh something was by the way it rattled around in its package. "Felty," she said, holding the tub of mints closer to her ear. She was only eighty-five, but she didn't hear as well as she used to. "I'm afraid there's trouble brewing at Mary Anne and Jethro's house. I can feel it in my bones."

Felty stood next to Anna in the candy aisle, listening to a tub of peanut clusters. "What kind of trouble, Annie-Banannie? Are you sure it's not your arthritis acting up?"

"*Jah,* I'm sure. My bones have never steered me wrong, except for that one time I thought there was a mountain man living in our attic."

Felty set the peanut clusters in the basket

hung over his arm and picked up a tub of Jersey cherry candies. They were very loud. "Trouble is nothing new for Mary Anne and Jethro. It's been four years since they found out they can't have a *buplie*."

"I know, dear, but this is something different. Something worse."

Felty furrowed his brow, either because he was concentrating on the sound of a tub of candy corns or because he was concerned for his granddaughter, Mary Anne. "What's the matter?"

"They've been married for six years, but I don't think they like each other anymore."

Felty put the candy corns in his basket. No pantry should ever be without candy corns. "Well, Annie, all married couples go through that. There was a time when I didn't like you very much."

Anna grinned. "And I didn't like you. You always had to be right."

"And you were so stubborn."

The bishop's wife, Christina Yoder, shuffled down the aisle and leaned past Anna to grab a tub of gummy worms. "You two don't like each other?" she said, a look of deep concern traveling across her features.

"Only when she hogs the covers," Felty said, giving Anna a wink. Anna scrunched her lips to one side of her face. Felty was the one who stole the covers.

"We used to not like each other," Anna said, patting Christina on the shoulder and sort of nudging her in the other direction. Some people just didn't know how to stay out of a private conversation.

Christina strolled away but kept her ear turned toward them. For sure and certain she'd try to listen in while she did her shopping.

Anna smiled at Felty. "Remember when I made you sleep in the barn?"

"Remember when I used to slam the door as hard as I could?"

"There was a time when I wished the Amish believed in divorce," Anna said. "You were the last person in the world I wanted to spend the rest of my life with."

Anna heard a sound behind her and turned to see Dorothy Raber staring at both of them. "Is everything okay?" Dorothy said, pasting a smile on her face as if determined not to act suspicious.

"*Jah,*" Felty said, sliding a tub of lemon drops into his basket. "We're picking out candy for the great-grandchildren."

Dorothy pursed her lips. "*Ach.* Okay. I'm *froh* to hear it." She hesitated, then reached out and snatched a tub of candy from the shelf above Anna's head. She obviously wanted them to believe she'd come down this aisle to get a treat instead of to eavesdrop on their conversation, but she didn't fool Anna. Nobody bought licorice gumdrops on purpose.

Felty shook a tub of peach rings. They didn't make much noise. "I'm *froh* you didn't divorce me, Annie. I was wonderful hard to live with."

"And so was I. It's easy to see why so many *Englischers* split up."

David Eicher marched down the aisle, grimacing as if he'd eaten a pickle for breakfast. David had never forgiven Anna for matching her grandson, Aden, with David's daughter, Lily, even though Aden and Lily were very happily married with a lovely organic farm and three children.

"*Hallo,* David," Felty said, setting the stale peach rings back on the shelf.

David shook Felty's hand, though he acted as if he were petting a snake. "My wife is in the bread aisle, and she is wonderful concerned. She wanted me to remind you that you'll get excommunicated if you get a divorce."

Anna couldn't help but be impressed. Gossip traveled faster than a runaway horse in Amish country, but it seemingly traveled like lightning in an Amish grocery store.

Unfortunately, Mary Anne and Jethro were in trouble, and Anna had no time for such nonsense. "Now, David," she said. "Nothing has been decided yet. We'll let you know the minute it is."

David narrowed his eyes and opened his mouth as if he wanted to give them a lecture.

Anna didn't have time for a lecture. "You'd better go find Martha. I hear they have a special on Friendship Bread."

He shook his head, turned around, and walked away. "It's against the *Ordnung*," he muttered.

She wanted to point out that gossip was against the *Ordnung* too, but she couldn't, because it wasn't.

When David disappeared from sight, Anna leaned closer to Felty so she could whisper, even though whispering was very inconvenient and Felty didn't hear well. Was it too much to expect of their neighbors to leave them alone for five minutes so they could have a private conversation? "There is going to be trouble at Mary Anne and Jethro's house. We've got to do something about it."

"What can we do, Annie? Jethro is already acting like an old man, and Mary Anne is unhappy in a way I can't begin to guess."

Anna studied the nutrition information

11

on a tub of chocolate taffy. It was a short read. "Jethro and Mary Anne can't stand each other. I'll have to play matchmaker."

"For two people who are already married?"

Anna nodded. "We had to fall in love with each other again."

"I don't know how we did it, but I love you now more than ever, Annie-Banannie."

Anna furrowed her brow. There seemed to be some sort of silent gathering on the next aisle over. She put her finger to her lips, took Felty's hand, and tiptoed to the end of the aisle. She peeked into the next aisle over. No less than fifteen people stood in a little clump with their ears turned toward the aisle where Anna and Felty had just been standing. Anna covered her mouth to stifle a giggle. "*Ach,* Felty," she whispered. "We've given them all a little excitement to start their day. It does my heart good to see it." They shuffled quietly to the front counter, where young Tobias Raber waited to total their ten tubs of candy. "How long before they realize we're not there anymore?" she said.

Felty stroked his beard. "We should probably run to the buggy just to be safe."

CHAPTER TWO

Mary Anne lit the candles and stood back to admire her work. Two salmon filets rested on a bed of herbed-butter asparagus with grilled lemon slices for garnish. The vegetable tray was a work of art, with crinkle-cut carrots and radishes cut in the shape of rosebuds. A hollowed-out cabbage held ranch dip, and the cucumbers looked like little flowers because she'd scored them with her special tool. She'd put extra cheese in the funeral potatoes so they were swimming in a pool of cheese sauce.

She'd even made her special rainbow Jell-O parfaits, with six kinds of Jell-O, for dessert. Rainbow parfaits took an indecent amount of time to make, but they were so beautiful and just right for a once-a-year event. Mary Anne was convinced Jethro had fallen in love with her over a rainbow parfait seven years ago. Today she'd made four parfaits just to be sure she got at least two perfectly right.

The vanilla-scented candles had been a spark of inspiration. The Amish didn't use candles much anymore. It was too easy to start a fire. But according to the package, vanilla "filled the air with romance." The perfect thing for a sixth anniversary.

Mary Anne glanced at the clock. Without fail, Jethro walked through the front door every day at five. He worked at a carpentry shop in Shawano, and the van brought him home right on time. She was always sure to have dinner ready for him as he walked through the door. He worked so hard. It was the least she could do.

Jethro seemed to have a lot on his mind lately, as if he barely even noticed her because he had so many worries floating around in his head. Tonight was going to be different. Tonight, his eyes would light up at the sight of salmon and asparagus, and he'd remember he was happy he'd married her. Maybe he'd call her his "precious ruby" like he did when they were first married. Maybe he'd hold her hand and run his fingers across her knuckles and tell her that she was the only woman in the world for him. Maybe he still loved her. Maybe the funeral potatoes would help him remember.

She flinched when she heard the door

open, and her heart did a little somersault. Jethro was going to be so happy.

"Mary Anne?" he called.

She was so excited, she ran into the living room and threw her arms around his neck. She loved how he always smelled of cedar and pine.

He raised both eyebrows and studied her face. "*Hallo.* Did you have a *gute* day?"

Mary Anne was practically bouncing. "The best day. Come and see what I made for dinner."

He hung his hat on the hook by the door and smoothed his fingers through his hair with a sheepish twist to his lips. "*Ach,* Mary Anne, I'm sorry. I already ate."

"You . . . already ate?"

He grimaced. "I should have told you this morning. Marty and I grabbed McDonald's right after work. Randall is picking me up in five minutes. We're going fishing. They both want to try out my new fishing pole."

Mary Anne bit down on her tongue. Hard — which was a very bad idea because it was difficult to eat with a severed tongue. She'd heard nothing but "the new fishing pole" for a whole week. Jethro had spent four hundred dollars on that new fishing pole, and he was so proud of it, you would have thought he'd given birth to a baby. "I hoped we could have a nice dinner together to-night."

Jethro patted his stomach. "It smells wonderful *gute,* but I couldn't eat another bite. I had two Big Macs and a large fries." He headed down the hall, no doubt to retrieve his fishing pole, which he kept on the bed in the spare bedroom. Why not? There wasn't any need for a spare bedroom in the Neuenschwander house. "Eat without me, and don't bother waiting up. We'll be out late."

Standing as if her feet were glued to the floor, Mary Anne watched Jethro tromp down the hall. It felt as if two invisible weights were attached to her shoulders and she couldn't shrug them off. She wouldn't be surprised if they dragged her right through the floor. She'd felt so heavy for such a long time.

Jethro came back carrying his fishing pole and tackle box. She didn't know how she managed to move, but she took his jacket and fishing hat from the hook and handed them to him. He smiled as if she'd made him very happy. "*Denki,* Mary Anne. I will see you in the morning."

He opened the door and blew out of the house like a whirlwind — just the way he'd come in. And then he was gone, having spent less than two minutes with her on their sixth anniversary. It hadn't quite gone the way she'd planned it.

She stood as still as stone in the silence, listening to the kitchen clock beat out its predictable, dependable cadence. She'd given that clock to Jethro for his birthday last September. Instead of numbers, the hands pointed to a different kind of fish for each hour of the day. Even though it had cost more than a regular clock, Jethro had loved it. It was the last real enthusiasm he'd shown toward her about anything. The familiar ache of guilt and anger and helplessness squeezed at her heart. Why did she even try anymore?

Mary Anne gazed through the front window curtains and watched as Jethro carefully laid his brand-new fishing pole in the back of Randall's truck, then climbed in the cab. Randall was the best kind of friend, an *Englischer* who could drive Jethro to all his favorite fishing spots. Mary Anne, on the other hand, was completely useless to her own husband. She made dinners he didn't eat and she couldn't give him the son he'd always wanted.

She wandered into the kitchen, wishing she had a camera. She'd take a picture of the beautiful food sitting on the lace tablecloth lit by the light of three vanilla candles. Then she'd post it on her blog so other people could appreciate all the work she'd gone to.

Mary Anne slumped her shoulders. She didn't have a camera or a computer or a blog. *Ach* — it was the life of an Amish *fraa,* having to keep all this wonderfulness to herself. Her husband hadn't even seen it.

The candle flames fluttered as Mary Anne sat down at the table and picked up her spoon. She scooped a spoonful of potatoes from the casserole dish and took a bite. The potatoes had probably been her first mistake. Who served funeral potatoes for an anniversary dinner?

She took another bite. She'd gotten the salt just right this time, and the hint of onion and cream of mushroom soup was *appeditlich.* Jethro would have liked them, funeral or no funeral.

She squared her shoulders. Because she was the only one eating them, it didn't really matter what Jethro thought, did it? She had made them to please him, but was his opinion any more important than hers? She liked the potatoes. That was enough to call her dinner a success.

Jethro wasn't here to scold her, so she ate her helping of funeral potatoes right out of the pan. She pressed her lips together and glanced behind her as if she might catch someone spying on her. With her fork, she skimmed all that golden, crusty, melted cheese off the top, and ate every oily bite. She'd never felt so rebellious.

She had craved Jethro's approval for years, but all she'd gotten was criticism. She'd ached for his affection, only to be rewarded with indifference. He paid more attention to that new fishing pole than he did to her.

The candlelight seemed to grow brighter as she finished up the last of her cheese and glanced at the veggie tray. It didn't matter if her radishes were shaped like roses. Vegetables were for well-behaved people, and tonight she was feeling a little disorderly.

She went to the fridge, took out one of her rainbow parfaits, and held it up to the candlelight. The different layers of Jell-O in the small cup sparkled like sunshine on a lake. She really had outdone herself. It was the most beautiful dessert anyone could wish for.

It was almost too pretty to eat. Mary Anne took the parfait to the table and admired it for a few minutes before picking up her spoon and eating the whole thing in seven bites, telling herself one thing she disliked about Jethro with every bite. Another parfait came out of the fridge, and then the last two. She ate every one, not even feeling guilty that she hadn't saved one for Jethro.

As her *Englisch* friend Pammy said, you snooze, you lose.

Maybe she was completely useless to Jethro, but she made a wonderful *gute* rainbow parfait, all the same.

She frowned. Maybe she *was* completely useless to Jethro, but wasn't it also true that Jethro was completely useless to her? Of course, he went to work every day to earn money, but then he spent it on fishing poles and worms and went fishing when he could have been home eating rainbow parfaits with her.

The truth hit her like a tree branch to the head.

Oh, *sis yuscht.*

She couldn't stand to live this life anymore.

Sometimes during the day, she felt so trapped that she would ball her hands into fists and scream at the top of her lungs at an empty house. Some nights she was so lonely, she'd sneak out to the barn and sit with the cow just to have someone to talk to — someone who wouldn't chastise her or tell her she was being silly for feeling the way she did. She'd tried, she'd really tried to stick with Jethro, to be a *gute* Amish *fraa,* but her desperation was mounting. She just couldn't do it anymore.

Should she be concerned that such a thought didn't make her feel guilty?

Jethro was a nice person, seldom grumpy, but often quiet and — might as well face it — boring — especially in the last four years. But more than that, she was a huge disappointment to him. She cooked for him and cleaned his house, but otherwise he didn't especially care whether she was around or not. How had she not realized this about him when they were dating?

She didn't love him.

And she wasn't going to wait for him to notice her. As of right now, she didn't care if he noticed her or not. Of course, there was the tricky thing about being married to him and being Amish. They were stuck with each other. But that didn't mean they had to stick by each other.

Sitting in her quiet kitchen feeling a little sick to her stomach, she had the terrifying thought that she wanted to live for her own happiness without regard to Jethro at all. Her heart all but leaped out of her chest. She had been sufficiently miserable for years, but was she brave enough to do something about it?

Did she have the courage to defy the *gmayna,* her family, and her husband?

Nae, of course she didn't.

But courage didn't matter. If she stayed in this house even for one more day, she thought she might shrivel up into a little, wrinkly ball and blow away with the wind. She might not have the courage to leave, but she didn't have the strength to stay.

Nothing mattered now but her escape.

Jethro woke with a start when the alarm clock rang. He'd gone to bed late last night or, more accurately, early this morning. He turned over, pressed the button on the clock, and stretched his arms over his head. He was exhausted, but it was a *gute* kind of tired after a *wunderbarr* night of fishing. His new fishing pole had performed better than he'd even dreamed. It was worth every penny he had spent on it.

His fishing pole lay beside him on the bed. He'd gotten in late and hadn't wanted to disturb Mary Anne, so he'd gone to sleep in the spare bedroom with his fishing pole beside him like a teddy bear. He couldn't really cuddle his fishing pole, but he took comfort that it was in a safe place. He had gotten the feeling Mary Anne hadn't been too happy about storing his fishing pole on the bed in the spare bedroom, but their dream for filling that bedroom with children was gone, so what was wrong with his fishing pole?

Even in the dim light, Jethro could still make out the faintest outline of Mary Anne's old artwork on the walls. Mary Anne had been so excited to have a baby that she had started painting the walls of the nursery before she'd even gotten pregnant. She loved to paint, though she hadn't done much of it lately. She'd drawn a whole farmyard of animals on the walls — orange and black chickens, fat cows with ribbons around their necks, shiny pink pigs with smiles on their faces. Jethro had teased her that pigs didn't know how to smile, but that hadn't stopped her from painting them with grins on their snouts. When she had the miscarriage and the doctor had told them they couldn't have children, Jethro had painted two coats of white over the whole scene, so Mary Anne wouldn't have a daily reminder of the pain. The whole thing was too bad. It had been a wonderful pretty farm scene.

Jethro dragged his feet into the bathroom where he showered and shaved any traces of a mustache off his face. He got dressed and made his way to the kitchen, where Mary

Anne would have breakfast and *kaffee* waiting for him.

It was their daily routine. Every morning, she got up and milked the cow while he got ready for work. Then she would make him breakfast and a sack lunch. When they were first married, she'd put all sorts of strange things in his lunch, like crackers with unusual cheese or hummus or a chicken salad with kale and something called quinoa. He always liked what she made him, but it had concerned him that she spent so much money on his lunch. After the miscarriage, he had told her not to bother with the fancy stuff. It was too much work for her and money she didn't need to spend. He'd taken a plain turkey sandwich to work ever since.

The kitchen was dark. No pot of *kaffee* on the stove. No bacon sizzling in the pan. Jethro drew his brows together. Was Mary Anne still milking? It wasn't like her to be late with his breakfast. That van came at 7:30 sharp every morning.

He went down the hall to the bedroom. The gray blanket was pulled tightly across the sheets and tucked in neatly at the corners. She must still be milking. He stomped back to the kitchen, trying not to let himself get irritated, but didn't Mary

Anne care that he needed his *kaffee* before he left? It had been a late night. How did she expect him to stay awake at work?

He pulled the *kaffee* pot off the shelf. How hard would it be to figure out how to make *kaffee*? Then again, how hard would it have been for Mary Anne to start the *kaffee* before she went out to milk? Mary Anne had always made the *kaffee.* He didn't know what to do. He shouldn't have banged the pot on the counter so hard, but what was taking her so long?

He reached out to open the fridge and noticed a note taped to the door. It was written on some of the bright pink notepaper Mary Anne had bought without consulting him. He couldn't convince her that plain white notebook paper was just as useful and much cheaper. Mary Anne's handwriting was neat and easy to read, even if she did dot her *i*s with hearts and put a curlicue on the tail of every word. *"Jethro, there is salmon and asparagus in the fridge left over from dinner last night. That should hold you over for a couple of days, plus a whole plate of vegetables and three-fourths of a pan of funeral potatoes. It turns out they were a very appropriate dish. There are no parfaits, but I am happy to report that they were delicious — all four of them. Good luck after that. Mary*

Anne. P.S. I've taken the two hundred dollars from the jar in your underwear drawer. I'll need it more than you do."

Jethro snatched the note off the fridge and read it again. He couldn't make heads or tails of it. Growling like a bear, he marched down the hall to the bedroom and opened his underwear drawer. The jar was there, but no money, though his underwear was folded neatly like always. If she'd taken the rainy-day money to buy pink stationery, he'd be very annoyed.

He marched back into the kitchen and opened the fridge. A platter covered in plastic wrap sat on the top shelf. Two plump salmon filets rested on a bed of grilled asparagus looking like something right out of a magazine. Why had she gone to all that trouble? He was perfectly happy with shepherd's pie and corn for dinner, or even his latest catch with a little salt, cooked on the grill.

He took the tray of vegetables off the refrigerator shelf. Mary Anne had cut the radishes into rose shapes. They looked pretty but had surely taken her hours to create. He couldn't understand why she wasted so much time trying to make the food look like something it wasn't. A radish tasted the same whether it was shaped like a rose or not.

Pure hunger drove him to tear the plastic wrap off the veggie tray, pick up a crinkle-cut carrot, and bury it halfway into the dip — the dip in a bowl made from a hollowed-out cabbage. He shook his head and finished the carrot off in three bites. Three radishes and four cucumbers later, he still had no idea what was going on.

Where in the world was his wife, and what had she done with his two hundred dollars?

The van would be here in fifteen minutes. He wouldn't get his *kaffee* now, and he needed to find Mary Anne before he had a nervous breakdown.

After grabbing one more carrot from the plate, he stormed out the back door to the barn. Daisy had been milked because a full bucket sat on the floor next to the door, but Mary Anne wasn't in the barn. He had just exhausted his list of places he thought to look for his wife. She might have left him a little more information in that fancy note of hers.

Growing more and more puzzled and more and more irritated, he stepped outside and scanned his backyard and the woods behind the house. Through the trees, he could just make out a light green tent and a wisp of smoke hanging in the air. Was somebody camping on his property? Was it Mary Anne?

He almost laughed at that thought. Almost. Mary Anne hated to camp. She'd rather go to the dentist than sleep in a tent.

Jethro jogged toward the tent. His time was running out, and he wasn't any closer to finding his wife — until he did.

His missing *fraa* sat on a generous-size boulder just outside the tent door, tending a fire in their small fire pit. How had she dragged the fire pit all the way out here? It wasn't light. A piece of toast sizzled on a griddle that sat on top of the fire pit grate, and a pot that looked suspiciously like it might contain *kaffee* sat beside the griddle.

Mary Anne furrowed her brow and pressed her lips together as if she wasn't all that happy to see him. And maybe she was feeling a little guilty for not brewing him his own pot of *kaffee.*

"What are you doing?" he snapped, not even trying to hide his irritation.

She poked at the bread with a spatula while doing a good imitation of a smile. "Making Gruyère-and-bacon-stuffed French toast. It's a recipe I've wanted to try for a long time. Doesn't it smell good?"

It did smell good, but Jethro wasn't going

28

to be distracted by the smell of an imported cheese that had probably cost twenty dollars a pound. "That's not what I meant, and you know it. Why are you out here?"

Her fake smile stayed in place, even though he could see the uneasiness in her eyes. "Did you get my note?"

"Didn't understand a word."

"*Ach.* I'm sorry. I tried to be plain. There's salmon and vegetables and potatoes in the fridge. You can eat leftovers for days, and then there's always McDonald's if you get desperate."

"Who cares about what food is in the fridge?"

"You might care tonight after work, when you're hungry." She flipped over her piece of French toast, and the melty cheese dribbled onto the griddle. The sizzle hid the sound of his stomach growling.

She wasn't making any sense, and he wasn't any closer to understanding why he hadn't gotten his *kaffee* this morning. He glanced inside the tent to see a pillow and a sleeping bag — one of his nice, hundred-dollar sleeping bags — sitting on top of his nice, hundred-dollar cot. "That's my stuff," he said.

She stiffened her spine so fast, he could almost hear it snap. "*Ach, vell.* When you bought it, you said it was for the two of us, so I think I'm entitled. You insisted on the eight-man tent because you wanted to have plenty of room even though there would only ever be the two of us. I'm *froh* you spent the extra money. The tent is very roomy."

"But you hate to camp." The strangeness of the conversation didn't escape him. Mary Anne was talking about tents and French toast and ignoring the fact that she was sitting on a boulder in the middle of the woods when there was no *gute* reason for her to be here and no explanation in sight.

She tapped her spatula against the griddle, three, four, five times, for sure and certain trying to annoy him. She must not have realized he couldn't have gotten any more annoyed if the neighbor's dog had done his business in the yard.

He clenched his teeth. *She* seemed to be annoyed with *him.* She had some nerve, especially when he was the one standing in the middle of the woods with no breakfast, no *kaffee,* and a crazy wife. "I *do* hate to camp," she said, as if she were confessing her deepest secret, "but the expensive cot is very comfortable, and I only had to hike to the barn once to go to the bathroom."

The previous owners of the property had

built a small bathroom with a toilet and a shower in the barn for their farmhands. "You used the bathroom in the barn?"

She nodded and seemed to regain some of her cheer, which only made him madder. "It really wasn't as bad as I feared, and it's better than an outhouse, for sure and certain."

He snatched his hat off his head and ran his fingers through his hair. It was still wet. "Tell me now. Why did you sleep in this tent last night?"

Mary Anne lowered her eyes and started that tapping thing again. "You'll be late for work."

"I still have three minutes."

"I didn't want to impose on the family, and I couldn't bring myself to ask any of my friends for a place to stay. I'm too proud. I suppose that's my greatest sin after all. A tent was the only thing I could think of."

"Mary Anne," he said, a warning note in his voice. She was being purposefully vague.

She slumped her shoulders and huffed out a long and heavy breath, as if surrendering to the inevitable. "I've left you, Jethro."

He drew his brows together in confusion. "Left me?"

"We can't get a divorce because it's against the church, but I don't want to live with

31

you anymore."

Something inside Jethro's head exploded. He couldn't possibly be hearing what he thought he was hearing. "I don't understand."

"I'm sorry to be so blunt, but you're boring."

It was like a blow right in the chest with a two-by-four. "Boring? I'm not boring. I used to do doughnuts in the parking lot with my buggy. I play Scrabble every Saturday night with my parents. And I bring home all sorts of delicious fish." His voice rose with his agitation. Soon only the wolves would be able to hear him. "A man who owns a four-hundred-dollar fishing pole is not boring." He pointed in the general direction of the house. "You get back in there right now. This is nonsense."

Mary Anne squared her shoulders and seemed to grow taller and fiercer. "You are the most boring man in Wisconsin, Jethro Neuenschwander, and I would have died of boredom."

"You just don't . . . you don't just . . . you don't leave someone because they're boring."

She shook her head. "It's been six years. I'm finished."

Jethro caught his breath. Yesterday was

their anniversary, and he'd forgotten it. How could he have been so *deerich*?

But how could Mary Anne be so touchy?

He bit down on any apology she thought she was entitled to and shoved aside the guilt that niggled at the back of his mind. This wasn't his fault. So he forgot an anniversary. Everybody forgot anniversaries and birthdays and special days. It wasn't a reason to leave your husband. Mary Anne was throwing a tantrum, plain and simple, and he wasn't going to indulge her.

He pulled the watch from his pocket. "I have to go." He took one last, longing look at the *kaffee* pot before turning his back on all of it. "You've made your point, Mary Anne. I expect all of this to be taken down and put away when I get home. Wipe down my tent and let it dry before you put it away. Read the instructions about how to fold it or you'll ruin it. Shake out the sleeping bag and hang it on a hanger. Don't stuff it in the bag."

The van honked for him just as he reached the edge of the backyard. He had no *kaffee* and no lunch. It was going to be a long day.

He hoped Mary Anne was satisfied with his misery.

CHAPTER THREE

There was no way a set of quilting frames was going to fit in the tent, and Mary Anne just had to have quilting frames. And her sewing machine. And a bookshelf for paint and brushes and sticks and strings.

It wasn't that she didn't appreciate what a spacious tent Jethro had purchased, but she was going to need a bigger one. She simply had to have more room for her imagination, which seemed to have taken wing in the last twenty-four hours.

And like it or not, she was going to need more money. Not only did she have big plans, but she needed to eat, and Gruyère cheese wasn't cheap. That was why she liked it so much. Jethro's two hundred dollars would only go so far, and he wasn't likely to fork over more money even if she asked, especially not after his reaction that morning. She didn't know what she'd expected. Of course he was upset at her leaving, even if he had practically ignored her for years. She was part of his routine, making breakfast for him every morning and dinner every night. She set his slippers by his chair every evening so he could enjoy his paper in comfort, and she cleaned the fish he brought home and cooked them up like any frugal *fraa* should. Maybe she had hoped he wouldn't mind her moving out so much. It would have made things easier for both of them.

Mary Anne lit the propane lantern with the lighter she had stolen from Jethro's tackle box. She hoped it wasn't a great inconvenience when he noticed it was missing. He had two others. The propane lamp sat on the small table that used to be in the living room next to Jethro's chair. She hoped he wouldn't be too inconvenienced by that either.

She glanced at the clock that hung from one of the tent poles. Mary Anne had made one irresponsible purchase today. It was a big kitchen clock with five brightly painted butterflies on the face. Each butterfly's wing was streaked with shiny gold highlights that sparkled in the lantern light. It was the most beautiful thing Mary Anne had ever seen at Walmart. She'd let Jethro keep his fish clock.

Seven o'clock. Jethro would be sitting in

his easy chair right now, reading the news-paper. She hadn't heard a peep from him since five, when he was supposed to have come home from work. Maybe he had accepted her decision to move out. Maybe he was trying to wait her out, sure she would grow tired of camping and move back into the house soon enough.

But he didn't know how determined she was, and he had no idea how nice it felt to be left in peace to do exactly what she wanted — without the expectations and judgments that weighed her down and made it hard to breathe.

"Mary Anne?"

She heaved a sigh. It really had been too much to hope that Jethro had given up.

"In here," she said, adding a little extra-chipper cheerfulness to her voice. She quickly unzipped the door to her tent and stepped outside. If she invited him in, she might never get him to leave. He could be like that sometimes.

She froze. Jethro had brought the bishop for a visit. *How very nice.*

"Mary Anne," the bishop said, looking like he'd just been to three funerals. "It wonders me if we could have a talk."

Jethro stood next to the bishop with his arms folded across his chest and his mouth twisted into a smug smile. Of course Jethro would fetch the bishop. Mary Anne had been expecting it, though maybe not quite this soon. She had no doubt the bishop would side with Jethro. She didn't feel clever enough to try to convince them otherwise, and she wasn't about to bear her soul to either of them. Jethro couldn't care less about her feelings, and the bishop thought she was just another fussy *fraa* who needed to be put in her place.

Why would she even try to make them understand?

It would complicate things if the bishop had her shunned, but she'd cross that bridge if she came to it. Living in a tent gave her confidence she could do anything she set her mind to.

Mary Anne's heart pounded against her ribs. She tried to pull herself taller. "Would you like to come in?"

The bishop nodded, and his gaze seemed to pierce right through to the back of her head. Who did she think she was? She was nobody, an insignificant, selfish *fraa* who liked to draw and couldn't have children.

Still, moving out of her house had been the first thing in a long time that had felt right, like shrugging off a heavy coat in hundred-degree weather. She might be going against *Gotte,* but what did it matter when *Gotte* didn't even know who she was? How much, really, did *Gotte* even care?

Mary Anne led the way as the three of them ducked into the tent. She sat on the end of the cot and motioned for Jethro and the bishop to sit on a small bench she had dragged from the house this morning. It was barely wide enough for both of them, and they had to squish. Mary Anne raised an eyebrow. She'd have to get more chairs if she wanted visitors.

Jethro pointed to the ceiling, where Mary Anne had hung her first creation. "What is that?"

She looked up and tried not to smile. She didn't want the bishop to think she was treating his visit with levity, and she certainly didn't want to appear proud. "*Ach.* It's a potato-chip mobile. I made it this morning. Don't you think it brightens up the tent?"

"What is it?" the bishop asked.

Mary Anne picked up the lantern and held it close to the mobile. She'd poked a dozen bamboo skewers into a Styrofoam ball and hung spray-painted potato chips from each skewer using fishing line from Jethro's tackle box. She'd spray-painted the chips blue and green and gold, with a little yellow dribbled on for an interesting pop of color. "Ruffles are the best because they don't break easily, and they're big enough to drill a hole through. And the ridges make a pretty design."

"You shouldn't spend good money on food if you're going to waste it," Jethro said.

She ignored his criticism. She didn't live with him anymore and felt no obligation to pay heed to his opinion. "And look," she said, setting down the lamp and picking up two chips from the table. She held them out for the bishop to see. "I found one in the shape of a tulip and one in the shape of a pig. The pig one isn't as good, but this really looks like a flower."

The bishop smiled. "*Jah.* You're right. I've never looked at a potato chip that closely before."

"Who has?" Jethro said, rolling his eyes.

That reaction usually hurt her feelings, but because she didn't love him anymore, she hardly felt the pain. Let Jethro think what he wanted.

Jethro's eyes widened as he took a second look around her tent. "That's my table! And my lamp!"

Ignoring any references to the furniture, Mary Anne set her potato chips on Jethro's table and sat back down on the cot, facing him and the bishop.

Bishop Yoder propped his elbows on his knees and laced his fingers together. "Now, Mary Anne, Jethro tells me that you have moved out."

"*Jah,*" she said, unable to keep her lips from curling slightly. That much should be obvious to anybody.

Jethro nodded. "I had hoped you'd have everything put away when I came home today, but instead my cooler is missing."

"I needed someplace to put my food."

The bishop patted Jethro's leg as if to stop him from saying whatever was about to come out of his mouth. He turned a concerned gaze back to Mary Anne. "Will you tell me why you moved out?"

Jethro glared at her. "She's throwing a tantrum because I forgot our anniversary last night."

Mary Anne raised an eyebrow. He'd remembered their anniversary — a day late, but still, it was something.

The bishop gave Jethro the kindly, patient smile he probably used on misguided young people in the *gmayna*. "I'd like to hear what Mary Anne has to say."

"She says I'm boring. A *fraa* shouldn't be allowed to move out just because she doesn't like something about her husband." Jethro sounded like he was preaching a sermon. If he didn't have such a difficult wife, he probably would have been a minister by now. He pointed a righteous finger at Mary Anne. "There are plenty of things I don't like about you, but I'm willing to stay together and work it out. That's what it means to be married."

Bishop Yoder studied Mary Anne's face. "You think Jethro is boring?"

Mary Anne looked down at her hands, which she had clasped in her lap. She wasn't about to tell the bishop or Jethro the real reasons for her leaving. Telling Jethro he was boring was much less painful for him than telling him she couldn't love someone who could hardly stand to look at her. She truly hated to hurt Jethro's feelings, but she also wanted to tell the truth — or at least a truth the bishop would be satisfied with. "I can't live like that for fifty more years."

Jethro was like a boiling teakettle. He stood up to keep from erupting. "But you made vows. You made a commitment to me."

"*Jah,*" she said. "I intend to keep those vows. Nothing says we have to live together to be married."

"But you're commanded in the Bible to love your husband. What about that?"

Jethro had just learned he was boring. She

wasn't about to tell him she didn't love him anymore. "I can love you from a distance."

"You're supposed to be at home. You're supposed to be a comfort to your husband. You can't do that when you're living in a tent and using my best sleeping bag."

She longed to point out that he never noticed when she was home so why should he notice when she wasn't. But she'd sound petty and bitter, when she just wanted Jethro to leave her alone and go on with his life.

"You'd rather live by yourself in a tent?" the bishop said.

She could tell he wasn't scolding her. "The woods are wonderful pretty this time of year. It's warm enough."

"What will you do when it turns cold?"

She didn't know if she was ready to share her plans, but she sensed that the bishop maybe wanted to help. At least he didn't seem inclined to lecture her. "I'd like to move into my own place."

Jethro scoffed. "You already have a house."

The lines on the bishop's forehead bunched together. "You're going to need money."

Jethro snapped his head around to scowl at Mary Anne. "She stole two hundred dollars from my underwear drawer."

42

Mary Anne couldn't fault Jethro for being mad. Money was more important to him than just about anything. "I plan to pay you back as soon as I can." She ignored the ache in her heart. "Do you remember the three quilts I made for the baby?"

That pulled him up short. "You don't have to talk about that."

"My *Englisch* friend Pammy has an Etsy shop, and she's going to sell them for me."

"What kind of a shop does she have?" Jethro said.

"I want to make more quilts to sell, but it won't be enough." She looked at the bishop. Would he help her? "I'm going to need to get a job."

"You don't need a job," Jethro said, all riled up again. "You need to come home. My wife should not live in a tent. It's embarrassing."

Even though Mary Anne was determined to keep her temper, Jethro was determined to push her to the limit. She gritted her teeth and took a deep breath. "If you're worried about what other people will think, just tell them that your wife is crazy. They can't blame you for that."

Jethro paced around the tent. Two steps forward, two steps back. "You're not crazy. You're selfish, and I won't stand for such wickedness in my home."

"Then it's *gute* I'm not living there anymore."

Bishop Yoder stood up and laid a firm hand on Jethro's shoulder. "Jethro," he said, his voice as mild as a summer day. How did he keep his composure? "Sit down, and we'll talk."

Jethro did as he was told, though his agitation couldn't be contained so easily. He bounced his knee up and down so fast it was almost vibrating.

The bishop sat down next to him. "These are hard times for husbands and wives. The world is changing, and we don't teach classes on how to have a *gute* marriage. No marriage is completely safe because it's easy to take each other for granted or to expect the other person to be someone they're not. I hear even your grandparents, Anna and Felty, have been talking about divorce."

Mary Anne frowned. "My grandparents?"

The bishop folded his arms. "One of my favorite passages of scripture is from the Last Supper. Jesus tells His disciples that one of them will betray him. Do you remember what the disciples ask him, Jethro?"

Jethro's face turned even redder than it already was. "*Nae.* Not really."

"They asked 'Is it I?' "

"What does that mean?"

"None of them said, '*Ach,* I'm sure Judas is the one who will do it. He's so greedy.' *Nae,* the disciples each examined their own hearts." The bishop looked Jethro squarely in the eye. "Maybe that is what you both need to do. When you want to blame everything on the other person, you should say, 'Am I the problem? Is it I?' "

Jethro turned to Mary Anne. "He's right, Mary Anne. You have to stop blaming me. Your weaknesses are not my fault."

"Jethro," the bishop said. "I'm trying to tell you that —"

Jethro focused squarely on Mary Anne. "Instead of accusing me of being boring, maybe you should say, 'Is it I?' You could very well be the one who is boring. You never join in Scrabble at Mamm and Dat's house."

"Now, Jethro," the bishop said, but Mary Anne raised her hand to stop him.

"Jethro is right. I'm the problem. I moved out so Jethro doesn't have to be offended by me anymore. I know this is all my fault."

Jethro's mouth fell open like a largemouth bass. There was no satisfaction in accusing her of things she already freely took the blame for. "But you said you moved out because I'm boring."

"And that's my problem, not yours," she said.

The bishop smiled that ministerial smile again. "Remember, before you try to change someone else, think how hard it is to change yourself." He stood up. "*Denki* for the visit, Mary Anne. I think I understand things better now."

Jethro jumped to his feet. "So, are you going to call her to repentance and make her move back in?"

The bishop chuckled. "I can't make anybody do anything, and I wouldn't want to. *Gotte* will force no man to heaven."

That obviously wasn't the answer Jethro had been expecting or hoping for. "But . . . but . . . she can't just live out here. She's my wife."

The bishop smiled so kindly, Mary Anne was compelled to smile back. "She is still your wife, and she doesn't want a divorce. I don't see how she's breaking any commandments. I'm tempted to camp in my own backyard tonight. I love sleeping under the stars."

Jethro sputtered and fussed like a wet cat as he followed the bishop out of the tent. The bishop had surprised both of them, and Mary Anne was overcome with gratitude. He was a *gute* man, and Mary Anne would always think well of him.

It wouldn't be so easy for Jethro, but he'd get over it. He'd pout for a few days and then go fishing. One good catch and he'd be right as rain. Fishing made him happy in ways Mary Anne never could.

CHAPTER FOUR

Jethro hadn't slept well last night. Mary Anne had stolen his favorite blanket, plus he was going on his second straight day without his morning *kaffee*. *Ach,* at work today he'd probably swigged a whole gallon of that liquid they tried to pass off as *kaffee,* but his head still felt as if someone had drilled a hole right between his eyes.

Randall had offered to pick him up after work for a little fishing trip, but Jethro turned him down. He just didn't have the heart for it. He hoped Mary Anne was happy. In one swift blow, she had single-handedly killed his desire for the one thing that brought him any happiness — all because he'd missed their anniversary to go fishing. If she had any forgiveness in her heart, she would not be putting him through this nightmare. His only hope was that in a moment of humility, she would remember what the bishop had said and ask, "Is it I?"

Her answer would definitely be *yes.*

Just walking into the house upset him. When Mary Anne was home, the smell of something delicious always greeted him as he came through the door. She would have a lamp lit in the kitchen, and he would tell her time and time again that it wasn't dark enough for a lamp. She said she liked the extra light and wouldn't give in, even when he complained about the cost of propane.

Tonight, he would gladly have forked over the money for extra propane, just to see Mary Anne softly moving about the kitchen, brushing the freshly baked loaves of bread with butter, taste-testing the soup, giving him an unexpected smile. The longing was an ache in his gut, a shard of glass in his heart, a sliver right under the skin.

Mary Anne's smiles had become less and less common over the years. She was devastated when she lost the baby, and even more upset when she found out she couldn't have more, and he hadn't known how to comfort her. He feared she'd see the disappointment in his eyes if he wasn't careful. And so he'd started being very careful. Things had never been the same between them.

Now they never would be. According to Mary Anne, he was boring. How could he ever get past that?

And all he had to look forward to for dinner were rose-shaped radishes and soggy asparagus. He wasn't even excited about the salmon. Nothing tasted good anymore.

He climbed out of the van. The driver said something to him like, "Have a nice night," but Jethro didn't respond. What was so nice about it? He trudged up the porch steps and stepped into the house. No lantern. No *gute* smells. Just emptiness.

A lot of emptiness.

The sofa sat under the window where it had always been, but Jethro's easy chair, the ottoman, and the bookshelf were missing. The books were piled in stacks looking like tiny crooked old men leaning against the wall.

The heat flared inside him. She could take his sleeping bag and even his favorite blanket, but he'd be plucked if he'd let her steal his easy chair. He took one second to be impressed that she'd managed to get it out of the house by herself, then stormed out the back door and into the woods.

He stopped short when he got closer to Mary Anne's encampment. What had Mary Anne done to his tent? The side facing the house had been painted with enormous, brightly colored butterflies. They hurt his eyes to look at.

Not only did that side of the tent look like some sort of windshield accident, but another tent, taller, wider, and greener, sat behind it. The back door of Jethro's tent connected with the front door of the new tent, as if Mary Anne was building her own mansion out here, piece by piece.

He walked around the other side of the tent, where his easy chair was sitting out in the open. Didn't Mary Anne care that it would get rained on? Mary Anne was bent over a Dutch oven — for sure and certain the one from the kitchen — stirring something that smelled too heavenly for words. It looked like a hearty beef stew with corn still on the cob and shiny green beans and plump potatoes. Maybe . . . was there any way she'd share it with him? There looked to be plenty. He closed his mouth, partly to keep from drooling and partly to keep from saying something he'd wish he hadn't, especially before asking for something to eat.

He could give her a lecture about the easy chair and the butterflies after dinner.

She looked up at him, not exactly happy to see him but not scowling either.

"What are you making?" he said, in the least boring voice he could muster.

Mary Anne lifted the spoon to her lips and

took a taste. "Braised beef and vegetables. I think I used too much garlic yet."

He laughed nervously, afraid she'd see right through him. "I love garlic. Never can have too much garlic."

She put the lid back on the Dutch oven, stood up, and studied his face, her frown etching deep lines around her mouth. "I'm not going to feed you, Jethro."

He nearly choked on his irritation. "You've got plenty."

"I've been wanting to try this recipe for months. I went to the market today and spent ten minutes picking out just the right cut of beef. I peeled the garlic cloves and even got fresh rosemary leaves. They come in a package with the roots still attached."

What did any of this have to do with whether she was going to feed him or not? "You should grow your own herb garden. It would be less trouble."

She smirked. "And less expensive."

"I suppose."

She huffed out a frustrated breath. "I'm not going to cook to please you anymore, Jethro. I want to try new things, new tastes, without worrying that you'll complain because I spent too much on the beef or be irritated that I bought green beans out of season."

"But you can't afford to spend all you've got on fancy meals. I'll never get my two hundred dollars back." He knew it was the wrong thing to say the minute he said it. What was two hundred dollars compared to the fact that his wife had left him?

She pinched her lips together until tiny lines circled her mouth. "You'll get your money back."

"I don't care about the money."

Her laugh was brief and unhappy. "That's *all* you care about."

"It is not. I want my wife to come home and quit stealing my furniture."

"I need places for visitors to sit."

"Visitors? You can't have visitors out here. My chair is going to get wet."

She looked at him as if he didn't have a brain in his head. "I was going to move it into the tent after dinner."

"It's heavy."

"I can manage."

"You'll ruin it, and then what will I sit on?"

She huffed out an even louder breath. "You'll get it back as soon as I have the money to buy my own."

"If you moved back in the house, you wouldn't need to buy another one."

"Pammy says she can sell every quilt I

make. On the computer. I brought the sewing machine out today, along with my fabric and scissors."

Jethro was wonderful impressed and wonderful irritated. She'd hauled her sewing machine from the house? "You shouldn't have the machine out here. It will get wet."

She lifted her chin. "It's safely under your tarp."

"My tarp? I use that for long fishing trips."

"I have to keep the machine dry."

"If you're so eager to live by yourself, you shouldn't keep taking my stuff. And because you've taken some of the dishes, you should at least offer to feed me."

She scrunched her lips together, as if she were trying very hard to keep her temper. "I gave up trying to correct my faults when I moved out. I feel no need to be the perfect wife."

"You're not being any kind of wife."

"That's right. I'm not even trying. So I don't have to feel guilty when I sew a baby quilt or paint my tent."

"It's my tent."

"It's our tent, and as soon as I get the money, I'll buy you a new one. I'm sorry, Jethro, but I need it right now."

"And yet you had enough money to buy a second tent."

"I don't have to defend myself to you. I'm not going to feel guilty anymore. But because you're so worried about it, it's my cousin Moses's tent. He let me borrow it."

"Does he know it might come back with butterflies painted all over it?"

"I asked them at the store. It's the kind of paint that won't hurt the tent. I wanted butterflies. They'll scare away the bears."

He folded his arms across his chest. "They look ridiculous."

She sucked in a breath and blinked back what looked like moisture in her eyes. He hadn't meant to hurt her feelings. He was simply trying to make her see. "I don't care what you think, Jethro. I painted those butterflies because I love butterflies. I did it to make myself happy because my husband doesn't even try anymore."

Doesn't even try *what* anymore? They were married. Wasn't that what happiness was? "Mary Anne," he said, cupping his fingers around his neck. "Come home. I won't say another word about the tent or the two hundred dollars. And . . . and you can buy beef once a week if you want."

She shook her head. "I'm not coming back."

The urge to lash out overtook him. "Then I'm taking back my chair."

"Fine. It smells like fish anyway."

Jethro picked up his easy chair, grunting at its bulk, and headed toward the house. He turned around with the chair in his arms. "I want my favorite blanket back."

She huffed out a breath, marched into the tent, and emerged with the blanket in her arms. She draped it over his shoulder and turned away, as if avoiding a bad smell. If she thought she was going to get away with clearing him out of house and home, she had another thing coming.

He was going to fight back.

CHAPTER FIVE

Mary Anne shimmied out the window, grateful she'd always been a little on the skinny side. Still, breaking into the house in a dress hadn't been easy, and she had a nice scrape on her left hip to prove it.

She lowered herself to the ground, made sure the window was tightly shut, and brushed off her shaking hands on her apron. She wasn't sure she'd even be able to lift a pan to make herself dinner tonight. It felt like she'd been hefting hay bales for two hours.

She hiked back to her tent with her plunder and couldn't help that the giggles tripped out of her mouth like birds from a cage. Who knew making mischief could be so fun? She didn't take pleasure in Jethro's unhappiness, so she had done her best to make it look like she hadn't even been inside the house. Besides, if he knew she knew how to get into the house, he might buy locks for all the windows, and she'd be sealed out for good.

This morning she had found that she needed tinfoil, spices, and the salad tongs to make dinner tonight, but when she'd tried to get into the house to fetch some supplies, she'd discovered Jethro had put locks on every door. He must have gone to the store very late last night, bought locks, and installed them before he went to bed. He'd put simple sliding locks on the side and back doors, but there was a fancier key lock on the front door. That he had been willing to spend the money on fancy locks was only a sign of how angry he was with her.

When she had found the doors locked, it hadn't taken Mary Anne long to find a window that was easy to open. The windows didn't have locks, and it surprised her that Jethro wouldn't have secured those too. Either he hadn't thought of it or he didn't imagine Mary Anne would be so nervy as to crawl through a window.

Oh, she was nervy all right. Nothing was going to stand in the way of her and a tinfoil dinner.

She had unlocked the back door because the chair wouldn't fit through the window. Surely Jethro wouldn't notice her sewing chair was missing. Then she'd gotten the other supplies she needed, slid the door lock into place, and climbed out the window. Lord willing, Jethro wouldn't notice anything amiss. If he did, she'd have to figure out how to pick that expensive dead bolt on the front door.

Mary Anne tried to ignore the twinge of pain and the pinch of guilt right at the center of her chest. Jethro had been tossed off his well-ordered life as if he'd been thrown from a horse into the river. He was simply doing all he could to keep his head above water. She bit her lip and quickened her pace toward the trees. Jethro's happiness was no longer her responsibility. She had already made up her mind about that. She was sorry he was upset, but she had her own happiness to look after. Nobody would do it if she didn't.

Her *mamm* would say Mary Anne was being selfish and spoiled and stubborn, and she probably was, but *ach,* the thought of sitting in that little house while the plain white walls closed in about her was unbearable. Jethro didn't understand. He was content to let her cook and clean and do his laundry, and so long as she didn't spend any money or paint any walls, he was happy.

But did his happiness have to come at the

expense of hers? Did her happiness have to come at the expense of his? Couldn't they both be happy in their own lives — never needing the other person's approval to chase their own dreams?

With the tinfoil, spices, and tongs in one hand and the chair draped over her other arm, Mary Anne walked as quickly as she could back to her double tent. Jethro would be home soon, and under no circumstances must he see her going from the house. Although Jethro didn't like to spend money, something told her he'd gladly lay down some cash for window locks just to teach her a lesson.

She didn't enjoy borrowing things from the house, and in truth, Mary Anne was going to need to earn some money. She'd started on three quilt tops, even though quilt frames weren't going to fit in either tent. Pammy had helped her sell those three baby quilts online for a hundred and fifty dollars apiece. Mary Anne had almost four hundred dollars of the quilt money left to buy more fabric, plus food and paint, but it wasn't going to go very far. Pammy said she could sell as many Amish quilts as Mary Anne could make. Mary Anne could sew them well enough, but she hadn't quite figured out where she would set up the frames to quilt them.

The living room in Jethro's house had plenty of space for a king-size quilt and a whole flock of quilters, but Jethro would never approve. She needed to start behaving as if she didn't have a house to go to whenever she needed. The sooner she was out of Jethro's hair, the better.

Mary Anne ducked into her tent, set the tinfoil, spices, and tongs on the bookshelf that now served as her pantry, and went through to her second tent, where she kept her sewing machine, fabric, and painting supplies. She scooted the sewing chair under the sewing table. At times like these, she was very glad the Amish didn't use electricity. The sewing machine was powered by a battery just bigger than a toaster. She'd carried the machine, the table, and the battery out the very first day. She hadn't sewn one quilt in more than three years, and she was determined to make up for lost time.

"Knock, knock," someone called from outside the tent. Mary Anne froze for a fraction of a second. Too bad Jethro had taken back his easy chair yesterday. There was nowhere for anyone to sit but the cot and the bench. And the sewing chair, if she got desperate.

"Yoo-hoo! Mary Anne, are you home?"

Mary Anne ducked back into her first tent, passed her cot, and opened the flap. Mammi and Dawdi Helmuth stood just outside her door, each cradling a casserole dish and smiling like Christmas morning.

"Mary Anne," Mammi said. She shifted the casserole dish into one hand and gave Mary Anne a one-armed hug. "We came to bring you some food and keep you company. Camping by yourself can't be very fun." Mammi drew her brows together. "Camping with other people isn't very fun either. I think we got here just in time."

"How . . . how did you know I was here?" Were they aware she'd left Jethro and that he'd locked her out of the house? Or did they think she was just on a camping trip?

"Ach," Mammi said. "The bishop told us what you were up to. He came over last night to try to talk us out of getting a divorce."

Mary Anne frowned. If Mammi and Dawdi were having marriage troubles, there was no hope for anybody. "You're getting a divorce?"

Mammi scrunched her lips together in exasperation. "Of course not, dear. Gossip is like a bag of feathers. Once you scatter them, you never know where they're going to end up." She handed Mary Anne the casserole dish. It felt like a pan of cement. "You painted butterflies on your tent. Did you see the butterflies, Felty?"

"I did."

"They're a breath of springtime on canvas."

Dawdi reached out and curled his fingers around the edge of the fire pit. "I like this fire pit. Moses and I helped Jethro pick it out. Nice and sturdy, but not too big to move around if you have to. You've got a nice place here."

Mary Anne relaxed. That was just like Mammi and Dawdi. There was no, "Why in the world are you living in a tent?" or "You should be ashamed for leaving your husband." They always noticed the beauty and ignored the messy stuff.

Mary Anne wasn't sure what proper tent manners were. "Would you like to come in and sit on my cot? Or would you rather stay out here where there's more room and fresher air?"

Mammi shook her head. "Much as we'd love to see the inside of your tent, I think we'd better get ours set up before dark. We borrowed it from Aden, and we're going to need to read the instructions."

"We don't need the instructions, Annie.

I've set up many a tent in my day. It's not hard."

"A tent?" Mary Anne said, completely perplexed now. "You brought a tent?"

"Jah," Dawdi said, pointing to a short, thin canvas bag sitting on the ground next to the fire pit. "We brought a two-man tent, two sleeping bags, some extra shoes, Anna's knitting, and our toothbrushes."

"I brought earplugs in case Felty snores," Mammi said.

Dawdi handed the other casserole dish to Mary Anne. "And these two casseroles for dinner. Do you still have that bathroom in your barn?"

"But why did you bring your tent?"

Mammi picked up the canvas bag and unzipped it. "It's Aden's tent. He let us borrow it because I don't especially enjoy sleeping under the stars, and it might snow tonight."

Mammi and Dawdi were both well into their eighties, but as far as Mary Anne knew, they were still sharp as tacks. "You're sleeping here?"

Mammi nodded and stretched herself to her full height of five feet zero inches. "We've come to show solidarity with our granddaughter."

Mary Anne resisted the urge to look

64

behind her to see if it was another grand-daughter Mammi was talking about. "Me? What does solidarity mean?"

"It is a Polish word, I think," Dawdi said, lifting the bottom of the bag and letting the tent and its poles slide out onto the ground.

Mammi was entirely serious about her solidarity. "Of course, you. I know how you hate to camp, and if things with Jethro have gotten so bad that you felt you had to move out, we're here to support you. It's why we brought two casseroles. Camping gives me an appetite."

Mary Anne's heart sank. She set the casseroles on the ground next to her tent. "*Ach,* Mammi. I love that you want to support me, but it's asking too much."

Mammi clicked her tongue. "You didn't ask, dear. I volunteered. And I made Felty come with me."

"But what if you have to get up in the middle of the night to go to the bathroom? It's in the barn. And the ground is hard. At least take my cot."

"I don't think a cot will fit in this tent," Dawdi said, studying the segmented poles in his hands as if he had no idea how they got there. "It's a two-man tent, but the men must be very little."

Mammi patted Mary Anne's arm. "What

do we need to do to get dinner started?"

Mary Anne gave her a weak smile. Was it possible to cook a casserole in a fire pit? She had no idea what they'd eat on. She'd only taken one plate from the house. Maybe Jethro would let her borrow two more just this once. "Could we pour the casserole into the Dutch oven? We could start a fire in the pit and warm it over the coals."

"That's an excellent idea, dear. It's my famous cheese and cabbage lasagna. The layers will get mixed, but I'm sure it will warm up beautifully in the Dutch oven."

Famous indeed. Cousin Titus had once thrown up for three days straight after eating it. No one had ever told Mammi.

"I'll build a fire," Mary Anne said, "while you help Dawdi set up the tent."

Mammi waved in Dawdi's direction. "*Ach,* he can put it together with his eyes closed."

"What's all this?"

Mary Anne nearly hopped out of her skin. She hadn't heard Jethro come up behind her, and the fact that she'd broken into his house today made her a little jumpy.

Jethro stood with his feet apart and his muscular arms folded across his chest. He had strong arms and a trim waist. Mary Anne had always liked that about him. Even after their fight yesterday, he didn't have a

66

scowl on his face — probably because her grandparents were here and he wanted to be polite. "I saw the buggy parked in front of our house," he said.

"*Ach,* Jethro." Mammi beamed like a lantern and moved in for a hug. She acted so happy to see him, someone might have thought Jethro was her favorite grandson-in-law. Maybe Mary Anne wasn't the only one Mammi was doing the whole solidarity thing with. "I hope you don't mind we put our horse in the barn with yours. We're going to be here for a while, and we didn't want her to get snowed on. And I must say, it's a very small barn. No wonder Mary Anne decided on a tent instead of the barn. There's barely room for our two horses and a cow. And it stinks."

Bless his heart, Jethro was doing his best not to turn hostile, which was the only emotion it seemed he had felt in the last three days. "What are you doing here?"

"We've come to support your wife in her time of need," Mammi said, putting a protective arm around Mary Anne.

Jethro's frown was like a deep gash on his face. "I've tried to be a *gute* husband, but Mary Anne is bent on embarrassing me."

Mary Anne shouldn't be surprised that shame was his biggest concern. Her moving out embarrassed him. The *gute* news for him was that once things calmed down and everybody got used to the idea of them not living together, his embarrassment would fade and he'd find just as much joy in fishing as he once did.

Dawdi tried to slide two tent poles together and nearly took his eye out. "This Swift-n-Snug tent isn't very swift. I can only hope it's snug."

Jethro strode to Dawdi's side and held out his hand. "I can help." There were two poles that folded compactly into seven equal pieces, connected with a cord that ran through the center of each. Dawdi handed them over, and Jethro easily connected the pieces. He and Dawdi spread out the tent, and then Jethro threaded the poles through the clips running criss-cross over the top of the tent. He had the tent up in less time than it took to say, "Mammi's famous cheese and cabbage lasagna." He took Dawdi's hammer and drove the four stakes to anchor the tent, then brushed off his hands and stepped back to inspect his work. He glanced at Mary Anne and quickly looked away, as if he would catch on fire if he stared at her too long. "Is this to hold more of Mary Anne's potato chip sculptures?"

Dawdi raised an eyebrow. "How many potato chips does she have?"

"Plenty," Jethro said, as if he was talking about how many mosquitoes there were in Wisconsin or how many times the cow had kicked over the milk bucket.

"This tent is not for potato chips," Mammi said, and Mary Anne detected a hint of a scold in Mammi's voice. Mary Anne was starting to like this whole solidarity thing. "Felty and I are sleeping here tonight so Mary Anne doesn't have to sleep outside by herself. At times like these, a girl needs the support of her family."

Jethro scowled with his eyes, but the expression didn't quite reach his mouth. He was trying to behave himself even if he was seething. "Anna, you're eighty-two years old."

"Eighty-five."

"Eighty-five years old. You won't get a wink of sleep, and you'll ache in places you didn't even know you had."

"I'm willing to sacrifice for my granddaughter, and I brought two casseroles."

Mary Anne wasn't sure what the casseroles had to do with sleeping outside, but Jethro didn't argue about it. He cupped his fingers around the back of his neck and sighed. "You two are reasonable people.

Can't you talk Mary Anne into moving back into the house?"

Mary Anne gave him the stink eye. "Don't talk about me like I'm not here."

Jethro raised his eyes to Mary Anne's face and quickly averted them. "I never wanted you to leave."

Dawdi stroked his beard. "Do you want Mary Anne back or do you just want her back in your house?"

Jethro narrowed his gaze in confusion. "What does that mean?"

Mammi's eyes twinkled merrily. "Mary Anne is of her own mind, and we wouldn't dream of trying to change it. We like her just the way she is."

Jethro all but growled. "I like her just the way she is too."

It was a nice thing to say, especially when he was so angry. But he didn't really like her just the way she was. He liked who she had pretended to be to please him, that woman who cooked plain, sensible meals and kept his plain, sensible house and never said or did anything to upset his well-ordered life. It wasn't who she ever wanted to be again.

"Of course you do, even if she doesn't currently live with you," Mammi said, as if it was the most natural thing in the world that

70

Jethro's wife had moved into a tent.

Jethro wasn't finished trying to convince Mammi or Dawdi to take his side. "Aren't you concerned that your granddaughter is going against the Bible? A wife is supposed to submit to her husband."

Dawdi chuckled. "And you're supposed to love your wife as Christ loves the church."

"I do," Jethro said, with a little less conviction.

Dawdi knelt to unroll his sleeping bag inside the tent. It was quite a feat for an eighty-seven-year-old man. "Like locking her out of the house?"

How did he know about that?

Apparently, Jethro wondered the same thing. He shot a glare at Mary Anne as if she had tattled on him. "She took my easy chair."

Dawdi finished spreading out his sleeping bag and stood up. "For sure and certain, I like my recliner."

Jethro picked up the other sleeping bag, untied the knot in the string around it, and spread it next to the other one in the tent. "Sleeping in here is going to be torture for your back, Felty. You need a cot."

Dawdi smiled, as if he was just humoring everybody. "Let us try it out tonight. Right, Annie?"

Mammi nodded. "I went through labor thirteen times. How bad can it be?"

Pretty bad, Mary Anne thought. She hated sleeping in a tent. It almost made her sad. She suddenly liked the idea of Mammi and Dawdi sharing her campsite, and they were only going to last one night, two at the most.

Mammi picked up one of the casseroles from the ground. "We should build a fire so we can warm up this casserole. I'm hungry." She glanced at Jethro. "Would you like to eat with us? Cabbage and cheese lasagna, my special recipe."

Jethro gave Mammi a weak smile, and Mary Anne could see the wheels turning in his head. He'd probably eaten all the anniversary leftovers, so he was forced to decide between cornflakes or cabbage lasagna for dinner. Mary Anne didn't know which one she would have picked. She would have preferred the tinfoil dinner she had planned on making, but it would have to wait until the casseroles or Mammi and Dawdi were gone — or both.

"I'd appreciate it if I could join you for dinner. I don't know how to cook much of anything. Mary Anne is such a *gute* cook, I've never had to learn."

Mary Anne tried not to show her surprise. Two compliments from Jethro in one day.

She couldn't remember the last time that had happened — probably about the time they had found out she couldn't have children and he had stopped taking any interest in her at all.

Mary Anne took a deep breath and turned her face away. She'd better be careful. Her hurt could so easily turn into bitterness. Maybe it already had. Maybe that was why she was living in a tent. "We'll need more plates and cups," she said, trying very hard not to sound smug. If he wanted to eat with them, he'd have to retrieve a few things from the house.

Jethro pressed his lips together. He obviously didn't like the idea of taking yet more things from the house, but if he wanted to eat, he'd have to be obliging. "Okay. And I'll make a salad."

He helped Dawdi build a fire in the fire pit while Mary Anne and Mammi transferred the lasagna from the casserole dish to the Dutch oven. The lasagna — red and orange and green — sort of seeped out of the pan like a slug oozing from its shell, and Mary Anne tried not to breathe in the smell. She comforted herself with the thought that Mammi and Dawdi couldn't last very long out here. She'd be cooking her own meals in less than forty-eight hours. And if Mammi and Dawdi managed to stick it out longer, Mary Anne would volunteer to be the camp cook. Solidarity was nice, but it didn't taste very good.

Mary Anne had hooked up a hose to the spigot by the barn, and she and Mammi washed and dried the casserole pan. Mammi wiped her hands on one of the dish towels Mary Anne had taken from the kitchen and then wiped the casserole dish and stowed it on top of one of the sleeping bags in her tent. Hopefully, she would remember to move it before she climbed in. Mammi gave Mary Anne a wide smile. "Now, dear. While we're waiting for dinner to cook, I'd like a tour of your tent, and so would Felty."

"*Jah,* I would," Dawdi said.

Mammi got that tricky glint in her eye that meant she was up to no good. "And so would Jethro, for sure and certain."

Mary Anne felt her face get hot. She didn't want Jethro looking down at her decorations and criticizing how she'd spent his two hundred dollars. He didn't care about her rock collection or the stack of quilt blocks sitting on her cot. And she certainly didn't want him seeing the sewing chair and getting suspicious about how she'd gotten it. She wasn't strong enough to withstand his disapproval. It was one of the reasons she had moved out in the first place.

Mary Anne folded her hands almost casually. "Jethro will want to make his salad."

Mammi seemed so eager all of a sudden. "Stuff and nonsense. A salad takes three minutes. He has time before the lasagna cooks."

Ach du lieva. Mary Anne's stomach fell to the ground. Mammi was a matchmaker at heart. Was she trying to get Mary Anne and Jethro back together? She would have to put a stop to that — without offending Mammi or making a big stink about it. Mary Anne was already making a big enough stink just living in a tent.

Well, she'd been brave enough to move out of the house. She could muster the courage to insist on things her own way without making a scene in front of Mammi and Dawdi. She had as much a right to be happy as anyone. "Jethro can come too, but he isn't allowed to say anything."

Jethro frowned. "What do you mean by that?"

She squared her shoulders. "Just that. I don't want you to say anything."

Mammi's smile got wider as Jethro's frown got thinner. "I think she means you need to keep your mouth shut. I've always found that to be very *gute* advice in almost

75

every situation."

Mary Anne tried to ignore Jethro altogether as she led the way into the tent. If she had her way, Jethro would be sitting in his house eating cornflakes. But Mammi had invited him to dinner, and Mary Anne couldn't very well uninvite him when it was Mammi who had done the cooking.

Jethro was the last to enter, and he turned and zipped up the screen layer of the door. "To keep the mosquitoes out," he said.

Mammi's eyes flashed in Jethro's direction. "You're not supposed to say anything. Surely you haven't forgotten already."

Jethro pressed his lips together and shot Mary Anne a scowl. She bit her tongue before she said something rude that would shock her grandparents. Something like, "Jethro, get out of my tent." Her grandparents wouldn't like it if she talked to her husband like that, even though she was sorely tempted to put him in his place.

Jethro had to remove his hat to keep it from brushing against the top of the tent and knocking down all Mary Anne's mobiles. Dawdi stooped over so as not to scrape his head.

She should have ignored him, but she couldn't keep from noticing how Jethro's eyes traveled from her cot to the table she'd taken from the house to the bookshelf that was now full of pots and pans and canisters of flour and sugar and oatmeal, chocolate chips and shortening. His gaze rested on the fish-shaped pot holders she'd made him for his twenty-eighth birthday. He had never used them. Did he want them back?

Mammi pointed to the ceiling, which wasn't all that far above her head. "*Ach,* Mary Anne. Look at what you've done! They're beautiful. Aren't they, Felty?"

Dawdi formed his mouth into an *O.* "What are they made of?"

Mary Anne reached out and gave her Ruffles mobile a little twirl. "This one is made of potato chips."

Mammi's eyes were wide with delight. "They're so colorful."

Mary Anne lightly tapped one of the delicate leaves on her nature mobile. "Spray paint. I especially like the gold ones. I pulled some new leaves off the trees and gathered sticks and pinecones for this one, then sprayed them gold and taped them to the ceiling."

"Duct tape will leave residue —"

One sharp look from Mammi, and Jethro shut his mouth. Resentment pulled at his lips as he eyed the seven mobiles Mary Anne had hung above her cot. Had he

77

noticed that she'd used his fishing line?

"This one is made of Ritz Crackers," Mary Anne said.

Dawdi carefully took one of the hanging crackers between two of his fingers. "I like blue. And green."

Mary Anne grinned. "Me too. I love every color. They're all so glorious." She pointed to the egg mobile, painted and decorated in every variety of pattern and color. "That is my favorite. I made a little hole on the bottom and top of each egg and blew out the yolk and egg white." She curled her lips. "My cheeks hurt for an hour afterward."

Mammi clapped her hands. "It's adorable, Mary Anne. Like Easter morning."

Jethro grunted, but he didn't say anything, so Mary Anne wasn't sure what it was specifically he disapproved of. It wasn't hard to guess, though. Jethro disapproved of everything. He disapproved of the mobiles. He disapproved of the money she'd spent to buy the paint. He disapproved of the stolen fishing line and the time she'd wasted to make her creations and the residue on the ceiling of his tent. Mostly, he disapproved of Mary Anne and the fact that she was an embarrassment to Amish *fraas* everywhere.

She shouldn't have agreed to let him come

inside. Making those mobiles had brought her so much happiness. The colors, the patterns, the textures invigorated her like nothing else had in a long time. And Jethro was being a stick-in-the-mud.

She folded her arms across her chest. "Go make your salad, Jethro."

"What?"

"I said, go make your salad. Mammi's lasagna is almost ready."

He looked as if he'd eaten a lemon. "I'm dying to see the rest of your mansion."

"You'll need to run to the market for some lettuce. The head in the fridge is probably slimy by now. And we don't have any tomatoes or cucumbers."

"I know how to make a salad," he said, the resentment dribbling out of his mouth like a cup of pebbles.

Mammi reached up and gave Jethro a grandmotherly pat on the cheek. "You had better go, Jethro. Your bad attitude is ruining the tour."

Jethro's indignation was almost as sharp as his surprise. "It is not."

"I'm enjoying the tour," Dawdi said, studying one of Mary Anne's eggs with his bifocals.

"We were having a lovely afternoon until you came along. You're making Mary Anne very uncomfortable."

Jethro was like a smoldering fire. "I'm her husband. She should love me, not feel uncomfortable around me."

Mammi sighed. "So true. It's going to take some time to sort things out, Jethro, and now is not the time. We only have so long before the lasagna burns. I want to finish the tour, and you need to make a salad and quit making a mess of things."

Jethro's nostrils flared, but he somehow kept his temper, unzipped the flap on the door, and ducked out of the tent.

"Leave your frown in the house when you come to dinner," Mammi said as he re-zipped the door.

It was almost as if the smoke cleared as soon as he left.

Mary Anne stifled a smile. Her sweet little *mammi* had just put Jethro in his place.

Thank the *gute* Lord for solidarity.

Mary Anne finished showing Mammi and Dawdi her living space. The tent in the back was for cutting and sewing fabric and sand-ing and painting furniture for Pammy to sell. She showed Mammi and Dawdi her rock collection and the book about rocks she'd borrowed from the library. They were impressed by her supply of oddly shaped chips and crackers. There were the tulip-shaped Ruffles chip and the Ruffles pig that didn't look all that much like a pig. But she had also found a potato chip that looked like a dog's head and a Cheetos puff in the shape of a little man with two outstretched arms. Mammi especially liked the Cheetos collection. She started talking about tuna Cheetos casserole. Hopefully, that would never really happen.

She had also started making quilt blocks for the first quilt to sell on the computer. The quilt squares were almost done, and Mary Anne would need to find a place to set it up for quilting.

When Mammi and Dawdi finished oohing and aahing over Mary Anne's collections, the three of them decided they'd better get dinner on. Surely Jethro would be back any minute with that salad, and Mary Anne wasn't about to let him in her tent again.

Mammi stoked the fire, and then she and Dawdi sat down for a little rest before dinner.

Mary Anne lifted the lid from the Dutch oven and dipped her spoon into the cheesy concoction. A glob of cheese and a soggy cabbage leaf came out with the spoon. Mary Anne blew on it and took a taste. Not too bad, if you didn't mind cabbage, and cheese made everything taste better. "The lasagna is ready," she said.

Mammi and Dawdi sat on a pair of camp chairs they'd borrowed from Jethro, enjoying the sunset that filtered through the trees in the west. Dawdi read a newspaper while Mammi did some knitting. Mammi hadn't thought to bring a nightgown, but she was never without her knitting.

Jethro had unlocked the house and let them get the folding table and four chairs from the closet, plus enough plates, cups, and forks for everyone. So Jethro wouldn't have one more thing to scold her about, Mary Anne hadn't set foot in the house, but had directed Mammi where to find the napkins and a red-and-white-checkered tablecloth to brighten up the table. Dawdi had set the table while Mary Anne had tended the fire and Mammi had tended her lasagna.

"Dawdi," Mary Anne said, placing the lid back on the Dutch oven. "How did you know Jethro locked me out of the house?"

Dawdi lowered his paper and stroked his horseshoe beard. "Titus saw him at Walmart last night buying an assortment of locks. I figured it out."

Jethro had been in the house for nearly half an hour. How long did it take to make a salad? Maybe he had decided he'd rather eat cornflakes than sit at the same table with Mary Anne. That was fine with her. She didn't even care about the salad. She'd rather be left alone.

Mary Anne lifted the Dutch oven from the fire pit just as Jethro strode across the lawn and into the woods. He carried a plastic bowl in one hand and a bottle of ranch dressing in the other and kept his eyes to the ground.

"Yoo-hoo, Jethro," Mammi called, as if Jethro hadn't seen them sitting there. "It's time to eat."

Jethro deposited his bowl and his dressing on the table. Mammi had told him to leave his frown in the house, but he hadn't heeded her advice. He frowned as if his face might break with the slightest touch.

Mary Anne put the steaming Dutch oven on the ground next to the table. It was too hot and heavy to put directly on the folding table. It would either make it melt or collapse. "Let's eat," she said.

Jethro made a point to sit across from her, for sure and certain because he was too mad to sit next to her, but it didn't matter. The table was small, and they seemed closer sitting face-to-face. They said silent grace and then Mary Anne used a fish-shaped pot holder to lift the lid of the Dutch oven and gave everyone a helping of lasagna.

Mammi took the lid off Jethro's salad, and her smile wilted. Jethro's salad was a pile of torn, slightly rusty lettuce and nothing else. "You didn't go to the store, did you?" Mammi said, obviously trying to keep the disappointment out of her voice.

Jethro's expression was hard, as if daring Mary Anne to make fun of him. "It's exactly how I like my salad."

Mary Anne had never made Jethro a salad like that, but she could almost believe he was telling the truth. It certainly was the cheapest salad anyone had ever made.

Mammi served everyone a helping of lettuce. "Jethro, while I'm here, I'm going to have to teach you how to cook."

"I know how to cook," Jethro said.

Mary Anne pressed her lips together. Jethro wasn't about to concede an inch, even to Mammi.

Mammi didn't believe him for one minute. "Stuff and nonsense. If this is your idea of a salad, you're in big trouble." She reached out and patted Jethro on the wrist. "I don't mean to hurt your feelings, and I'm proud of you for trying your best. It's always important that we try our best. Unfortunately, with the way you're handling things so far, I can see you're going to be living on your own for quite some time. I won't have you starve because of sheer stubbornness."

Jethro looked positively mulish. "I can eat at McDonald's."

Mammi was positively shocked. "McDonald's? *Ach,* Jethro. You'll get fat *and* burn yourself. Their *kaffee* is wonderful hot."

Jethro set his cup on the table a little too forcefully. Water jumped out onto the tablecloth. "I don't need cooking lessons. I want my wife back."

Mary Anne lifted her chin. "I don't want to come back."

"The wife should submit to her husband. Her husband rules over her."

Mary Anne knew those scriptures by heart. She just didn't have a heart for them. A husband who tried to force cooperation from his wife by quoting scripture was not a godly man. She felt no obligation to obey him. "You can rule over me from a distance."

"That's not what marriage is."

"Well, Jethro, what is marriage? Is it me waiting patiently at home while you go fishing? Is it me doing my best to be the perfect wife while you ignore me? To you, I'm an unused piece of furniture unless you want to be fed."

"That is not true."

"I'm less than a piece of furniture. Furniture doesn't spend money."

Mammi pasted an awkward smile on her face. "This salad isn't half bad, Jethro."

"Be honest, Jethro. You like your easy chair more than you like me. If you hired a maid, you wouldn't even notice I was missing."

"I'd notice my two hundred dollars was missing."

It was a low blow, and she could see he regretted it as soon as he said it, but she wasn't about to let him apologize or take it back. "Then why should you care if I move back into the house as long as you get your money? I'm sorry about how embarrassed you are, but of what use am I really? I can't give you a child. It's better if I'm not there to remind you."

Jethro jumped to his feet, and the chair collapsed behind him. "Don't throw that in my face. I never treated you differently because you couldn't have a baby."

"Didn't you?"

Dawdi reached down and scooped himself another helping of lasagna. "This is the best you've ever made, Annie-Banannie."

"*Denki,* Felty."

Mary Anne got to her feet and locked her

86

gaze with Jethro's. "I could smell your disappointment every time you came into the house."

"Of course I was disappointed," he yelled. He took a deep breath and lowered his voice. "There. I said it out loud. I'm disappointed you can't have a baby. That doesn't make me a bad husband. We're stuck with each other. Shouldn't we make the best of it?"

And there it was — a moment of complete honesty. She'd known it for a very long time, but to have him come right out and say it stung like a slap in the face. Jethro felt stuck, trapped even. If he had married someone else, he'd have two or three little ones by now.

It was why she had moved out. She was tired of trying to make it up to him, tired of being the perfect, cheerful wife when she knew how much he resented her. She didn't love him enough to keep trying, and she was through torturing herself. She wanted them both to be happy. Moving out was the only thing she could think of to do, despite her parents, Jethro, and the church.

Mary Anne sat down and twirled a piece of cheese around her fork. Everything was better with melted cheese. "You may be stuck, Jethro, but I'm not. I have a new quilt business, seven cheery mobiles hanging in my tent, and a potato chip that looks like the governor of Wisconsin. I have plans for my life."

"Plans that don't include me."

"Jah."

He took off his hat and ran his fingers through his hair. "All because I'm disappointed you can't have a baby? Or because you think I'm boring?"

He'd been honest with her. She owed him the same. "Because I don't love you anymore."

For half a second, he was speechless. He just stared at her as if she'd taken out an ax and chopped off his arm. He finally snapped out of whatever shock he felt, picked up his salad bowl, lid, and dressing, and turned his back on all of them. "*Denki* for dinner, Anna," he said, even though he hadn't taken a bite. He trudged away from them without looking back. At least he had a salad he could eat if he got hungry.

Mammi strangled the napkin in her hands. "Oh dear, Felty. I think we made things worse."

Mary Anne slid her arm around Mammi's shoulders. "*Nae,* Mammi, it wasn't your fault. Jethro's mad at me, no one else."

Dawdi was as cheerful as a fisherman with

a whole can of worms. "I think we made progress, Banannie. All *gute* marriages need honesty and forgiveness. They're halfway there."

Mary Anne frowned. "You're such dear people, but I don't want you to believe for a minute that I'll ever go back to Jethro. Please don't try to match us a second time. I won't go along with it. Ever."

Mammi waved her napkin in front of her face. "Why would you think I want to get you back together? I'm here to show solidarity and nothing else."

Mary Anne didn't believe it, but she wasn't going to argue when Mammi had been so supportive. It didn't matter what Mammi and Dawdi tried. She and Jethro were through. She smiled reassuringly at Mammi. "I think he understands me now. For sure and certain he'll see the wisdom in what I've said and give up."

Dawdi winked at her. "*Ach,* Mary Anne. That boy may be mad as a bee with a boil, but he'll never give up."

"But now he knows I don't love him."

"Well, he loves you. And he's a fisherman. He knows how to be persistent."

CHAPTER SIX

Mary Anne felt a little pinprick of guilt as she pulled the buggy up to Lily and Aden Helmuth's house. She didn't feel guilty about being at Lily's, but she did feel guilty for taking Jethro's buggy. She'd never felt guilty about it before, but now that she was living in a tent in the backyard, it was getting harder and harder to justify using his things without permission. She'd used the buggy every day last week and she needed it again today, but she'd have to find another way to get around town or her sins would just keep piling up and she'd end up owing Jethro a lot of money she couldn't begin to pay back.

Mammi and Dawdi had offered to let her use their buggy, but she didn't want to impose on them any more than she already had. They wouldn't be in the woods with her forever. She needed to learn to solve her own problems.

Aden was Mary Anne's cousin. Her *fater,* Peter, and Aden's *fater,* Emmon, were *bruders,* sons of Mammi and Dawdi Helmuth. Both Mary Anne's parents and Aden's parents lived in Ohio.

Aden's wife, Lily, was one of Mary Anne's best friends. Lily didn't mind that Mary Anne didn't have children, like some of the women in the community did. Not that anyone was particularly unkind, but some few seemed to believe infertility was a punishment from *Gotte,* and they looked at her as if trying to guess what sins she had committed that she hadn't yet repented of. More often than not, however, the women of the community included her in their canning frolics and quilting bees, but Mary Anne was painfully aware that having children bonded women in a way nothing else could. She simply didn't fit into the group though they did their best to include her.

Lily and Aden lived on a tidy farm on the outskirts of town. Their barn roof was smothered in solar panels, and at least three dozen chickens ran every which way around the barnyard. Mary Anne couldn't imagine how those chickens survived. Aden's dog, Pilot, was as big as a bear and as mischievous as a raccoon. Surely he was always on the prowl for a good chicken leg.

Mary Anne got out of Jethro's buggy and nudged aside a few chickens with her foot on her way up the sidewalk. Lily opened the door before Mary Anne could knock and squealed in delight. She gave Mary Anne a hug, immediately lost her smile, and pulled Mary Anne into the house as if there was an angry bear just outside the door. "I can barely breathe, I'm so curious," Lily said, leading Mary Anne into the kitchen, where her three-year-old son, Aden Jr., sat on the floor playing with the one-year-old twins.

Mary Anne always got a thrill walking into Lily's kitchen. The variety of plants and flowers Lily and Aden kept in their house was astounding. They had their own indoor garden every day of the year. Aden had told Mary Anne it was to improve the indoor air quality. Mary Anne just loved all the colors.

Pulling a chair from under the table, Lily motioned for Mary Anne to sit. Lily sat down next to her and wrapped her fingers around Mary Anne's wrist. "Now," she said, leaning in eagerly, "I want to hear every-thing. Is it true you moved into a tent in your backyard?"

Mary Anne pressed her lips together and braced for Lily's disapproval. A *fraa* shouldn't leave her husband. No matter how nice the bishop had been about it, Mary Anne knew she was going against the church, the Bible, and the *Ordnung*. Jethro, the person who was supposed to love her most in the whole world, hadn't taken it well. There was no telling how her friends would react. "It's true. I'm camping in the woods with my grandparents."

Lily's mouth fell open. "Anna and Felty?"

"*Jah.* They set up their own tent and moved in on Thursday."

Lily put her hand to her mouth to cover a giggle. "*Ach!* What a sight to see."

"We're doing solidarity together."

Lily's smile wilted. "There's rumors that Anna and Felty are thinking of getting divorced."

"I think they're just rumors, but Mammi is wonderful insistent that they're only going to leave when I do, and Dawdi has already had enough. Last night the wind flattened their tent while they were still inside it, and they made quite a fuss. Jethro was asleep in the house, and he heard Mammi squealing. We tried to resurrect their tent so they could go back to sleep, but the poles had blown away. Jethro took Mammi and Dawdi into the house and let them sleep in the spare bedroom. It was a big sacrifice. He had to move his fishing pole."

Lily heaved a big sigh. "Oh, dear. I'm *froh* Jethro was there to help." She reached down and pulled a marker from Aden Jr.'s fist. "Aden Junior, don't color your *schwester.*" Estee, one of the twins, contentedly sucked on her binky, oblivious to the wide gash of color down the side of her face. Emily, the other twin, pounded a little wooden hammer into a pile of blocks. Lily hadn't caught Aden Jr. in time. Both of Emily's cheeks were covered with green scribbles. Lily heaved an even bigger sigh. "*Ach, vell.* That mess isn't going anywhere." She leaned closer to Mary Anne. "So, tell me everything. How long ago did you move out?"

"Monday night."

Lily gave her a look of the deepest sympathy Mary Anne had ever seen. "*Ach.* On your anniversary. Didn't he like the dinner?"

Mary Anne traced her finger along the line in the table. "He didn't eat it. He went fishing."

"*Ach du lieva,* Mary Anne. No wonder you moved out."

Mary Anne dared to raise her gaze to Lily's face. "You aren't mad at me?"

"Mad at you? Jethro has had blinders on for years. I don't know how you stood it."

Mary Anne let out a breath she didn't even know she'd been holding. "I know it's wicked, and I'll probably go to hell."

Lily frowned. "I wish I knew the answer to that, but I'm not the bishop. I think you did a very brave thing, but for sure and certain the *gmayna* won't approve. You know how my *dat* feels about the Helmuths."

"Your husband in particular."

"Jah," Lily said, grinning in spite of herself. "He wasn't happy when I married Aden, and he blamed Aden's whole family, especially Anna and Felty. But he's being less grumpy about it all the time. He even comes to dinner sometimes, though he always gives us a long lecture on Aden's shortcomings when he comes over." Estee started fussing, and Lily picked her up and set her in her lap. *"Dat* thinks you should be shunned for setting a bad example for all the *fraaen* in the community. He's not the only one. Jethro has talked to the elders."

"That doesn't surprise me. He's wonderful angry."

Lily lowered her voice, as if someone was eavesdropping. "Jethro has talked to just about everybody, mostly to get sympathy but also to get ammunition. If he gets the community behind him, it will be hard for you to do anything but move back in with him."

Mary Anne slumped her shoulders. Because of what she'd done, it was unlikely anyone in the Amish community would hire her. "I know, and I was hoping to find a job. I owe Jethro two hundred dollars."

Lily nodded. "You need money."

Mary Anne squeezed her hand. "Will you help me?"

"Of course. We have almost a hundred dollars in the cookie jar."

"*Nae,* I don't want your money."

"It's a loan, Mary Anne, and we can buy the egg sorter next year."

Mary Anne shook her head. "I need your help more than I need your money. My friend Pammy at the library is selling my quilts on the computer. I've already finished one quilt top and I need people to help me quilt it. I don't think any of the women in the *gmayna* will come to one of my quilting frolics."

Lily bounced Estee on her knee. "Of course I'll come. Where are you going to set up a quilt? I'm guessing Jethro won't let you do it in the house."

"I suppose I'll just do it out in the woods next to my tent, but first I have to steal the quilt frames from the cellar."

Lily giggled again. "It sounds so exciting, but it's not stealing if it's yours."

"Jethro bought them with his money. Everything is his."

"*Ach,* Mary Anne, when you get married you're supposed to become one flesh with your husband. One flesh means the money too."

Mary Anne scrunched her lips together in mock confusion. "I've never heard that in a sermon."

"And you never will," Lily said. "Not as long as my *dat* is preaching." She got to her feet and went to the sink, where she did what she could to wipe the green smudge off Estee's face.

Mary Anne picked up Emily and transported her to the sink as well. She got a little soap on a dishrag and gently scrubbed Emily's cheeks. It took the top layer of color off, but marker was notoriously stubborn. "Emily might have light green cheeks for *gmay.*"

"Oh, *sis yuscht,* Mary Anne. Maybe you had better stay away from church tomorrow. They're not going to be nice. At the very least, they'll give you the cold shoulder."

Mary Anne swallowed the lump in her throat. She'd take her medicine like a *gute*

Amish girl. "Jethro has given me the cold shoulder for four years. It's nothing I haven't borne before."

"But everyone will stare at you. My *dat* will scowl for sure and certain. He might even chastise you in front of everybody." Mary Anne didn't doubt it. Lily's *dat* was one of the ministers and quite proud and protective of his importance.

"As long as they let me in the door, I'll be there. It might keep me from hell, when all is said and done."

Lily shook her head. "*Ach,* Mary Anne. I wish I had your courage."

"You do. As I remember, you stood up to your *dat* when he wanted you to marry Tyler Yoder. He kicked you out of the house."

"I almost chickened out."

Lily and Mary Anne set the twins on the floor, where they immediately crawled away in search of adventure. "I'll have the quilt set up on Monday afternoon in the woods behind the house," Mary Anne said.

"I'll come after naptime." Lily opened a drawer in the kitchen and pulled out a little pouch. "Impatiens seeds. They grow well in the shade. You can plant some around the tent." She gave Mary Anne a hug. "I hope you find a job. You should go look for one today. Maybe news hasn't spread yet and someone will accidentally hire you."

"I'll do that," Mary Anne said, even if they both knew there was no hope.

News in an Amish community traveled faster than a horse in a buggy race.

Mary Anne knocked on her sister's door and listened for any sign of life inside the house. Mary Anne's sister Mandy and Mandy's husband, Noah, lived in a brand-new house Noah had built himself from foundation to roof. Of course, a slew of Amish neighbors had helped put up the walls, taped and sanded the Sheetrock, and lay the wood floors, but Noah had done just about everything else, including digging the well and installing the plumbing. Noah was very handy that way. Noah and Mandy also had solar panels — Aden's idea — to heat water that ran in pipes under the floorboards and heated the house. They had no problem getting approval from the bishop. He had the same heating system in his house.

Mandy had moved to Bonduel two years ago when she'd married Noah Mischler, and Mary Anne had been overjoyed to have her *schwester* in town, even though Mandy liked to stick her nose in other people's business.

Well, she was about to be neck deep in

Mary Anne's business. Mary Anne needed quilters, and Mandy was her *schwester.* Of course she'd say yes.

Mandy opened the door with her arm resting protectively on her stomach. Mary Anne always felt a twinge of pain whenever she saw someone close to having a baby, but she would never begrudge anyone their happiness. Every baby was a miracle, a gift from *Gotte.* Just because Mary Anne couldn't get pregnant didn't mean she couldn't rejoice with her *schwester,* even if that rejoicing came with a little hurt attached.

Mandy gasped. "Mary Anne. Noah says you've left Jethro. Is it true?"

Mary Anne's lips curled involuntarily. "It's so nice to see you too."

Mandy flicked her wrist in Mary Anne's direction. "Don't tease. You know I've heard the gossip. Have you left Jethro?"

"*Jah.*"

"And you're living in a tent?"

"In the backyard."

Mandy pressed her lips together and shook her head in righteous indignation. "I told you to go see a counselor. Noah wouldn't have survived without a counselor to help him with his *dat.*"

"I don't need a counselor, Mandy. The

bishop would never approve, and it wouldn't do any good. I've left Jethro, and that's that."

Mandy narrowed her eyes. "Do you want me to go talk to him? I don't mind putting him in his place. He needs to treat my *schwester* better. I'll tell him. Do you want me to tell him?"

Mary Anne had expected Mandy's righteous indignation. There wasn't a problem in the world Mandy didn't think she could fix. "*Nae,* Mandy. I need your help, but I don't want you to scold my husband. I need money and —"

"We've got a little in the bank. You can have it."

Mary Anne was going to have to stop telling people she needed money. Her family would give away all their savings if she let them. "I don't want your money. I'm going to sell quilts, and I need quilters. Can you come and help me quilt?"

"*Ach, vell,* I'm not a very *gute* quilter, but I'd be happy to help until the baby comes."

"How are you feeling?"

Mandy smiled. "Sore all over, and my stretch marks are getting stretch marks. I've never seen Noah so happy and so terrified at the same time, but there will never be a better *fater.*" She narrowed her eyes. "Is

Jethro giving you a hard time about not having a baby? I'm going over there right now to give him a piece of my mind."

Of course Jethro was giving her a hard time about not having a baby, but in ways he didn't even recognize himself. "*Nae.* Don't talk to him. Just come and quilt."

Mandy glanced behind her, then stepped out of the house and shut the door. "I don't want to worry you, but Noah was very upset when he heard you'd moved out. His *mater* left his *fater* because his *fater* wouldn't stop drinking, and it very nearly crushed Noah. He doesn't understand. Jethro is a *gute* man."

Mary Anne couldn't argue with that. Jethro was a *gute* man, but he was also blind and indifferent. "You don't have to come if it will make Noah unhappy."

Mandy blew a puff of air from between her lips. "You are my *schweste*r. Noah would want me to help, even if he isn't all that happy about it. The eye can't see what quiet sorrows dwell in our hearts. He knows that better than most." She leaned over and gave Mary Anne a kiss on the cheek. "When should I come to quilt?"

"Monday afternoon."

"Where are we quilting?"

"In the woods," Mary Anne said.

102

Mandy frowned. "We'll get rained on."

"We can't go in the house."

Mandy thought about that for a minute. "Sarah Beachy has one of those big canopies they use at auctions. It has walls, and it's big enough for two quilts if you need."

"Do you think she'd let me use it?"

"She's our cousin. It wouldn't hurt to ask."

Mary Anne grinned as it felt like the clouds might part to let in a little sunshine on her life. "It's a *gute* thing Mammi and Dawdi had so many children. We've got cousins all over the place." Sarah was Mammi and Dawdi's oldest granddaughter, old enough to be Mary Anne's mother and more likely to give Mary Anne an earful for her bad behavior. But she was still family. And she had a canopy for Mary Anne's quilts. Mary Anne gave Mandy a sideways hug. "I'll ask Sarah."

"I'll be there on Monday," Mandy said. "Let me know if you change your mind. I'm not afraid to give Jethro a *gute* rebuke."

Mary Anne paused momentarily and pinned Mandy with a stern eye. "Promise me you won't go near Jethro."

"I can't promise that. It's church tomorrow. Besides, the Bible says to swear not at all."

103

"Mandy," Mary Anne said, putting an extra dose of warning in her voice. "Leave him alone."

Mandy twisted her lips into a pout. "Okay. I won't scold Jethro, even though he deserves it."

Jethro didn't deserve any such thing. He was already suffering enough.

Mary Anne tried to ignore the hitch in her heart when she thought of Jethro sitting alone, miserable in that gloomy, lifeless house. She didn't love him anymore, but she suddenly felt wonderful guilty about what she was putting him through. "Jethro will be all right," she said, more to convince herself than anyone else.

"But will you?" Mandy placed her hands on Mary Anne's shoulders. "At least be sensible and skip church tomorrow."

Mary Anne sighed. "I'll have to go sometime, and I may as well get it over with."

Mandy looked positively stricken. "What about Jethro's parents? Do they know?"

"I don't know."

Mandy clicked her tongue. "They'll be at *gmay*. Aren't you afraid of Lois? I am."

She didn't want to admit it, but Mary Anne was terrified of Lois. Jethro's *mater* was fiercely loyal to her family, and she would not be happy that Mary Anne had left her son. "Maybe staying home is a *gute* idea."

"Of course, that will give them one more sin to add to your pile." Mandy scrunched her lips to one side of her face. "Or maybe your pile is so tall already, it won't matter."

Mary Anne squared her shoulders. She'd known the consequences of her choice when she made it. Angry mothers-in-law, disapproving neighbors, and unhappy husbands would not weaken her determination. "The sooner they get used to seeing me without Jethro, the better. I'm still a part of the *gmayna,* and I'm going tomorrow."

"Even if Jethro's *mamm* yells at you?"

"Lord willing, it won't come to that."

Mandy shook her head. "*Ach, schwester.* It definitely will come to that. I admire your bravery. But then, a *fraa* who leaves her husband is no shrinking violet. Just don't let Lois Neuenschwander see you cry."

"I won't. I've always been *gute* at hiding my emotions."

Sarah Beachy was a no-nonsense kind of woman, a midwife, and the mother of eight children, and Mary Anne wasn't altogether sure Sarah wouldn't throw Mary Anne out on her ear as soon as she stepped into the house.

Mary Anne pulled up to Sarah's place, where dogs and goats and boys ran amok in the yard. The boys — there had to be at least a dozen of them — were playing Annie I Over, and one of Sarah's younger sons had just run around from the backyard and was trying to hit someone from the other team with a big rubber ball. The best Mary Anne could hope for was that she didn't get tackled on her way up the sidewalk.

She successfully dodged two boys who were in turn trying to dodge the ball, but another one of Sarah's sons wasn't paying attention and backed into her. Fortunately, he didn't nudge her very hard. She probably wouldn't have a bruise.

Sarah's boy — Mary Anne didn't know his name — turned around, and surprise popped all over his face. "*Ach.* I'm sorry. I didn't see you."

"Hello. I can't remember your name."

"It's Pine."

"Okay, Pine. Is your *mamm* home?"

"She's in the house. Just walk in."

Mary Anne wasn't all that comfortable with walking in, but it seemed the kind of house where people *would* just walk in, strangers and friends alike. She opened the door and entered an empty great room with sparse furniture but plenty of room for church when it was their turn. *"Hallo,"* she called, still unsure of the reception she'd get. Maybe she'd walked in where she wasn't welcome.

"Who's there?" Sarah called back from the kitchen. "Come farther in. I'm up to my elbows in dough."

Mary Anne tiptoed across the great room as if she didn't want to get caught, and into the kitchen, which had three large windows and a skylight in the ceiling. Sarah was indeed up to her elbows in dough, kneading a ball as big as her head.

"I hope I'm not interrupting. Pine said I could walk in."

Sarah looked up from her kneading and raised an eyebrow in Mary Anne's direction. "I hear you're making all kinds of trouble, Cousin."

Mary Anne's mouth was already dry. Now she thought she might choke on her own tongue. "I . . . I don't mean to."

"Of course you do." Sarah rolled her dough into a thick rope, lifted it onto the cutting board, and cut it into five pieces. "We can let that rest for a few minutes." She rinsed her hands and wiped them on a towel hanging on the fridge. Sarah had big, capable hands that suited her well. She was almost six feet tall with a perpetual frown on her face and a good-natured gleam in her eye.

Mary Anne didn't know Sarah well. There was such a big difference in their ages. But she knew Sarah didn't put up with nonsense from anybody without being grumpy about it. Mary Anne liked her because she told you exactly what she thought. Everyone knew where Sarah stood, and it made her the most trustworthy person in Wisconsin.

"*Cum* and sit," Sarah said, leading Mary Anne to the massive table that took up half the space in the kitchen. Mary Anne sat while Sarah poured two cups of steaming *kaffee.* Mary Anne nearly swooned with pleasure. She hadn't had *gute kaffee* in a week. Sarah set down the two cups and sat at the head of the table. "I tell you, Mary Anne, folks around here haven't had this much excitement since the tornado hit the school. And you can only gossip so long about a tornado."

Mary Anne wrapped her hands around her cup but didn't dare take a sip. She wanted to be alert if Sarah decided to throw her out. "I'm sorry."

Sarah shifted in her chair to face Mary Anne head-on. "Why are you sorry?"

"I'm sorry I've upset so many people."

"You're not sorry you left?"

"Nae." She hated that she sounded like a little mouse.

Sarah grunted and gave Mary Anne a curt nod. *"Gute.* You never have to apologize for being brave."

"You . . . you aren't mad at me?"

"Of course not, though it doesn't matter if I am or not. Plenty of other people are. Barbara Yutzy practically had a conniption fit in the market, and Rose Mast and Scilla Zook are mad as wet hens. I'd stay away from them for a week or two. Barbara can get pretty mean."

"But you're not mad?"

"Nae. Husbands need to be put in their place once in awhile — just like wives do, I suppose. Husbands put their wives in their place all the time, but most Amish *fraaen* don't dare do it to their husbands. That's why the men of the church get too big for their britches."

"But you said everybody's mad at me."

"You're helping every last woman in Bonduel, though hardly nobody sees it that way. The men of this town are shaking in their boots, wondering if their wives are going to leave them too, considering that maybe they need to be better husbands, hiding their tents. You've done the women of the community a great service, even if they'll never thank you for it."

Mary Anne furrowed her brow. "I don't suppose . . . I didn't intend to do all that. I just moved out."

"A big door moves on a very small hinge."

Mary Anne took a sip of her *kaffee,* which turned out to be pumpkin spice. She sighed. "This is delicious. And so warm."

"I'll bet that tent gets wonderful cold at night."

"There was frost on my sleeping bag Tuesday morning, and the wind almost took Mammi and Dawdi with it last night."

Sarah raised an eyebrow and puckered her lips. "Mammi and Dawdi? What about Mammi and Dawdi?"

"Thursday night they set up a tent and sleeping bags next to mine. I tried to talk them out of it, but they said they came to support me."

Sarah snorted. "And you believed them?"

"I don't know." Did Sarah suspect the same ulterior motive Mary Anne suspected?

Sarah covered her mouth to cough and seemed to wipe a smile from her face with her hand. "*Ach, vell.* Of course they're there to support you. Why else would they come? But I can't imagine that's going to last very long. Two eighty-year-olds shouldn't be sleeping in sleeping bags."

"I agree."

"Then again, Mammi is stubborn. It's her best and worst quality."

"*Jah.*"

Sarah took a swig from her mug. "Now, Mary Anne, how are you going to support yourself? I don't wonder but Jethro has cut you off. I hear he's wonderful angry — not that you should feel bad about that. He got what was coming to him."

Mary Anne couldn't quite agree with that, though she wasn't sure why. She hadn't moved out to punish Jethro, had she? She just wanted to find her own happiness and let Jethro find his. "I took two hundred dollars from him. It's understandable he'd be angry."

Sarah blew air through her nose. "You're more forgiving than I am."

"I have a few plans for making money. I'm making a quilt to sell. The top is done, but I need quilters to help me finish it."

"I don't like quilting, but Mammi taught me how to do it all the same. I can help."

Mary Anne wasn't ready for how emotional Sarah's kindness made her. "Oh, *denki.* I so appreciate it."

"Don't say that until you see how wide my stitches are."

"It wonders me if I could borrow the

111

canopy you use for auctions. I don't have room in my tent to set up the quilt, and Jethro won't let me in the house."

Sarah nodded. "You can use it, but you'll need help setting it up. It's as heavy as a horse. I'll send my boys over. You can keep them if you feel so inclined."

Mary Anne giggled. "I'm willing to let them stay if they bring their own food. I can't afford to feed them."

"I can't either, but here we are. I shouldn't have kept trying for another girl. All it got me was five boys at the tail end." Sarah finished off her *kaffee.* "Quilt making isn't going to bring in enough money, I'm afraid."

"I'm going to find a job too."

Sarah shook her head, her mouth drooping like a wilted flower. "No one around here will hire you. We'd give you a job if we could, but we've already got too many sons to work the farm as it is." Sarah cleared both cups from the table. "*Cum.* I'll have the boys get the wagon hitched up and bring the canopy to your house."

They walked outside together, where the gaggle of boys was now playing some form of tackle football without a ball. "Boys," Sarah barked.

Her four youngest sons immediately peeled themselves from the group and came running.

"I need you to hitch up the team and take the canopy to the woods behind Mary Anne's house and set it up for her."

The youngest Beachy boy, who was probably about twelve, slouched his shoulders and groaned. "Aw, Mamm. We just started a new game."

Sarah wagged her finger at her son. "No complaining, young man. Mary Anne needs our help. Take your friends with you and get them out of my hair. There'll be pizza waiting for all of you when you get home."

"Yes, Mamm."

"And, Pine," Sarah said, pinning her son with a stern eye. "The next time someone comes to the house, don't just send them in like you don't have any manners. I taught you better than that."

"Yes, Mamm."

The four boys gathered up their friends and disappeared around the side of the house.

"His name is Pine?" Mary Anne said. "I didn't remember that."

"His real name is LaWayne, after his *dawdi,* but none of us liked the name much. His hair stuck out like a porcupine when he was born, and we started calling him Pine. We all like it better." Sarah propped her

113

hands on her hips. "You better get home so you can show those boys where you want that canopy."

Mary Anne nodded. "*Denki,* Sarah. You don't know how much I appreciate it."

Sarah smiled for the first time since Mary Anne had come. "Consider it a thank-you gift. My Aaron made breakfast this morning. He's one of the best as far as husbands go, but do you know how long it's been since he made breakfast?"

CHAPTER SEVEN

Oy, anyhow.

Mary Anne couldn't say she hadn't been warned. Her sister Mandy had been quite insistent that Mary Anne shouldn't go to church today. Mary Anne had anticipated some dirty looks and curious stares from everyone, but she hadn't expected the almost hostile reception she received from the women — most especially her mother-in-law — as soon as she alighted from Mammi and Dawdi's buggy. This morning Mammi had stuffed half a dozen pot holders into her white apron pocket and said something about buttering up the enemy.

Mary Anne's most dreaded encounter was with Jethro's *mater,* Lois. In truth, she was surprised Lois hadn't been to the woods to chastise her already. Maybe Lois was biding her time, thinking Mary Anne would move back into the house before the week was out. Maybe Lois was so angry she couldn't look at Mary Anne without spitting at her, and she was waiting until she had cooled down to have a talk with her. Maybe Lois and Jethro and Chris, Jethro's *fater,* were making plans to lock all the windows in the house and didn't want Mary Anne to suspect anything.

Lois and four of the other *fraaen* stood together on the porch. As soon as Mary Anne glanced in her direction, Lois turned her back, as did the women standing by her. It was a deliberate snub, and Mary Anne felt it right down to her bones. She'd have to grow a thicker skin immediately or she'd be reduced to tears before the first prayer of the day.

Mary Anne swallowed the very large lump in her throat and did her best to pretend Lois and her friends had all just turned around at the same time for no reason at all. She craned her neck while trying not to seem like she was looking in any particular direction. There was Jethro, surrounded by at least half the men in the *gmay.* They looked to be engaged in a serious conversation, each man frowning and stroking his beard as if trying to work out an impossible problem. For sure and certain Mary Anne was the problem they were trying to work out. Her face got warm. What had Jethro told them?

It didn't matter. He couldn't paint it any worse than it was. She had left her husband. Aside from divorce, that was as serious as it could get.

Earlier Jethro had hitched up Mammi and Dawdi's buggy and then his buggy and gone by himself to *gmay* without saying a word to either Mary Anne or her grandparents. Mary Anne hadn't expected him to be anything but unfriendly to her, but he usually had a kind word for her grandparents. Mammi had even made Jethro *kaffee* for the last two mornings in a row. Mary Anne couldn't begin to imagine that it was very *gute kaffee,* but even Mammi's strong brew was better than nothing. Probably. Jethro could at least show a little gratitude.

Mammi climbed out of the buggy after Mary Anne, pulled her shoulders back, and hooked her elbow around Mary Anne's, practically squeezing her arm off. "Don't you worry, dear," Mammi said, smiling as if the corners of her mouth had been fastened to her ears with clothespins. Her eyes flashed like she was ready for a fight. "We can't fault Lois for being offended for Jethro's sake. I don't wonder but that a red pot holder will soften her right up."

Mary Anne mustered a weak smile. "I

don't wonder that it will."

Cousin Sarah Beachy immediately crossed the yard to greet them, which made Mary Anne like her all the better. Sarah didn't much care about appearances. "Did my boys get the canopy up for you okay yesterday?"

Mary Anne smiled in spite of her growing uneasiness. "They had it done in less than ten minutes."

Sarah nodded. "Of course. They knew there was pizza waiting at home."

Dawdi unhitched the horse and led it toward the pasture, where the other horses grazed.

A deep line etched itself between Sarah's eyebrows. "What's wrong with Dawdi's leg? He's limping."

"*Ach,*" Mammi said, smoothing a pot holder in her hands. "He slept on his hip wrong last night."

The line between Sarah's eyes got deeper. "Mammi, I know you want to help Mary Anne, but you and Dawdi shouldn't be sleeping in a tent. You'll end up in the hospital."

Mammi sighed. "I know. Camping is the most miserable activity in the whole world. But we're willing to sacrifice our own lives if necessary for Mary Anne's sake."

Sarah smirked. "It's not as serious as all that."

"Really, Mammi," Mary Anne said. "I appreciate your support, but your health is more important. I'm fine living by myself in the woods. It's only temporary anyway." There was a certain comfort in having Mammi and Dawdi close by in the middle of the night, but if they moved back home, Dawdi's hip would quit bothering him and the camp food would definitely get better.

"We know it's only temporary, dear. That's why we're staying until the bitter end. We hope the end is close, but Jethro is being wonderful thick."

Sarah sighed. "Some men are like that."

"Who will help him if we don't?" Mammi said, glancing in Jethro's direction. "Lois is squarely on his side, and the men are stoking his indignation. It will do him no good."

Mary Anne's mouth got dry. Jethro's indignation was *gute* and hot. But he wasn't the only one. It seemed all the adults but Mary Anne's cousins and grandparents were glaring at her as if she were an *Englischer* with a camera — *ach, vell,* everyone but Lois and her friends. They were glaring at the front door of Barbara Yutzy's house.

Sarah heaved a sigh as she surveyed the

119

church members standing in the yard. "*Ach.* They're sharpening their knives, Mary Anne, but I don't wonder that you expected that."

Mary Anne swallowed hard. "I was hoping to talk one of them into giving me a job."

"I wouldn't advise it," Sarah said. "You can cut the hostility with a knife, and you haven't even tried to speak to anyone yet."

"Barbara Yutzy always seems to need help sorting eggs. And the harness shop has a 'Help Wanted' sign in their window. Dorothy Raber might need an extra pair of hands in her fabric shop, especially with a little one coming."

Sarah pressed her lips together. "You can try, but you're going to get your feelings hurt."

"They'll be nice if you give them a pot holder," Mammi said. She reached into her pocket and handed three to Mary Anne. "No one can resist a pot holder."

Sarah didn't seem convinced. "I don't wonder that your pot holders have worked miracles, Mammi, but they won't cure self-righteousness."

Mammi furrowed her brow. "I should have brought scarves."

Lily, with one of the twins in her arms, came to Mary Anne and gave her hand a squeeze. "It's going to be all right. Dorothy Raber said she's on your side." Lily's smile faded. "But she doesn't want anyone to know."

"I won't tell." Mary Anne's heart sank. She had hoped Dorothy might give her a job.

Her cousin Moses's wife, Lia, practically ran to them and threw her arms around Mammi's neck. "Mammi, I've been so worried about you. Moses says you and Dawdi are thinking of getting a divorce. Please tell me it's not true."

Mammi tapped her finger to her chin and looked up at the sky, as if thinking about it really hard. "I can't say one way or the other yet."

Lia's mouth fell open before she burst into laughter. "*Ach,* Mammi. What are you up to?"

"Everyone is having a wonderful *gute* time gossiping about it. I hate to ruin the fun."

Lia gave Mammi a wry smile. "You're always thinking of others." She put an arm around Mary Anne. "Are you okay? I hate to tell you this, but some of the *fraaen* are wonderful mad."

"I know. All I can say is that I didn't do this to hurt anybody, even Jethro."

"He's still hurt." It seemed Lia was doing

her best to keep her smile in place.

"He's not hurt. He's angry, and he'll get over it. He needs to go fishing more often." Mary Anne pressed her lips together to keep the bitterness from falling out of her mouth and onto her shoes.

"Of course," Lia said. "He shouldn't let his anger get the better of him." She patted Mary Anne's hand. "How is the extra tent working out?"

Mary Anne had borrowed her second tent from Lia's husband, Moses. "Wonderful *gute.* I put my sewing machine in there with all my fabric."

"Mandy says you're going to make quilts to earn some money."

"*Jah.* Do you want to come help us quilt?"

Lia nodded. "I'm wonderful busy at the store and with Crist, but I'll come when I can."

Mary Anne caught her breath. "Does Moses need any help at the cheese factory? I'm desperate for a job."

"*Ach,* Moses just hired two helpers, and we can't afford more just yet. I suppose we could fire one of them, but that doesn't seem very nice."

Mary Anne shook her head. "*Nae.* I wouldn't want to put someone out of a job. I'll think of something else."

Mammi handed Mary Anne another pot holder. "Lord willing, someone will hire you. Give them an extra pot holder or two. I can always make more."

Everyone but her cousins did their best to ignore Mary Anne as they lined up and marched into church. After "Das Loblied," Lily's *fater*, David Eicher, gave a sermon on Paul's letter to the Ephesians about how wives should submit to their husbands. Out of the corner of her eye, Mary Anne could see Jethro staring at her, as if trying to bore a hole through her head. Maybe he thought he could stuff the sermon inside her if he stared hard enough. Jethro wasn't the only one. It felt like everyone was staring at her, the people behind as well as the ones in front, as if everyone had eyes in the back of their heads. Feeling an unexpected sense of calm, Mary Anne slipped her hand into her apron pocket and fingered the pot holders Mammi had given her. Maybe she had come to terms with her own wickedness. Maybe she didn't care about her soul. The sermon had no effect on her except to make her very sleepy. A week of camping had taken its toll.

Mary Anne frowned. It wasn't that she didn't care about her soul. She just didn't care about Jethro. Was it so wrong to want her own happiness? Maybe her neighbors in the *gmayna* would call her proud, but she didn't regret for one minute her decision to move out. If they knew the heartache she had already lived through, they wouldn't be so quick to judge.

To her great satisfaction, the bishop's sermon was about how husbands should cherish their wives as Christ loves his church. She liked it when the bishop talked. He wasn't long-winded like David Eicher, and he always had something interesting to say. Mary Anne seldom had trouble staying awake when Bishop Yoder spoke.

Jethro was still scowling in her direction after services when the men set up the tables and the women readied the fellowship supper. Mary Anne tried to insert herself into the food preparations, but the other women wouldn't have it. She was begrudgingly impressed at how they excluded her with so much subtlety. Was that Lois's doing? In the kitchen, Mary Anne reached for a bread knife, and Martha Eicher grabbed it before Mary Anne could lay a hand on it. Mary Anne had made a loaf of bread in her Dutch oven, but it was the only loaf that didn't get sliced. She picked up a bowl of church spread to take to one of the tables, but Sadie Yoder snatched it from her hand. "I'll take this," Sadie said, and she practically flounced away.

It happened three times with three bowls of church spread. Did they not even want her touching the food? Were they afraid she'd contaminate it? Mary Anne pursed her lips together and tried not to let unpleasant emotions overwhelm her. Of course they were mad. It was silly of her to be hurt, and it was a *gute* lesson for another day. They weren't going to convince her to change her ways by treating her unkindly. She might be bullied into changing her behavior, but persecution would never change her heart.

How many *fraaen* had been browbeaten into submission with a few choice scriptures? How many husbands had forgotten the commandment to love their wives?

Mary Anne frowned. She didn't want her neighbors to judge her, yet here she was, judging them. Harshly. It was another *gute* lesson. She still had so much to learn.

Martha must have gotten distracted. She set down the bread knife, picked up a plate of vegetables, and walked out of the kitchen. Mary Anne sliced her bread quickly, before someone noticed she was using the bread knife. The Dutch oven bread had turned out wonderful *gute.* If she could slip it into one of the baskets without anyone noticing, it might get eaten after all.

Mandy was suddenly by her side, a basket of bread in her hands. "Put it in here, Mary Anne. Quick. No one will know." She smiled and pumped her eyebrows up and down.

Mary Anne couldn't help but laugh. Her sister would always be on her side. She glanced around furtively to make sure no one caught her, then slipped her slices of Dutch oven bread into the basket.

Mandy nudged Mary Anne with an elbow. "Barbara Yutzy is standing all by herself over there. You should ask her about a job. They've got over two thousand chickens. For sure and certain they could use an extra pair of hands."

Mary Anne's heart bounced like a rubber ball ricocheting back and forth between the floor and ceiling. Barbara was a plump woman with wiry salt-and-pepper gray hair and bushy eyebrows. She had a reputation for being blunt, and Mary Anne didn't know if she could bear blunt today. On the other hand, she was desperate for a job. Maybe Barbara would take pity on her.

Barbara stiffened like a post when she saw Mary Anne coming toward her. Mary Anne gave Barbara her friendliest smile and pretended not to notice the cold reception.

She shouldn't even bother asking. It was as plain as the mole on Barbara's neck that she was going to say no.

"Barbara, *wie gehts*?" Mary Anne said.

Barbara stared persistently at the far wall with her arms folded tightly around her waist. "I am fine, though I hear you are not."

Mary Anne tried hard not to let her smile slip. "It's true. I have moved out of my house."

"It is Jethro's house."

"All the more reason for me to be out of it."

Barbara snapped her head around to glare at Mary Anne. "No need to poke fun at me. There is no *gute* reason for you to move out. You are Jethro's wife, and a vow breaker."

It was no use defending herself. Neither Jethro nor Barbara nor Lois cared about her reasons for leaving, and they certainly didn't sympathize with her either way. Trying to make them see was just a waste of breath. Asking for a job was a waste of breath too, but that didn't stop her from making a fool of herself. "It wonders me if you need someone to help you sort eggs. I'm looking for a job." She wasn't just looking. She was desperate, but Barbara would probably gloat if she knew that.

Barbara pressed her lips together. "I wouldn't give you a job if you were the only *fraa* on earth with hands. You have disobeyed your husband. You don't deserve any such kindness. I shouldn't even be talking to a sinner like you."

"Jesus talked to sinners."

Barbara reacted with a start, as if Mary Anne had insulted her entire family. "*Jah*, he did. He said, 'Go and sin no more.' "

Mary Anne resisted the urge to heave a sigh. Barbara was only behaving as Mary Anne had expected her to behave. Mary Anne couldn't be cross with her, even though she really wanted that job. She wouldn't even need to borrow Jethro's buggy. She could walk to the Yutzys' house.

Barbara turned her back on Mary Anne and strode into the kitchen as if something very important was going on in there. Mary Anne leaned against the wall and tried not to be stung by the little darts everyone was shooting at her with their eyes. Was it worth the pain to ask Max Nelson about a job at the harness shop? Should she talk to Dorothy Raber even though Dorothy didn't want her to? Maybe it would be better to wait until tomorrow and go to the harness shop and the fabric store and the market when five dozen pairs of eyes weren't watching

128

her. No one wanted to be seen being nice to her.

She nearly smiled at the absurdity of it all.

Lois passed her with a basket of bread in her hands — the basket containing Mary Anne's bread. For sure and certain Lois had no idea she was serving bread made by wicked hands. She might have dumped it in the trash. Lois inclined her head in Mary Anne's direction without looking at her. "Go out the back door to the barn. I'll meet you there in two minutes."

It was frustrating that Mary Anne suddenly felt so unsettled. She was the brave one who slept in a tent and asked her hostile neighbors for jobs. She was the one who chose to find her own happiness instead of waiting hopelessly for it to come to her. She was the one who ate every bite of Mammi's cabbage and cheese lasagna and painted butterflies on Jethro's tent. Lois shouldn't have any power to upset her.

She didn't have to go out there, didn't want to go out there, but she couldn't avoid Jethro's parents forever, no matter how badly she wanted to. If she didn't talk to Lois now, Lois would come to her tent and make fun of her egg mobile and admonish her for her potato chip collection. She wouldn't even care that Mary Anne had found a cracker yesterday that looked just like a horse's head. It was better to meet in Yutzys' barn.

Besides, maybe Lois knew where Mary Anne could get a job. She really needed a job.

She'd only been given two minutes, so she hurried out the back door, only to realize she still had the bread knife in her hand. Lois wouldn't take kindly to Mary Anne wielding a weapon. She left the bread knife in the kitchen and patted her hand to her apron pocket. She still had Mammi's pot holders. Mammi said a red one would soften Lois up in no time. Too bad she only had one blue, one gray, and one fluorescent pink. Did Lois like fluorescent pink?

The Yutzys' barn was spick-and-span, with swept cement floors and the enticing smell of fresh straw. Families spent weeks getting ready to host *gmay,* and even the barn was cleaned. At least she and Lois would have a pleasant place to visit, though Mary Anne suspected it wasn't going to be a visit and there wouldn't be anything pleasant about it.

Mary Anne ran her hands over the smooth wood of the barn walls. They would be perfect for a mural of smiling children or a field of sunflowers or even a herd of cows.

Wouldn't Jethro's barn look darling with a flock of birds painted on the outside west wall? Or a series of quilt squares. A whole patchwork quilt would be *wunderbarr.* Where could she get some extra paint? It would take a lot of paint.

Her gaze traveled to the ceiling. How high could she go on Jethro's ladder?

It had been nearly ten minutes. Was Lois purposefully making her wait? Maybe she'd been cornered by Gloria Stutzman. Gloria liked to talk about her arthritis and her kidney stones, and it was hard to pry away from her once she got going.

Mary Anne strolled to the stalls and petted the Yutzys' two horses. She loved drawing horses. Maybe Jethro would like a picture of his horse painted on his barn. *Nae.* Jethro didn't like any of her projects. They were a waste of time and money and kept her from important things like cleaning his latest catch.

Mary Anne had just about decided Lois was playing a dirty trick on her when the side door opened, and Lois walked into the barn, followed by her husband Chris, Jethro, and Jethro's *bruder,* Willie Jay. Mary Anne's heart sank all the way to her toes — maybe farther. It was very unfair of Lois to plan an ambush. Mary Anne hadn't brought enough

131

pot holders.

Willie Jay had always been Mary Anne's least favorite relative. She couldn't quite put her finger on why she disliked him so much, but it probably had something to do with the air of superiority that hung about him like a sharp smell. He thought he knew the Bible better than anyone and soundly defeated anyone who debated him about it. He became insufferable when he was made a minister a year ago. Mary Anne found his pride very un-Amishlike.

Willie Jay was eight years older than Jethro, with a wonderful nice wife, Naoma, who barely said three words at one sitting, and seven orderly children who never seemed to get their clothes dirty, even when doing chores on Willie Jay's farm. Mary Anne hadn't noticed Willie Jay at services. He and Naoma lived in Appleton, and Mary Anne and Jethro didn't see them much. He was a very unpleasant sight indeed. "Willie Jay, it's wonderful *gute* to see you," she said, adding lying to her list of sins. She couldn't very well say what she was really thinking. She wouldn't give them the satisfaction of believing she was anything but indifferent.

Willie Jay shut the door behind him and shook his head. "I am disappointed in you, Mary Anne. I truly am."

"So am I. Very disappointed," Jethro chimed in, probably feeling the need to make it clear who was the most upset by Mary Anne's leaving.

Mary Anne bit her tongue on the need to defend herself. They didn't care about her reasons.

Lois propped her hands on her hips. "We've talked about it — all of us — and we agree that you must move back with Jethro immediately."

How nice to see a family so in harmony with one another.

Mary Anne was going to make her tongue bleed if she kept clamping down on it like this. The only thing she could think to do was distract them. "Do any of you know where I could get a job, preferably one I can walk to?"

They weren't so easily distracted. Jethro's *dat* found the milking stool, set it on the floor in front of Mary Anne, and motioned for her to sit. "Jethro says you painted one whole side of his tent."

"And she hung potato chips and crackers all around the inside," Jethro said.

Lois gasped. Chris and Willie Jay were rendered speechless.

Jethro and his *fater* were quite a bit alike. They both wasted hours at the river with a fishing pole, and Chris had no regard or patience for nonsense like fish-shaped hot pads or rainbow Jell-O desserts.

Chris again motioned to the milking stool. "Why don't you sit down, and we'll talk about it."

Mary Anne wasn't about to fall for that trick. All four of the Neuenschwanders were taller than she was. They weren't going to bring her lower. If they wanted to browbeat her, they could do it eye to eye. *"Nae, denki,"* she said. "I'm not going to stay much longer."

Lois, Willie Jay, and Jethro wore matching scowls. Chris seemed confused.

Mary Anne couldn't have hoped to have a *gute* relationship with Lois after moving into a tent, but it made her very sad all the same. She and Lois had always gotten along well. Mary Anne might even have said they were *gute* friends. Lois had come to the hospital after the miscarriage and spent two weeks after that at the house every day just to make sure Mary Anne was okay.

Willie Jay glanced at Jethro. "Do you understand the danger you're in, Mary Anne? What *Gotte* has joined together, no man or woman can put asunder. *Gotte* said that man must leave his father and mother and cleave unto his wife. Paul said that mar-

134

riage is honorable for everyone." He then proceeded to quote several other scriptures about marriage, making sure Mary Anne knew he was familiar with every chapter and verse. He'd practically memorized the entire New Testament. It was quite impressive — not likely to convince her — but impressive.

Mary Anne smiled and nodded in all the right places during Willie Jay's speech. She wasn't going to argue with Willie Jay about what the Bible said. He knew it much better than she did, and she had no scriptures to defend herself with. She was more than willing to admit that.

Maybe it was time to start handing out pot holders.

Willie Jay finally wound down, and Mary Anne laced her fingers together. "You're right about everything, Willie Jay. I am wicked and ungrateful and not worthy of Jethro's love. He doesn't deserve such a wife. It is better that I moved out."

Jethro narrowed his eyes. "I told you that you couldn't convince her that way. She won't ask, 'Is it I?' "

The urge to laugh grabbed Mary Anne around the throat. Had Jethro not just heard her take responsibility for everything? To him, asking "Is it I?" meant "Mary Anne has finally given in and moved back into the house." She found it funny, in a sad way, that none of them cared to ask how she felt. Her feelings didn't matter to any of them. Jethro had made that very clear year after miserable year.

It really was time for those pot holders. She retrieved them from her pocket. "Here," she said, handing them to Lois. "Mammi wanted you to have these. I'm sorry to have caused such a fuss."

Lois looked at the pot holders as if she wasn't quite sure what pot holders had to do with tents and husbands and Mary Anne. "Anna gave these to you? Does she know what you've done?"

Jethro scowled. "Her grandparents are camping out in my woods too. They say they're on her side."

Lois's mouth fell open. "Well, they've got to stop it. No good can come of indulging such wickedness. I'll talk to Anna immediately."

"It won't do any *gute,*" Jethro said. "Anna is as stubborn as Mary Anne."

Chris nodded. "And I hear Anna and Felty are splitting up. You can't talk them into anything."

Lois stuffed her pot holders into her pocket, more to get them out of the way than anything else. "You've got to move back home, Mary Anne. I know you're upset about the baby, but in a marriage, you work things out. You don't just leave. I don't care how often Jethro goes fishing or how many anniversaries he misses, you stay because you've made a promise, no matter how hard it gets." Mary Anne's ears must have been playing tricks on her. She thought Lois's voice shook just a little. "The rest of us *fraaen* stay no matter what. What makes you so special?"

It was unfair of Lois to assume Mary Anne thought herself anything but a nobody. "I'm not special. I simply don't have the courage to live a joyless life."

Lois's eyes flashed with something deep and painful, and then the emotion was gone, replaced with the righteous indignation of a *mater*. "Jethro says you think he's boring. You should thank *Gotte* you have a godly, steady man."

Willie Jay nodded. "You should be grateful he still wants you, even though you can't have children."

For the first time since she'd walked into the barn, Lois looked unsure of herself. "Hush, Willie Jay."

Willie Jay didn't know how close he had come to the mark. He knocked the wind right out of her. "Jethro *doesn't* want me, and it *is* because I can't have children. Can you blame me for leaving?"

Her in-laws fell silent, as if someone had turned off the sound on an *Englischer*'s television. She should have bitten her tongue. They didn't care about her reasons, and she'd just given them another stick to beat her over the head with. Oy, anyhow. She'd put too much confidence in those pot holders.

"I do want you, Mary Anne." Jethro's voice was nearly a whisper, which told more truth than his words did.

Willie Jay pasted a fake smile on his face. "There. You see, Mary Anne. Jethro does want you."

"He's more concerned about his money."

Jethro very nearly jumped out of his skin. "I am not!"

Mary Anne nodded, as if she agreed with him. "I've promised to pay him back as soon as I can. That's why it would be to your advantage to help me find a job."

"You wouldn't need a job if you moved back home," Willie Jay said.

"I've got quilts to sew and murals to paint, flowers to plant and potato chips to collect. There is so much of life I want to live before I die. I'm sorry to be the cause of so much pain, but I'm not moving back."

138

The side door flew open as if blown by a stiff wind. Mammi swept into the barn as if she were a firefighter trying to save a cat from a burning building. "Mary Anne, I thought I'd lost you. I didn't want you to think your camping partner had abandoned you." She smiled and gave Mary Anne a private wink, her lips forming the word *solidarity* before she turned to Lois. "I have a special gift for you, Lois."

Lois's mouth curled into a smile, as if she had no choice. Mammi had that effect on people. "There's no need for presents, Anna. Mary Anne has already given me some of your lovely pot holders."

Mammi nodded at Mary Anne as if she couldn't be prouder. "Good job, dear." She studied Lois's face. "Do you like pot holders? If not, I also make scarves and Minion beanies."

Lois gave Mammi an indulgent smile. "Anna, I'm concerned that you're camping in Jethro's backyard."

Mammi scrunched her lips to one side. "I'm concerned too. I don't particularly like camping, and that toilet seat is wonderful cold in the morning. And Felty's snoring has gotten worse."

Lois cleared her throat. "What I meant was, I'm afraid it sends Mary Anne the wrong message. For sure and certain you don't want her to think you approve of her leaving her husband."

Mammi waved her hand in the air. "*Ach*, I approve of everything Mary Anne does. Last night she made us Parmesan Chicken Ranch tinfoil dinners with real Parmesan cheese."

Mary Anne waited for Jethro to say something about how expensive real Parmesan cheese was, but he didn't make a peep. He was probably wishing he'd been invited to dinner, even if Mary Anne had spent too much money on it.

Willie Jay's nostrils flared. "So, you don't care that your granddaughter is choosing a life of sin?"

Mammi looked at Willie Jay as if he were a pesky mosquito buzzing in front of her face. "Camping is not a sin, Willie Jay Neuenschwander, though it should be against the law." She took Mary Anne's hand. "We really must go. Mary Anne is making Italian horsey spinach soup for dinner tonight in the Dutch oven."

"Italian *orzo* spinach soup," Mary Anne said, lest Jethro think she was going to do anything bad to his horse.

"Whatever it is, it's going to be delicious," Mammi said. "It was nice seeing you, Willie

Jay. Give Naoma my love, and all those adorable children. Tell her she's welcome to pick huckleberries again when the weather turns."

The argument Willie Jay was going to make died on his lips. Mammi disarmed even the most hostile neighbor with her sweet, grandmotherly kindness. Maybe it was because Mammi had just invited his wife to pick huckleberries or had called his children adorable. Or maybe Willie Jay was worried about Jethro's horse. Whatever his reasons, Mary Anne was grateful that he didn't start quoting Bible verses. Mary Anne had had enough Bible for one day.

Jethro would call her very wicked for having such a thought.

Ach, vell. She was fully aware of what Jethro thought of her. She wouldn't let it ruin her day.

CHAPTER EIGHT

Two weeks since Mary Anne had set up a tent, and the woods behind Jethro's house were beginning to look like the circus was in town. Not only had Mary Anne decorated both sides of his tent with disorderly butterflies, but she had painted the side of his barn with a six-foot-by-six-foot quilt square, and there was nothing he could do about it. If he had seen her painting the barn, he would have stopped her, but one of the people in this family had to work, and she made a lot of mischief when he was at his job all day.

Last Saturday, he'd sneaked into her tent while she was off to the market with Anna and Felty, no doubt spending his hard-earned two hundred dollars. Her strange collection of mobiles hung everywhere, and she'd stolen two rickety benches from the barn to use as shelves for her ridiculous collections. Standing in her crowded tent, he had considered getting a lock for the barn, but Mary Anne still milked the cow every day and Anna and Felty used the bathroom in there. He couldn't lock them out.

In her tent, Mary Anne had a pile of unusual rocks, a collection of oddly shaped potato chips and crackers, even a group of walking sticks leaning against the tent wall. It was a jumbled, chaotic mess of art and garbage. She had been in the process of sanding one of the old benches, probably to paint butterflies all over it and sell it on the computer. So much trouble for so little profit. Why wouldn't she just move home?

Jethro gazed out his back window and scrubbed his fingers through his hair. Mary Anne had attached Jethro's butterflied tent to Moses Zimmerman's eight-man tent. She had quite a bit of living space out there. Not only that, but a huge canopy had shown up two Saturdays ago under which Mary Anne had set up her quilting frames, and all sorts of cousins had shown up to help her quilt. There were three cousins out there now, visiting and laughing with Mary Anne while their children played at their feet. Anna was quilting too, and even Felty sat at the quilt holding a needle but not doing anything with it. Jethro would have given anything to be invited to sit with them, if only to feel included in Mary Anne's circle of friends.

Even though he was still ferociously mad at her for abandoning him and taking his money and embarrassing him in front of the whole district, he missed her something wonderful. And yes, he admitted to himself, he hadn't appreciated her as he should have. She made the best *kaffee* in the whole world, and he had completely forgotten what her sweet rolls tasted like.

Since the night Anna and Felty had shown up, Jethro hadn't been invited back to Mary Anne's campsite for dinner — probably because Mary Anne had been the one doing the cooking, and she wouldn't have cooked for him if he'd been starving to death, which he was. Except on the nights he went to his parents' house, he ate cold cereal for breakfast, McDonald's for supper, and cold cereal for dinner. When he was feeling especially sorry for himself, he pulled a Pop-Tart out of the cupboard and toasted it over the open flame of his stove for dessert.

He went to dinner every Sunday and Wednesday night at his parents' house, but there was only so much scolding he could take before he longed for home; even an empty house was better than listening to his *mamm*'s lectures.

Didn't they know he'd tried everything? He'd yelled at Mary Anne and tried to make her see reason. He'd put locks on the doors and brought the bishop to talk to her. He'd made sure everyone in the *gmayna* was on his side and that no one would hire her. He didn't want her to find a job, even if it meant he'd never see his two hundred dollars again. If she got a job, she'd move out of his woods and somewhere far away. He'd made it as hard for her as he could, but she stubbornly insisted on sleeping in a tent. He had hoped she would grow tired of camping, but if anything, she seemed to be hunkering down, preparing for a long stay.

Life with him must have been very miserable indeed if camping held more appeal than his comfortable house. That realization was a knife right to the heart. And Mary Anne didn't care how much it hurt.

Jethro fingered the letter in his hand, reluctant to open it, knowing exactly what it was going to say. Willie Jay had sent him three letters in the past week. They were full of scripture, hellfire, and brimstone, as if Jethro was the one who needed convincing instead of Mary Anne. He had lectured her until he was blue in the face, and he didn't know what else to do. He felt helpless and useless and desperate. And Willie Jay's letters weren't helping.

Jethro glanced at the clock. For some reason, Mary Anne hadn't taken it. Anna would be here soon for their first cooking lesson. He'd avoided it as long as he could. Anna was wonderful sweet and very thoughtful, but her lessons would be a complete waste of time. He'd been to enough family dinners at Mammi and Dawdi Helmuth's house to know Anna knew even less about cooking than he did. At the very least, maybe she could teach him how to use the *kaffee* pot. Surely he could teach himself how to make a *gute* cup of *kaffee* if Anna pointed him in the right direction. His *mater* could probably teach him, but he'd been too ashamed to admit to her that he didn't already know how. Anna would have to be the one to help him.

A knock at the front door made him jump. Lord willing, it wasn't another cousin come to join the quilting party or some *Englisch* friend of Mary Anne's here to buy a potato chip mobile.

He opened the door to his *bruder* Willie Jay, standing on the porch with *Dat,* David Eicher, Norman Coblenz, and Adam Wengerd, and none of them were smiling. *"Wie gehts?"* he said, the anger rising in him like bile. They were here to give him what-for about his wife, but if they thought they could do any better at convincing her to come home, they were welcome to try.

"Hallo, bruder," Willie Jay said, laying a hand on Jethro's shoulder. It was all Jethro could do not to pull from Willie Jay's grasp. Willie Jay had an obedient, submissive *fraa.* He didn't need to act superior about it.

"How did you get up here?" Jethro asked. Appleton was only half an hour away by car, but the trip by buggy was long.

"I hired a driver," Willie Jay said. "I'm concerned that Mary Anne hasn't seen the error of her ways, and I thought you could use my help."

"And mine," *Dat* said. Hadn't he grown tired of lecturing Jethro yet?

"Can we come in?" David Eicher asked. David was one of the ministers in the district, and he'd given a wonderful *gute* sermon at *gmay* on how a wife should reverence her husband — not that Mary Anne had listened. But at least David was on Jethro's side. Most of the men in the district were, and most of the women too. He could at least take comfort in the fact that Mary Anne was the one who was in the wrong.

Jethro reluctantly stepped back and invited them into the house. Maybe they wouldn't lecture him. Maybe they'd come up with a way to convince Mary Anne to move back. He motioned to the easy chair and the sofa. They were the only furniture left in the front room. *"Cum reu,"* he said. "Mary Anne took the bench and my footrest, but you can sit on the sofa and the floor, if you like."

Willie Jay's frown deepened. "You shouldn't let her do that. If things are easy for her, she won't care to come back."

Jethro scrubbed his fingers through his hair. "I bought locks for all the doors. She can't take anything else."

David took Jethro's easy chair, Adam and *Dat* sat on the sofa, and Norman, Willie Jay, and Jethro sat on the floor. It wasn't comfortable, but the floor wasn't much worse than the backless benches they sat on every other week for church. Adam was the deacon of the church. It was comforting to have a minister and a deacon sitting in his living room, offering their help to get his *fraa* to come home. As Mary Anne's cousin, Norman Coblenz was another strong ally. Norman had always rubbed Jethro the wrong way with his rigid and immovable opinions of the church and the *Ordnung,* but now it seemed he was the only one of Mary Anne's relatives who wasn't blind to her sins.

David settled into the easy chair. "Jethro, something has got to be done about your *fraa*. She is setting a bad example for the *gmayna*."

"I know," Jethro said. Mary Anne had already led many of her cousins astray. What would David think if he knew his daughter Lily was in the woods right now, working on one of Mary Anne's quilts?

Adam Wengerd leaned back and folded his arms across his chest. "*Die youngie* watch her behavior and think that when they are married they will be able to leave anytime they want." Adam had two unmarried sons and a teenage daughter. He knew what he was talking about.

"The Helmuths have always been a troublesome lot." David inclined his head in Norman's direction. "Not all of you."

Norman shook his head. "Don't mention it. I agree with you." Norman's sister Cassie had left the church, and Anna and Felty had matched her up with an *Englisch* doctor. Norman would probably never get over it.

David's daughter Lily had married Mary Anne's cousin Aden, and the whole thing was still a sore spot for David. "Not a month ago I heard Anna and Felty in the market arguing like children. If I had known about the Helmuth family problems before you married, Jethro, I would have warned you off all of them."

Such a warning wouldn't have mattered to Jethro. He had been so turned over every which way for Mary Anne, the angel Gabriel himself couldn't have talked Jethro out of marrying her. The memory of their wedding day stole his breath. Mary Anne had worn a blue dress that had made her eyes look like cornflowers sitting on a snow-covered hill. She was like the sunshine and the evening star and the first bud of spring all in one person. He'd never forget her smile or how completely happy he had been. *Ach,* how things had changed!

"Some of our *fraaen* are discontented," David said. "We men are not perfect, and I fear Mary Anne's behavior has given the women an excuse to leave their husbands if we make even a tiny mistake. They'll think they can get better gifts if they threaten to move out of the house when we forget a birthday."

Jethro swallowed the lump in his throat. "I shouldn't have forgotten our anniversary."

"It's not your fault, Jethro," David said. "Who hasn't forgotten a special day or neglected to clean off his boots before coming into the house? We all make mistakes.

Wives and husbands are expected to forgive each other."

"I would forgive Mary Anne with all my heart if she'd only move back in."

David nodded. "Of course you would. We all would." He leaned forward and propped his elbows on his knees. "Mary Anne has got to move back home before she upsets the whole applecart. That's all there is to it."

Jethro threw up his hands. "What can I do? I've tried everything."

Norman flared his nostrils. "You need to go out there right now and tell her she is going to hell."

Jethro pressed his lips together. Mary Anne wasn't going to hell, was she? She didn't love him anymore, and *fraaen* were commanded to love their husbands. Maybe she *would* go to hell for breaking the commandments, but who was he to pass that kind of judgment on anybody? Not even the bishop had done that. "I've talked and talked until Mary Anne is sick of my voice. I've quoted every scripture I can think of. I've reminded her of her duty as a *fraa*. If David's sermon at *gmay* didn't convince her to change her ways, I don't know that anything will."

David was obviously pleased with the

compliment, but it didn't solve their problem. David stroked his beard, which held a few wiry strands of gray hair. "The only thing I can think to say is that you need to be firm. Joshua told the children of Israel, 'Be strong and of a good courage.' That is your task. Be a man. Your wife will respect you if you stand up to her."

"Getting locks was a *gute* start," Adam said. "She knows she can't just do anything she wants and get away with it."

Norman narrowed his eyes. "And don't apologize for forgetting your anniversary. It only makes you seem weak."

Jethro slumped his shoulders. "I already apologized."

"Well, don't do it again. Your word is law, and she has to truly believe it or she will never choose the path of obedience." Norman laced his fingers together. "You need to put your foot down. I saw her in town the other day in your buggy."

Adam shook his head. "You can't let her use the buggy."

"In your heart, you know what you have to do," David said. "We cannot tell you exactly what, but if you remember to show your *fraa* strength instead of weakness, she will change her ways. She has to have confidence in your judgment and strong hand. She has to know that you are the capable leader of this family."

Jethro nodded, even as his heart ached. There was no family, and there never would be. Jethro couldn't be a leader when there wasn't a flock. Besides, was that the kind of leader he wanted to be?

One nice thing about a meeting where some people sat on the floor: it tended to be short. Everyone stood up and shook Jethro's hand in turn. David gave him an especially firm handshake. "We are counting on you, Jethro. If you don't solve this, more *fraaen* will start to get bad ideas, and then where will we be?"

Dat shook hands with Jethro and leaned close to his ear. "Don't mention to your *mamm* I was here."

Jethro watched through the front window as Willie Jay and *Dat* got into one buggy and Adam, Norman, and David got into another. They had just set the weight of the world on his shoulders. What was he going to do with it? The *gmayna* was depending on him not only to save his own marriage, but all the other marriages as well. It was a greater task than he could ever accomplish.

Jethro trudged into the kitchen and took a look out the back window again. Mary Anne, her three cousins, and Anna and

153

Felty were sitting around the quilt on six of his kitchen chairs, putting stitches in the quilt as if they were born with needles in their hands.

Six of his kitchen chairs? How long had they been gone? He drew his brows together. Hadn't they all been inside the house on the day he'd put in the locks? *Jah,* he was sure of it.

Had Mary Anne somehow gotten into the house? Had he forgotten to lock the doors one day last week?

His heart pounded against his chest, and he straightened his spine in righteous indignation. How dare she? How dare she think she could still come into this house and take whatever she wanted? She had lost that privilege when she moved out. No matter how uncomfortable, she had made her bed, and he expected her to lie in it. One thing was for certain: He was going to be a man, firm and unyielding, and he was going to get his chairs back. Now.

He slammed the door behind him and rattled every window in the house. Halfway across the lawn, it hit him. He had locked the doors, but he hadn't locked the windows. Would Mary Anne stoop to climbing through a window? Of course she would. She had stolen his money. She was smart enough for anything, and he was going to stop indulging her.

Before he reached the edge of the woods, he slowed his steps and wiped the scowl off his face. Mary Anne deserved his wrath, but three cousins and her grandparents were also there. He would temper his reaction in front of them. Besides, he didn't want to scare *die kinner.*

Anna's dog, Sparky, barked at him as if he was a robber, and ran around and around Jethro's feet, nipping at his pant leg. He had to tiptoe to keep from stepping on her. Lily and Aden's giant dog, Pilot, loped around Jethro's backyard playing tag with Lia's little boy, Crist. Pilot barked at Jethro but was too busy to attack. *Gute.* Pilot tended to jump on people, and Jethro was in no kind of mood.

Anna and Mary Anne's sister Mandy glanced up from their stitches when Jethro approached and smiled as if they were happy to see him. Mary Anne ignored him completely, though she'd seen him coming for sure and certain.

"*Hallo,* Jethro," Mandy said. "It's a wonderful nice day for quilting. Have you ever seen such a beautiful quilt top? Mary Anne made it."

Jethro had no interest in quilt tops, not

155

when chairs were disappearing from his house and Mary Anne was painting everything that stood still. He had to be a man.

"Do you want to join us?" Felty said. "I'm threading needles because I've got the strongest trifocals money can buy."

Lily Helmuth was trying to quilt and bounce a baby on her lap at the same time. "*Wie gehts,* Jethro? Did you have a nice day at work?"

"*Gute* enough," he said, knowing no one really cared what kind of day he'd had at work, especially not Mary Anne. She didn't even care that her husband was starving or that he'd been saving that two hundred dollars for something special.

Lia, Moses Zimmerman's wife, was a tall brunette who seemed to have more than her share of *gute* sense. Jethro used to like her until she had shown up for one of Mary Anne's quilting parties last week. She looked a little embarrassed that she had come to help Mary Anne defy her husband. "*Denki* for letting us have a quilting frolic in your backyard. I hope we're not making too much noise."

Anna tugged at her thread. "Jethro doesn't care if we're out here. Do you, Jethro?"

Jethro cleared his throat. He wasn't going to pretend that everything was pies and cakes. "Of course I care. I want Mary Anne to stop this nonsense and come home." Should he mention the part about hell?

Mandy stretched a smile across her face. "But Mary Anne loves to camp."

Lily nodded and hid her smile behind her baby's head. "I've never seen anyone take to camping the way Mary Anne has."

Mary Anne's lips curled into an involuntary smile, as if amused by some private joke. Maybe they were secretly sharing a laugh about the stolen kitchen chairs. Probably they were making fun of him.

He knew what they were up to, and he refused to let them think they'd pulled one over on him. "I want my chairs back."

All hands stilled and all eyes turned in his direction, even Mary Anne's.

"Your chairs?" Anna said, her brows drawn together in concern. "Are they missing?"

"Mary Anne stole them."

Mary Anne suddenly became very intent on her quilting. Mandy pressed her lips into a hard line, and Lia lowered her eyes and stabbed her needle into the fabric.

Anna stiffened her spine. "Mary Anne doesn't have a dishonest bone in her body. Who is she supposed to have stolen them from?"

Jethro growled. "From me. She climbed through my window and took them from my kitchen. There are only two left."

Anna didn't seem to understand how serious this was — how serious all of it was. "*Ach,* are you having folks for dinner? I haven't taught you how to cook anything yet."

Jethro tried to remain calm. Besides Norman Coblenz, none of Mary Anne's relatives were on his side. Was there any way to make them see reason? "I'm not having anyone for dinner. I want my chairs back. I can't live in an empty house."

"Your house is far from empty," Anna said, as cheerfully as if she was talking about an upcoming party. "You have two wonderful nice beds I am very envious of."

Jethro clenched his teeth. "Until Mary Anne steals them."

Mandy looked as if she were on the verge of laughing out loud. "Why would she steal them when she has such a nice cot to sleep on?"

It was too much to bear. "A nice, hundred-dollar cot I bought for fishing trips, not for Mary Anne's temper tantrums."

Mary Anne hunkered down in her chair and attacked the quilt with her needle. Maybe her conscience nagged at her. *Gute.*

Lord willing, she would realize how *deerich,* foolish, she was being. Jethro had just about had all he could take. Maybe she could see she'd pushed him too far. Maybe she could sense he was determined to be a strong and capable leader in their family.

Mandy seemed to be having fun at his expense. Her expression set his teeth on edge. "You're not going to take our chairs, are you, Jethro? How will we help Mary Anne get her quilt done without chairs?"

Anna nodded. "They're not only your chairs. They belong to both of you. I remember your *onkel* Perry gave you the set as a wedding present."

"Maybe you should take some tape and a pen and label all the things in the house that are yours," Mandy said. It sounded more like she was taunting him than giving him a suggestion.

"It's all mine," Jethro said, knowing that wasn't entirely true. Onkel Perry *had* given them both the dining set on their wedding day. The dishes had come from Mammi Zook. Mary Anne had brought several pillowcases and three blankets to the marriage. Still, he was the one who earned the money. He was the head of the household. Everything belonged to him as part of his stewardship.

Mandy pursed her lips as if she'd taken a hearty bite of a lemon. "So, the husband and wife become one flesh, but the bank account is all yours. Is that what you think?"

Everyone but Mary Anne stared at him as if he had a bad smell hanging about him — and he hadn't done a single thing to deserve it.

Mary Anne finally spoke. "I'll return your chairs as soon as I can buy my own." She didn't sound at all sorry she'd stolen his chairs. She didn't sound sorry for anything.

"Ach," Mandy protested. "You don't need to buy chairs, Mary Anne. I can spare two from my kitchen."

"I've got three folding chairs I can bring over," Lily said.

Lia smoothed her hand along the quilt top and shot Jethro a conciliatory smile. "You can always find old chairs at yard sales, Mary Anne. It would be another way to make money if you painted and sold them."

Jethro huffed out a breath. "I'll never get my chairs back, or my money." He hoped the same couldn't be said about his *fraa.*

Mandy smiled so Jethro could see all her teeth. "You'll get your money back. Mary Anne found a job."

Mary Anne slowly raised her head and gave him a hesitant smile. "I'll be able to pay you back."

Jethro felt as if he'd stumbled backward even while he was standing still. Why had he mentioned the money? It wasn't about the money, and surely Mary Anne knew that. It wasn't about how many chairs she could buy at a yard sale or the fancy waders at the sporting goods store. Mary Anne's poverty was the only thing keeping her in his woods. "Who . . . who gave you a job?" He'd pay a visit to them tonight and have a little talk. Everyone in the community should know not to encourage Mary Anne's nonsense.

"It's at a little senior center in Shawano."

Mary Anne desperately wanted to earn some money, but he'd never thought she'd be brave enough to work *out*. There was no one in the community to blame for this.

He couldn't forbid her to work for an *Englischer* — she had made it very clear she didn't care what he thought — but he could still stand firm and keep her from taking the job. "You'll have to tell them *nae* because you don't have any way to get there. You've taken my chairs, but you can't take my buggy." Jethro felt the unkindness of it before it was even out of his mouth, but it had to be done. He refused to lose Mary Anne.

She gazed at him, her eyelid twitching slightly like it always did when she was angry. "Your buggy is safe. Someone is going to pick me up three days a week. Tuesday, Thursday, Friday, starting tomorrow." She bloomed into a smile, as if she hadn't just shattered his already upended world. "It's *wunderbarr.* I'll get to help them do crafts and make quilts, and they'll give me a ride."

"We're going with her tomorrow," Anna said. "It's free for anyone over sixty-five."

Mandy gave Mary Anne's hand a squeeze. "It's just what you were looking for."

"It's wonderful *gute* they're going to pay you to do what you love," Lily said.

"Jah." Mary Anne seemed to forget Jethro was even there. Her smile was dazzling, like a sunrise over the lake. She was still the prettiest woman Jethro had ever known, even if he was mad at her. She reached out and patted Anna's arm. *"Ach,* Mammi, I've never been happier."

Jethro felt as if he'd been hit squarely between the eyes with a baseball. *She'd never been happier?* Not even on their wedding day? Not even when he made that cradle for the baby and surprised her with it on her birthday? Not even when he'd told her he loved her for the first time, and she'd twirled around the room like a leaf dancing in the wind?

She was living in a tent in the middle of the woods, stealing furniture from the house where she used to live, barely scraping by on Jethro's two hundred dollars, and she had never been happier?

Jethro thought he might be sick. Had she been pretending all these years? Had she deceived him into believing something that wasn't really there? His insides felt like a shack in a tornado. He had to get out of there or he was going to lose every shred of dignity he had left. Turning his back on all of them, he stomped to the house, being careful not to plow into the very large dog and the small children playing in his backyard.

It was time to stand firm and refuse to let Mary Anne stomp all over his life and his heart.

He was finally going to be a man.

CHAPTER NINE

"Mary Anne, dear," Mammi said, holding up a pair of scissors. "Where would you like me to put these?"

"In that drawer over there, Mammi. *Denki.*"

"No need to thank me. Felty and I had the time of our lives today. Didn't we, Felty?"

"Yes, we did." Dawdi swept the floor — which he didn't need to do — but he liked being helpful more than anything else in the world. Mary Anne couldn't say no to that. He and one of the seniors who came to the center had spent nearly two hours today playing checkers. He'd definitely had a *gute* time.

Dawdi was in such a *gute* mood, he'd been singing ever since they'd closed the center. "I'll help someone in time of need, and sweep the floor with rapid speed."

Her grandparents were the most *wunder-*

barr people in the whole world.

The senior center was one big room with chairs and tables on one end and shelves and drawers and plenty of floor space on the other. The room was big enough for a wedding party or even a game of basketball, with shiny wood floors and a high ceiling. They could set up a king-size quilt on one end without any problem at all.

Mary Anne put the pins back in the drawer where they belonged, and stacked the squares of fabric on one of the shelves. It was only her first day of work at the senior center, but she had already started a quilting club, and she was going to organize a painting class, a gardening group, and a Dutch oven cooking class. She was getting very *gute* at that Dutch oven, and her boss, Charlene, told her she could teach any classes she wanted, as long as she was within budget.

Mary Anne didn't mind a tight budget. It was the reason she'd gotten this job in the first place. No one else but a desperate Amish woman was willing to take a job as activities director for minimum wage. Some of the senior ladies in the group said they could donate fabric, and they'd voted to make a quilt for the children's hospital in Milwaukee.

Working for minimum wage wasn't going to get Mary Anne anywhere very quickly, but at least she would have some money coming in. If she sold one quilt every month and made a little money off her painted benches and chairs and milk cans, she might be able to save up enough to rent a small place of her own before winter came. She'd rather not be living in the woods come November. The nights were plenty chilly at the first of May. And under no circumstances were Mammi and Dawdi to be camping in the winter. None of the relatives would forgive Mary Anne if Mammi and Dawdi froze to death in the name of solidarity.

There had been eight ladies at the center today and three men, including Mammi and Dawdi. They'd never had an activities coordinator before, so the senior center for most of them was just a place to pass the time playing cards or visiting. Mary Anne was looking forward to bringing a little more creativity to their lives. She probably would have volunteered at the center for free if she didn't need the money so badly. She couldn't think of anything more fun than making quilts and painting pictures and helping others find and create beauty for themselves. It was going to be a *gute* job, working with people who appreciated her.

Alice Swanson, a white-haired grandmother of sixteen, was already one of Mary Anne's favorite people, and they had only met today. Alice had a ready smile and a loud, boisterous laugh that told Mary Anne she wasn't afraid of being noticed or heard. Mary Anne liked that Alice could just be who she was without apologizing to anybody.

Alice and Mammi seemed like best friends already. Mammi told Alice all about Mary Anne, and Alice gave Mary Anne a big hug when she found out she was living in a tent. Mary Anne wasn't especially eager for everyone at the senior center to know her living situation, but Mammi didn't think it was anything to be ashamed of. By the end of the day, everyone knew that Mary Anne was living in a tent and that she showered in a bathroom in the barn.

Judy and Dennis VanderSleet had been the only married couple at the center today. Judy drove to Green Bay every week to dance with the Tap Dancing Grannies, and Dennis liked to watch football on TV. Dennis was especially looking forward to the painting class because he'd once been a graphics designer. Margaret Baumann's husband was in a care facility for Alzheimer's, and she came to the senior center for a weekly break. Helen Jensen had lost her husband in the war over forty years ago and had never remarried. She had worked for the state and now lived with her only son and his family.

Mary Anne could barely contain her excitement. Besides Pammy, she hadn't had much to do with *Englischers* before now, and the seniors at the center had all lived such interesting lives. Bob Hennig used to go salmon fishing in Alaska. For sure and certain he'd have some stories for Jethro. Jethro enjoyed a good fish story. She loved the way his eyes lit up whenever he talked about battling a certain trout that had gotten away. He still thought about that fish.

Charlene came out of her office jangling her keys. "Are you ready to go?"

Charlene lived on the east side of Shawano and was more than happy to drive Mary Anne and her grandparents to and from the center. It was probably her concession for not paying Mary Anne more money. Mary Anne was more than a little grateful for the ride. She'd pushed Jethro's patience too far already. He wouldn't be letting her use the buggy again.

Mammi and Dawdi followed Mary Anne

out the door, and Charlene turned off the lights and locked up. They climbed into Charlene's minivan and pulled out of the parking lot.

Charlene was older than some of the seniors who came to the center. She had told Mary Anne that volunteering there kept her young. A total of three people worked at the senior center — Mary Anne, Charlene, and Marco, who was the janitor and the building supervisor. Charlene ran the center, Marco scheduled special events, and Mary Anne was the only one who got paid. She was very grateful for the work.

Dawdi and Charlene struck up a conversation about the president of the United States. Mary Anne didn't even know who it was. Not that she cared to, but she was constantly amazed at how much she didn't know and how much she still had left to learn.

Charlene dropped them off at the house, and Mary Anne practically ran to the backyard. Lily and Sarah would be here at four to quilt, and she needed to get the fire going before they came. She'd found a recipe at the library for Dutch oven New England clam chowder, and she had to get it started before quilting time.

Mary Anne went around to the back of

the house and came to a dead stop. Was she in the right yard?

She stared into the woods for a full minute, not believing what she was seeing — or rather, not believing what she *wasn't* seeing.

Mammi gasped. *"Ach du lieva."*

Mary Anne's beautiful, butterfly-decorated tent was gone, as was Mammi and Dawdi's tent and the fire pit. Moses's tent had disappeared too. The canopy, the kitchen chairs, even the quilt were all missing. She stumbled slowly across the lawn and stopped directly on the spot where the front door of her tent used to be. Not a trace of the camp was left except for Mammi and Dawdi's sleeping bags, which were neatly rolled and tied and standing on end next to each other like two fat badgers guarding the forest. The delightful quilt square she'd painted on the barn had been covered over with a flat, manure-brown paint, and the pansies she had planted around the perimeter of her tent had been trampled to bits.

She'd known Jethro was angry, but she'd had no idea he could be so spiteful.

An icy hand seized Mary Anne's throat and squeezed until she couldn't breathe. She was choking and suffocating and retching all at the same time. Where were her

170

mobiles? What about her quilt and sewing machine, her potato chip collection, and the bench she'd been painting? How would she get anything back? She couldn't make quilts without her machine, and she couldn't buy more fabric without the quilt money.

The thought of starting over nearly buried her. She'd spent an hour setting up Jethro's tent. She didn't even want to think about the effort it had taken to drag her sewing machine or the fire pit into the woods. She'd taken so much joy in creating her mobiles and hanging them up. She'd never be able to replace her potato chip collection or the walking sticks or the pansies. She'd spent the last of Jethro's two hundred dollars on those pansies. How would she eat? She certainly wouldn't be allowed in the house to borrow back her utensils.

As she stood there in breathless shock, trembling like a match in the wind, she could sense Mammi and Dawdi behind her, stunned into silence by Jethro's thorough purging of the campsite.

She was seconds away from breaking down, from falling on the ground, curling herself into a little ball, and weeping like a child. Out of the corner of her eye, she spied Jethro tromping across the lawn, no doubt coming to exult in her pain. She drew a deep breath, bit down hard on her tongue, and squared her shoulders. He wouldn't get the satisfaction of seeing her disintegrate like a delicate pansy, no matter how exhausting it was to hold back the tears. He would never know he had crushed her.

Mammi stepped forward and wrapped her arm around Mary Anne's waist. "That boy deserves a *gute* spanking," she said, growling her displeasure and blinking back moisture from her eyes.

Mary Anne's heart swelled until she thought she might weep out of sheer gratitude. Mammi would always be on her side. She took great comfort in such fierce loyalty.

Jethro stopped at the edge of the woods, barely missing an already hopeless pansy with his boot. "I hope you've learned your lesson," he said, in a voice so mild, Mary Anne might have thought he felt sorry for what he'd done, even though she knew better.

She had to wait a few seconds before responding, just to make sure she could speak without losing her composure. "And what lesson is that?"

"The lesson that it's time to come home."

"Why would I have learned that lesson?"

He lifted his hat and scrubbed his fingers through his hair. "Because you shouldn't be living in a tent."

Mary Anne was glad for the anger that welled up inside her. It kept her from bursting into tears. "For sure and certain it's been wonderful embarrassing that you can't control your *fraa*."

He pressed his lips together, as if he was choosing his words carefully. "I don't want to control you, but you need to understand how selfish you're behaving. Your silly camping idea has hurt more people than just me. *Fraaen* in the district are discontented for no reason, and the husbands are fretful. Your selfishness has upset the applecart, and the elders aren't happy about it."

Mammi tightened her grip around Mary Anne's waist but didn't say anything. She was either lending her support or trying to hold Mary Anne back from giving Jethro a *gute* shove.

"I'm sorry the elders are upset, Jethro, but they shouldn't blame you. You haven't done anything wrong. It's not your fault your wife is unrepentant." She had found that if she took all the blame, he had fewer things to argue with her about.

"It's not about what the elders think."

"Then why did you say it was?"

He ran his fingers through his hair again and growled. "Surely you see how hard it is to make quilts in a tent. Your sewing machine is back where it's always been, and I've set up the quilt in the living room so you can work on it, even though Willie Jay told me not to. It will get dirty sitting out here in the woods. Your cousins are invited to come in anytime they want to work on it."

She longed to know about her walking sticks and the mobiles but didn't want him to sense they meant anything to her.

Mammi was looking at Jethro as if he'd burned all her recipe books. "Where is my dog, young man? Is he running free in the woods somewhere?"

"I took him to Aden's house, along with the tent you borrowed. Aden agreed to watch her until you came to fetch her."

Mammi narrowed her eyes. "Does Aden know what you've done?"

Jethro didn't seem to like Mammi's accusation. He lifted his chin. "I didn't explain myself. They'll all know soon enough when Mary Anne moves back in and everything is set to rights."

"I'm not moving back in."

"You have to. There's nothing left for you out here, and I've done up all the windows with dowels. You can't get in." Jethro came closer and dared to cup his hand around

Mary Anne's upper arm. Wasn't he afraid it might get bitten off? "I know you're mad, but in time you'll come to see I did this because I love you."

Mary Anne was fairly certain love had nothing to do with it.

"I did this for you, Mary Anne. You hate to camp. You cook your meals in a fire pit and then have to wash all the dishes with the hose. I love you too much to let you live in a tent, and I want to protect you from the gossips."

He was just rejoicing in how kind and caring he thought he was. Mary Anne bit harder on her tongue.

He finally dropped his hand from her arm and gave her a kindly smile. "I do love you, Mary Anne, and I want both of us to work on the things you don't like about our marriage. I can help you." The corners of his mouth curled upward. "I'll even try to be more exciting." Poor Jethro. He still thought being boring was the reason she'd left him. "But we can't work together if you're living in a tent. That's why I pulled up your camp. You have to come home."

"You trampled my pansies."

Jethro shook his head in resignation. "It was for your own good."

Mary Anne clasped her hands together so

Jethro wouldn't see how badly they were shaking. "Do you honestly think I'd come home after what you've done? I'd rather sleep on the ground in the pouring rain."

She saw pain in his eyes and something else — remorse perhaps. She was definitely imagining things. "Mary Anne, please come home." He sounded so sincere.

She got even madder at him for making her feel sorry for him. "I'll sleep in the barn."

"The barn is locked."

She folded her arms. If she didn't end this conversation soon, Jethro was going to notice the shaking. "You're going to milk the cow from now on?"

"I'll unlock the barn and milk the cow every day if you come home."

Mammi ignored Jethro. "You can stay at our house. You'd have a nice, comfortable bed and a toilet that flushes."

"I don't want you to think I don't appreciate it, Mammi," Mary Anne said, "but I want my own space. Something to call my own."

Jethro sighed. "You don't have anything to call your own out here. Everything you've been using is borrowed from me or one of your cousins."

"Not my frying pans."

"Don't forget about the dining set," Mammi said. "That was a wedding present."

Jethro reached out and took Mammi's hand in his. Mammi scrunched her lips to one side of her mouth, but she didn't pull away. "Anna, don't you think it would be better if you and Felty went home? Felty is limping something wonderful, and I don't mean to be rude, but you're only making things worse."

Dawdi seemed to be secretly laughing at a joke that only he found funny. "Worse for whom?"

Mary Anne struggled to keep her voice under control. "You can't keep my sewing machine. My *fater* gave that to me when I got baptized."

"You can use it if you come back home like a faithful, loving wife."

Was this what happened when people got divorced? Did they start fighting over things that didn't matter because their lives were falling apart? Mary Anne hadn't felt this low in years, even though until this morning, she'd been living in a tent. She wanted to sit down on the damp ground and bawl her eyes out, but she'd prefer that Jethro not be here to see it.

She lifted her chin. "Then I will just have

to borrow one."

"We have a sewing machine at home," Dawdi said. "You can still come live with us."

Jethro frowned. "You don't need to borrow a machine when you have a perfectly good one sitting in the spare bedroom."

"In your house," Mary Anne said.

Jethro gave her that pained look again. She ignored it. "You're always welcome back into the house."

"*Ach, vell.* Not really. You locked me out."

She could have drawn a map of unhappiness on the lines of his face. "You know what I mean."

"*Ach.* For sure and certain I do."

She clamped her lips together to keep from saying anything that would prove her weakness. *Jethro, I know you don't want me using your stuff, but could I borrow some bolt cutters to cut that lock on the barn door?* She was alone in the woods with her grandparents to take care of, and she had no idea what she was going to do about the bathroom situation. It should have been a small problem amid all the upset and anger, but Mary Anne was almost tempted to move back in with Jethro just for the luxury of using his toilet. Knowing there was a flushable toilet in the barn had made it easier for

Mary Anne to move into the tent in the first place. What was she going to do now? Mammi and Dawdi wouldn't survive without a toilet, and Mary Anne would die before she stooped to squatting in the woods.

"What happened here?"

Mary Anne looked up to see Cousin Sarah carrying Lily's twins, Estee and Emily, with Lily and Aden Jr. and Pilot in tow. Mary Anne's sister Mandy followed a few steps behind.

Lily's eyes were as wide as saucers. "Your . . . your camp is gone."

Mammi shot Jethro a look that could have killed every mosquito in Wisconsin. "Jethro took it down while Mary Anne was at her first day of work."

Jethro's eyes flared like a forest fire. "You all know it was for her own good."

Sarah narrowed her eyes. "You're slyer than a snake, Jethro Neuenschwander."

The muscles of Jethro's jaw twitched fiercely. "You should be ashamed that you're encouraging Mary Anne to sin. You may not care about her soul, but I will fight tooth and nail before I see my *fraa* go to hell."

Sarah snorted so loudly, the sound echoed up through the trees. "Unless you are the blessed Lord Himself, you have no right to pass judgment on who is going to hell and who isn't." She put the twins down, and they promptly ran to Jethro's lawn and started chasing Pilot around. "I'm sorry, Mary Anne. Jethro and his *bruder* brought our canopy back and said you didn't need it anymore. I should have been more suspicious."

Jethro was going to lose a lot of hair if he kept scrubbing his fingers through it like that. "Doesn't anybody else see that Mary Anne is breaking the commandments? No *fraa* should just move out on her husband."

"Why?" Sarah said, taking a step closer to Jethro. She was almost six feet tall and could just about look him straight in the eye. She intimidated a lot of people. "Because you say so?"

Jethro probably didn't even realize he took a step back. "Because *Gotte* says so."

"I'm . . . I'm horrified, Jethro. How could you do this?" Mandy said, sounding as breathless as if she had jogged all the way from her house.

Mary Anne had never seen Jethro so upset. He looked at Mary Anne. "You've made your point. I've learned my lesson. If you'll try to be a better wife, I'll be a better husband. There's no camp anymore. You have to move home."

Mammi straightened to her full diminuitive height. "Don't you worry, Mary Anne. We're not giving up. We'll sleep on the ground under a pile of leaves if we have to. And we'll use trees instead of the toilet."

Dawdi cleared his throat. "*Ach* . . . yes . . . that's right. We're with you to the bitter end. And just remember, you're always welcome to stay at our house."

"Because the barn is locked, we're going to have to start using the trees," Mammi said, "and we're going to need toilet paper. You're going to have to unlock the barn so we can steal some toilet paper."

Jethro gritted his teeth. "The camping trip is over."

Sarah grunted. "The camping trip is far from over. I'm going home to get my tent."

Mammi brightened considerably and clapped her hands. "Does this mean you're going to do solidarity with us, Sarah?"

"You bet your grandpa's galluses, I am," Sarah said.

Lily pressed her lips into a firm line and took a deep breath. "Me too. Me and *die kinner*. I'll bring our other tent. And an extra sleeping bag."

Mandy was already stomping in the direction of her buggy. "I'm going home to get my tent and my husband. He'll dig a latrine for us."

"You shouldn't sleep on the ground," Mary Anne said, her heart swelling with gratitude for her sister and her cousins.

Mandy didn't even break stride. "We've got a cot."

"I won't camp without toilet paper," Sarah said. "I'll bring some from home. And some wet wipes. I don't go anywhere without wet wipes." Sarah pointed at Jethro. "The boys will be back with the canopy. Don't take it down again or I'll get very testy. My boys have plenty to do on our farm without having to set up the canopy every week."

Jethro shook his head. "You don't have to do this, any of you. Why are you so mad when I did this for Mary Anne's own good?"

If he said that one more time, she was going to explode. "Go away, Jethro." *Before I disintegrate into a puddle of tears.*

His eyes were full of longing. "Please come back, Mary Anne, and I'll let you use all your stuff, extra toilet paper if you want."

It was too much. He didn't understand her heart at all. He hadn't ever tried. "You think I care about my *stuff*?" Her voice broke into a million pieces, and she could no longer hold back the tears. "You took down my tent and painted over my artwork.

You stole my sewing machine and trampled my flowers."

"Won't you try to understand?" His voice sounded as if he'd swallowed a bowl of gravel.

"Won't *you* try to understand?" Her crying was uncontrollable now, but she would say exactly what she wanted to say, even if Jethro thought she was weak, even if it gave him a reason to gloat. "You didn't do this because you want me to move back in. You did this to hurt me."

"I didn't."

"Well, you should be wonderful happy." She sobbed like a lost puppy. "I'm broken, Jethro. You've broken me."

"That's not what I want at all," he said.

Even though Mammi had her arm firmly around Mary Anne's waist, her legs were going to give out on her any second. She stumbled to the boulder she sat on to tend to the fire. It was the only solid, flat thing in the near vicinity, and if she didn't sit down now, she'd fall over. She had lost her tent, her rock collection, and any shred of hope in a matter of minutes. Jethro had never been so cruel, and at that moment, she hated him — hated him with a fierceness that frightened her and a despair that shattered her heart. She'd never trust in Jethro's goodness again. "I want a divorce," she said, shoving the words out of her mouth like poisonous darts.

Mandy and Lily both gasped, and one of the twins started crying.

Mary Anne might as well have slapped Jethro. His face went deathly pale, and he stumbled backward a few steps. "Mary Anne, *nae*. Please don't say that. I love you."

Dawdi limped to Jethro's side and placed a firm hand on his shoulder. "It wonders me if you shouldn't maybe go back in the house and let Mary Anne be. It's been a hard day, especially now that she doesn't have a toilet."

How did Mammi manage a scold and an affectionate smile at the same time? "I think we'd better cancel cooking lessons tonight, Jethro. We're going to be a little busy out here."

With a stunned and lost expression on his face, Jethro nodded slowly, as if he was trying to figure out what Mammi had just said, then turned and walked back to the house. It seemed they all held their breath as they watched him go. As soon as he closed the door behind him, Mary Anne buried her face in her hands and wept.

CHAPTER TEN

Jethro poured himself a bowl of cornflakes and sank into a chair at the kitchen table. After retrieving all his furniture from Mary Anne's campsite, he'd had the choice of any of eight chairs he wanted to sit in. Willie Jay had come back this morning and helped him break down the tents and erase any sign Mary Anne had been living in the woods. It had been Willie Jay's idea to paint over the quilt block Mary Anne had drawn on the side of the barn, just so she would know "she couldn't do this to her husband."

The shadows grew long as he took one bite and then another of his cornflakes. They got soggier and soggier as his heart grew heavier and heavier. Willie Jay had told him it was the right thing to do, but now he realized how horribly wrong he had been. The sight of Mary Anne's tears had knocked the wind right out of him. No husband should make his wife cry. Ever. He felt as if he'd cut off his own arm.

The last time he'd seen Mary Anne cry was after she'd lost the *buplie* — *they'd* lost the *buplie.* She had clung to him and wondered aloud why *Gotte* had seen fit to take her baby. At that time, it had been nearly a year after the miscarriage, and she had still been crying about it. Jethro had found her tears unbearable. He had urged her to get over the loss and to trust that *Gotte* had something *wunderbarr* in store for their future, even if she wasn't meant to have children.

He had never seen her cry again. He used to be glad about that. Now he wasn't so sure. She knew he didn't want her to cry. Did she think he didn't care about their *buplie*?

He sat as still as a stone for fifteen minutes while his cornflakes turned to mush, in turns ashamed and heartbroken and numb. He had done everything wrong. Mary Anne hated him, and there wasn't a thing he could do to make it better. Everything he had tried made it worse. Much worse.

A firm knock on the front door made his heart do a somersault. Could it be Mary Anne? Maybe she was here to offer her forgiveness or say she hadn't really meant what she said about wanting a divorce.

186

He hurried to the door, stepping around the quilt frames that took up most of the space in the living room. He didn't care if Mary Anne wanted three dozen quilters at a time in the house. He'd agree to anything. He'd let her buy that twenty-dollar cheese she was so fond of. And if she wanted to carve their radishes into flowers, he wouldn't tell her *nae.*

His heart crashed to the floor when he opened the door to Felty with a crowbar in one hand, a small cardboard box in the other, and a twinkle in his eye. "Can I use your bathroom? The crowbar didn't work."

Jethro tried to talk himself out of his profound disappointment. "I . . . I suppose so."

Felty stepped into the house and hurried down the hall to the bathroom. Jethro heard the crowbar clatter to the floor. Felty must have dropped it in his rush. Lord willing, he hadn't dropped it on his toe. Jethro went back to his bowl of cornflakes and stirred them around with his spoon. He should buy Lucky Charms. At least he could eat the marshmallows when the cereal got soggy.

He heard Felty open the bathroom door and march down the hall like a man twenty years younger. Ever since he'd been camping, he also walked with a slight limp, but he was still as spry as any sixty-year-old. Felty always seemed to have a song on his lips, and Jethro could hear him singing softly. "Springtime in Glory, we'll have springtime in Glory, where the pansies are blooming in the bright, fresh air. Where the rivers are rushing, and all toilets are flushing, it is springtime always there."

Felty came into the kitchen, set the crowbar and the box on the table, and pulled out the chair opposite Jethro. "May I sit?" he said. "It's been a trying afternoon."

Jethro nodded, too numb to ask Felty about the crowbar or the cardboard box.

Felty cocked his head to one side and studied Jethro's bowl of cornflakes. "That looks like a very nourishing dinner. Nothing like a bowl of corn paste to fill you up." He took off his hat and laid it next to the crowbar. "We didn't have it so *gute.* Anna and I walked to the market while Mary Anne gathered wood for a fire. We roasted hot dogs and marshmallows and called it good enough."

"You walked? The market is three miles from here."

"My horse is locked in your barn. I didn't want to impose."

"Ach," Jethro said, feeling worse and worse by the minute. "I'm sorry. I'll go out after

188

dinner and take off all the locks. Mary Anne isn't going to come back just for the toilet." His heart scraped on the floor. She wasn't going to come back, period.

Felty leaned back in his chair and grasped his beard as if it were a handle. "I should have put a stop to this two weeks ago."

Jethro eyed Felty doubtfully. "Do you think you could have talked Mary Anne into coming home?"

One side of Felty's mouth curled upward, and he shook his head. "You misunderstand, Jethro. You're only my grandson-in-law, so I didn't know if it was proper to stick my nose in your business, but I can't sit by and watch you make a bigger and bigger mess of things."

Jethro cradled his head in his hands. "I was doing what I thought was right, but I made her cry. I never wanted to make her cry."

"You thought she'd come to her senses and realize you were right all along."

Jethro winced. "I thought . . . I thought she was throwing a tantrum. She's the one who went against the Bible."

"Will that be a comfort to you when she moves away?"

"The truth is always a comfort," he said, not even believing it himself. There would

189

be no comfort if Mary Anne left him for good.

Felty stood up, and the chair legs scraped against the floor. They were covered with grit from being outside. Jethro would probably have to refinish the floor when this was all over. His heart stopped beating. Would this ever be over? "Have you seen what's going on outside?" Felty drew the curtains open and motioned for Jethro to come to the window.

The woods behind his house weren't empty anymore. In addition to Aden's Swift-n-Snug tent, there were four — four! — other tents out there, plus Sarah Beachy's canopy with a quilt set up under it. Where had the quilt come from? Mary Anne's quilt was sitting in his living room. The tents stood watch around a glowing campfire, and at least five people sat around the fire on camp chairs. Jethro resisted the urge to check on the camp chairs he stored in the shed. It didn't matter if they were there or not.

"Mandy told Lia and Moses, and they rounded up their camping gear. They don't even care that we have no bathroom. Moses and Aden helped their *fraaen* set up their tents, and Aden set up Mary Anne's tent." He pointed to two big trees standing twenty feet to the left of the campfire. "Sarah brought her giant hammock, and Moses strung it between two trees for us. We're going to sleep out under the stars. Lord willing, it's more comfortable than those sleeping bags."

"I . . . uh . . . I have some cots."

Felty shrugged. "I hear the hammock is wonderful soft." He tapped on the window. "Noah dug a hole and is building an outhouse about a hundred yards that way, but Anna isn't real sure about it. I tried to break into your barn with my crowbar, but it didn't work. Moses is coming back with some bolt cutters."

Jethro swallowed the lump of shame in his throat. "He doesn't have to do that. I'll unlock it. Or maybe I should let you unlock it. I'm the last person anyone wants to see right now."

Felty stroked his beard. "That's for sure and certain."

Jethro couldn't comprehend the number of cousins who had moved into his woods in a matter of hours. It looked like a small city out there. "They really hate me, don't they?"

"They love Mary Anne and don't like the way you treated her."

It was like a crowbar right to the chest. "I

was trying to show her that I would do anything to get her back."

Felty raised an eyebrow. "You haven't done anything to get her back, Jethro. You've only done things to get back *at* her. I love you like a grandson, but I've never seen anyone quite as slow-witted as you are. I don't know how you convinced her to marry you in the first place."

He wanted to argue. He ached to defend himself, but there was nothing he could say. What did it matter if he was in the right and Mary Anne was in the wrong or if the minister and the deacon admonished him for his wife's sins?

Mary Anne was gone.

All the righteous indignation in the world wouldn't bring her back. The embarrassment, the tent, the hunger, the need to be right, none of it mattered. All that mattered was that he loved Mary Anne.

His throat felt as if it had been scoured with sandpaper. In the last two weeks, he hadn't done anything to make Mary Anne believe anything other than that he hated her. He'd yelled and scolded and locked her out of the house and scoffed at her paintings and rock collection. It was no wonder Mary Anne would rather use an outhouse than move back in with him.

The sight of Mary Anne's tear-streaked face had been devastating. There was a time he would have lain down his life for Mary Anne, would have done anything to make her laugh or show that beautiful smile of hers.

He hadn't taken down the campsite for Mary Anne's own good. He'd done it because, for some crazy reason, he'd thought it would fix his wounded pride and broken heart. He nearly fell over when he realized that in the deepest part of his heart, he'd been trying to get revenge on Mary Anne for hurting him. What kind of a husband would do that to his *fraa*?

Felty gazed out the window. "If I were you — and I'm wonderful *froh* I'm not right now — I wouldn't try to take the camp down again or you'll have some very angry cousins on your hands. You don't want to see Sarah when she gets angry. She gave Josiah Zimmerman a dressing-down for losing track of time and arriving late to the birth of his *buplie*."

Jethro turned from the window and collapsed into the nearest of his eight kitchen chairs. He covered his face with a trembling hand. The thought of losing everything important to him nearly buried him. "I love Mary Anne, and she used to love me. What did I do wrong?"

Felty sat down next to him and wrapped his fingers around Jethro's wrist. "You need to love her."

"I do love her."

"Do you?" Felty's gaze could have punctured a hole through a tin can.

"Of course I do. More than anything."

Felty pressed his lips together. "Love isn't a feeling, Jethro. Love is something you do."

"That doesn't make sense."

"The Bible tells husbands to love their wives as Christ loves the church. How did Christ love the church?"

Jethro didn't especially want a lesson in scripture tonight, but Felty was trying to help him, so he would go along with whatever Felty had in mind. "With all His heart, I guess."

"You've been quoting that passage to Mary Anne for two weeks, and you haven't thought about it any more deeply than that?"

Jethro frowned. He needed words of comfort, not another lecture. "It says He gave His life for the church."

Felty bloomed into a smile. "You can love Mary Anne deeply, Jethro, but if you don't practice love, she'll never know. Were you trying to show your love when you took down her campsite?"

"Willie Jay said it was a *gute* idea."

Felty raised an eyebrow. "Ah. So you wanted to show Willie Jay you loved him?"

"Nae," Jethro said. "I was angry and wanted to be right." He pressed his fingers to his forehead. "She'll never forgive me."

Felty gazed at Jethro with a sympathetically amused gleam in his eye. "*Ach.* It's not as dark as all that, but you've got your work cut out for you."

"What can I do?"

Felty stood up and rummaged through Jethro's cupboards until he found the neglected *kaffee* pot. He took it from the shelf and filled it with water at the sink. Jethro felt a tiny spark of warmth right in the center of his chest. Was Felty going to make *kaffee*? Would it be Anna Helmuth *kaffee* or Mary Anne Neuenschwander *kaffee*? Did Jethro even care? It had been so long since anyone had done anything for him. He caught his breath. "Do you think Mary Anne made *kaffee* for me because she loved me?"

Felty set the pot on the stove. "At least until it became more of a duty than an act of love."

Jethro jumped to his feet, opened one of the drawers, and pulled out the pair of fish-shaped hot pads. "Mary Anne made these for me." He curled his lips upward. He'd never noticed the careful hand stitching around the edges. "She must have loved me once."

"What about you? Did you love her?"

"I always have."

Felty turned and leaned against the counter. "Did she know?"

"Of course she did. I'm her husband."

"Do you think that was enough?"

"I used to think it was." Jethro ran his fingers through his hair. "When could she have stopped loving me? She made me dinner every night and did the laundry and planted the garden. She loved me with her actions, just like you said."

"What happened on the night she left you?"

"I forgot our anniversary. I didn't know she'd made this fancy meal to surprise me, and I went fishing."

"Maybe she thought you loved fishing more than you love her."

Jethro wanted to protest until he thought about his four-hundred-dollar fishing pole sitting in its place of honor in the spare bedroom. On the night of their anniversary, he had barely given Mary Anne a second thought.

Felty squinted, as if he were thinking wonderful hard. "Would you have appreciated the meal if you had stayed home?"

Jethro took a deep breath as something heavy pressed down on his chest. "Probably not. All that work, all that time she spent was so unnecessary. She didn't have to make fancy dinners to show me she loved me. It was a waste of money, and I was perfectly satisfied with a plate of chow chow and grilled fish. She carved her radishes into rose shapes. She used to buy expensive cheese and strange fruits until I told her not to."

"You told her not to?" Felty poured the *kaffee* grounds into the pot.

"She was making too much work for herself, especially after she lost the *buplie.* She was so sad all the time. I did everything I could think of to make her forget. I painted over the farm animals she'd drawn on the nursery wall. I put the homemade baby quilts away so she wouldn't be reminded. I finally had to tell her to quit crying all the time."

Felty widened his eyes as if Jethro had taken a match and set his own house on fire. "You told her to stop crying?"

Once again, he felt the need to justify himself. "It was like a funeral in here every day. I hated to see her cry, and I wanted her to get on with her life. It was for her own good."

Felty's lips twitched, whether in amusement or exasperation, Jethro couldn't tell. "You've said that three times today already."

The air drained from his lungs. He stuffed the fish-shaped hot pads back into the drawer and sat down at the table, in a different chair this time. After all, he had eight to choose from. He'd paid a high price for having all eight of his chairs back.

Felty poured himself and Jethro a cup of *kaffee,* and set both cups on the table. It smelled like heaven itself. Felty opened the mysterious cardboard box, pulled out two jelly-filled doughnuts, and placed them in front of Jethro. "Two for a dollar at the market today," he said. "Anna said you like this kind."

Jethro's stomach growled at the bounty before him. He would have eaten the cardboard box if Felty had spread frosting on it. He took a sip of *kaffee* and then a gulp. He didn't care that it burned his tongue. It was the best thing he'd ever tasted. Where had Felty learned to make *kaffee*? For sure and certain Anna hadn't taught him.

Felty sat down and picked up his cup. "Everything you've done is for Mary Anne's own good, but maybe nothing you've done has been good for her. She certainly doesn't think it's because you love her — and I can't say I blame her. I'm not convinced. It's not hard to see how her love faded, and then even her sense of duty wasn't enough to keep her here. She probably felt guilty for not loving you anymore, and that was one of the reasons she moved out."

"What can I do to get her to come back? I'll do anything. I'll buy her all the cheese in Wisconsin if I have to."

"Don't try to get her back. Just love her."

"I do love her."

Felty shook his head. "You're not usually this thick, Jethro. Christ gave His life for the church. If you're not willing to dedicate your life to Mary Anne's happiness, then all the cheese in Wisconsin won't be near enough."

"But what about my happiness? Shouldn't Mary Anne want the same for me?"

"If you truly love her, then hers is the only happiness you should care about. That means your embarrassment doesn't matter, or your anger. To be sure, she has hurt your feelings. Can you forgive her and love her anyway, because if you can't, there's no reason to go to all that trouble? Winning her love will be near impossible as it is.

You're even further behind than when you first met her. Right now, she's willing to leave the church to be rid of you."

Not even the steaming cup of rich, black *kaffee* and a raspberry-filled doughnut could make Jethro feel better. In a thousand different ways, he'd hurt Mary Anne deeply. Even the strength of his love might not be enough.

Jethro set his cup on the table with a little too much force. A drop of *kaffee* jumped out of the cup and landed on his hand. He wouldn't lose Mary Anne. He'd been foolish and cruel, trying to force her instead of persuade her, but he wouldn't be so blind again. If he knew anything as a fisherman, he knew how to be patient, even if he hadn't shown much patience in the last two weeks.

No matter how long it took, he would win her back. He couldn't imagine life without her. She was beautiful, smart, kind, and creative. She was everything to him.

She was the light of his life.

There would be no happiness left for him if he failed.

CHAPTER ELEVEN

Mary Anne crawled into Aden's two-man tent and tried to press out the lumps in the ground with the heel of her hand. Sleeping in a sleeping bag with only a tarp between her and the ground was a far cry from Jethro's nice cot in the eight-man tent. It was an even farther cry from her own bed in her nice, warm house not two hundred feet away. No matter how adamantly she had protested that she would be fine camping for the rest of her life, she truly didn't know how long she would last out here. Sleeping was almost impossible already, but adding the smells of an outhouse, a persistent owl, frost on the ground in the mornings, and the noises of her cousins' young children into the mix, and she might never sleep again.

Lia and her children were sleeping in the tent Mary Anne had originally borrowed from Moses, which was only fair. They needed the space. Mammi and Dawdi slept in the hammock Sarah Beachy had given them, although that couldn't last long. There was no shelter from the rain, and it was so cold out tonight, one of them might suffocate under that pile of blankets they were covered in. The only tent left for Mary Anne was Aden's Swift-n-Snug tent that Mammi and Dawdi had been using. At least it was shelter, but she would miss the space for her mobiles and her sewing machine.

She still had no idea what she was going to do about her sewing machine. She needed it something wonderful, and Jethro didn't seem likely to budge, especially after the way she'd broken down in front of him. He could sense he was getting to her. At this point, he was no doubt determined to wait her out. The hurt and frustration felt like a raw wound on her skin. It had been a long, trying day, and she was too exhausted to solve the problem of her sewing machine or the toilet or her camping cousins tonight. Things always looked better after a *gute* night's sleep. Too bad she wasn't going to get one.

Mammi and Dawdi had already gone to bed in their deluxe double hammock. For tonight, they seemed comfortable enough.

Mary Anne could already hear Dawdi snoring.

Lily had brought her three little ones and the dog. Even though Lily's husband, Aden, had been very helpful in setting up the camp, Lily had told him to go home and sleep in the house. Lily felt very strongly that this "protest," as she called it, was just for the *fraaen,* even though Dawdi had been here for almost two weeks and Noah was staying with Mandy in her tent. Cousin Sarah had set up a tent right next to Lily's, and two of Sarah's boys were sleeping at the edge of the clearing in their sleeping bags under the stars. Mary Anne didn't think they knew anything about solidarity. They just liked an excuse to camp.

Mary Anne wished she liked to camp. It would have made things so much more pleasant. But maybe it was better that camping was hard. The difficulty made it plain to Jethro how badly she wanted to live by herself. She couldn't give up, especially now that all these relatives were living in the woods with her. Her lips curled involuntarily. She had moved out of the house, but for sure and certain she wasn't living by herself.

It was shaping up to be a chilly night. She could see her breath in the air. *Gute* thing

Aden's sleeping bag was warm to thirty degrees below zero. She probably wouldn't freeze to death, even on the cold ground.

"Mary Anne," someone whispered behind her.

She backed out of her tent on her hands and knees and stood up, only to come face-to-face with the last person in the world she wanted to see. It was dark, but he held a bright flashlight pointed at the ground, and Mary Anne could see him well enough. Just being near Jethro made her want to cry all over again, but her nose got stuffy when she cried right before bed and made it hard to sleep. "What do you want, Jethro?"

He lowered his eyes and stared at the circle of light made by the flashlight on the ground. "I'm sorry, Mary Anne."

"For what?" He certainly wasn't there to apologize for anything that mattered.

"I'm sorry I took down your camp. It was mean, plain and simple."

"*Jah.* It was."

"I'm sorry I painted over your quilt square and threw away your mobiles. I'm sorry for everything."

In the dark, she couldn't tell if he was being honest or just trying another trick to get her to come home. It was probably a trick, and she didn't know how to respond. "I'm sorry too."

"I never wanted to hurt you."

She didn't believe it, but he sounded sincere enough to plant a seed of doubt in her mind. "It doesn't matter."

"It's the only thing that matters." He reached out as if to take her hand but suddenly pulled back. *Gute.* He knew better than that.

"Why are you out here? It's late, and most everyone is already asleep."

"I hate to think . . . I know how you feel about camping, and I hate to think of you sleeping out here by yourself. Please go in the house, and I'll sleep out here in the tent."

Mary Anne swallowed the lump in her throat. She couldn't let the deep richness of his voice get to her. She had always found it irresistible. "You'll say anything to get me back into the house." It wasn't very nice to accuse him of lying, but he had to know she didn't trust him.

"This isn't a trick. You don't want to live with me, so let me live in the tent. You deserve a roof over your head and a *gute,* sturdy bed."

Mary Anne shook her head. She didn't believe he'd had a change of heart in less than four hours, and she'd be foolish to listen to him, no matter how much she missed her bed. "My cousins wouldn't like it if they woke up in the morning to find I'd abandoned them."

He closed his eyes, as if overwhelmed by some unbearable pain. "I'm sorry, Mary Anne. I'm sorry I hurt you. No matter what you decide, I'm going to be sleeping out here from now on."

She tried to ignore the hitch in her breath. "I don't want that."

"No husband with a decent bone in his body would let his *fraa* sleep in a tent while he was warm and comfortable inside. I've unlocked the barn, so everyone can use the bathroom. And everyone is welcome to use the bathroom in the house too."

She reminded herself that he was only trying to trick her and hardened her heart. "I moved out here to get away from you, Jethro. I don't want you closer."

If what she said hurt him, he didn't show it. "I'll set up out by the ditch. It's farther away than the house."

She wanted to argue but didn't quite know how to contradict a man who claimed he was moving into a tent because he loved his *fraa.*

Jethro shined his flashlight on a light green canvas bag sitting on the ground a few feet away — his tent, the one Mary Anne had painted with butterflies. "Will you at least sleep in the bigger tent? I brought out the cot and a sleeping bag and that soft blanket you like. It won't take but ten minutes to set up."

The bigger tent was a great temptation. Great indeed. "I . . . I don't know if I should."

He tilted his head to study her face and cracked a smile. "Your cousins won't think less of you for taking the bigger tent. You need room for the cot and the sewing machine."

The sewing machine? Surely he didn't mean to give it back. Why was Jethro being so nice all of a sudden, and how could she resist the lure of a bigger tent? Still, she hesitated.

"If you're worried that you'll be betraying unhappy *fraaen* all over the world, let me put your mind at ease. They'd say you're smart to make your husband sleep in that puny thing. It looks very uncomfortable."

Mary Anne bit down hard on her tongue to keep from grinning. Jethro used to be able to make her laugh like no one else could, but she wouldn't be fooled by his easy charm. He wanted her to move back into the house. It seemed he was just going about it in a new way. "Okay," she said. "I'll take the big tent."

Even in the dark, his smile lit up his face. He put the flashlight down on the ground, pointing it in the direction of the canvas bag. "I'll set it up right over here a little closer to the barn, so you won't have to hike so far to the bathroom."

Even though she was fully aware of what he was doing, she couldn't help but be grateful to him for bringing back her tent. She so loved the butterflies painted on it, and that cot was wonderful comfortable.

Jethro pulled a tarp from the canvas bag, found a flat, smooth piece of ground close to the barn, and spread the tarp over it. Then he tugged the tent from the bag and laid it out on top of the tarp. Even though he'd taken down her tent without her permission, she admired how neatly he'd folded it. Jethro was very particular about his things. He'd never been one of those husbands who left his socks in the living room or made a mess at the dinner table. It was one of the few things she still liked about him.

Mary Anne bent over and unfolded one side of the tent so Jethro could thread the poles through the top. She extended one of the support poles and put it into place, then lifted and secured it when Jethro did the same on his side. Putting up a tent went a lot faster when you knew how to do it and when you had a little help.

Jethro brushed off his hands and smiled at her. "I've got the cot right here, and the sleeping bag. And the lantern." He took a couple of steps toward the house then turned back. "Is there anything else you need? I can bring the other things back in the morning, but it's dark and I don't want to wake everybody up."

"Other things?"

"The bookshelf, the food, the pans and utensils. The bench you were working on is sitting in the spare bedroom. Do you want me to bring out the quilt? There's already another one under the canopy."

"It's for Sarah's new grandbaby. That won't take long to finish. Mandy and I will come get the quilt and frames in the morning, if that's all right with you."

He practically jumped to give his consent. "Of course it's all right. You don't have to ask my permission. It's your house too, and you should come in anytime you want. I won't lock it again." He lowered his eyes as if he was embarrassed he'd locked it in the first place. Maybe he recognized how unreasonable he'd been.

Or maybe he was trying to fool her into thinking he'd had a change of heart. She'd be wise to be on her guard.

"I'll bring your sewing machine too, unless you want to just keep it in the house and use it there. It would stay dry."

She wasn't about to let him talk her into anything, even something sensible. "I'd like it in my tent, please. But don't bother. I can move it."

"It's heavy. I'll move it. It wonders me how you got it out here the first time."

She curled one side of her mouth. "There was a lot of grunting involved."

"You must have really been desperate." He lost his smile as soon as he said it. She had been desperate — desperate and angry and unhappy — and he knew it. He cleared his throat and jabbed his thumb in the direction of the house. "I'll set up the cot and then move my tent."

He picked up the flashlight, and her gaze followed the beam of light to the edge of the woods where the cot, sleeping bag, and a pillow sat in a pile on the grass. She drew her brows together until her forehead ached. Jethro was harder to resist when he was nice, but he was still Jethro and she still wanted to live alone. She sighed. It was plain he still held out hope for their marriage. Why else would he give her sewing machine back?

She'd have to set him straight or his hopes would soar like an unstaked tent on the wind. Unfortunately, if she set him straight, she'd never see her sewing machine again.

What was she to do?

It took Jethro five minutes to set up the cot where it had taken Mary Anne almost half an hour. She could paint and draw and quilt, but she couldn't fix a toilet or build a storage shed. Jethro could fix anything. It was a skill that came in handy when you had to set up a tent and a cot in the dark.

Mary Anne watched from outside the tent as Jethro turned on the lamp, situated the cot, and spread Mary Anne's sleeping bag on top of it. He laid their fuzzy blanket over the top of the sleeping bag and set her pillow at the head of her new bed. Was she imagining things, or did his hand linger on her pillow a second too long? *Ach.* She wasn't going to let him do that. His hopes were too high. She blew a frustrated puff of air from between her lips. She was never going to get her sewing machine back.

When Jethro ducked out of the tent, she squared her shoulders and tried to stand taller. "Jethro, if you're being nice because you want to convince me to move back in, it's not going to work. I don't want you to go to all this trouble and then be upset when I don't do what you want."

His hesitation told her all she needed to know. That sewing machine was as good as lost. "Mary Anne." He ran his hand across his forehead, as if trying to wipe away the anger that was surely bubbling just below the surface of his pleasant expression. "I won't deny I want you to come back. I love you, and I don't want to live without you."

Something heavy like guilt pressed down on her chest. She wished he wouldn't say that. It sounded like he meant it, and she hated the thought of hurting his feelings.

"I know I haven't treated you like a husband should treat his *fraa* — especially after you moved out. There's no *gute* excuse for how I acted except that I felt like you'd taken a rock and thrown it at my head. I was confused and wonderful unhappy."

Mary Anne pressed her lips tightly together as another wave of guilt washed over her. She couldn't blame Jethro for being mad. She hadn't given him any warning, and then suddenly she was gone. For sure and certain it had felt like a blow right to the head. "I don't wonder that you reacted like any normal husband would react."

"That doesn't excuse what I've done.

You're the person I love most in the whole world, but I haven't treated you that way."

She laced her fingers together. "I know it was hard on you. You were embarrassed when the *gmayna* found out, but I thought you would be happier once I was out of your hair."

He winced. "Then I've failed as a husband." He took off his hat and scrubbed his fingers through his hair. "I want to do better."

"That doesn't mean I'm going to move back in."

Pain filled his eyes, but there was resignation in the lines of his face. "I know. But when this is over, I don't want you to have any doubt in your mind that I love you."

When this is over. Jethro couldn't know how significant those words were. Did he know what *over* meant to her?

Mary Anne nearly jumped out of her skin when Mammi's voice rang loud and clear through the darkness. "Felty, there's a spider on my neck!"

Dawdi's sleepy, muffled voice was a little harder to hear. "Huh? What are you saying, Annie?"

Mammi's voice got louder and more insistent. "Can you get this spider off my neck?"

"I can't see it," Dawdi said.

"Kill it!" Mammi squeaked.

"I can't kill it. Spiders are very helpful in the garden." Dawdi always did have a heart for the animals.

"*Ach*! It's crawling down my back. Help me, Felty. Help me."

Mary Anne heard a thud and a thump and some general struggling coming from the direction of the hammock. She and Jethro glanced at each other before Jethro retrieved his flashlight and they sprinted to the twin trees.

Mary Anne gasped as Jethro shined his light in the direction of the hammock. Arms and legs stuck out in every direction, flailing as if trying to find purchase on anything solid. Somehow Mammi and Dawdi had managed to trap themselves in their own bed, tangled beyond any knot Mary Anne could begin to untie.

"Hold on, Mammi and Dawdi," Mary Anne said. "We're coming."

"I'm stuck," Mammi panted. "We're both stuck, and I think I've lost one of my feet."

"Ouch! That's my beard, Annie-Banannie," Dawdi said. His arm hung from one of the holes in the netting, and he waved it around as if he was paddling through the water — probably hoping he could swim to the nearest tree and save both of them.

"Kill it, Felty!"

Both of Dawdi's arms stuck out from either side of the hammock. He wasn't going to get a chance at that spider unless he trapped it with one of his feet.

Sparky the dog, who had been asleep under the hammock, woke up and started barking as soon as Jethro got within ten feet. If Mammi's squealing didn't wake up the whole camp, Sparky's barking would. Sparky was soon joined by Lily's dog, Pilot, two tents over, who sounded more like a wolf than a dog. Mandy and Noah's Polish hound dog, Chester, joined the chorus. One — or more likely both — of Lily's twins started crying. The sounds of Mammi's squealing, babies' crying, and the dogs' barking echoed up through the trees and into the night sky.

"Can you stop struggling?" Jethro said, running his hand along the hammock, trying to find where they'd gone wrong. "It looks like it twisted completely upside down and around itself."

"I did a flip when that spider landed on me," Mammi said.

Mammi was spry, but surely she couldn't have flipped the hammock all the way over on itself. Mary Anne could understand Mammi's reaction, though. She didn't like spiders either. She wasn't sure how high she would jump if one landed on her.

Sarah Beachy emerged from her tent carrying a hissing lantern. Her hair fell in a long braid down her back, and she wore a black shawl around her shoulders. "Jethro Neuenschwander, what are you doing? Haven't you stirred up enough trouble for one day?"

"It's not Jethro's fault," Mary Anne said, though why she bothered to defend him was a mystery. She shone the flashlight in the direction of the hammock. "Mammi and Dawdi got tangled all on their own."

Sarah raised both eyebrows, as if annoyed but not surprised that her grandparents were stuck in her hammock. "I told you, Mammi," she said, talking to the east side of the hammock at the spot where Mammi's head was most likely to be. "People your age should be at home sleeping in a bed. You're going to get sciatica or lumbago. Or arthritis."

Dawdi sounded like he had a blanket lodged between his teeth. "And probably shingles too."

"Now, Felty," Mammi scolded. "We've had the shot for shingles. No need to worry

216

about that."

Noah, Mandy's husband, came out of his tent quickly buttoning his shirt. Chester followed, barking as if a herd of cats was sneaking around, maybe crouched behind the surrounding trees. "What happened?" Noah asked.

Jethro simultaneously tried to fend off Sparky and figure out how to free Mammi and Dawdi. "They're tangled in the hammock, and I can't quite see clear how to rescue them."

"Help us, Jethro," Mammi called. Her face peeked out from under one of the blankets and her bare foot stuck out from the hammock not five inches from Jethro's face. Mary Anne shivered involuntarily. Mammi's toes had to be freezing.

Noah glanced at Jethro and frowned. Noah probably wondered if he was allowed to be nice to his own brother-in-law. He ran his fingers along one side of the hammock while Mammi and Dawdi struggled mightily inside their cocoon. "I think we're going to have to take the whole thing down," he said.

Jethro nodded. "Do you want to untie the knot or hold them up?"

Noah thought about it for a second. "You're strong. I'll untie, and we'll both lower them to the ground."

Jethro handed Mary Anne the flashlight. "Anna and Felty, we're going to have to take your hammock down. Noah is going to untie one end, and we'll lower you to the ground. Then we can get you out of there."

"Okay," Mammi said. "If you're sure you won't drop us."

Jethro patted one of Mammi's hands, which stuck out from the hammock. "I won't let you fall, Anna. You're my favorite grandmother-in-law."

Mary Anne smiled to herself. Jethro had such a comforting voice and a calming way about him. He could talk an angry bear into trusting him. His untroubled manner had pulled her through those first few weeks after the miscarriage. It was only later that he seemed to quit caring how she felt and started treating her with indifference instead of fondness.

"Be careful, Jethro," Mammi said. "I've lost track of that spider, and he might turn on you next."

Noah nodded to Jethro and held the rope taut with one hand while he untied it with his other. Jethro braced his back and shoulder against the sagging hammock and gripped the rope with both hands. Noah loosened the knot and held on tight as

Jethro slowly lowered his end of the hammock to the ground. Mammi and Dawdi rolled out of the hammock like marbles from a bag.

"Ach du lieva," Mammi said. "Now I know what a burrito feels like. I'm never eating one again, even though I have a very *gute* recipe."

Mary Anne had tasted Mammi's burritos. She could only hope Mammi would be true to her word and never pull out that recipe again.

As soon as her grandparents were safely on the ground, Mary Anne and Sarah rushed to Mammi's side and helped her up. Jethro pulled Dawdi to his feet. Mammi was barefoot, wearing a cream-colored nightgown with a fluorescent pink nightcap. Her braid had fallen apart, probably during her hammock ordeal, and her snowy-white hair frolicked about her head like wispy clouds on a windy day. But she had a smile on her face, which, after being attacked by a spider and tangled up in a hammock, was quite a miracle. *"Denki,* Jethro. *Denki,* Noah." She reached up and patted Jethro on the cheek. "You were always such a nice boy, even if you are a bit thick sometimes."

Sarah took off her shawl and placed it over Mammi's shoulders. "I suppose this is my fault. I thought the hammock would be more comfortable, but I should have known better."

Mammi waved her hand as if swatting a fly — or a mosquito. They were plentiful in the woods in the springtime. "I got attacked by a spider. I had to defend myself." She scrunched her lips to one side of her face. "Come to think of it, it might have been a nightmare." She turned to Jethro. "Did you see any spiders running away?"

Jethro shook his head. "He probably sneaked away when he heard you tell Felty to kill him."

Mary Anne loved Mammi's laugh. It sounded like Christmas morning and birthday parties. "Jethro, you're such a tease. Spiders don't speak *Deitsch*."

Sarah wasn't in any kind of mood. "I wholeheartedly support solidarity, but those dogs have got to go or none of us will get any sleep."

Mammi smoothed her hand down her nightgown. "Now, Sarah, you know in your heart I can't leave Sparky home. When she gets lonely she sheds and chases the chickens." Mammi took in a breath sharply. "Oh dear. I forgot all about the chickens, Felty. There's probably a mountain of eggs in that coop, and the chickens have no doubt run into the woods and been eaten by the bears."

"I don't think bears eat chickens, Banannie."

"Well. That's a relief." She brushed her fingers across her neck, as if remembering the spider that may or may not have been there. "We had a bear in our huckleberry patch once. It nearly ate Pilot, but Pilot got away."

"Huh," Sarah grunted. "That's too bad."

"I heard that," Lily called from inside her tent.

Dawdi straightened his nightshirt. He was still wearing his trousers and socks. "Not to worry, Annie. I asked Titus to keep watch over our chickens and milk Iris twice a day. He takes the milk home to Katie Rose so she can make cheese."

Sarah folded her arms. "We still need to do something about the dogs."

Noah wrapped his fingers around Chester's collar and led him quickly back into the tent. He probably didn't want to be around for any talk of banishing the dogs. Mary Anne liked having a few dogs in the camp. They were noisy, to be sure, but they probably kept the bears away. And the foxes. And for sure and certain the raccoons.

Mammi sighed. "I'm afraid you'll just

have to wear earplugs, Sarah. I can't do without Sparky."

"But now you have no bed," Sarah said. "I'll hitch up your buggy and take you home right now if you want."

Jethro pointed to the Swift-n-Snug tent. "I would really appreciate it if you would take my bed in the house, Anna. I'm sleeping out here tonight."

Dawdi's eyes lit up, but he didn't say anything.

Mammi smiled as if she was very pleased — either pleased about Jethro sleeping outside or pleased she would get a nice bed tonight. The smile faded as quickly as it had appeared. "*Ach,* Jethro, that's a wonderful nice offer, but Felty and I would never dream of abandoning Mary Anne in her time of need."

"We wouldn't really be abandoning her," Dawdi said. "It's cold out here, and we don't have a tent or a hammock, and you forgot your stockings."

"And there are no spiders," Jethro said.

Mary Anne clasped her hands together. "You wouldn't be abandoning me, Mammi. Sarah, Lily, and Mandy are all here."

A deep line appeared between Mammi's brows. "But solidarity was my idea. What will happen to the protest if the captain gives up?"

"You're not giving up," Sarah said. "You're being practical, and we'll keep the solidarity going until you get back."

Mammi pursed her lips. "I suppose you're right, especially if it's just for one night. And my feet are like ice cubes. Do you have any slippers, Jethro?"

"*Jah,* right at the foot of my bed."

Mammi smiled. "I'll do my best to keep Sparky from chewing on them."

Jethro's hesitation was so brief that only Mary Anne noticed it. "They're lined with sheepskin. They'll keep your feet warm." Mary Anne was impressed. He didn't complain or take back his very generous offer or make a face, even though he loved those slippers.

No matter what Jethro thought of her, he was always so kind to her grandparents. It was one of the few things she still liked about him.

CHAPTER TWELVE

Mary Anne dipped her brush into the dollop of ruby red paint on her palette, crinkled her nose, and squinted at her canvas. She had thought to paint a whole flock of butterflies, but Dennis wanted them to start with something easy so they could learn the basic elements of oil painting. Mary Anne's gaze traveled from her canvas to the deep red apple sitting on the table next to the *kaffee* mug. *Green Bay Packers* was written across the bottom of the mug, but Dennis said to pretend the mug was plain white. The lettering was too complex for their lesson today.

It was just Mary Anne's second day at work, but she had been eager to start the painting class as soon as possible. Charlene had purchased ten small blank canvases out of the center's budget, and there were plenty of paints and brushes and easels to go around. Dennis, Bob Hennig, Dawdi, and

Josie Monson — who didn't have a great deal of artistic talent — were the only ones who had been interested in painting. The other women and Mammi were on the far side of the room tying a quilt.

It had only taken Mary Anne two minutes of trying to instruct her students how to paint a butterfly to realize she was completely unqualified to teach a painting class. She liked to paint farm scenes on her walls and butterflies on her tent, but she'd never taken a course or read a book on painting. She wasn't even sure how to tell her students how to hold the brush properly. Josie held her brush between her index finger and thumb the way Mary Anne had seen *Englischers* hold their cigarettes. Dawdi held his brush like a pencil. Margaret had raised her hand and asked if they shouldn't sketch something on the canvas in pencil first, and Mary Anne hadn't been able to give her an answer.

At that point, Dennis — bless his heart — had stood up and gently taken over the class. He had smiled and told Mary Anne that he knew a little about painting because he'd studied art in college, and could he maybe give everyone a few pointers? Mary Anne had been humiliated for about half a second, and then she'd decided that if she wanted to learn anything, she'd better be humble enough to own up to her shortcomings.

Dennis had offered Mary Anne his chair and then he gave them a lesson on the basics of oil painting. Mary Anne was soaking it in as fast as she could. She'd never even guessed she needed to know line and shape, texture and light. She had always just enjoyed the creativity without learning the skills.

Her heart raced at the possibilities, at the exhilaration of learning something new, something that opened a whole world for her that she never even knew existed. *Ach,* the things she'd been missing!

Even concentrating as hard as she was, it was easy to hear the conversation Mammi, Alice, and Judy were having on the other side of the room, while they tied a baby quilt for the hospital. Mary Anne hadn't had time to put together a patchwork quilt for them to work on, so she'd found some cute flannel at the store, cut it into two panels, and stretched it onto the quilt frames at the senior center. Once she finished her latest quilt top, she'd bring it for the ladies to work on. They seemed excited about helping her make quilts for Pammy's Etsy shop, and they balked when she offered to share the profits with them.

"We should be paying you," Alice had said. "We love to quilt, and it's all the better if we can help you make a little extra money. Camping isn't cheap."

Nae, camping wasn't cheap, not with the food and other supplies she had to buy. She needed to make as many quilts as possible because she wanted to save enough money to be in her own place when the weather turned cold. October at the latest. And she needed to repay Jethro his two hundred dollars. She didn't want to feel guilty about it anymore, and it would be better if he quit fretting about it. Maybe it would be easier for him to forgive her if his money jar was comfortably full again.

Mary Anne took a deep breath to clear the weight that settled onto her chest. Thank the *gute* Lord, Jethro had given her back her sewing machine and the half-painted bench she planned to sell on Etsy. As long as she could earn some money with her handicrafts, she would be okay. And so would Jethro, Lord willing.

Dennis came around to Mary Anne's side of the canvas and took a look at her work. "I like the shape of your apple," he said. "Can you make the gradations of color more subtle?"

Mary Anne pressed her lips together. She was so ignorant yet. She didn't even know what *gradations* or *subtle* meant. "What . . . what do you mean?"

Dennis bent down to her eye level and pointed to the apple on the table. "The apple isn't just one color of red. Do you see how the red gives way to green around the top by the stem, or how the shadows at the bottom make the color darker? There's even a little fleck of white where the light shines on it yet."

Mary Anne nodded. "Okay. I'll mix more colors."

Dennis smiled. "The best part is that you can always paint over your mistakes."

"I like that when you're tying a quilt too," Judy called from across the room. "I seem to be making a lot of knots."

"Ach," Mammi said. "You should learn how to knit. It limbers up your fingers for quilting, except you can't knit while you're camping because your fingers get cold and seize up, and spiders like to lurk in the yarn."

Judy tried to thread her needle and look at Mary Anne at the same time. "How is the camping going?"

Mary Anne didn't quite know how to answer that. Camping itself was terrible, but being out of that house and on her own was heavenly.

Mammi answered for her. "*Ach,* our hammock twisted itself into a knot with Felty and me inside it. I'll never eat a taco again. Or a burrito."

Alice's laughter filled the entire space. "I prefer enchiladas."

"We've slept in Jethro's house for two nights, but it doesn't seem right," Mammi said. "We should be out camping with Mary Anne. True solidarity means sharing the misery."

"I think we're wonderful miserable in Jethro's bed," Dawdi said. "The sheets are itchy. I don't see any reason to move out. We've got our share of tribulation."

A scold pulled at Mammi's mouth. "Now, Felty. Suffering for Mary Anne's sake is a sign of our love. We don't want Mary Anne to think we don't love her."

Mary Anne smiled. "I know you love me, Mammi. It's better for you to sleep in the house. It's not that far from my tent."

Mammi squared her shoulders. "I wouldn't hear of it. I'm determined to make myself miserable for your happiness. That's what grandparents are for."

"Why were you sleeping in a hammock?" Judy said.

Mammi snipped the end of her yarn. "There aren't enough tents. And now that Lia has moved out to the woods with us, we can't borrow Moses's tent. Emma and Ben set up a tent yesterday too." Mammi looked up at Mary Anne from across the room and grinned. "All this solidarity warms my heart."

Mary Anne tried to smile back. She was happy for the company and even more grateful for the support, but she hated that her relatives were living in tents when they could have been sleeping in comfortable beds and using their own private toilets. They were putting up with a lot of misery, as Mammi said, for Mary Anne. And in some ways — though she hated to admit it to herself — it was like a slap in the face to Jethro every time someone new set up a tent in the woods. She might not love Jethro anymore, but she didn't especially like to see him humiliated — not that the cousins were out to purposefully humiliate Jethro, but Mary Anne felt it keenly all the same.

She tightened her fingers around the palette. Why should she feel guilty? He'd practically ignored her for four years. He'd taken down her campsite and put locks on all the doors. He only had himself to blame for stirring up the wrath of the Helmuths.

A quiet sigh escaped her lips. Mary Anne just wanted Jethro to go on with his life and be happy. If only she could make him understand. It wouldn't do any *gute* for him to move into the woods or even try to be nice to her. She wanted to live her own life. She wanted to draw farm scenes on her walls and collect rocks. She wanted to make baby quilts and paint butterflies, buy expensive cheeses and experiment with strange recipes. Maybe she was more like Mammi than she imagined. Mary Anne wanted to create, and she couldn't do it with Jethro's disapproving eye always on her.

She got a little carried away with the black, and before she knew it, she'd painted several black-red slashes across the bottom of the apple. That would never do. She mixed her colors again and painted over the dark.

"We have a tent you can use," Judy said, reaching for the scissors Mammi had just put down. "Don't we, Dennis?"

"We do," Dennis said. "We haven't used it for ten years, but I don't think it has any holes in it."

Mammi bloomed like a morning glory in the sun. "You do? Well, that's wonderful *gute,* Felty. We can move back into the woods tonight."

Dawdi heaved a sigh, for sure and certain missing Jethro's bed already. Was it any wonder his apple looked like red, lumpy banana? "Wonderful *gute*. With all the suffering we're going to do, Mary Anne will surely be the happiest girl in Wisconsin."

Mammi nodded her approval. "She will."

Bob Hennig glanced up from his painting. In forest green paint, he had written "Green Bay Still Life" across the top of his canvas, and his mug was so big, there wasn't going to be any room for an apple. He'd definitely need a lesson about size and following directions. "You could use my RV."

Dawdi perked up like a horse on a bag of oats. "Your RV?"

"I take it on fishing trips with my son, but I'm not going anywhere for a couple of weeks. Is there a road into Mary Anne's woods? I could park it right there and you could sleep in it. It has a toilet and a shower too."

Mammi frowned. "Well, Bob. That's wonderful kind of you."

"Wonderful kind," Dawdi said.

"But we can't accept," Mammi added. "It doesn't seem fair to live in an RV while *die youngie* suffer in tents. It's not real camping, and I can't see that it's in keeping with the spirit of solidarity."

"Nine million people own RVs," Bob said. "You can't tell them it's not real camping. They'd get offended."

Dawdi abandoned his painting altogether and dragged his chair across the room next to Mammi's. "He could park it right next to Mary Anne's tent, and we could still do all our cooking outside. Wouldn't it be nice not to have to hike to the barn to go to the bathroom?"

Mammi drew her brows together and nibbled on her bottom lip. "But what about the suffering, Felty?"

Alice chimed in. It was probably obvious to everyone that an eighty-five-year-old woman might end up in a body cast if she camped out much longer. "You'll suffer plenty, Anna. RV toilets are disgusting, and it can get pretty stuffy in there at night. Plus, you won't be able to hear the crickets to lull you to sleep. It's a little crowded in an RV. You and Felty will do a lot of bumping into each other."

Dawdi nodded, as if resigned to sleeping in the RV. "It's going to be miserable."

"You won't have to set up another tent," Judy said.

"An RV's not likely to get blown away in the wind."

Concern lined Mammi's face. "We had a

233

tornado once at the school. In an RV we might get knocked about a bit in a tornado."

"That's plenty of suffering for me, Mammi," Mary Anne said. "I'll never doubt your love, even if you sleep in the RV."

Mammi's expression relaxed. "I suppose it would be okay if we slept in Bob's RV as long as we cook over the fire."

"Of course," Dawdi said, slapping his knee. "I love your tinfoil dinners, Banannie."

"What would you think if I came camping for a few days?" Alice said. "It sounds like you've got quite a party going on over there."

Mammi nodded vigorously. "You'd be welcome."

"My grandkids tell me we never do anything fun," Alice said. "I'll bring them with me."

Mammi smiled. "Mary Anne needs all the solidarity she can get."

Mary Anne chuckled. She liked the solidarity for sure and certain, but she'd have to start sending people to the house to use the bathroom. It was *gute* Mammi and Dawdi now had their own toilet. That would help.

That toilet in the barn probably couldn't take all those extra flushes.

■ ■ ■ ■

Jethro set his fishing pole on the bed and stowed his tackle box in the closet. He might be sleeping in a tent, but he was keeping his fishing pole in the house. He didn't want it to get ruined out in the woods. Besides, neither of the beds in the house were being used. He might as well spread out the contents of his tackle box too for all the good it would do him.

His heart skipped around like a wild colt, and he felt almost giddy with excitement. It was an emotion he hadn't felt in a long time, not even when he had bought his fishing pole. He'd caught two fat trout in the river, and he was going to give them to Mary Anne. He couldn't wait to see her face light up when she saw the size of them. She could eat fish for three whole days, even if she shared some with Anna and Felty. Jethro didn't even expect her to cook any for him. He wanted her to have both fish all to herself. For sure and certain she'd be happy at the money she would save on fish from the grocery store.

Two trout, no matter how plump, probably weren't going to make Mary Anne fall in love with him again immediately, but he hoped they would soften her up a little. When they were courting, he would bring her asparagus from the field by the ditch and goat cheese from the dairy. Anna and Felty had even let him pick berries from their huckleberry patch to give to Mary Anne. She liked making huckleberry pie.

Jethro loved the way Mary Anne's eyes used to dance whenever he came into a room. With her golden hair and shocking blue eyes, she looked like an angel when she smiled, and he loved how her face bloomed into freckles whenever she spent too much time in the sun. He used to tease her that he wanted to kiss those freckles one by one. His toes curled inside his boots. Maybe she'd let him do that kissing thing if she really liked the fish. He cleared his throat. Mustn't get his hopes up, even with a pair of trout in his hands.

Jethro walked out the back door in the muted light of the approaching sunset and looked toward the woods. Mary Anne's tent was the easiest to spot, with the bold, bright butterflies painted on the outside. Even though she'd ruined his tent, he liked that she was painting again. After she'd lost the baby, painting seemed to make her sad, and Jethro had advised her to quit. There was no use dredging up all those bad feelings.

Jethro looked to his left and nearly dropped his precious fish. If he'd been chewing gum, he would have swallowed it. A shiny white monster of an RV was parked on the dirt path that led to his barn. It was a newer model, and Jethro didn't doubt that that thing had cost more than his house. But the RV wasn't the only addition to their already crowded campsite. At least seven new tents had sprung up like toadstools under the trees. For three days, there hadn't been one tent within fifty yards of Jethro's. Now there were five. He had no idea what to make of it. Not only were there five tents near his, but a Porta-Potty stood in the midst of them like a shepherd keeping watch over his flock.

He tucked the paper bag containing the fish under his arm. He'd have to get to the bottom of the growing population of tents before giving his fish to Mary Anne. And who had brought a Porta-Potty?

Jethro marched to his tent, unzipped the flap, and stuck his head inside. No one in here. Okay. At least he still had a place to sleep. He rezipped his tent and studied the tent right next to his. It looked familiar. *"Hallo?"* he said.

Someone unzipped the flap from the inside, and Jethro's *mamm* and *dat* crawled

237

out of the tent. Mamm pinched her lips as if she had a sour stomach, and Dat didn't look much better. It was plain they were both in wonderful bad moods. "So," Mamm said. "You finally decided to come home. Where have you been? Anna says you get home at five o'clock every day. It's almost seven."

Jethro held out the paper bag but didn't open it, even though those fish were something to be proud of. "I went fishing with my friend Randall."

Mamm narrowed her eyes. "Your *Englisch* friend?"

Jethro gritted his teeth. It wasn't against the rules to have *Englisch* friends. Why was she so testy? "He has a nice truck," was all he could think to say. Jethro glanced at the olive-green tent he and Dat had taken on many a camping trip when Jethro was a boy. "What are you doing here?" He suspected he wasn't going to like the answer.

Mamm folded her arms across her chest. "The better question is, what are *you* doing here?"

"I live here."

"Not in this tent you don't," Mamm said. She had the uncanny ability to make any sentence sound like an accusation. "We'd heard you'd moved out to the woods, and

238

we were shocked. I told Chris, 'Jethro hasn't done anything wrong. Why would he have moved into a tent?' "

Jethro hadn't wanted his parents to find out he was living in the woods. They were furious with Mary Anne. How would they ever understand? "I'm not going to sit in my comfortable house while my *fraa* lives in a tent."

Mamm opened her mouth to argue and promptly closed it again. She seemed to be digesting his words. "I suppose that's quite thoughtful of you." She paused, and a line appeared between her brows. "But the tent was her choice, not yours."

"It doesn't matter. Until she moves back home, I'm staying here."

"You don't have to pay for her mistakes," Dat said. "If she's wicked enough to leave her husband, she should suffer the consequences alone. This isn't your fault."

"Maybe it is." Jethro slumped his shoulders. It was probably more his fault than he wanted to admit.

Dat pointed to Mary Anne's side of the camp, where two new tents had appeared since last night. There were six tents in all, plus the giant RV, which could probably house a dozen people. "Mary Anne's relatives are supporting this nonsense — as if

239

they hope to prove Mary Anne is right and you're wrong. I sincerely hope one of them doesn't die while camping and go straight to hell for their wicked ways."

"It's not as bad as all that, Chris," Mamm said. "Mary Anne has done wrong. We're here to help her see there's a right way to treat her husband and a wrong way. I can't see that she's going to hell just yet. There's still time for repentance."

Dat hooked his thumbs around his suspenders. "But the Helmuths need to know they can't get away with supporting sin. They're standing by a woman who's left her husband. We've come to show the Helmuths there are still people who believe in righteousness. We aren't afraid to stand up to evil, and neither are the rest of the men who came with us. They're going to see we won't turn a blind eye to such behavior. When the *fraaen* understand how their husbands feel about wives moving out of their homes, they'll learn a valuable lesson."

Jethro shuffled his feet. "Maybe the Helmuths just want to show they love Mary Anne." He couldn't blame them. He loved her too.

Mamm seemed to dig in her heels without moving. "Well, then. We love you just as much as they love Mary Anne. They need to see you have allies."

Mary Anne wouldn't like it. She hadn't liked it when he'd moved into the woods, but Mamm might have a point. Jethro didn't agree with Dat that Mary Anne was sinful, but when she saw him camping all by himself, did she think it proved he was wrong and she was right? Did she believe that because no one had come to support him, everyone agreed with her?

Jethro eyed the other tents. "Who else is here?"

Dat pointed to the tents standing in a circle around the Porta-Potty. "David Eicher, even though he's wonderful busy being a minister. Norman Coblenz, Adam Wengerd, and Willie Jay. He came all the way from Appleton because he's so upset about what Mary Anne did to you."

Mamm nodded. "Naoma was very understanding. She's taking up Willie Jay's chores because she knows how important this is to all of us."

Jethro furrowed his brow. Willie Jay had talked him into tearing down Mary Anne's camp. Mary Anne wouldn't have asked for a divorce if it hadn't been for Willie Jay. Maybe this was a mistake. Maybe their being here would make things worse. Then again, how much worse could they get?

He'd be foolish to turn away friends who only wanted to support him.

Dat patted the wall of the Porta-Potty. "We all pitched in, and David rented this. He thought it would be better if we didn't share a bathroom with the enemy." He glanced at Mamm, then Jethro, and cleared his throat. "I mean, no one is the enemy. We're all here to help Mary Anne."

Jethro wasn't sure about a lot of things, but he was sure Mamm and Dat and the others weren't here to help Mary Anne. It would be okay as long as they stayed away from her and left Jethro to court her on his own. He didn't point out that the Porta-Potty had no shower. They were all going to stink something wonderful. Well, Mamm and Dat were going to stink. Jethro planned on showering in the house. He couldn't make Mary Anne fall in love with him if he smelled like a skunk.

"Where's David? And what about Willie Jay?"

Mamm brushed her hand down her apron. "Norman and Adam went home to eat dinner. David and Willie Jay went to the market to get food. I've agreed to cook for all of us."

Jethro nodded, his stomach already tying itself into a knot. He'd eaten nothing but cold cereal and McDonald's for several days. He was suddenly overjoyed that Mamm and Dat had decided to come camping.

Mamm took a look around and heaved a great sigh. "I hope Mary Anne comes to her senses soon. I don't think I can stand to be here for more than a week."

Dat patted Mamm on the shoulder. "It won't be long, now that we're here. Lord willing, you'll help her see a better way."

Jethro didn't want to discourage them, but Mary Anne wasn't going to budge in a week. Of course, he might be underestimating the power of his gift. Who could resist two fine trout from the Wolf River? He held out the bag to show Mamm and Dat. "I caught some fish."

"Wonderful *gute*," Mamm said. "I'll fry them up for dinner."

"I thought I'd give them to Mary Anne."

Mamm frowned. "Okay, then. They'll remind her what a *gute* provider you are."

"She always liked it when I brought home fish. I'm hoping it might make her remember some of the happy times we had."

"If she has any goodness left in her, she'll be touched," Dat said.

Jethro showed his parents a *gute* place to build a fire and pointed out where they could collect firewood. "If I'm not back in ten minutes," he said, "it's because Mary Anne has invited me to eat with her."

Mamm grinned. "No one can resist that smile of yours. We won't wait."

Jethro straightened his jacket around his shoulders and headed for Mary Anne's tent. It was a little late, and there was the risk she'd already eaten dinner, but it couldn't be helped. He hadn't gotten off work until five, and catching the fish had taken almost an hour. If she'd already eaten, she could put the fish in her cooler and cook them up tomorrow. That might be even better. She'd probably invite him to dinner if she had a little more time to prepare.

As he got nearer her tent, Jethro could hear the sewing machine humming inside. Mary Anne never spent one moment in idleness. The coals in the fire pit were still warm, but it was obvious she'd already cooked dinner and cleaned up after herself. Sometimes she ate with Mammi and Dawdi, sometimes with the cousins, but never with him. Maybe his fish would change all that.

"*Hallo,* Mary Anne?" he said, loud enough so she could hear him but soft enough that he wouldn't startle her. When she got to sewing, she was oblivious to anything else.

The sewing machine stopped, and he

heard the crackle of the tent fabric as she made her way to the front opening. She unzipped it, poked her head out, and hesitated for a second before stepping out of the tent. Jethro got a brief glimpse inside. A mobile of pink and green Ritz Crackers hung on the ceiling like a bough of cherry blossoms in the spring. Because she only had one tent now instead of two, the sewing machine and the little chair from the spare bedroom were crammed against one side of the tent, and her cot and sleeping bag sat against the other side. If Jethro hadn't taken down her campsite, she'd still have both tents and plenty of room for sewing. He'd made things harder for her, and a pair of trout weren't going to make up for all his mistakes.

She wore her black shawl and gloves with no fingers. It was only May 11, and the days and nights were still wonderful chilly. He wished she'd move into the house. She'd be so much warmer. For a moment, Jethro was distracted by a strand of golden hair that had escaped the confines of her *kapp* and was hovering a breath away from her cheek. He ached to reach out and wrap that silky strand around his finger. She stared at him, and he tried to stuff the urge to touch her hair deep into his chest. He didn't want her to see the longing in his eyes.

Suddenly his tongue felt as if it weighed ten pounds. "You look so pretty tonight."

"Okay?" She gave him a pleasant look, as if she was having a conversation with a checker at Walmart. It was *gute* she didn't scowl at him, but he was her husband, for goodness sake. Was politeness the best she could do?

Maybe not, but he'd be greedy to wish for more.

"I always thought you were the prettiest girl in the *gmayna.*"

She acted like she didn't even hear what he'd said. "Your parents are here. And my cousin Norman. They brought their own bathroom."

Jethro kicked the dirt at his feet. "They . . . uh . . . they want to support me."

"Your *mater* hates me."

"She doesn't hate you. She's just concerned, and maybe a little protective of her son."

Mary Anne huffed out a breath, as if surrendering the argument. She looked very unhappy. Jethro resisted the urge to pull her into his arms. "I don't blame her for hating me, and they're your woods just as much as they're mine, but your *mamm* is here to scold me, and I don't want to talk to her.

Will you tell her?"

He forced a painful smile onto his face. Mary Anne didn't like his parents being here, but they were going to help Jethro win Mary Anne back. "Of course I'll tell her. She's not here to argue. She loves you as much as she loves me."

Mary Anne nodded, but it was plain she didn't believe him. "Okay. *Denki.*"

He wanted to reassure her that Mamm really did love her, but Mary Anne hadn't said anything he could argue with, so he let it go. Besides, he didn't want anything to overshadow his gift. He showed her the paper bag and couldn't help the wide grin that stretched across his face. "I brought you some fish. I thought you might like it for dinner tomorrow night."

She expelled a long breath. "That's very kind of you, but I don't like fish. Save it, and make dinner for yourself."

He drew his brows together in confusion. "You don't like fish?"

"*Nae.* I've never liked fish."

"But . . . but I used to bring fish home at least once a week. You cooked it and ate it with me. I thought you liked it."

"I did that to make you happy, but I don't have to pretend to like it anymore."

Jethro couldn't believe what he was hearing. "But you made up all those new ways to cook it. You cleaned and fileted every fish I ever brought home."

"I was afraid one of the bones was going to get stuck in my tonsils. And you like to catch fish, but you don't like to clean them."

She made their marriage, her life, sound like such a chore. "Why didn't you tell me?"

She hesitated, as if weighing whether she should trust him or not. "It would have been one more reason for you to be disappointed in me."

Her words sliced him to the bone. Was that what she truly thought of him? "How can you blame this on me? I wouldn't have brought fish home if I'd known."

She didn't even seem upset. "I'm not blaming you. It's my fault. Everything is my fault. Does that make you feel better?"

Of course it didn't make him feel better. *Lord, is it I?*

What did it matter if he was right and she was wrong? Did he love her or didn't he? Did he want her to come home or not? How could he fall back into the same pattern of arguing with her when three days ago he'd promised himself he'd never again do anything to hurt her?

Jethro shut his mouth so fast, she probably heard his lips smack together. He was

248

beginning to realize that everything he thought was Mary Anne's fault was turning out to be his. Maybe she should have told him about the fish, but it disgusted him that he hadn't known something so important about his own wife. He had started fishing after they lost the baby because fishing took his mind off the pain, and it got him out of the gloomy house where Mary Anne had done nothing but cry.

He'd been a coward.

"I was never disappointed in you, Mary Anne," he whispered, even though she wouldn't believe him. He hadn't given her a reason to believe in him for four long years.

"Okay," she said, looking past him as if he weren't even there.

"I talked myself into believing you liked to clean the fish, mostly because I didn't like to do it, and I really hoped you did. You were willing to do it, but I never even asked if you liked to."

"It doesn't matter."

He picked up the edge of her shawl and fingered the tassel at one of the corners. She stiffened like a prairie dog at the sound of a fox. "I was disappointed about the baby but never about you. I loved you, Mary Anne. I still do, more than ever."

"You don't have to lie to me, Jethro. I saw

it in your eyes."

"I don't know what you saw, but I'm not lying."

A stifled and short moan came from Mary Anne's throat.

"Please don't cry," he said. "I hate to see you cry."

Mary Anne wiped a hint of moisture from her eyes. "I don't have to do what you say anymore, Jethro Neuenschwander. I'll cry if I want to . . . and I'm not crying."

His heart hurt for her, for the pain of lost dreams and the longing of empty arms. "Of course you don't have to do what I say. You never did."

"I did if I wanted to keep from disappointing you."

How could she say that? How could she not know how he cherished her? Even though a thousand protests were on the tip of his tongue, he wasn't about to argue with her. He'd done enough arguing to last him until Christmas three decades from now, and his words only hurt Mary Anne. He didn't want to be right anymore. He just wanted his *fraa* back, and he didn't know the words to say to make it so. "I love you so much, Mary Anne," he finally said, because anything else he could think of to say might have further hurt her feelings.

But what did he know? Maybe telling her he loved her brought her pain too.

She sniffed back her tears. "What's done is done."

He dared to reach out his hand and wrap his fingers lightly around hers. "It would mean very much to me if you would talk. Would you tell me all the ways I've hurt you so I can have a chance to say I'm sorry?"

She pressed her lips together and shook her head, but she didn't pull her hand away.

That was enough encouragement for him. "This first thing I need to apologize for is the fish. I'm sorry you ate fish for four years, and your husband kept bringing it home. You probably hated the sight of my fishing pole."

She expelled a puff of air from between her lips. "I still do."

His chest tightened until he found it hard to breathe. She'd withheld so much of herself for so long. Would he ever be able to get it back? "So you'd be happier if I got rid of the fishing pole?"

She pulled her hand from his grasp and laced her fingers together. "I don't care what you do. We don't live together any-more."

She kept slapping him across the face with that one. He paused until he could breathe again. "Randall will buy it. He'd probably even be willing to give me what I paid for it."

She pressed her lips together and blinked twice. "I don't want you to sell your fishing pole."

He caught a hint of something in her eyes, a deep emotion that gave him hope, even though he couldn't name it. "You don't?"

The emotion disappeared as quickly as it had come. "Don't sell your fishing pole on my account. You'd resent me for the rest of your life."

"You're the only woman I've ever loved. How could I resent you?"

She snorted her disapproval. "You do nothing *but* resent me. I see how you look at Mattie Byler at *gmay*. She already has three children and one on the way."

Mary Anne had surprised Jethro before, but now he was truly speechless. Mattie Byler? What did he care for Mattie Byler? His mouth fell so far open, he could have caught every mosquito in the woods.

Mary Anne lowered her eyes. "I'm sorry. That wasn't nice."

"But you wanted to say it." He made sure she heard the gentleness in his voice. She had surprised him, but he felt only curiosity and pain for what she had said.

She looked up and took a deep breath. "*Jah.* I wanted to say it. You don't have to tell me. I already know what a wicked person I am."

"Mary Anne, you babysit your cousins' *kinner.* You make those striped Jell-O treats for new mothers and shut-ins. You're always at someone's sickbed, and you used to do my laundry every week." He gave her a self-deprecating smile. "Until you told me I was boring, I'd never heard you say a bad word about anyone, even your cousin Norman. If you're wicked, then most of the *fraaen* and all of the men in the *gmay* are wicked too, and there's no hope for any of us. Hell is going to be very crowded."

That coaxed a reluctant smile out of her.

"*Cum,*" he said, tugging playfully on her shawl. "Let's sit down by the fire pit, and we can talk about Mattie Byler."

She resisted his pull. "I have to finish my quilt top."

"Mary Anne, you just accused me of something terrible. I want to understand why." He tilted his head to the side to study her face at a different angle. "Don't you think I deserve that much?"

"I shouldn't have said it. We can leave it at that."

"You know me well enough to know I

could never leave it at that." He motioned to one of the camp chairs, and she took it, obviously reluctant to say another word about Mattie Byler and how Jethro did or didn't look at her at *gmay.* Jethro pulled a chair close to Mary Anne's and sat. "Will you tell me why you said that about Mattie?"

"You dated Mattie for almost a year. If you'd married her, you would have all the children you could dream of."

The urge to contradict her felt like bile in his throat, but he clenched his jaw and took a deep breath. Felty would have been proud of him. "But how do I look at her?"

Mary Anne was altogether too serious, as if she'd just revealed her deepest, darkest secret and she feared Jethro was going to rebuke her for it.

He narrowed his eyes to slits and puckered his lips into a pout. "Like this? Do I look at her like this?"

Mary Anne turned her face away to hide a hesitant grin.

"What about this?" Jethro formed his mouth into the shape of an *O* and widened his eyes until they could have popped out of his head. "Do I look at her like this?"

Mary Anne's smile escaped, and she cuffed him on the shoulder. "It's not something to laugh at, Jethro. Every time she gets up to tend to one of her *kinner* at *gmay,* your eyes follow her until she leaves the room."

Jethro let out the breath he'd been holding. Had he made Mary Anne insecure about her worth, about her place in his heart? He had to fix it. He leaned a little closer to Mary Anne, but not close enough to annoy her. "I'm going to tell you a secret that Mattie and I have never told anyone." He stroked his hand down his short beard. "That might not be true anymore. I don't wonder but Mattie has told Vernon, but I never told you, out of consideration for Mattie. I hope she won't be cross that I'm telling you."

Mary Anne hardened like cement. "You don't have to tell me anything."

"I want you to understand." Jethro draped his hand over Mary Anne's armrest. He couldn't resist trying to get as close to Mary Anne as she'd let him. It helped ease the ache in his chest. "One night, Mattie and I sneaked out to a bar in Shawano. We were both in *rumschpringe,* but we knew neither of our parents would approve. Mattie had more of an adventurous streak than I did, so she was the one who talked me into going — not that I blame her. I could have stayed home." Maybe Mary Anne wouldn't think he was so boring once she heard his story. Unfortunately, she'd also know he wasn't so righteous either.

"As I remember, Mattie was wonderful mad at her *dat* for something, and she brought fifty dollars to spend on alcohol. I wasn't brave enough to have even one drink, but she had seven or eight. I didn't keep track."

Tiny lines gathered around Mary Anne's eyes, and she didn't seem quite so far away from him anymore. "She got drunk?"

"I finally dragged her out of the bar, but she could barely walk. She took a hard step and rolled her ankle off the curb. She threw up three times in my buggy before I got her home. I've never been able to completely get rid of the smell."

"I guess she was okay."

"I sneaked into my house before I took her home and got a Diet Coke from my *mamm*'s hidden stash. We sat in my buggy while she drank the whole thing. I didn't know how to make *kaffee*, but I thought she should have something with caffeine. Buck Poulter died from drinking too much alcohol. I didn't want that to happen to Mattie."

One side of Mary Anne's mouth curled

upward. "I guess a Diet Coke is better than nothing."

Jethro chuckled. "*Gotte* was trying to tell me something, but I didn't listen. I still don't know how to make *kaffee*." He pulled his hand off her armrest and sat back in his camp chair, just in case she felt he was smothering her. "The next day, Mattie's ankle swelled up like a waterlogged hen. She could barely walk on it, but she was somehow able to hide it from her parents for a week. She finally asked them to take her to the hospital, but she didn't tell them how she hurt her ankle. She'd broken it in two places, and her family didn't want to pay for surgery, so the doctor put her in a cast."

Mary Anne raised an eyebrow. "What does this have to do with the way you look at her at *gmay*?"

She smiled when she said it, and Jethro smiled back. He'd been honest with her. She was ready to believe him. "That ankle never healed right. Every time I see her, I feel sort of guilty, like if I had supported her better with my arm, she never would have rolled her ankle. I watch her at *gmay* to see if the limp is getting better. Keep an eye on her on Sunday, and you'll see."

"Sunday is Mother's Day. I'm not going to church."

"Ach." Jethro's gut clenched. Mary Anne always skipped church on Mother's Day. "Don't tell anyone that Mattie got drunk. Even though we were in *rumschpringe,* I think she'd be embarrassed."

Maybe the crinkles around her eyes softened just a bit. *"Denki* for telling me."

"I dated Mattie for nearly a year, sat with her faithfully every other Sunday, and tried to talk myself into loving her, but then *Gotte* saw fit to send me to Charm, Ohio, for a funeral. The moment I saw you, I promised myself I'd marry you."

Her face turned a pretty shade of pink, and she twisted her mouth into a wry grin. "I'll bet you wish you would have gotten to know me first."

"It just got better and better once I knew you, but it was a big scandal here in Bonduel. Mattie's parents were wonderful mad, and I don't think they've forgiven me yet. Mattie wasn't nearly as upset as her parents. She sort of had her eye on Vernon Byler anyway. I think she was relieved she didn't have to break up with me."

"Mattie is wonderful nice."

Jethro grinned. "Not as nice as you. I always felt so clumsy when I was around you. You could cook and sew and draw like a real artist. You knew the names of five-dozen cheeses. I knew orange and white."

"I still can't believe you moved to Charm so we could date." She eyed him doubtfully, as if wondering if he regretted that decision.

He rested his elbows on his knees. "I couldn't stand the thought of being without you. I would have moved to Florida if you'd lived there. Do you remember when we hiked to the waterfall and you kept finding interesting rocks that you wanted to take home and paint?"

"I used them to line my *mamm*'s flower bed."

"*Jah,* but I had to carry them home in my backpack. It was thirty pounds of rocks."

Mary Anne grinned. "I knew you didn't mind because you wanted to impress me with your muscles. The rocks were beautiful in my *mamm*'s garden."

"You should paint some for our garden," he said, before changing the subject in hopes she wouldn't notice what he'd said. "You were always doing something creative. You made beautiful quilts, and there were leaves and bird's nests all over the house."

He used to think all that was junk, but now he would have done anything for a pile of painted pinecones spread out on his kitchen table.

Or painted rocks lining his garden path.

After the *buplie,* Mary Anne had bought some round, smooth stones from a local *Englisch* farmer. She'd told Jethro she was going to paint rocks and lay them into a path to the barn. Jethro had told her it was silly to buy rocks. What fool paid *gute* money for something you could dig up on your own property? Besides, painting only reminded her of the baby. Who needed a daily reminder every time she went to milk the cow? She'd taken the rocks back to the farmer and gotten her money back.

He'd gotten his way, but Mary Anne had stopped doing much in the garden after that. Flowers were expensive, a fact he'd pointed out to her many times over the years. If she planted anything, she got starts from her cousins or seeds from her neighbors. He pressed his lips together. Was his love of money the root of all his marital problems?

"You didn't mind my projects so much at first," she said.

I don't mind them so much now, he wanted to say, but since he'd torn down her mobiles and painted over the quilt square on the barn, he couldn't really justify himself. Mary Anne's projects cost money, and the older he got, the more frivolous it seemed to spend money on paint and potato chips.

He swallowed hard, not sure he would like the answer to his next question, but if he wanted to win Mary Anne back, he had to know. "When did I start to get boring?" It was probably around the time he'd started worrying about paying the medical bills.

She shifted in her chair. "I don't know."

He was making her uncomfortable, when he really wanted to see her smile. "I wasn't always boring. You and I almost got arrested by the Shawano police."

Her blush got even deeper, even though she tried to suppress a smile. "*Ach*, Jethro, that was your fault, not mine."

His mouth fell open in mock indignation. "It was your idea to go to the lake. You wanted to see the sunset. Is it my fault the sunset was so romantic?" In the first few months of their marriage, he hadn't been able to get enough of her. Things had gone a little far in the buggy — not that Mary Anne minded — but that overeager policeman had. Still, it was a *gute* memory.

Mary Anne laughed. Jethro drank in the sound like a thirsty man gulps up water. How long had it been since he'd heard her laugh? "You kept telling the policeman we were married, but he didn't believe you. He was a grumpy one."

"Grumpy?" Jethro protested. "He made

me get out of the buggy, walk a straight line, and close my eyes and touch my nose. Then he followed us to my parents' house and asked my *dat* if we really were married."

"He told me it was his job to keep the Amish kids from getting pregnant."

"I can't believe that was his only job. What about bank robbers?"

"There aren't that many banks in Shawano."

"I don't know who my *mamm* was angrier at, the policeman or me. It didn't matter to her that we were married. She insisted there are just some things you don't do in a buggy."

Mary Anne shook her head. "I couldn't look your parents in the eye for a month."

"After an adventure like that, I can't believe you would ever think I was boring." He stood up and emptied out the pockets of his trousers. He held out his hand. "Look. Would a boring man carry a pocketknife *and* half a roll of breath mints? And look at this. A rock that looks very much like a button."

Mary Anne's ears perked up at the thought of a rock in the shape of a button. She took it from him and turned it over in her hand. "Wonderful *gute.* But it looks more like a tire."

"Tire, button. They're both very exciting things to carry in my pocket."

Mary Anne lost her smile and sighed with her whole body. "*Ach,* Jethro. We both know I didn't leave because you're boring."

He nodded and tried to pretend her words hadn't cut his legs off. "You said you stopped loving me, but I thought you stopped loving me because you think I'm boring."

She stiffened her spine. "*Ach.* Maybe that was part of it."

Mary Anne wasn't shallow or selfish. She never would have left him just because he was boring. She'd told him she didn't love him anymore. How had that happened? Jethro again fought the urge to argue with her. *What did I do wrong? Why didn't you tell me?*

He knew the answer without having to ask.

She didn't tell him because he wouldn't have heard her. He hadn't truly listened for a very long time. The morning he had found her in the woods making Gruyère-and-bacon French toast and some sort of gourmet *kaffee,* he had assumed she was throwing a tantrum. It was easier and less painful to accuse her of being childish than to try to understand her reasons for leaving. He was just discovering how deep her reasons were, and it made him ashamed. "What did I do that made you want to live in a tent even more than you wanted to live with me, *heartzly*?"

If she cared that he called her *heartzly*, she didn't show it. "I left because you love your fishing pole more than you love me."

Jethro clenched his teeth to keep from shouting out a denial. He could tell she wasn't being petty or trying to make him angry. The truth of what she said was written plainly in her eyes. He had obviously done something to make her believe it. "I only bought it a few weeks ago. Is it because I keep it on the bed in the spare bedroom?"

She lowered her eyes and shook her head. "You might as well keep it in there."

"I'll move it if that would make you feel better."

"It's not really about the fishing pole, Jethro. It's just that when the fishing pole went where our baby was supposed to have slept . . . I don't know . . . It was like all my hopes and dreams were dead, and I realized it had been that way for a long time."

"I'm sorry. I didn't think of it that way."

"Until I moved out, how long had it been since you thought of me as your wife, your helpmeet?"

Again, Jethro held back. He wanted to give

her a chance to tell her truth, no matter how painful it was for him. Humility had never been an easy pill to swallow. "Help me understand what you mean, Mary Anne."

She pulled back. "I don't want to hurt your feelings, Jethro. My faults and sins are a hundred times what yours are. I should pull the beam out of my eye before I go pointing out the mote in yours."

"I want to know how you feel. I don't care about motes or beams. I don't even know what those are exactly." He propped his elbows on his knees and tried to make himself look as teachable as possible. He didn't quite know how to do that, so he pressed his lips together as a sign that he wasn't going to interrupt her and looked at her intently.

"You'll be mad."

"Probably, but you have nothing to fear from me."

She furrowed her brow. "I know."

Of all the things she could have done, this little gesture was significant to him in ways Mary Anne didn't know. She wasn't afraid of him. The thought sent a ribbon of warmth snaking up his spine. "What did I do that made you stop loving me?"

She sighed in resignation. "I started to feel like I was just another thing that made your life easier, like a piece of furniture or the clock on the wall. You paid attention to me when you needed dinner or *kaffee* or clean laundry, and as long as I did what a godly Amish *fraa* should, you had nothing to complain about. You went fishing or sat in your easy chair and read the newspaper every night, and as long as your slippers were by your chair, you didn't have much to say to me."

Jethro stroked his short beard. "You've gotten so quiet the last few years."

"I didn't want to say anything that would disappoint you. I had disappointed you so much already."

"I suppose I didn't want you to see how disappointed I was about the baby. When I was fishing, I didn't have to hide my disappointment, and I didn't have to watch you grieve."

Mary Anne nodded. "You were doing what you thought would bring you the most happiness. The problem was that you were all I had, and your love was shrinking. My life shriveled like a dried apple. I was the submissive, steady *fraa* you wanted me to be, but I wasn't Mary Anne anymore. I moved out before I lost myself altogether."

He knew he shouldn't push her, but he understood things so much better than he did just a week ago. "I'm different than I was, Mary Anne. I've been insensitive and distracted, but I can't bear the thought of losing you. Can't you give me another chance?"

She stared at him for a few seconds. "How long would it last, Jethro? Two or three weeks? Six months? You like your predictable life, and I love butterflies and fancy cheese. I'm not going to try to please you anymore. You wouldn't be able to put up with me for more than a month. You may not believe this, but I moved out as much to make you happy as I did for me."

He couldn't keep a hint of bitterness from his voice. "You're right. I don't believe it. Maybe you just wish it was true."

She took a deep breath. "I'm sorry. I said more than I meant to. My faults and sins are a hundred times what yours are. You can take comfort in that."

"I can't take comfort in anything, Mary Anne. Right now, except for the fact that you're living in a tent, I can't think of one thing I don't like about you."

"I can jog your memory if you need." She stood up and turned toward her tent, signaling an end to the conversation. There was nothing he could do but stand as well. "I've got to get to that quilt. It's got to be done on Tuesday so the ladies at the senior center can work on it." She turned back and gave him an I'm-really-sorry-for-you smile. Even Mary Anne felt sorry for him, and she was living in a tent sewing quilts for extra money. "*Gute nacht,* Jethro. Enjoy that fish."

She ducked into her tent, and Jethro stood like a stone as he heard her turn on the lamp. He watched as her muted shadow moved about her tent, listened as the sound of her soft movements drove him crazy with the need to go in there and kiss her. He tightened his fist around his package of fish and tried to distract himself with thoughts of Porta-Potties and parents and pansies. It was no use. Thoughts of Mary Anne were so painful and potent, he couldn't even stand up straight.

Mary Anne was at the sewing machine now. After a few breathless seconds, it began humming at the speed of his heart.

Even though he could barely stand the thought of dinner with his parents and David Eicher, Jethro stumbled in the direction of his tent. Smoke curled up through the trees in the distance. Mamm and Dat had found some firewood.

Jethro pressed his fingers to his temple, but nothing would keep a headache at bay. There was nothing quite as painful as coming face-to-face with the truth about who you really were. Jethro felt it all the way to the marrow in his bones. He'd slowly pulled away from her in the months after the baby. He'd spent three or four nights a week fishing, sometimes getting home so late that Mary Anne was already in bed. No wonder she wanted a divorce. He had abandoned her months ago. He had thought he was protecting her from the painful memories when he encouraged her to stop quilting. He hadn't been able to see the value in painting rocks or walls and had talked her out of spending the money. And then there was the food. Mary Anne was an exceptional cook. She could make chicken and rice taste like a meal fit for a king. That was why he thought her buying fancy foods was unnecessary. Her simple meals were *gute* enough. Fancy cheese and gourmet olive oil cost too much money, and he hadn't seen the need.

He had forgotten how important these things were to Mary Anne. In his eagerness to help her forget her heartache and save money, he had disregarded his dear *fraa*. She thought she was a disappointment to him, and so she had tried as hard as she could to be the wife she thought he wanted. And in truth, she *had* become the *fraa* he'd hoped for — never complaining, never grieving for their baby, never spending money for frivolous things. He'd been able to buy that fishing pole because of her thrift. The irony of it was not lost on him. He had strained at a gnat when he wouldn't let Mary Anne buy exciting cheese but had swallowed a camel buying that fishing pole. And the tent. And the sleeping bags and cots.

He was so ashamed, he could have crawled into that Porta-Potty and never come out. But there was also a little bit of hope mixed up in all that murky despair. He knew what he'd done wrong, so maybe he could fix it. If Mary Anne had truly lost hope for their marriage, why would she have been so honest with him? Of course, that might mean she didn't care anymore, but Jethro preferred to think maybe deep down inside she wanted to love him again.

He hoped and prayed it was so.

He couldn't bear the thought of a fishing pole destroying his marriage.

CHAPTER THIRTEEN

Mary Anne jumped from her sleeping bag, gasped at the cold, and threw on her dress and shawl so fast, she could have won a race. She quickly donned her *kapp* and tied her bonnet underneath her chin with stiff fingers. It was supposed to be getting warmer. Wasn't summer little more than a month away?

She liked to get up early and make the *kaffee* before Mammi and Dawdi had a chance to do it. She felt guilty enough about her grandparents staying in the woods. She'd feel terrible if one of them ended up in the hospital or flat in bed with a bad back. The *gute* news was that this was Tuesday morning, and her grandparents had slept in the RV for four straight nights without a peep. Mary Anne said an extra prayer of thanks for Bob Hennig and Charlene Johnson. Charlene had given Mary Anne the job at the senior center where

Mammi and Dawdi had met Bob, who had been kind enough to offer his RV for them to sleep in. So far, the arrangement seemed to be working out.

The RV was warm and comfortable and insulated, so no one in the camp could hear Dawdi snoring at night. They'd all gotten a lot more sleep. Mammi and Dawdi had their own toilet and shower, which freed up the crowded bathroom in the barn, and Mandy and Lily and their families had started using the bathroom in the house. It was a lot warmer in there, and it would do no one any *gute* if one of *die kinner* got pneumonia.

Mary Anne unzipped the flap, ducked out of her tent, and got the shivers all over again. A light blanket of snow dusted the ground. No wonder she'd been able to see her breath this morning. Just another balmy Wisconsin spring day.

The good news was, there was already a cheery fire going in the fire pit. She smiled as she warmed her hands near the flames and glanced in the direction of Jethro's camp. Smoke rose from their fire pit too. Since Jethro had moved into the woods, he had been starting both fires before anyone else got up in the morning. Jethro was thoughtful like that — more so in the first years of their marriage than the last. Still, he didn't have to build Mary Anne's fire. It was a sign of his kind nature that he did.

Of course, it might be just another trick to get her to move back into the house, but what did it matter why the fire got made? Might as well let him do it, no matter his reasons.

For four days, Jethro's and Mary Anne's camps mostly had nothing to do with each other, except when one of Jethro's friends or family needed to use the shower in the barn. Mary Anne hadn't even seen Lois except for a glimpse of her on the first day. Jethro must have told Lois that Mary Anne didn't want to talk to her, and Mary Anne was wonderful grateful. Lois could keep her righteous indignation to herself. Mary Anne already knew how Lois felt. She didn't need a daily lecture about the evils of leaving her husband.

The door of the RV creaked open, and Mammi stepped out onto the small step that was the only thing between her and falling flat on her face. Mary Anne always held her breath when she watched Mammi and Dawdi get out of the RV. It was too high off the ground for two eighty-something-year-olds, especially for Mammi, who couldn't even touch her feet to the ground when she sat on a normal-size chair. This RV had a step that pulled out from under the door. It didn't look all that sturdy, but Mammi and Dawdi seemed to have no problem with it.

Mammi kept hold of the doorknob as she lowered herself to the ground. She was in a black dress with a black apron and a lime-green sweater. Mammi was a famous knitter, and she liked to create all sorts of colorful sweaters for herself. No one had the heart to tell her that lime-green sweaters weren't exactly in keeping with the *Ordnung*. With her white *kapp* and snowy hair, she looked like a piece of Key lime pie.

Sparky bounded out of the RV after Mammi, barking and carrying on as if she was going for a ride in the car. Mammi caught sight of Mary Anne, burst into a smile, and waved. Then, like she had done every morning for the last four days, she narrowed her eyes in the direction of Jethro's camp and huffed out a breath. "Are they still here?"

"I suppose they are, Mammi," Mary Anne said.

"I wish they'd go home. Solidarity was my idea. They're a bunch of copycats."

Mary Anne wished they'd go home too. On Saturday night, she had overheard David Eicher giving Lily a very loud piece of his mind about how she needed to go home and be a comfort to her husband.

"But Dat," Lily had said, "you don't even like my husband."

Mary Anne had nearly laughed out loud. Lily was too clever for her *dat* by half. David was in a difficult position. He would rather get a tooth pulled than say anything in support of his son-in-law, but the only leverage he had over Lily was to invoke Bible verses to urge her to go back to Aden. David had no idea Aden was firmly on Lily's side of the argument. On Sunday night, Aden had moved in with Lily. He'd told Mary Anne that he wasn't going to allow David to scold his *fraa* again. If David wanted to yell at someone, Aden wanted David to yell at him.

Mary Anne hated that she'd been the cause of so much contention and unplanned camping, but she loved seeing how her married cousins took care of their spouses. Jethro hadn't watched out for her for years. She drew her brows together. He had made a fire for her every morning for a week, and he had kept his *mater* away from her. Maybe in his own way, he was trying to watch out for her. Or maybe he was just trying to convince her to come home.

"I don't wonder that they'll all be gone soon," Mary Anne said. "Except for maybe

Lois and Chris. They might stay until Jethro gives up."

Mammi sighed pitifully and shook her head. "I'm afraid they'll be here until one of them dies of old age. Jethro isn't going to give up. He's in love with you."

Mary Anne frowned. Jethro only thought he loved her because he didn't know how to cook his own meals and do his own laundry. Now that Lois was cooking for him, he wouldn't be so desperate to get Mary Anne back. Maybe he'd move in with his parents when all was said and done.

That thought made Mary Anne sort of sad. Jethro should stay in the house. He'd built it with his own two hands. Before the wedding, they'd worked hard to save every penny to put into it. They couldn't afford anything bigger, but Jethro and Mary Anne had designed it together, thinking that when their family began to grow, they would build an addition on the back.

She had picked out the kitchen sink and the shower curtain, and he had picked out the toilet. It had been one of the happiest times of her life, dreaming of the day when they'd be married and making plans for their future. She'd been convinced that no one would ever love a boy the way she loved Jethro, that her love was the greatest love the world had ever known. It was funny how fast affection could die when those dreams didn't come true. Some heartache couldn't be healed with the power of love.

Poor Jethro thought he could fix it, like he fixed a toilet or a buggy wheel, but he was wrong. Some things and some people just couldn't be fixed.

Dawdi stepped down from the RV, singing at the top of his lungs. "Some sweet day, I'm going away. When camping is done, I'm going home. Some sweet day, I'm going away." If anyone was still asleep, they were awake now. He stretched his arms over his head and opened his mouth for a wide yawn. No matter what the song said, it looked as if he was sleeping better. Anything had to be better than a tent. Behind Mary Anne, the children in Lily's tent stirred. She needed to get breakfast going before *die kinner* got ornery with hunger. One *gute* thing about Jethro's *mamm* being in camp was that Mary Anne didn't feel guilty about not making Jethro breakfast. Lois was a capable cook. Jethro wouldn't starve.

Mary Anne hurried to the barn to take a shower and use the bathroom. The shower was as cold as ice, but at least it woke her up every morning. Mary Anne refused to take a shower in the house, even if the thought of warm water made her giddy.

After her shower, she dressed quickly and practically ran back to the fire pit. Lily and Aden and their children, plus Sarah and her boys, were standing around the fire. Sarah was making *kaffee,* Aden was helping Lily wrestle the twins, and Mammi had somehow gotten her hands on a bowl and a whisk.

"*Gute* morning, Mary Anne," Aden said, balancing one of the twins on his knee while feeding her a jar of baby food — organic, of course.

Mary Anne's teeth chattered involuntarily. Lord willing, she'd warm up before bedtime. *"Gute mariye."*

"I think I'll scramble some eggs," Mammi said, tapping the whisk against the bowl as if summoning the eggs to come to her.

Sarah shot Mary Anne a horrified look. Mary Anne pursed her lips. Under no circumstances was Mammi to make eggs. When she made them on the stove, they turned out runny and gooey and slid down your throat like a slug on a playground slide. When Mammi made them on the griddle over an open fire, they came out black and leathery and smoking, like a firefighter's glove.

"Now, Mammi," Mary Anne said, "you

know it's my turn to make breakfast. I bought all the ingredients for caramel banana French toast."

Mammi held her whisk at the ready. "Do you need help?"

What jobs could Mammi do without ruining the French toast? "I saved the bacon grease from breakfast yesterday. Do you want to find it in the cooler?"

Sarah set the *kaffee* pot into the coals on the edge of the fire. "We'll need more wood." She turned to her sons, who were warming their hands. "Pine, Johnny, go gather more firewood. Take the ax, but be careful you don't cut anything off that won't grow back. And don't dawdle. Johnny has to get to school."

The only thing more exciting to a teenage boy than fire was the unlimited use of an ax. Pine grabbed the ax from Sarah's tent, and he and Johnny jogged into the woods.

"Don't carry the ax like that, Pine Beachy," Sarah called after them. "If you trip, you'll take your neck off."

Besides Mary Anne and Mammi and Dawdi, there were now seventeen relatives living on Mary Anne's side of the camp: Sarah and her two youngest boys; Lily, Aden, and their three children; Mandy and Noah; Emma and Ben and their toddler;

and Lia and Moses and their two little ones. Lia had told Moses she wanted to camp by herself, but it hadn't lasted too long. She needed Moses's help with the children in the middle of the night.

Moses and Ben left early in the morning for work. Mary Anne seldom saw them, even for breakfast. Aden and Noah always saw that the fire was out and that the women and children were settled before they left for their farms and chores.

They all took turns cooking meals, and the shared cooking helped with food expenses. Sarah had told Mammi and Dawdi that they were the leaders, and it wasn't the leaders' job to help with the meals, though Mammi still managed to make her mark on every meal. Yesterday, she'd put a "little extra" salt in the beef stew, and it had taken Mary Anne three extra glasses of water to finish off her bowl. It had felt as if her tongue would shrivel up and fall out of her mouth.

They had to watch Mammi like a hawk.

Emma and Lia helped Mary Anne soak the bread and get it on the griddle coated with bacon grease. In another saucepan, she stirred the brown sugar into the butter, then set it on the grate above the fire to melt. Once the sugar and butter were melted, she added four sliced bananas to caramelize. Mammi and Dawdi had bought one giant package of paper plates, a hundred paper cups, and a huge box of napkins.

Emma put a piece of French toast onto each plate, and Mary Anne topped each piece with a spoonful of caramelized bananas. It smelled heavenly. She had a little bottle of syrup for Pine, who didn't like bananas, but everyone else raved about the topping and nobody said one word about how expensive bananas were.

Mary Anne and Emma served the others before they sat down to eat. Nearly everyone but *die kinner* had seconds. Pine, Johnny, and Noah had thirds. "*Denki* for the French toast," Sarah said. "We eat so *gute* in this camp, my boys are never going to want to go home." She raised an eyebrow. "But it can't last forever. Their *dat* wants them for chores, and I'll get scoliosis if I sleep on that cot much longer."

"It's okay with me if you need to go, Sarah. You've been more than kind to stay as long as you have."

Sarah grunted. "*Ach.* I'm not going anywhere. Maybe I'll stay and send the boys home. They can cook for themselves for a few weeks. It would almost feel like that vacation I've been meaning to take."

Mary Anne smiled. "Don't sacrifice on my account. Nobody wants to live in a tent for their vacation."

Sarah scrunched her lips together. "There's plenty of people who consider sleeping in a tent a vacation. I'm just not one of them."

Mammi sat in her camp chair and licked her fingers. "This French toast is the most *appeditlich* breakfast I've ever had. How did you make those parsnips taste so sweet?"

"They're bananas, Mammi, and I used lots of brown sugar."

Mammi nodded. "I bet parsnips would be good in that recipe."

That must be how Mammi collected her recipes. She ate something delicious and decided to make her own "improvements." In Mammi's mind, parsnips were enough like bananas that they might just work.

Mary Anne took a bite. Everything cooked over a campfire carried a slight taste of smoke, but she had outdone herself with the French toast. The flavor of eggs with a hint of citrus and the sweet bananas was worth every penny she'd spent on those bananas and real butter. Even the bacon grease had made a difference. What wasn't good with a little extra bacon grease?

Lia thanked Mary Anne and threw her

family's plates into the fire. The Zimmermans went back to their tent. Lily and Aden did the same. They had plenty to do just getting *die kinner* ready for the day.

Mary Anne watched Lily duck into her tent just as Jethro crossed to her side of the camp, carrying a medium-size box. Jethro loved bananas. Maybe he'd like to try a piece of French toast. Maybe not. He'd probably complain about how much money she'd spent on ingredients. Still, he'd built her a fire this morning and probably kept her from getting frostbite. Even if he'd already eaten, she'd be ungrateful not to at least offer.

When he caught sight of her, he smiled as if he was seeing his first butterfly. "Mary Anne, *wie gehts?*"

"*Hallo,* Jethro," Mammi said, standing on her tiptoes and patting him on the cheek.

Jethro winked at Mammi. "You look as green and fresh as springtime, Anna."

Mammi laughed. "And you look wonderful handsome. I've always thought you had very nice eyebrows and teeth. Don't you think so, Mary Anne?"

Jethro turned his dazzling smile to her, and Mary Anne was glad she was sitting. Lois was very particular, and she had always been insistent that her children be careful

283

of their dental hygiene. The persistence had paid off. Jethro wasn't missing any teeth, and he'd never had a cavity in his life. "Jethro has *gute* teeth," she said, wanting to be truthful but not encouraging. She didn't want Jethro to get the wrong idea.

Mammi threw Dawdi's plate in the fire. "Mary Anne, dear, Felty and I are going back to our RV to take a nap. Let us know when you're ready to go."

"What time do you have to be to work?" Jethro said, betraying no emotion at the fact she had a job and was working *out.*

"Charlene will be here at 9:45. What about you?"

"I've got another fifteen minutes before the van gets here."

Jethro pulled up a camp chair next to her and set his box on the ground. After sitting down, he studied her face as if trying to memorize her freckles. "Your cheeks are bright red. Do you want me to get the blanket from your tent?"

"I'm warm enough by the fire. *Denki* for building it."

She could have warmed her hands by the glow in his eyes. "I didn't want you out in this weather trying to light a fire. Going to the bathroom in the barn is cold enough."

She gave him a half smile. "I'll bet the

Porta-Potty is worse."

"Oy, anyhow, you don't know the half of it. The smell destroys your appetite for breakfast, and when you sit down, a breeze blows in from underneath. Let's just say I don't lollygag in there."

"It's wonderful close to your tents."

Jethro winced. "*Jah.* We tried to move it last night, but it's heavy, and you don't want to risk that thing tipping over. It would be a mess beyond anything bearable."

"You tried to move it?"

"We're going to move our tents fifty feet to the north. Willie Jay isn't happy about it, but because he's the one who told the deliveryman where to put the Porta-Potty, he's the last person who's allowed to complain."

Mary Anne smiled to herself. Willie Jay had no idea how entertaining he was from a distance. She shouldn't be so smug, but Mary Anne took secret pleasure in Willie Jay's annoyance. He was too sure of himself by half. "It wonders me if you wouldn't like some French toast."

He raised an eyebrow. "French toast?"

"Caramel banana. Unless you've already eaten or the Porta-Potty made you lose your appetite."

He grinned so wide, she could see almost all those perfect teeth. "I'll never turn down caramel-banana French toast, no matter how many Porta-Potties I've been in recently, especially if it was made by you."

Mary Anne stifled a smile. Jethro usually only got this excited about a fish on his line. "Will your *mamm* be offended if you eat my breakfast?"

Jethro snapped his head around and looked in the direction of his tent, as if making sure he wasn't being watched. "She doesn't have to know."

Mary Anne giggled. "Just make sure she doesn't smell bananas on your breath."

Emma had filled the plastic tub with water and was washing the griddle, but there were still two pieces of French toast left on a paper plate, plus an ample helping of caramelized bananas. Mary Anne handed the plate to Jethro, who gasped as if she'd just given him a plateful of gold coins. She gave him a plastic fork, then spooned the last of the banana topping onto the French toast. "They've cooled down a bit yet."

He raised the plate to his face and breathed in the scent of warm bananas. "It's *wunderbarr.*" He stabbed his fork into the French toast and took a hearty bite. "Mmm. This is like everything *gute* about Christmas Day on a fork."

"They turned out well." Warm liquid

pleasure threaded up her spine, and she immediately chastised herself for caring what Jethro thought about her French toast.

Jethro finished off his French toast in about five bites. He scraped up the leftover banana sauce off the plate with his fork. "That was *appeditlich,* Mary Anne. It's been so long since I've eaten your cooking, I almost forgot what perfection is."

"Perfection is expensive," she said. "The bananas were almost two dollars a pound." She didn't mean to snap at him, but she refused to let him soften her up with a kind word and a little appreciation. The last thing she needed was a weak spot in her heart where Jethro might be able to find an entrance. She wouldn't let him hurt her again. Better to remind him why she'd stopped fixing fancy food in the first place.

He didn't scowl at her like she'd hoped he would — a bad reaction from him would put her on safer ground. Unfortunately, she was standing close enough that he could reach out and take her hand. For some reason, his touch sent a tingle of energy all the way up her arm, and it irritated her to no end that she didn't pull away.

Jethro tugged her gently into the chair next to him and promptly let go of her hand. Her irritation cooled to a simmer.

"Do you want to know what I did on Saturday?"

Not really. "What?"

He grinned and shifted in his chair so he faced her. "*Vell,* the Porta-Potty is nicer than using a tree in the woods, but it still leaves a wonderful lot to be desired. There's no soap or water in there, so you have to wash your hands with hand sanitizer. When I use hand sanitizer, I feel like I'm just pushing the dirt around in my hands. So I hooked up a hose to the spigot in our yard to run some water to our campsite. Then I took one of my long stockings, put a bar of soap in the toe, and tied it to the branch of a tree. When you get the stocking wet, you can work up a lather and wash your hands without needing a place to set the soap."

"Wonderful *gute,*" Mary Anne said, with a note of hesitancy in her voice. Why was he telling her this nice little story?

"Neither David Eicher nor Willie Jay had a nice thing to say about it. David said the bar of soap was too little and the stocking was too thick and asked if I'd just been wearing it or if it was clean. Willie Jay complained I'd hung it too far away from the Porta-Potty and the water was too cold to get anything clean."

Mary Anne curled one side of her mouth.

"They're not so happy to be camping, but they're determined to teach me a lesson. It wonders me how long they'll hold out."

"It made me finally understand something. I'd given Willie Jay and David this wonderful smart contraption so they could wash their hands, and all they did was find fault with it." He laced his fingers with hers. "Your whole life was a gift you gave me every day, and I didn't even see it. You sprayed lavender water on my handkerchiefs when you ironed them. You made me egg salad sandwiches with avocado and some sort of green, leafy plant."

"Watercress," she said.

"I loved it. You sewed me fish-shaped pot holders for my birthday, and do you remember what I said?"

It shouldn't have been such a painful memory. They were just pot holders.

He pressed his lips together into a rigid line and studied her face. "I said I loved them. I did say I loved them first."

"*Jah,* you did."

"And then I said, 'You shouldn't have spent so much time making these. Regular pot holders will do just fine.' And then I accused you of making them for yourself and not really for me because I never cook."

Mary Anne nodded. *"Jah."* She couldn't

289

have said another word if Jethro's hair had been on fire.

Jethro rubbed his thumb along the back of her hand. She didn't know why she allowed it, except that his touch was oddly comforting. "You gave me gift after gift with your quilts and your rose radishes and your paintings, and all I did was complain or point out a way you could do something better. You did whatever I suggested because you didn't want to be a disappointment to me. But I stole a little bit of your happiness every time I criticized you or took you for granted or ignored you." He expelled a long sigh. "I'm sorry, Mary Anne. I didn't even see it."

"It doesn't matter," she whispered, but it did. At this moment, his remorse mattered very much.

He gazed at her and she held her breath, afraid of the vulnerability he might see in her eyes. "Maybe it will matter to you someday. I hope you'll remember I'm sorry."

"Okay."

"*Ach,* Mary Anne. I have to go to work, and I brought you a present."

"A present?"

He leaned over and picked up the cardboard box at his feet. "There was an icicle hanging from the eaves of the Porta-Potty yesterday morning. I got you a space heater for your tent. It's battery powered."

A space heater? Mary Anne shivered at the thought of a space heater. What would it be like to finally feel warm? "You didn't have to do that," she said, even though she was wonderful glad he had. It couldn't have been cheap.

With his pocketknife, Jethro cut the tape and pulled out a smaller box the size of a toaster. A black grill protected the inner workings of the space heater, and the rest of the heater was made of shiny orange metal. Jethro smiled, obviously proud of how clever he was. "Shall we try it?" he said, pointing to her tent.

"Right now?"

"You'll want warm fingers for all that sewing."

Mary Anne unzipped her tent and let Jethro duck in first. Pulling the small bench from the foot of the cot, he set the space heater on it. He pressed a button on the front, and it beeped. A muted orange light appeared at the heart of the machine.

Jethro widened his eyes in excitement and put his hands up to the grill. "It's warmer already. Can you feel it?"

Mary Anne waved her hand in front of the heater. A stream of air no stronger than a puff of wind blew from behind the grill. It wasn't warm, but it wasn't cold either. Maybe it took a few minutes to heat up. "It's wonderful kind of you, Jethro, but don't you want to give it to your *mamm*?"

He scrunched his lips together. "Nah. Mamm's got Dat to keep her warm."

The space heater was definitely warming up. A low, hissing sound from the bottom of the machine got louder and higher the longer they stood there. Jethro held out his hand to test the airflow. "It's coming out harder now."

"Very nice," Mary Anne said, loud enough so Jethro could hear her over the screeching noise coming from the space heater. She wouldn't be able to sleep with all this racket. Being warm enough was one thing; being deaf was quite another. Did Jethro have earplugs in his tackle box?

A loud pop from inside the space heater made them both jump. "What was that?" Jethro bent over to get a better look at the machine. He went to touch it, and a tiny spark jumped from the grill to his finger. He snatched his finger away and shook it vigorously. *"Ach du lieva!"*

Mary Anne gasped as a tendril of smoke curled up from the space heater. "Is it supposed to do that?"

Her question was answered when they heard another pop and the space heater burst into flame. Mary Anne squeaked in alarm. Jethro jumped back so fast, he fell backward onto Mary Anne's cot. The force of his fall and the awkward angle at which he hit the cot caused the whole thing to collapse.

Thick black smoke started pouring from the space heater along with the flames. Her Ritz Cracker mobile was going to catch fire if she didn't do something, and then the whole tent might go up in flames. "Put it out. Put it out," Mary Anne yelled, with no idea how to do it. She'd burn herself if she touched it.

Jethro quickly fought his way out of the tangle of Mary Anne's sleeping bag and got to his feet. "We need to get it out of here." He grabbed the long-handled potato masher from the shelf. "Open the flap!"

Coughing and gagging at the smoke, Mary Anne quickly unzipped the tent door and held it open for him. Jethro took aim, swung the masher like a bat, and whacked at the blazing space heater. He'd always been a *gute* athlete. The space heater flew out the door as if it had wings, bounced just outside the tent, and rolled for another ten feet on the ground lightly dusted with snow.

The trip hadn't managed to put out the fire. They followed the space heater out of the tent. "I'll get the hose," Mary Anne said.

Jethro held up his hand to stop her. "*Nae.* If it's an electric fire, you'll get zapped."

"Is it an electric fire?"

"I have no idea." Jethro decided to deal with it like any cook worth his salt would do. He raised the potato masher over his head and brought it down on the space heater with a heavy blow. Again and again, he struck the heater until he'd reduced it to a pile of smoking rubble. He'd managed to put the fire out, but there was no hope for the space heater. It was nothing but a pile of scraps.

The potato masher, on the other hand, had done Mary Anne proud. It was made of thick stainless steel with an extra-long handle for reaching into big pans. She had bought it right before they were married for "all those times when we have family over and I need to mash a lot of potatoes." Jethro had laughed and told her they'd never need to mash that many potatoes, but she'd tied a ribbon around it and given it to him as an early wedding present. He hadn't been so stingy back then.

"What's going on?" Emma said, drying

the last of the dishes. "Did something catch fire?"

"All is well," Mary Anne said, giving Emma a reassuring smile. Emma was a little accident-prone. She was extra-cautious around fire.

With the masher securely in his fist, Jethro raised his hands over his head in a victory sign. His hat had fallen off somewhere back in the tent, and his dark hair stood out in unruly tufts all over his head.

Mary Anne laughed at the look of pure exultation on his face. "Congratulations. You killed it."

He pumped his fists in the air again. "I killed it."

She couldn't resist teasing him. "And you thought we'd never have use for that masher."

He studied the masher in his hand, as if checking for injuries. "I take back all the bad things I ever said about it." He nudged the remains of the space heater with his toe. "Do you think I can get my money back?"

"Did you keep your receipt?"

Their eyes met, and they laughed in relief and maybe a little bit of shock. She loved Jethro's laugh when he wasn't trying to force it. "Are you okay?" he asked.

"I smell like smoke and so does the tent."

"*Ach, vell,* we all smell like smoke, and you know a tent has gotten some *gute* use if it stinks inside. Painted butterflies are even better."

She smiled at him, not even trying to guess if he was sincere about the butterflies. It was a nice moment. She wouldn't let her suspicions ruin it.

He touched his hand to his head. "What happened to my hat?"

"I think you lost it when you did a somersault over my cot."

She followed him back into the tent. The air was smoky, but with the flap open, it was quickly clearing out. The small bench had a three-inch scorch on the seat, but other than that, it had come through the disaster all right. Her cot was tipped on its side, and the sleeping bag and blanket were in a heap on the floor. "Oy, anyhow," Jethro said. "I made a mess."

They both heard the honk. Jethro glanced at Mary Anne. "Oh, *sis yuscht.* It's the van. I have to go."

"Don't worry, it won't take but a minute to put back together." She eyed him and scrunched her lips to one side of her face. "You might want to comb your hair before you go."

He cocked an eyebrow and pulled a comb

out of his pocket. "A comb is a wonderful exciting thing to keep in your pocket." He grinned and winked at her, and she didn't even try to ignore the butterflies that took wing in her stomach. He combed through his hair and smoothed it with his hand. "Okay?"

She made a face, as if she was less than enthusiastic about his combing job. "Eh. Keep your hat on."

He chuckled while he searched through the rubble to find his hat. "*Gute* suggestion."

The van honked again. Jethro tapped his hat onto his head and gave her a serious look, as if he wanted to say something important or big or . . . mushy. She quickly pushed open the flap and stepped out of the tent. It was too stuffy in there.

He followed her out. "Good-bye, Mary Anne. I hope you have a *gute* day at the senior center. Will you tell the RV man *denki* for letting Anna and Felty use the RV?"

She nodded. "Dawdi was even singing this morning."

"*Jah.* I heard."

She grabbed his arm and stopped him before he walked away. "*Denki* for the space heater. It was wonderful thoughtful of you."

His smile was warmer than a space heater on fire.

It was a strange dream. Mary Anne couldn't see anything, but someone was eating breakfast — cornflakes, it sounded like — and he was chewing very loudly, right next to her ear. Didn't he have any consideration for people who were trying to sleep? She rolled over, only to get slightly tangled in her sleeping bag, but the chewing didn't stop.

She opened her eyes to the soft light of the moon filtering through her tent window. Jethro had brought her another space heater two days ago, but she hadn't used it once, and not because she was afraid she'd catch fire in her sleep. May was finally behaving like spring, and the weather the last few nights had been perfect for sleeping. The tent wasn't perfect for sleeping and the cot wasn't perfect for sleeping, but the weather was definitely ideal.

Mary Anne closed her eyes. It was just a dream. She rolled to her other side to untwist her sleeping bag.

It had been just a dream, except she knew she was awake and she still heard the chewing. Her heart leaped into her throat. Was there a bear out there looking for a snack?

Nae, it didn't exactly sound like a bear. It sounded more like the steady chomping of a beaver.

She sat up and reached for her shawl. Might as well investigate. She wouldn't be able to sleep until she found the source of the noise. If it was a bear, she could probably scream loudly enough to wake the dogs. Pilot was big enough to scare a bear away, but maybe not before the bear had taken a big chunk out of Mary Anne's leg.

Clutching the shawl to her chest as if it would give her some protection, she unzipped her tent and stepped outside. She squinted into the darkness. The sound was coming from the direction of Mammi and Dawdi's RV. Mary Anne caught her breath as she realized the sound was tire on gravel — as in the tires of the RV crunching along the tiny pebbles that covered the driveway. Bob Hennig's RV slowly, ever so slowly, rolled down the gravel path that ran from Jethro's barn to the road. It was nearly three hundred yards from the barn to the road, but the path ran on a slight downward slope, and the RV was picking up momentum. Blissfully unaware, in untroubled slumber, Mammi and Dawdi were headed straight for the road and the gulley on the other side.

Mary Anne dropped her shawl and ran as fast as her legs would take her. She stumbled as she stubbed her toe on something hard and sharp, but she barely felt the pain. She had to save Mammi and Dawdi. Reaching the RV, she tried to open the side door, but it was either locked or stuck. In hopes of waking someone inside, she slapped her hand several times against the wall of the RV. Did either of her grandparents know how to stop a moving vehicle? RVs had brakes like buggies, didn't they?

Mary Anne didn't even have to walk particularly fast to keep up with the rolling RV, but it wouldn't take long for it to reach the road, and it didn't sound like she'd managed to wake anyone inside.

She raced for the driver's side door, caught her foot on a rock, and fell flat on her face. She gasped as a pair of strong arms grabbed her around the waist and wrenched her back and away from the tire that would have rolled over her leg. She didn't have to say a word. Jethro had already released her and was reaching for the door to the cab.

"*Ach du lieva,* Felty! We're moving." Mammi had finally woken up, and Mary Anne could hear her squealing through the open window. "We're being kidnapped!"

"Mammi," Mary Anne called, "can you

go to the front of the RV by the steering wheel and press on the brake?" There was too much commotion going on in there. Mammi didn't hear a thing Mary Anne said.

Thank the *gute* Lord the cab wasn't locked. Jethro opened the door and, in one fluid motion, jumped inside and grabbed the steering wheel. Jethro had never driven a car, but he must have known something about them. He immediately pressed on one of the pedals, and the RV came to a shuddering halt.

His ragged breathing matched her own as their eyes met in shocked silence. If Jethro hadn't been there, it could have been a terrible disaster.

The ruckus inside the RV made up for the deathly stillness outside. "Felty, go up there and find out who kidnapped us."

"I think it was our imagination, Banannie. We're not moving."

Mary Anne knocked on the side door. "Mammi, Dawdi, are you okay?"

She heard some shuffling, and the RV rocked from side to side like a boat on calm waters. After a few tries at the doorknob from the inside, Dawdi finally opened the door and stuck his head out. Strands of gray beard stuck out from his face like the branches of a creeping juniper bush, and his eyes were glazed over, like someone who'd been rudely awakened in the middle of the night. "Why, *hallo,* Mary Anne. Do you need to borrow a cup of sugar?"

Jethro climbed out of the cab and sidled close to Mary Anne. His breathing came fast and hard, and his hands trembled so violently, he folded his arms.

Mammi, with her hair covered in a pink knitted nightcap, nudged Dawdi aside, stepped down from the RV, and pulled Mary Anne in for a stiff hug. "You saved us from the kidnappers."

"*Nae,* Mammi. There weren't any kidnappers."

Mammi tugged herself out of Mary Anne's embrace and studied her face in confusion. "There weren't? Was someone trying to steal our RV?"

"I woke up and saw your RV rolling down the lane."

Dawdi's expression matched Mammi's. "By itself?"

"I don't know," Jethro said, his voice as shaky as his hands. "Maybe one of you accidentally put it into gear or released the emergency brake before you went to bed. A slight movement could have started it rolling."

Mammi clapped her hand over her mouth.

"Last night we sat in the two seats up front because we wanted to know what it might feel like to drive the thing. We let temptation get the better of us, Felty."

"It's okay, Banannie. I don't think *Gotte* was mad."

"Of course He was," Mammi said. "He tried to kill us."

Mary Anne pulled her *mammi* in for another hug. "*Gotte* doesn't work that way, Mammi. He loves us. He's not out for revenge."

"Of course you're right," Mammi said. "I know that better than anyone. Still, I think I'd better go repent right quick, just in case."

Mary Anne kissed her *mammi* on the cheek. "All is well. Jethro stopped it before it went into the road."

Dawdi nodded his approval. "Jethro is very strong."

Jethro let out a shaky chuckle. "I hopped in the cab and hit the brake, that's all."

Mammi patted Jethro's arm. "*Ach,* Jethro, I've always thought you were a little thick, but you're also very brave. We could have died."

They paused to eye the RV and where it had ended up. It wasn't more than ten feet from the road. A shudder tripped down Mary Anne's spine. If Jethro hadn't been there . . .

Jethro tapped the side of the RV. "I set the emergency brake. As long as you don't touch anything near the steering wheel, it shouldn't roll again. We'll move it back closer to the barn in the morning. You're far enough from the road tonight."

Mammi's lower lip trembled ominously. "What are you saying, Jethro?"

Jethro obviously didn't recognize Mammi's distress. "You're far enough from the road tonight. You'll be fine to sleep right here."

"*Ach,* Jethro dear, I'll freely admit that you're brave and kind and quite handsome, but you're still thicker than a slab of bacon. You must know I'm never sleeping in that thing again. When the *gute* Lord takes me to heaven, it won't be in an RV."

"But, Banannie, what about your sciatica?" Dawdi said weakly. It was obvious he didn't want to give up his comfortable bed, but he must have recognized it was a lost cause.

"Now, Felty, you know very well I don't have sciatica. I've never even had the measles, and I won't get a wink of sleep in that thing ever again." She pointed to the RV as if it was the cause of all her troubles. "We're moving back into a tent."

Mary Anne knew better than to try to talk Mammi into anything. She was more stubborn than Mary Anne.

"Why don't you sleep in the house for the rest of the night?" Jethro said. "We can set up another tent for you in the morning."

Dawdi perked up at bit — at least as much as could be expected in the middle of the night. "There's nothing else for it, Annie. We'll have to take Jethro's bed for the night."

Deep furrows lined the part of Mammi's forehead that wasn't hidden by her floppy pink nightcap. "*Ach*, Mary Anne. What should we do?"

"Sleep in the house, Mammi. It won't roll away."

Mammi wrung her hands in unnecessary distress. "I don't want you to think for one minute that I'm not committed to solidarity, but it's either the house or the cold, hard ground, and I think for Felty's sake, we'd better choose the house." She leaned in and whispered in Mary Anne's ear, "He doesn't have the stamina I do, and it smells like rain."

Mary Anne linked elbows with Mammi. "*Cum*. You've had quite a scare. You should be in a nice, warm bed, and I still count this as solidarity. I know you'll never fail

305

me, Mammi."

Mammi seemed satisfied. "Okay, but I'll do my best to toss and turn all night and be miserable so you don't feel abandoned."

Mary Anne grinned. "*Denki.* That's very thoughtful of you."

"Do you need anything from the RV before we go in?" Jethro said.

Mammi formed her lips into an *O.* "Would you mind getting my toothbrush? It's on the cupboard in that tiny bathroom. I can't go back to sleep unless I brush my teeth."

Jethro climbed into the RV and soon returned with two toothbrushes, a tube of toothpaste, and Sparky, who was nipping at his heels, probably annoyed at being awakened in the middle of the night.

"*Ach du lieva,*" Mammi said. "In all the excitement I forgot Sparky." She bent over, picked Sparky up, and cradled her in her arms like a *buplie.* "Were you scared? I thought we were being kidnapped."

They slowly made their way to the house, which was a lot closer to the RV since the RV had rolled so far. Mary Anne and Mammi led the way, and Dawdi and Jethro followed close behind.

Mary Anne winced every time she put weight on her left leg. She'd fallen hard back there, and she'd stubbed her toe before that. As soon as she remembered the toe, it started to sting something wonderful. She stole a glance at her foot. *Ach du lieva.* She couldn't see her toe for the blood. She'd be limping for days.

Mary Anne opened the back door, and she and Mammi walked into the kitchen. Jethro had left everything tidy, as he usually did. She had always been grateful she hadn't married a slob. Mary Anne sighed. She loved this house, but she wouldn't be living here ever again. What did it matter how clean Jethro kept it?

Jethro and Mary Anne got Mammi and Dawdi settled in, which mostly consisted of Jethro putting out clean towels while Mammi brushed her teeth. When Mammi's teeth were clean, Mammi and Dawdi shuffled into Jethro and Mary Anne's bedroom, obviously exhausted from their ordeal, and shut the door behind them.

Mary Anne gave Jethro a weary smile. "*Denki* for taking care of my grandparents again."

Jethro looked even more worn out than she felt. "I thank the *gute* Lord I couldn't sleep. I confess I was strolling around your camp, wanting to make sure the space heater was working properly."

She lowered her eyes, unsure if the

thought of Jethro watching out for her brought her pleasure or embarrassment. She'd put everyone through so much. "You took all the Styrofoam and plastic out of the package this time. There isn't much danger of fire now."

"I didn't notice the rolling RV until you popped out of your tent and started chasing it."

"*Ach.* I would have broken my leg — or worse — if you hadn't been there."

He took a step toward her and seemed to come about three miles closer. She held her breath as he stroked her cheek with the back of his fingers. "*Ach, heartzly,* my heart stopped when I saw you fall."

"I'm wonderful *froh* you were there to grab me."

His fingers felt like fine sandpaper against her skin. "You got your toe something wonderful."

She nodded slowly. "I . . . I wasn't . . . wearing shoes."

"Most people don't when they sleep."

For five breathless seconds, he traced his thumb along the curve of her jaw, staring down at her lips as if he thought they might taste good.

"Jethro," she said. She meant it to sound like a warning, but it came out more like a question.

Jethro seemed to come to himself. Frowning, he squared his shoulders and pulled his hand away from her face. He cupped his fingers around the back of his neck and sighed. "*Cum.* Sit at the table, and I'll tend to your toe."

She remembered to breathe before she fell over. "It only needs a Band-Aid."

He cocked an eyebrow. "You left a blood trail all the way down the hall. I might need to amputate. *And* give you a tetanus shot."

She sat down at one of the eight kitchen chairs Jethro was so particular about. Or *used to be* so particular about. These days he was sleeping in a tent just like she was.

At the sink, he filled two bowls with water and retrieved some towels and soap from the cupboard. He set the towels, soap, and a small bowl on the table, and the bigger bowl on the floor at her feet. "Here. Soak in this, and we'll see how bad it is."

She did as she was told and gasped as her toe touched the water.

He drew his brows together. "*Ach.* Do you want some Advil?"

Pulling in deep, measured breaths, she managed to get her entire foot into the bowl. "This is my favorite bowl. I won't ever be able to use it to cook in again."

Jethro shrugged and bloomed into a wide grin. "It's the only one big enough for your whole foot. I'll soak it with bleach in the morning. I hate to tell you this, but I've used that as a throw-up bowl before."

"*Ach,*" she squeaked in mock indignation. "I'm throwing it away."

His smile was infectious, and she couldn't help but laugh. He was joking about the throw-up bowl. Probably. When they were first married, he could never resist teasing her. Maybe the early hour and his weariness had made him a little punchy.

He chuckled as he disappeared down the hall and came back with the first aid kit from his tackle box. He pulled another chair from the table, turned it to face her, and sat down. "Here, put your foot on my knee."

"You'll get wet."

He reached over and snatched the towel from the table. "I came prepared." He spread the towel over his leg, and Mary Anne pulled her foot from the water. Without all that blood covering it up, it looked like raw hamburger. Jethro grimaced. "Ouch. You took off at least three layers of skin on the top."

"How many layers of skin do I have?"

"I don't know. None to spare."

She'd skinned the top of her big toe but

good, and the toenail had a scrape down the center, but it hadn't broken or come off. It was a tender mercy for sure and certain. Jethro dipped the corner of a towel in the small bowl and pumped some soap onto it.

He dabbed at her toe with the towel and drew his brows together when she flinched at the pain. "Sorry, but you don't want an infection."

"It's okay. You're doing a *gute* job. My toe hasn't been this clean for weeks." A few weeks ago, she would have expected him to remind her that it was her own fault her feet were always dirty or that if she hadn't insisted on living in a tent, none of this would have happened. But these days he was just as likely to keep his mouth shut.

He didn't keep his mouth shut, but he didn't say what she'd come to expect from him either. "You overestimate my skills. Hopefully, it will be clean enough that you won't get gangrene." He gently patted her toe dry. "Do you remember when I got that fishhook stuck in my thumb? You cleaned it out very well, but my thumb still swelled to twice its size and I had to get an antibiotic and a tetanus shot."

Mary Anne examined her toe, still oozing blood but clean enough to see the deep layers of pink skin. "I'm *froh* I'm up-to-date."

Jethro traced his fingers down her foot until his hand came to rest on top of her ankle. The touch sent a warm sensation radiating up her leg. She shifted in her chair and tried not to think about how nice it felt. It was the middle of the night, she was exhausted, and her nerves were pulled as tight as a rope in a tug-of-war contest. For sure and certain that was why every little brush of Jethro's fingers and every caress against her skin affected her like a bride on her wedding day. A *gute* night's sleep would put everything to rights. Of course, she wasn't going to get another wink of sleep tonight. She couldn't have fallen asleep if her life depended on it. She'd be playing the near-accident over in her head for days.

Jethro's hand lingered on her ankle for a few seconds too long, but she didn't have the will to pull away. It felt *wunderbarr,* and she was so weary. He sat breathlessly still, but she couldn't know what he was thinking because his head was down and his gaze was riveted on her ankle. He slowly worked his fingers around her heel and cupped it in his hand, as if her foot was the most precious thing he had ever held.

She shifted in the chair. "Pine has an extra toe on his left foot."

He looked up at her as if he hadn't quite heard what she had said. "Who?"

"Sarah Beachy's boy. I noticed it when he sat by me at breakfast this morning."

His lips curled upward, and he casually removed his hand from her foot. "I can see a boy like Pine trying to cut his extra toe off with that ax he likes."

She smiled back. "Don't give him any ideas."

Jethro squeezed a generous glob of antibiotic ointment onto her toe, then covered it with a gauze pad and wrapped it with some stretchy tape to keep the gauze in place. "I'll change this every morning for you, if you want."

"I can do it. I usually don't have a hard time reaching my feet."

He wadded up the paper package the gauze came in. "While I've got the first aid kit out, does it hurt anywhere else?"

Her left hip stung something wonderful. It was likely she had a wide, bright red scrape down the side of her leg, but she wasn't about to mention it to Jethro. She wasn't letting him near her hip, even with a Band-Aid. She stood up and took a few steps around the kitchen, trying to walk as normally as possible, even with a sore toe. She couldn't do it without limping.

"Do you need crutches?"

"*Nae*, but I might have to wear my slippers to work."

"You might start a new style with the old folks."

She grinned. "Josie wears her slippers to the center every day." She glanced at Jethro's fish clock. "*Ach.* Four thirty. It's hardly worth going back to bed."

"I won't be going back to sleep. Seeing that RV almost run you over was enough to scare me awake for a month."

She felt that warm sensation down her spine again. The way he looked at her left no doubt that he cared about her. It was a pleasant little surprise. Of course, in the last few days he'd told her over and over that he loved her, but words didn't have nearly the power of the truth in his eyes. She did her best to look anywhere else. "I can't go back to sleep either. My heart is still pounding, and my arms feel like jelly."

His eyes lit up like two vanilla-scented candles. "Can I take you to breakfast?"

"Breakfast? What do you mean?"

Jethro pumped his eyebrows up and down. "Betty's Bakery in Shawano has maple-bacon doughnuts. We could get doughnuts and *kaffee* and take them to the lake and watch the sun rise."

She laughed at the expression on his face. He was suddenly so eager. "Shawano? Jethro, the van will be here at seven thirty to pick you up for work. It's an hour to Shawano and another hour to the lake."

His expression fell like an undercooked chocolate soufflé. "We could just get doughnuts and skip the lake."

"Okay, I guess. I don't want you to miss the van."

He raised his eyebrows so high, they were halfway up his forehead. "What if we took the RV?"

"The RV? You *are* tired."

"Bob left the keys in case we needed to move it. It's practically sitting on the road. What will it hurt if we take it into town? It's a lot faster than a horse and buggy, and we can get doughnuts and make it to the lake and back before the van even drives down our road."

She was momentarily speechless. The RV? What was he thinking? "You know perfectly well we couldn't. Neither of us knows how to drive."

He smiled that mischievous smile she hadn't seen for years. "Oh, I know how to drive. I don't have a license, so if a policeman pulls us over, we'll probably go to jail, but I know how to drive."

"You do not."

"I do too. During *rumschpringe,* Elmer Lee Kanagy bought a car, and five of us learned how to drive it. I got wonderful *gute* on the back roads."

Her mouth fell open. "You never told me that."

"I didn't want you to know how wicked I'd been. What with the car and breaking Mattie Byler's ankle, you never would have married me."

She smiled. "You didn't break Mattie's ankle, and of course I would have married you. Your driving skills would only have added to your appeal." Jethro had been the whole world to her. She would have loved him even if he'd spent time in jail.

His smile widened. "I really want to take you to breakfast."

She growled, wanting to give in but knowing they absolutely, positively shouldn't do it. There were too many disasters that could befall them between here and Shawano. "We shouldn't. It's Bob's RV."

Jethro opened the fridge, pulled a key chain from the vegetable crisper, and jangled it in front of her face. "He left me the keys."

"Driving that thing would be more like trying to maneuver Noah's ark."

He cocked an eyebrow. "I'm a fisherman. I know how to steer a boat." He jangled the keys again, and the look on his face made her laugh. He looked so happy, she didn't even want to put her foot down.

"We're going to die," she said, a giggle tripping from her lips.

"Lord willing, we'll get to eat our doughnuts first."

He took her hand and tugged her out the back door to the RV, which was still sitting right where they'd left it half an hour before. Her heart did a somersault as she went around to the passenger side and got in. Jethro might know how to drive, but he hadn't been behind the wheel for over a decade, and an RV was probably like driving a house. Could he drive a house?

This was a very bad idea, even if she hadn't been this excited about anything for years. It was an adventure like the ones they used to have, before Jethro had stopped loving her.

"We shouldn't do this," she said, without an ounce of conviction in her voice. Maybe Jethro would come to his senses even if she couldn't.

He shut the door and fumbled with the key before getting it to fit in the little hole where the key went. Grinning in her direction, he turned the key and the motor came to life, like a bear awakened from a long nap. This was definitely not a *gute* idea, but she pressed her lips together and smiled at Jethro as if she had all the confidence in the world that he would get them there and back in one piece.

In the semidarkness, Jethro studied the handles and sticks and knobs that stuck out every which way from the steering wheel. After a few seconds of examination, he turned a knob that looked like every other knob, and the headlights came on. The panel in front of him lit up like a starry night. Mary Anne didn't know if he knew what any of those lights or instruments meant, but at least he could see them now.

He turned to Mary Anne with a grin as wide as the motor home. "Do you want to find us a *gute* radio station?"

"A radio station? Jethro, you *have* gone crazy."

"You should always listen to the radio when you're cruising the back roads. It's what all the *Englischers* do."

She rolled her eyes, but leaned in for a closer look at something that looked like it might be the radio on the dashboard. She'd seen *Englischers* turn on their radios before when she'd ridden in their cars. Charlene, the woman who ran the senior center, had turned on the radio once or twice when she'd picked up Mary Anne for work.

She eyed the buttons until she found one that said "On/Off." She turned it, but nothing happened.

"Push it," Jethro said.

She did as he said, and they both jumped as loud music sung by a very angry man burst from a speaker in the ceiling. *"Don't turn away from me. I won't be ignored!"*

"Do you want to turn it down?" Jethro yelled.

She shook her head. "I want it to make me go deaf. It's what all the *Englischers* do."

He laughed — or at least she thought he did. It was impossible to hear much of anything over that music. "Okay, then."

Jethro pulled down on the stick to the right of the steering wheel and the motor home lurched forward. Mary Anne quickly buckled her seat belt and grabbed onto the handle that hung directly over the passenger-side window. Whoever built this thing must have known that a nervous wife would need something to hold on to while her husband drove them off a cliff.

Jethro gripped the steering wheel like a lifeline and turned the RV onto the road that ran in front of their house. Without

319

speeding up, he let the RV roll slowly down the pavement, just like they were being carried downstream by a gentle current. The good news was that their house was on a back road and never saw much traffic anyway. At 4:30 in the morning, there wasn't a soul in sight.

The RV got going a little faster, and he slammed on the brakes, sending Mary Anne flying forward until her seat belt caught her. It hadn't been a violent forward motion because they weren't going that fast, but it was enough to take Mary Anne's breath away and make her rethink this whole adventure. Were they going too fast for her to open the door and jump out? Probably not, but with the way things had gone so far this morning, Jethro would run over her as soon as she hit the ground.

She reached out and figured out how to turn down the volume on the radio until they could barely hear it. Jethro needed all his wits about him, and the loud music was a huge distraction.

He slammed on the brakes four times before they got to the end of the road, smiling sheepishly at her every time he did it. The squealing tires and the pitch and roll of the motor home didn't seem to discourage him. He managed a relatively smooth stop at the stop sign and, with reckless abandon, turned onto the main road. Well, it wasn't exactly a main road. This was Bonduel. There weren't really any main roads, but it was wider and longer than the road they'd just been on. Mary Anne's heartbeat increased with the speed of the RV.

Jethro threw caution to the wind, stepped on the gas, and got the motor home going twenty-five miles an hour. He made an impressively smooth stop at the next stop sign and glanced at Mary Anne, as if hoping for acknowledgment of his achievement. Even though she was near to hyperventilating, she gave him what she hoped passed for a smile. "You're getting the hang of it."

He turned onto the road that went the back way into Shawano. "I don't think we should try the highway just yet."

She nodded and relaxed her grip on the handle above her head. "*Gute* idea."

With one long, loud blast on its horn, a small car came from behind and passed them on the left. Jethro instinctively slammed on the brakes, and the seat belt tightened across Mary Anne's chest again.

Jethro grunted his disapproval. "So I'm going slow. I'm a motor home. You don't need to get so huffy about it." He pressed on his horn and held it down, sending a roar of sound into the night. He flinched in surprise and snatched his hand off the horn. "*Ach.* I just woke the whole county."

A giggle burst from Mary Anne's lips. "For sure and certain."

He took his eyes off the road long enough to smile at her, then started laughing himself. "Next to getting caught in the buggy by the policeman, this is the most exciting thing I've ever done."

"We're not there yet. Things are bound to get more exciting, especially when we hit a tree or someone's mailbox."

He winked at her. "I won't hit a tree, but I can't guarantee I won't hit a mailbox. They never look both ways when they cross the road."

They didn't see another car until they got to Shawano, where a few stray automobiles were crawling along the roads in the half light of morning.

Jethro made three expert turns in a row, then maneuvered the motor home down an alley between two narrow buildings. The RV pitched and rolled, as if it would tip over at any moment.

Mary Anne tightened her grip on her trusty handle and tried to breathe normally. "Where exactly is Betty's Bakery?"

"Just down this way. They have a drive-through," he said, looking very pleased with himself. He veered right around what looked like a very tight corner, then turned left between two more buildings that seemed even closer together than the first two.

"The mirrors aren't going to fit!" Mary Anne said.

They both rolled down their windows and pulled their mirrors in so they didn't stick out. Thank the *gute* Lord the mirrors were bendable. He smiled at her. "Nothing to worry about."

"Uh, Jethro, the arrow on the ground is pointing in the opposite direction."

Jethro furrowed his brow. "Am I going the wrong way?"

The buildings were so close together and the motor home so big, they didn't have enough room to open their doors and get out if they needed to. Jethro certainly wouldn't be able to turn around. They pulled forward to a small window. Unfortunately, it was on Mary Anne's side of the RV. They were going the wrong way. Jethro tapped on the brakes a little too forcefully, but Mary Anne was ready, and the lurch didn't even bother her.

A girl with curly blond hair, not more than seventeen or eighteen, slid open the window, and her peppy smile faltered just a bit at the corners. "Um, oh my gosh. Um. Welcome to Betty's Bakery. You're going the wrong way."

Mary Anne covered a giggle that was threatening to pop out of her mouth. Jethro leaned over Mary Anne and raised his voice so the girl could better hear him. "Sorry about that, but could we get two maple-bacon doughnuts and two large coffees?"

The girl took a second and a third look at both of them, and then her gaze slid across the RV. "Um. Um, sure. Are you guys Amish?"

"*Jah,*" Jethro said.

Mary Anne thought it might be best to distract the girl from where her thoughts were likely going. They didn't need to try to explain this to a policeman. "We hear your maple-bacon doughnuts are famous."

"I didn't know Amish could drive motor homes."

"I can," Jethro said. It was a *gute* answer. True, but vague.

With an arm still resting on the counter, the girl turned and motioned to someone inside the bakery. "Uncle Gary, did you know Amish could drive motor homes?"

"They can't. It's not allowed."

"These Amish can."

Uncle Gary appeared at the window. He

324

was a short, middle-aged man with intelligent brown eyes and deep smile lines around his mouth. He wore a Green Bay Packers baseball cap and a Minnesota Vikings T-shirt. Mary Anne couldn't distract this one. She didn't know anything about football. Maybe they should make a quick getaway before the police were called in.

Uncle Gary gave Bob's RV a look-see, then peered into the cab and stared at Jethro and Mary Anne. Jethro gave Uncle Gary a friendly wave. Mary Anne pasted on a smile that probably looked more like a painful grimace.

"Well, how about that," Uncle Gary said, smiling as if he'd just met some long-lost cousins. "I didn't know you folks were allowed to drive motor homes. It's nice to meet you."

Mary Anne hated to give this nice man the wrong impression of the Amish, but she'd rather not spend the rest of what was left of the night in jail. She glanced doubtfully at Jethro.

Jethro winked at her — which was an oddly comforting gesture — then grinned at Uncle Gary. "The truth is, we're not allowed to drive RVs. This is a friend's RV, and we're just having a little adventure."

Uncle Gary nodded, as if he was in on the

secret. "No need to say another word. You people have to do something to relieve the boredom of your dull lives."

Mary Anne closed her mouth on another giggle. The *Englisch* had some funny notions about the Amish. Her smile faded, and she pressed her lips together. Up until a few weeks ago, her life was as dull as a sack of potatoes. Maybe some people were willing to settle. She wasn't.

"That's why we came here for doughnuts," Jethro said. "To get some excitement."

"You came to the right place, even though you came in the wrong way." Uncle Gary pointed to his right, where three cars were waiting in line in front of the motor home. One of the drivers tapped on his horn and spread his hands in a gesture of irritation. He didn't look too happy to be staring at the front end of an RV.

Uncle Gary handed Mary Anne two lidded cups of *kaffee* and a white paper sack. "You're going to be sad you only got two. Those doughnuts are so good, you'll want to buy a dozen next time. Our best seller."

Mary Anne relaxed a little. They weren't going to get arrested today. Probably.

Jethro handed Uncle Gary some money and got his change. "*Denki.* We'll be back sometime."

"I know you will," Uncle Gary said. "Just come in the right way next time."

Jethro eyed the three cars in front of him. They didn't seem willing to move. He gave Mary Anne a wry smile. "I think we're going to have to go backward."

Mary Anne nodded, as if she had all the confidence in the world in his driving skills. How was he going to back this house on wheels out of the alley?

Jethro put the RV into Reverse and turned to look over his right shoulder. There wasn't much to see except the small kitchen and the door that led to the even smaller bedroom. He wouldn't be able to navigate that way, and his side mirror was folded in to keep from scraping against the brick wall.

"Keep your tires straight and back out slowly," Uncle Gary called.

Looking straight ahead — because there really wasn't anywhere else left to look — Jethro eased his foot off the brake, and the RV crawled backward. "What did I tell you?" Jethro said, suddenly very pleased with himself. "You have to admit the motor home was a wonderful *gute* idea. We got our doughnuts, and it's only 5:10."

Mary Anne smiled. He was like a boy eager to show his *mamm* the frog in his pocket.

They backed slowly down the alleyway as the cars in front of them inched forward. Jethro stuck his head out the open window and looked behind them. "Almost there." Still going as slowly as a turtle on a stroll, he turned the steering wheel to the left to maneuver the RV around the tight corner.

"You're going to hit . . ."

Once again, Jethro slammed on the brakes as the left front bumper of the RV tapped ever so lightly against the building on the left. "Oh, *sis yuscht!*" he said, pulling the stick down and cranking the steering wheel to the right. "Do I have to turn it left to go right or right to go right?" He'd pulled forward barely a few inches when Mary Anne heard a sickening scrape behind them.

She poked her head out the window. "Stop, Jethro. The back end is up against the corner of the building."

Jethro looked like a schoolboy who'd been caught doing something naughty. "Oh, *sis yuscht.*" He pushed the stick up again and turned the steering wheel to the left, taking his foot slowly off the pedal. The RV moved backward, but there was more scraping noise behind them, and the front of the RV nearly hit the brick wall again.

He stepped on the brake as the car in front of them started honking with vigor. He'd gotten his doughnut and was stuck between an RV and a red sports car. Jethro winced and gave the irritated *Englischer* a friendly wave. "Do you think we could get them to tear these two buildings down? The man in front of us is getting a little testy, and I don't want to put any more scratches on Bob's RV."

Mary Anne couldn't help but smile as she watched the blush creep up Jethro's neck. "I think you need a few more driving lessons."

His mouth fell open in mock indignation. "I'm a *gute* driver."

"That must be why we're stuck at the doughnut shop facing the wrong way." It was all so strange. Mary Anne couldn't help but laugh.

Jethro laughed with her. "I missed the day they taught us how to back up."

The driver in front of them must have thought they hadn't heard him honk the first fifty times. Either that or he'd fallen asleep with his head pressed against his horn. Between the two buildings, the noise was deafening. Mary Anne and Jethro rolled up their windows.

"*Ach, vell,*" Jethro said with a dramatic lift of his eyebrow. "I can't open my door to escape." He took Mary Anne's hand and gazed into her eyes with a pathetic look that almost made her laugh out loud. "Save yourself, Mary Anne. The senior center isn't far from here. If you get out and walk, you might make it in time for work, even with a sore toe."

She grinned and batted her eyelashes. "I can't leave you, not after you went to all this trouble to steal a motor home and buy me breakfast."

A warm, breathtaking smile formed on his lips. "We could be stuck here for weeks."

"We've got a full kitchen and a bathroom."

He laughed. "What about the angry *Englischer* with the sparkly beads hanging from his mirror?"

"He can use our kitchen too," Mary Anne said.

Smiling like the cat that ate the canary, Jethro turned off the engine and picked up the sack from where she had set it on the armrest between them. "In that case, we might as well eat our doughnuts."

Before they could open the sack, Uncle Gary appeared in front of them, standing between the RV and the little white car that was still honking like an angry goose. He propped his hands on his hips and tilted his head to study the motor home from a few different angles. The man in the white car didn't seem to notice. He was still trying to bring down the walls with his horn.

Uncle Gary turned around and shouted at the driver of the white car. Mary Anne didn't hear what he said, but the honking stopped. She smiled to herself. Some people would only mind their manners if they were scolded into it.

Uncle Gary turned back and called to Jethro. Mary Anne and Jethro opened their windows so they could hear him. "You've got to turn your steering wheel hard to the left and then immediately to the right yet," he said.

Jethro stuck his head out the window and nearly scraped his forehead on the wall. "I can't do it. I'm not that good a driver." He glanced at Mary Anne and curled his lips. "I'll sacrifice my pride for the sake of Bob's RV."

She smiled. "That's very thoughtful of you."

Uncle Gary shook his head. "You Amish should learn how to drive your RVs." He came around to Mary Anne's side and opened her door, but since the RV was wedged between buildings, the door wouldn't open all that far, and Uncle Gary was too wide to slide into the cab.

"You could go in the side door," Mary

331

Anne said.

Uncle Gary puckered his lips as if he'd eaten a pickle. "It's on the other side. I'd have to go all the way around the building." He shut Mary Anne's door. "Okay. I'll get Natasha. She's a skinny little thing, and she drives her dad's tractor all summer long."

The car in front of them honked again as Uncle Gary walked past it and around to the front of the building. He smacked his hand against the side of the white car, probably as a warning to the driver not to honk again. Gary soon returned with Natasha, the curly-headed slip of a girl who'd filled their doughnut order. She looked too young to drive anything, let alone to be able to unstick a huge motor home from between two buildings.

Natasha slipped between the wall and the motor home, and Uncle Gary opened Mary Anne's door for her. Mary Anne stood up and moved back as Natasha slid into the cab. It was a tight fit. Mary Anne could hear Natasha sucking in her breath. "Okay," Natasha said, "I need to sit there." She pointed to Jethro's seat. He practically jumped out of her way, no doubt embarrassed that he hadn't moved sooner, or mortified that an *Englisch* teenager was going to have to get them out of their predicament.

Natasha settled into the seat and turned the key. She looked comfortable behind the wheel, as if she'd been driving motor homes all her life. Uncle Gary stood in front calling out directions, pointing and gesturing and flapping his arms every which way. To Mary Anne, it looked like a strange dance, and she had no idea how Natasha could understand what he was trying to tell her.

Whatever communication passed between them, it worked. Natasha turned the wheel hard one way and then hard the other, all the while letting the motor home roll without pressing on the gas pedal. There was only one screech as she dislodged the back bumper from the corner of the building. Other than that, the motor home didn't so much as caress the walls again, even though they came within half inches a couple of times. Mary Anne and Jethro stood just inside the RV kitchen and held on tight as Natasha pushed the side mirror into place and used it to back the rest of the way out of the alley and onto the street. Uncle Gary followed her all the way, still gesturing wildly, even though Natasha didn't seem to be paying him any heed.

She pulled onto the street and drove around the corner, then stopped the RV right in front of the bakery. Mary Anne and

Jethro gave her a big round of applause. Natasha didn't say anything, but the corners of her mouth curled upward as she put the RV into Park.

There was a line of more than a dozen cars at the bakery stretching out of the alleyway and onto the street.

Jethro made a face. "I caused you a lot of trouble this morning."

Mary Anne held the bag of doughnuts in front of his face. "But we got our doughnuts."

Natasha grinned. "They're totally worth it."

"Thank you for getting us unstuck."

"No problem, but next time you should park on the street and come in. That alleyway is too narrow." She rolled her eyes with an affectionate smile on her face. "Uncle Gary *had* to have a drive-through."

Natasha climbed out of the cab, and Jethro sat back down in the driver's seat. He glanced at Mary Anne doubtfully. "Do you dare drive to the lake with me?"

She lifted her skirts and bounced back into the seat beside him. "I almost got run over, we bought bacon-maple doughnuts, a teenage girl drove us around Shawano, and it's only 5:25. Why cut our adventure short? I'm expecting to nearly drown at the lake.

It'll be fun."

His face relaxed into the sweetest, toastiest smile she had ever seen. "It would be a shame to go home just when it was getting fun."

He started the motor home up again and, in his unbridled enthusiasm, tapped on the horn. If he hoped tapping would make the horn quieter, he was greatly mistaken. He could have summoned all the geese on the lake. It probably startled the *Englischer* in the white car. He was no doubt sitting in the alley wiping *kaffee* from his white shirt.

Jethro took it slow, but it was still much faster to the lake than going by buggy. He drove them up to the overlook, and although he parked far from the water, Mary Anne was certain the motor home would lose its brakes and roll right into the lake — especially after the mishaps they'd already had.

They found a nice patch of grass, and Mary Anne pulled a blanket from the motor home bed for them to sit on. They sipped their lukewarm *kaffee* and ate their maple-bacon doughnuts while they watched the sun rise. The rhythmic rat-a-tat of a woodpecker echoed in the air, as well as birdsong from at least half a dozen different birds. Mary Anne caught sight of a stunning yellow-headed blackbird and an even more rare red-breasted grosbeak darting among the safety of the budding trees.

The air felt still and fresh, and the sky was lined with long, thin clouds that caught the light of the sunrise and changed it into a thousand different shades of orange and pink. Mary Anne never in a million years would have been able to paint the beauty of that sky.

Jethro leaned back on one hand while holding the *kaffee* cup in the other. He was sitting close, but Mary Anne didn't mind. The morning air was a little chilly, and she appreciated the warmth that radiated from his body. They had often joked that he was like a furnace and she was like an icebox. She was always cold and slept with two blankets. He was always warm and kicked the blankets off anytime he got a chance.

His gaze was turned toward the lake, probably searching for fish jumping out of the water to eat their breakfast. She stole a look at him out of the corner of her eye. She had always liked his profile. His dark eyebrows brooded over his eyes like storm clouds, and his jaw was square and firm. She reached out and ran her fingers over the beard on his chin. He liked to keep it as short as was allowed in the *gmayna*.

He held perfectly still as she took off his

hat and lightly ran her fingers over his thick, dark hair. She loved the look of it, even if he kept it under his hat most of the time. "You need a haircut," she said, feeling that familiar twinge of guilt and sadness and affection she often experienced when she thought of him. He was so handsome, so steady. So safe.

"I . . . uh . . . I haven't thought about it for weeks."

Just in time, she remembered she lived in a tent and didn't love Jethro anymore, no matter how handsome he was. She pulled her hand away. "You should ask your *mamm* to cut it."

He turned to look at her, his expression a mixture of pain and hope. "You used to cut my hair."

"I don't do that anymore."

Instead of pulling away from her in irritation, he raised her hand to his lips and slowly kissed each of her knuckles. He put down his *kaffee* and smoothed his palm up her arm. She didn't take her gaze from his face as the warmth of a summer breeze seemed to penetrate her skin. She held her breath to keep from trembling, but it didn't work. She hadn't trembled at his touch for years, and here she was, unable to pull away, shaking like a flame in the wind.

It didn't make any sense, but she didn't want the sensation to stop. His rough skin felt so *gute* against hers, and it had been so long since his touch had made her feel anything but cold. It was almost as if he adored every little piece of her — her hands, her arms, her potato chip collection. Her quilts, her neck, her throat. Her lips.

A soft, barely audible sigh escaped her lips as he slid his hand behind her head and kissed her with a gentleness she hadn't thought possible. His touch was so soft, she wondered if she was just imagining it. She raised her hand to his cheek. *Jah.* He was there, and the touch of his lips against hers felt almost like the only gift she wanted for the rest of her life.

And then, her blood pulsed like a swollen river. This was insane. How could she be feeling these feelings for someone she didn't love anymore? She probably knew the answer, but she couldn't, wouldn't look closely enough to see what it was. Her confusion raised too many questions she didn't want to face.

He pulled away but stayed too close and ran his thumb down the contour of her neck. "I love you, Mary Anne, my precious ruby."

"I . . . I . . ." *I don't love you.* She couldn't

338

say it out loud. She didn't even know if it was true anymore. He'd bought her a maple bacon doughnut and a space heater. He'd driven a motor home to Shawano and saved her from getting run over. She was sure his efforts had something to do with love.

He gave her a weary smile, seemingly unconcerned about what her reply might have been. "You got some sun yesterday."

"Is my face burned?"

"You've got a few more freckles on your nose."

Mary Anne smirked. "My nose is nothing but freckles."

"Nae," he said, looking at her as if she was the only person in the whole world. "I've memorized your face, every freckle, every line. You've got more freckles today than you had yesterday."

She didn't know what to say to that. Maybe it was even true — the part about memorizing her face.

He let go of her hand, finally. "You're tired. The sheer terror of that motor home ride has worn you out."

"Nae," she said, unable to stifle a yawn. "It was wonderful exciting."

He smiled cautiously. "You think so?" He straightened his legs out in front of him. *"Cum.* Rest for a minute. We don't have to be back for almost an hour."

She didn't want to get so close to him and his aggravating warmth, but she was almost dizzy with fatigue — fatigue or the lingering effects of that kiss swirling in her head. Reluctantly or eagerly — she couldn't tell which — she laid her head in his lap and closed her eyes. Just as she expected, his lap was warm and comfortable. How had she gotten herself into this? And how would she get herself out?

She drifted off to sleep to the sound of the lake lapping against the shore and the tingle of Jethro's fingers stroking her cheek. Plenty of time to stew about it when she could think straight, if she ever wanted to again.

CHAPTER FOURTEEN

The other men in the van were irritated beyond endurance, but Jethro couldn't help himself. He had whistled all the way to work this morning. He'd whistled while he sanded cabinets and drove nails. He whistled during the lunch break and then all the way home in the van. When they finally stopped in front of Jethro's house, his cousin Marty practically shoved him out of the van. "Aren't you living in a tent?" Marty said.

Jethro nodded as he retrieved his lunch box from the seat. "Still in a tent."

"Then you have no business being so happy. Try to put a lid on it tomorrow or you'll be walking to work."

Jethro chuckled and gave Marty a wave as he shut the door. Nothing could mar his *gute* mood. Mary Anne was starting to warm up to him. He could feel it. He should have told her years ago that he could drive.

Their adventure with the motor home had

been almost a week ago, and things between them had improved dramatically. Maybe Mary Anne realized Jethro wasn't as boring as she had thought he was. Maybe she had liked the way he'd wrapped her toe. Maybe it was the maple bacon doughnuts that had made the difference. Never again would he underestimate the power of a maple bacon doughnut.

On Saturday, Mary Anne had asked him to help her plant pansies around her tent. Then they'd worked together in the garden, even though Mary Anne had made it clear the tomatoes and cucumbers were for Jethro because she didn't plan to be there to harvest them. Her determination to leave had made him more than a little unhappy, but then he'd realized that maybe she was digging in her heels because she could feel herself drifting back to him.

They'd planted tomatoes and cucumbers, peppers and cantaloupe. And milkweed, because Mary Anne was determined to save all the butterflies in Wisconsin. Jethro didn't see how a few stalks of milkweed were going to help, but it was a nice gesture for the butterflies all the same.

Last Sunday was off Sunday, and Mary Anne had specially invited Jethro to have supper with her and her camping cousins.

She *had* gently reminded him not to ask about the cost of the five pot roasts she'd bought to feed everyone, but she had still invited him. The invitation was very encouraging, considering she thought all he cared about was money. If only she knew how little he cared about money now that he was at risk of losing his wife. *Ach,* how he regretted the hundreds of times he'd used money as a justification when all he'd really been doing was suffocating Mary Anne's dreams.

No sense dwelling on past mistakes. He was determined to be a better man and a better husband. He wanted to treat Mary Anne the way she deserved to be treated and to show her that he wasn't a lost cause. He wanted to make her love him again. And maybe his efforts were working.

Surely the birthday present he'd made for her would melt her heart if anything would. He couldn't wait to give it to her.

Jethro strolled around to the back of the house, whistling all the way. Mary Anne had painted three giant flowers on the barn where the quilt block had been. Each flower was a different bright color, and each was as big as a buggy wheel. They were a cheery addition to the campsite. Mary Anne worked at the senior center, tended the garden, sewed quilts, and painted furniture

343

for that Etsy shop. Jethro marveled at all she got done in a day. Had it always been this way and he just hadn't noticed? *Nae,* more likely she had suppressed any desire to create because she thought that was what he wanted.

He made his way to the east side of the camp, where Mamm and Dat and the others were still camping. It was a much more somber place than Mary Anne's side. Mary Anne's camp had giant flowers, laughing children, and huge butterflies. The east side had dingy gray and green tents and an austere Porta-Potty. Jethro propped his hands on his hips and surveyed his campsite. Mamm fed the fire in preparation for dinner. Willie Jay was adjusting his tent stakes and airing out his tent. None of the other men had arrived from their farms or jobs yet.

Jethro had to admire everyone's dedication. They'd been there almost two weeks, and for sure and certain things wouldn't be resolved any time soon. How long would any of them last?

Mamm looked up and didn't even try for a smile. He knew her back ached from sleeping on a cot, and she said her mouth always tasted like dirt. Nothing but her loyalty to her son kept her in the woods.

"Anna thinks we should make peace," she said, her lips twitching in annoyance. "She's invited all of us to Mary Anne's birthday party tonight."

Jethro's heart jumped up and down for joy. He had been hoping for an invitation. "That's very nice."

Mamm scowled. "She had the nerve to insist that if Willie Jay comes, he isn't allowed to say a word to Mary Anne. How dare she say such a thing? Willie Jay is a perfectly nice man, but when he sees sin, he can't help but rebuke the sinner. He wouldn't be doing his job as a minister if he didn't."

Jethro took a deep breath. He loved his family, but Mary Anne was more important to him than a dozen *bruders.* "Anna is right. I don't want Willie Jay to make Mary Anne uncomfortable."

Mamm narrowed her eyes. "Jethro, this has gone on long enough. You're making it too easy for Mary Anne. She has to learn she can't leave her husband without suffering the consequences."

Jethro squared his shoulders. "*Ach,* she's learned her lesson all right. She's lost her comfortable home, the respect and support of the *gmayna,* and the love of her in-laws.

I'd say she's suffered plenty of consequences yet."

The lines around Mamm's mouth deepened until they seemed to be etched into her face. "She hasn't lost my love. I still think of her like my own daughter."

"You don't treat her that way."

"Just because I've tried to give her correction doesn't mean I don't love her. If you remember, you scolded her too."

Jethro scrubbed his hand down the side of his face. "You're right, but I only made things worse. If I want her to come back, I shouldn't do things that will push her away."

"Then let Willie Jay do the talking, and you be the nice one. She needs to hear it from somebody."

"In that case, Willie Jay can't come to the party." Jethro pressed his lips together, determined to do right by Mary Anne. "And neither can you."

Mamm harrumphed her indignation. "Anna invited me. It's not your place to uninvite me." She drew in a long breath and softened her expression. "It pains me that you think I would do anything to ruin Mary Anne's birthday party."

"So you won't say anything?"

Pain flashed in her eyes. "I won't speak unless spoken to."

He hated to hurt his *mamm* like that, but Mary Anne's feelings were the most important. If Jethro had anything to say about it, she would have the best birthday ever. She was going to love his present.

Adam Wengerd trudged around the side of the house, across the lawn, and into the woods like a scholar on his first day of school. With his head down and shoulders slumped, he seemed more like an old man than a newlywed of only eight months. "*Hallo,* Adam," Jethro said, unable to contain a smile. He'd been invited to Mary Anne's birthday party. It was a *wunderbarr* day. "*Wie gehts?* Did you have a *gute* day at work?"

Jethro felt a twinge of guilt that Adam was living out here in solidarity and Jethro didn't even know what Adam did for work. Was he a lumberjack? A teacher? A buggy maker?

Adam's beard was coming in nicely for eight months' worth of growing. He hooked his thumbs into his suspenders and squinted at Jethro against the bright afternoon sun. "Jethro, I really wanted to support you in your fight, but I'm afraid I'm going to have to break camp and go home."

This wasn't horrible news. Jethro hadn't asked anybody to camp in the first place, and Adam was the least useful, laziest camper of the bunch. He never helped clean up the dishes or gather firewood. He ate more than his share of food and complained about everything. Jethro pasted a concerned look on his face. "Is everything all right?"

Adam leaned closer and lowered his voice. "I stopped by my house after work, and *mei fraa* was making pies and eating ice cream right out of the carton. She's having a quilting frolic at our house tonight, and she told me to go back to the woods because she said I'd ruin the fun. I can't understand it, but I'm beginning to suspect she likes it when I'm gone. This never would have happened if I hadn't moved out in the first place."

Jethro nodded, his heart swelling in gratitude for the painful lessons Mary Anne had taught him. Maybe Mary Anne's moving out would make some of the other men in the *gmayna* realize they needed to cherish their wives more than they did. Lord willing none of them would have to learn it the hard way like Jethro had. "I appreciate all the support you've given me, but I agree. You need to go home."

Adam frowned. "She's not going to like it. She's having a quilting bee."

Jethro curled one side of his mouth. "Shut

yourself in the bedroom and don't make a peep."

"Can I take the ice cream with me?"

Jethro chuckled. "You'll need to get permission." He put a firm hand on Adam's shoulder. "If your wife is happier when you're out of the house, maybe you need to find out why."

Adam pursed his lips. "Maybe I do."

"Try to remember it's probably your fault."

Jethro helped Adam take down his tent and pack up his gear. Jethro couldn't regret Adam's leaving. One fewer camper would ease the strain on the Porta-Potty. And the food supply.

After dismantling Adam's tent, Jethro sprinted into the house to take a quick shower. He wanted to smell good tonight in case, Lord willing, he was ever alone with Mary Anne. He wanted to kiss her again and again, and someone who smelled like an Irish spring was much more pleasant to kiss than someone who smelled like a Porta-Potty. The kiss last week at the lake had only whetted his appetite for more. He'd forgotten how nice it was to kiss his *fraa*. He'd never take it for granted again.

David Eicher refused to cross the distance to attend Mary Anne's birthday party. He didn't like the Helmuths, and he was holding firmly to his position that Mary Anne was a sinner who didn't deserve any compassion. Celebrating her birthday was out of the question. It wouldn't surprise Jethro if David moved back home soon. He was getting grumpier by the day, and Mary Anne hadn't shown any signs of budging. David could probably guess there was no end in sight.

Norman Coblenz was nowhere to be seen, so they left without him. He was Mary Anne's cousin. Maybe he'd already gone to the party.

Jethro carried the rectangular pan that held Mary Anne's birthday present while Dat hefted the Dutch oven of cheesy potatoes that was Mamm's contribution to the meal. Everybody loved Mamm's Dutch oven potatoes. Surely they would soften a few hearts tonight. Willie Jay and Mamm followed a few steps behind. Jethro had never seen such a petulant look on Willie Jay's face, but he had assured them that he would keep his mouth shut, even if he was duty bound to call Mary Anne to repentance. He'd do it some time other than her birthday.

The campfire danced merrily, and it looked as if the whole Helmuth family had turned out for the celebration. Sarah Beachy's husband was there, as were two or three more of her sons. All the camping families surrounded the campfire, plus seven or eight other cousins and their families who must have been invited. Three *Englischers* Jethro didn't recognize sat in three Green Bay Packer camp chairs trying to get some of *die kinner* to join them in a camp song that nobody knew but the *Englischers.*

Jethro counted six long tables with benches set up on his back lawn. Had they been stolen from the *gmayna*? He pressed his lips together and looked away. He had enough to worry about without wondering about the church benches. There was a lot of chatting going on, as well as children running all over the place. There were at least three dogs and fifteen *kinner* running around on his lawn, dodging tables and benches.

Anna caught sight of Jethro and his family ambling toward the campfire, and her eyes lit up like a sky of fireworks. "Jethro, Chris, Lois!" she called, working her way through the crowd of cousins, then grabbing Jethro's sleeve and pulling him toward the circle of camp chairs. "I need to show you something." Mamm, Dat, and Willie Jay followed.

"Oh, and you brought Willie Jay. How nice."

There was barely room to move closer to the campfire, and he couldn't see Mary Anne anywhere. Jethro handed his casserole dish to Pine, who stood at the fringes of the circle and seemed to need something to do. "I'll come right back for this," Jethro said.

Pine nodded. "Okay."

Anna turned to Mamm. "I'll return him shortly."

Mamm arched an eyebrow, but she stayed behind with Dat and Willie Jay as Anna pulled Jethro through the group at the campfire and over to the large canopy that housed Mary Anne's latest quilt project. "You're going to be so surprised."

A stunning red, white, and blue quilt, halfway quilted, sat under the canopy on a set of frames Jethro had made for Mary Anne a few months after they were married. Mary Anne had finished the quilt top last week. Jethro was in awe of her talent. Everything she touched bloomed with beauty.

Anna pulled Jethro closer to the quilt. "Now, Jethro, before I show you, I want you to know I adore your parents — Lois makes the best spaghetti sauce in the *gmayna* — but I'm counting on you to keep Willie Jay well fed. He has good manners and won't talk with his mouth full, so you've got to keep his mouth full. He's the dearest man and I love him like I would a distant, unpleasant cousin, but I don't want him upsetting Mary Anne."

Jethro nodded. "I'll keep careful watch. We've already told him he's not to talk about sin, marriage, Mary Anne, me, hell, or camping."

Anna drew her brows together in deep thought. "That should do it." She suddenly bloomed into a smile. "Now, let's talk about more exciting things." She tugged him farther back, where the canopy walls had been rolled clear to the ground, and motioned into the dimness. "We can finally do solidarity again."

Jethro's mouth fell open. A queen-size bed, complete with sheets, blankets, two fluffy pillows, and a headboard stood under the canopy next to two end tables and a dresser. There was even a hat stand holding two straw hats in the corner. Sparky lay at the foot of the bed, asleep in probably the most comfortable place he'd been for weeks.

Anna patted the worn patchwork quilt on the bed. "I wanted to be a support for Mary Anne, and it felt like cheating to sleep in the house. Sarah finally gave in and had her boys fetch our bedroom. They left the rug and the calendar. I can't see that we need them."

Felty had to be elated. Camping had not been good to either of Mary Anne's grandparents. Anna and Felty had been sleeping in the house ever since the motor home had almost driven away with them last week. Anna was afraid of being kidnapped, or worse, rolling all over the county in a driverless vehicle. But she hadn't been satisfied with staying in the house long term.

"Of course, we have to share our room with Mary Anne's quilt, but there's plenty of space. Our only problem will be when they need to use the canopy for the Labor Day auction. As long as it doesn't rain that day, we should be fine to sleep under the stars."

Jethro jumped when a plump white chicken flapped out from under the bed, squawked in panic, and ran out of the canopy in the direction of the barn.

Even in the dim light, Anna's eyes twinkled. "I was wonderful worried about our chickens. Pine and Johnny brought all seventeen of them. It took four boxes. They're such dears."

"They put the chickens in boxes?"

Anna nodded. "Cardboard with air holes in the top. But I'm afraid we've lost at least

354

three of them. Noah's dog, Chester, chased them into the woods. Lord willing, they'll come back. If not, you might have a flock of wild chickens in your woods come next spring."

More likely he'd have a flock of dead chickens come next spring. Chester was an obedient dog, but Jethro couldn't blame him if he had an appetite for chickens. And then there were the foxes. There was a reason people had chicken coops. Jethro wouldn't have told Anna that for the world. She was so happy to have her very own bedroom. She might not even notice the chickens disappearing during the night.

Bob Hennig had come last Saturday to get his motor home. Jethro had shown him the damage done by the two brick walls, but Bob had said it would be easy to fix with some sandpaper and touch-up paint. He didn't even seem troubled that Jethro had taken his RV to Shawano and back. "Motor homes are for driving," he had said. He probably wouldn't have been so cheerful about it if he had seen the way Jethro drove, but what he didn't know wouldn't hurt him.

Anna hooked her arm around Jethro's elbow. "Now, dear, we've spent enough time looking at my new bedroom. We don't want to miss the birthday party. Mary Anne is making her famous rat-a-tat-two-ee. It's some kind of soup, but you don't have to worry about a thing because it doesn't have rats in it. Felty is grilling hamburgers, and Lia made six loaves of honey wheat bread. She even brought raspberry jam. Sarah and her boys cut fruit all afternoon." She pointed to a huge bowl of watermelon and strawberries sitting on Jethro's card table.

Jethro would trust Sarah Beachy with his life, but he had seen the dirt under Pine's fingernails when he'd handed him the tray with Mary Anne's birthday present. Jethro wasn't going to take any risks with that fruit salad. "Looks delicious," he said. Should he warn Anna?

"Lily baked three different kinds of cake, and I made a special treat just for Mary Anne."

Jethro tried not to look concerned. It usually didn't turn out well when Anna tried to make something special. "What treat did you make?"

Anna clapped her hands. "I've only partway made it. You hollow out a grapefruit and pour cake batter into the rind, then you wrap the rind in tinfoil and set it in the coals to cook. It's her own personal vanilla birthday cake with just a hint of grapefruit flavor. She's going to be so excited."

Jethro smiled. It didn't sound too bad, especially because Anna had used a cake mix. Things usually went awry when she tried to concoct her own recipes.

Anna patted his arm. "Do you have a birthday present for Mary Anne? You're not going to make any headway without a birthday present."

"*Jah,* I've got one, and she's going to love it."

"*Gute.* I think I might have thought about giving up on you if you hadn't brought a present. I can work with *thick,* but I can't work with *completely oblivious.*"

Jethro followed Anna out from under the canopy, and she immediately led him to the *Englischers* sitting on the Green Bay Packer chairs. The two women smiled at Jethro as if they already liked him. Maybe they wouldn't be so friendly if they knew who he was. The man seemed a little more reserved, but not inclined to dislike anybody. "Jethro, this is Alice Swanson and Dennis and Judy VanderSleet from the senior center. They've decided to move into the woods with us for a few days."

"I brought three of my grandchildren with me," Alice said, waving her hand in the direction of the campfire. "They wanted an adventure."

Jethro tried not to act anything other than happy that more people had moved into the woods, but he'd already swallowed so much pride, his gut was bulging. It was nice that people wanted to support Mary Anne, but it was almost as if they were saying, *We've decided to camp here because you're a rotten person.* There was only so much humiliation a man could bear.

Jethro swallowed yet another lump of pride in his throat. "It is wonderful *gute* to meet you. I'm glad Mary Anne has *gute* friends. If we get any more campers, we'll be able to start our own town."

Alice laughed, and despite his distress, Jethro immediately liked her. She laughed like she meant it, not just because she was trying to be nice. "You're not as bad as I thought you'd be, Jethro."

Jethro tried to ignore the weight pressing into his chest. *Jah.* Alice, Dennis and Judy, Sarah Beachy and her sons, Mary Anne's cousins — they all thought he was a monster.

Alice leaned to her right so she could see past Jethro. "He's not so bad, Mary Anne," she called.

Jethro turned and caught sight of Mary Anne. Finally. She was tending to five Dutch ovens standing in a row a dozen feet away from the nearest tent and down the slope from the barn — in almost the same place Anna and Felty's RV used to be. Gray and smoking charcoal briquettes surrounded the Dutch ovens, with several briquettes sitting on top of each lid.

Mary Anne held a lid lifter in each hand and wore the prettiest blue dress Jethro had ever seen. The color matched her eyes perfectly, and the glow of her smile took his breath away as she glanced at him. "He's not bad at all. I never said he was."

Alice raised an eyebrow. "Then why in the world are you living in a tent?"

Alice had a point there. But Mary Anne was just being kind. Jethro knew exactly what she thought of him. That she was willing to move into a tent spoke volumes about their relationship. He was hoping to change that. Soon.

Jethro strode toward Mary Anne, overjoyed just to be in her presence. He could have kicked himself for all the time he'd wasted living in the same house with her and barely even noticing. Six years ago, this beautiful, strong, feisty woman had chosen to share her life with him. If she saw fit to come back to him, he'd never take that sacrifice lightly again.

And it *was* a sacrifice, an incredible risk

for any woman to put her life in the hands of another, trusting that he would cherish and protect her and give her wings to fly. Jethro now saw her sacrifice for what it was, a sacred trust *Gotte* had given him. So far, he hadn't been doing a very *gute* job of keeping that trust.

Who was he kidding? He'd failed miserably.

"Happy Birthday, Mary Anne."

Her smile was like balm to a festering wound. "I'm *froh* you could come to my party."

"*Denki* for inviting me. If you hadn't, I think I would have been rude and invited myself. I ached all day to see you."

Was she blushing? "You always were the worst tease."

He raised his hands as if stopping traffic. "No kidding. I had to take two Motrin at lunch." He stepped over one of the hot Dutch ovens so he could be closer to her. "Can I help?"

She smiled as if she liked him near. "Give them about ten more minutes and we'll be ready, then you can help me douse the hot coals. With all *die kinner* running around, I don't want anyone to get burned."

He wanted her to smile at him like that all the time. It was time to show her the birthday present. "I . . . I got you a gift."

Her cheeks turned a darker shade of pink. "You didn't have to do that."

"There was nothing I wanted to do more." He scanned the crowd of cousins for Pine and saw him standing exactly where he had been with the rectangular casserole dish still in his hands. *Gute* boy. Sarah's sons were responsible like that. "Pine," Jethro called, waving his hands to get the boy's attention.

Pine looked in Jethro's direction and raised the dish, as if to show he'd taken care of it just like Jethro had asked. Jethro motioned for Pine to come to him, and Pine nodded and weaved around the groups of cousins blocking his path.

Jethro couldn't contain his excitement. "Mamm and Dat and I ate Cheetos until we couldn't stand it anymore. I took Cheetos to work every day and shared them and gave the rest to Lily and Lia. I think Lia ended up burying most of her share."

Mary Anne's lips curled in amusement. "I didn't know you liked Cheetos."

He grinned. "I love Cheetos. Or I used to. I think if I give myself a year, I'll be able to bear the taste of them again." He took Mary Anne's lid lifters from her hands and set them on the ground, then entwined his fingers with hers. It felt like heaven. "*Cum.*

I'll show you."

They walked around the Dutch ovens and met Pine on the other side. Pine held out the dish for Jethro to take. Jethro took one look and gasped. He coughed. He nearly choked. "Where . . . what happened to the Cheetos?"

Pine frowned. "There were just a few leftovers in the bottom. I didn't think you'd mind if I ate them."

"You . . . you . . . *ach!*" Jethro was struck dumb. A whole week of eating crunchy Cheeto after crunchy Cheeto, feeling like his tongue was going to dry up and fall out of his mouth, expecting to give himself a heart attack with all the sodium he'd consumed — not to mention the orange-stained fingers from handling about three thousand Cheetos. On Monday, Jethro's *Englisch* friend Randall had asked him if he had jaundice. That stuff wouldn't completely come off without fingernail polish remover.

Gone. It was all gone.

Pine must have guessed he had done something wrong — probably by the look of abject despair on Jethro's face. He grimaced. "I . . . I'm sorry, Jethro. I thought you needed the pan for dinner. I wanted to do you a favor by eating the leftover Cheetos."

Jethro's knees got wobbly. He sank to the ground and sat cross-legged, as if he'd chosen where he was going to stay for the rest of the party. He very nearly crushed one of Anna's chickens on the way down, and it squawked and flapped its wings and ran into the woods. For sure and certain there'd be another dead chicken by morning.

Mary Anne leaned over and put a hand on his shoulder. "Are you okay, Jethro?"

That present would have made Mary Anne fall in love with him again. But he couldn't very well tell her that. He nodded and forced a pleasant look onto his face. He didn't want Mary Anne to know how upset he was, but a smile was impossible. He propped his elbows on his knees and sort of cradled his face in his hands.

Mary Anne took the casserole dish from Pine. "It's okay, Pine. I think he's just a little ferhoodled."

A lot ferhoodled.

Pine gave Jethro a look of uncertainty, shrugged his shoulders, and ambled away as quickly as he could while pretending he didn't have anywhere in particular to go.

Cradling the empty casserole dish in her arms, Mary Anne sat down next to Jethro in the dirt and nudged him with her elbow.

A sympathetic smile played at her lips. "So, Pine ate my birthday present?"

"It wasn't his fault. I should have told him not to eat it."

"Nobody can resist a Cheeto."

He gazed sadly at the dish in Mary Anne's arms. The only thing left of his present was a piece of paper towel cut perfectly to fit the bottom of the dish. A slight dusting of cheese and oil was the only clue to where each of his special Cheetos had been placed. He wanted to growl like a bear and then crawl in his tent and sleep for a week.

She tilted her head to meet his eye. "Do you want to tell me about my present?"

Jethro heaved a great sigh. "It doesn't matter."

"It looks like it might have been *wunderbarr.*"

Jethro cracked a weak smile. It was a *gute* sign that she was trying to cheer him up. "Thirty-one bags of Cheetos."

Her eyes grew wide. "Thirty-one?"

"You like potato chips shaped like flowers. I thought you might like a collection of shaped Cheetos."

She grinned and pointed to the oil spot in the upper right corner of the paper towel. "What was this one shaped like?"

He rubbed his fingers along the whiskers

on his face. "The president of the United States. I found a picture at the library."

She pointed to a stain of cheese powder. "And this one?"

"A giraffe. I almost ate it before looking closely."

"A giraffe? That would have been something to see. I found a rock once that looked exactly like a beaver."

He touched another oil spot. "This one looked like a rock. And this one was a man with his arms outstretched. It would have made you smile."

"It makes me smile just thinking about it."

"I found the letters *T* and *S* and *Y,* but the *Y* also looked like a tree. I thought you would want to decide what it was."

"It could have been two things at once." A bright light glowed behind her eyes. "How long have you been working on this?"

He couldn't remember the exact day he'd started, but he could still taste Cheetos every time he brushed his teeth. "A few weeks. The *Y* was the first one I found. It was in the second bag I opened. I thought it would make you happy."

Mary Anne gave him the most dazzling smile he had ever seen, turning him inside out and upside down and rendering him unable to remember his own name. What would that smile have been like if Pine hadn't eaten the Cheetos? His heart probably would have jumped right out of his chest. "I love it, Jethro. It's the best birthday present anyone has ever given me."

"But Pine ate it before you could see it."

"It doesn't matter. You wanted to make me happy. I can't believe you spent all that time." She looked away, as if something by her tent had caught her eye. "And money."

He wrapped his fingers around her wrist. "I would spend every last dime on Cheetos if that's what you wanted. Even the flaming hot ones, though my throat was numb for days."

She grinned even as her gaze lingered on his hand. "What about Ruffles? They're my favorite."

Jethro chuckled. "Okay, but you have to spend your own money on pork rinds."

Mary Anne nodded and giggled at the same time. "Agreed."

"You two comfortable?"

Jethro and Mary Anne looked up. Sarah Beachy stood in front of them with her hands on her hips. She didn't look all that cheerful.

"Comfortable enough," Jethro said. Why was Sarah irritated? If anyone should be irritated it should be Jethro. Sarah's son had eaten all his Cheetos.

Sarah huffed out an annoyed breath. "There are forty hungry people waiting on the rata — the rata — the soup, and Mary Anne is playing in the dirt."

Even though it had been outdoors around a campfire and the air had gotten chilly when the sun went down, it really had been a nice birthday party. Neither of Jethro's parents nor Willie Jay had said one word to Mary Anne besides "Happy Birthday," and almost everyone liked the ratatouille. It had too many green things in it for the young ones, but the adults finished off every last bite. Lily had gone home this morning and made three cakes: a German chocolate, a pineapple coconut, and an Oreo cookie cake. Mary Anne had gotten a sliver of each.

She sat in her camp chair, because Mandy wouldn't think of letting her do the dishes, and tucked her fluffy blanket around her chin. It was really Jethro's fluffy blanket, but he had laid it over her lap as soon as the sun had dipped below the horizon.

Mary Anne gazed into the fire, trying to make sense of her swirling emotions. Flames licked at a single piece of firewood that hadn't yet crumbled into the glowing coals.

Judy and Dennis sat in the chairs across from her, but Alice had gone off to put her grandchildren to bed. Most of the other cousins had gone home or back to their tents. Mandy and Jethro finished up the dishes while Lois, Chris, Willie Jay, and Mary Anne's grandparents sat around the campfire. They didn't have any children who needed tending to, and Jethro's parents seemed determined to outlast Mammi and Dawdi at the party.

Were they planning to pounce after Mammi and Dawdi went to bed?

Ach, vell. It *had* been a nice party. Maybe she should be the one to go to bed first.

"Now, Mary Anne," Mammi said, struggling up from her chair. "I secretly made you one more special treat for your birthday."

Mary Anne pretended to be enthusiastic, even though she'd already had three pieces of birthday cake and even though Mammi was the one who had made the special treat. It was a challenge just keeping Mammi's food down in the first place. "You didn't need to do that. I got three birthday cakes."

Mammi beamed like a lantern. "I know. But this is going to be the very best one." She shuffled to the table and found an oven mitt and the tongs, then went to the fire

368

and pulled a tinfoil package the size of a softball from the coals. "Hold this, dear," Mammi said. She slid the oven mitt onto Mary Anne's outstretched hand, unclasped the tongs, and dropped the tinfoil ball into Mary Anne's oven mitt. It was surprisingly heavy.

Mary Anne didn't dare ask what it was. Surely Mammi hadn't roasted a cow kidney or a soccer ball. Soccer balls were made of leather, which was technically edible. She wouldn't put it past Mammi to try to cook anything if she had a mind to. "*Denki,* Mammi." If she sat there holding it long enough, maybe someone would divert Mammi's attention, and Mary Anne would be able to get rid of it.

Of course, this was just wishful thinking. Mammi stood over her, clicking her tongs open and shut and looking as eager as a beaver under a pine tree. "Open it from the top, dear. Pull back the tinfoil, but be careful because I don't want you to burn your fingers. And don't turn it upside down. There's no telling what might happen."

Mary Anne didn't want to guess what might happen, so she cautiously held the bottom of the ball in her oven mitt and peeled back about seven layers of tinfoil. Steam rose from whatever was in there, and she caught the aroma of vanilla and citrus. "It smells delicious, Mammi," she said. At least that was true.

Mammi clapped the tongs together like hands. "*Ach!* I just knew it would turn out. I'm a very experienced cook, but I've never made something like this before."

Mary Anne finished pulling back the tinfoil to reveal what looked like a grapefruit with batter oozing out of the hole sliced off the top of the rind.

"It's called 'Cake in a Rind,' " Mammi said, beaming from ear to ear. "You mix up some cake batter, hollow out a grapefruit, and pour the batter into the rind. Then you put it in the coals and bake for ten minutes." She furrowed her brow. "Or did the directions say thirty minutes? *Ach, vell,* it doesn't matter now. It seems to be done."

Not exactly. The edges were flaky, but batter seeped out of the hole at the top of the grapefruit when Mary Anne gave it a slight squeeze. Nothing like a whole grapefruit full of raw batter to make your stomach want to roll over itself.

Mary Anne pasted what smile she could onto her mouth. Maybe Mammi would go to bed in her nice new bedroom before Mary Anne ate her special treat. Maybe Mammi wouldn't care to watch her eat every bite.

"What a brilliant idea," Judy said. "Dennis, we need to try that with our grandchildren. They'd love it."

"That looks very good," Lois said. Willie Jay and Chris didn't seem to have an opinion.

Dawdi leaned back in his camp chair and stroked his beard. "Annie is the best cook in the world. The king of Mexico hasn't never eaten hotcakes as good as hers."

Mammi pulled her chair closer to Mary Anne's and sat down. "Take a taste and tell me what you think."

"She needs a spoon." With two spoons in his hand, Jethro pulled his chair even closer than Mammi's. He handed Mary Anne one spoon and raised the second spoon in the air. "Can I have a bite?"

Mary Anne curled one side of her mouth. Jethro was so kind. "Of course."

"Now, Jethro," Mammi said. "It's Mary Anne's birthday cake. Let her eat it."

Desperation bubbled up inside her. If Jethro ate some, she might just be able to get through this without hurting Mammi's feelings. "But I want to share it with him, Mammi. He gave me the most *wunderbarr* birthday present, and he . . . he's my husband, after all."

Mammi seemed overjoyed to find out that Jethro was Mary Anne's husband, or maybe she was just overjoyed that Mary Anne would admit it. She smiled so hard, her wrinkles piled up like gathered fabric. "Of course he's your husband. Let him eat as much as you want."

Mary Anne glanced at Jethro. His eyes were all soft and mushy, as if she'd given him back his two hundred dollars plus a new tackle box. Why did he have to look at her like that? It had been a perfectly fine birthday party. She didn't need him to complicate things with his unmistakable admiration.

So he loved her. Why should she care?

Her throat tightened, and she could barely draw a breath. She cared, all right. She cared more than she wanted to admit, but she wouldn't fall in love with Jethro again. She wouldn't. He'd eaten his weight in Cheetos and helped her plant flowers, but no matter how kind or lovable or good looking he was, she wasn't about to rearrange her plans to include him.

He nudged his foot against hers, and she immediately forgot every last plan she had. She hadn't sought his touch for years, but suddenly there it was, the deep longing to savor his lips against hers and feel his strong, capable arms around her. She shouldn't need him like this, not when the life she'd always wanted was within her reach. But with his foot grazing hers, she found it impossible to talk herself out of him.

"I know Jethro is your husband, Mary Anne," Mammi said. "But I still think you should take the first bite."

Mary Anne pried her gaze from Jethro's mouth. "Okay." She skimmed a little dough off the top and put it in her mouth. It wasn't bad if you liked undercooked cake. Some people loved licking the batter out of the bowl. *"Appeditlich,"* she said.

Jethro grinned at Mammi and took the entire grapefruit from Mary Anne. It had cooled down enough that he didn't burn himself. He scooped a generous, dripping spoonful right from the heart of the grapefruit and shoved it into his mouth. Mary Anne could almost hear it slide down his throat.

Mammi's smile grew wider and her wrinkles grew bunchier. "Now, Jethro. Save a little for Mary Anne."

Jethro tilted the grapefruit so Mary Anne could stick her spoon in and get a little bite, little enough to lick it off the spoon with her tongue. Jethro winked at her and ate another giant spoonful of goo. Mary Anne was so grateful, she could have kissed him right in front of Judy, Dennis, and the in-laws.

Jethro ended up eating nearly the whole thing, while Mary Anne got away with three piddly bites. Her stomach was more grateful than Jethro would ever know. He had always been thoughtful that way, even though she hadn't seen that side of him for several months.

Mammi smiled and stifled a yawn. "I suppose that's the end of the party."

"It was wonderful *gute,* Mammi. *Denki.*"

"The rat-a-tat stew was delicious, and Sarah was especially glad it didn't have rats in it."

Judy stood and folded up her chair. "You could serve that ratatouille at a fancy French restaurant, Mary Anne. It was that good. Your grandma isn't the only one who knows a thing or two about cooking."

Jethro gathered up the rest of the trash and took it to the barn, where they stored it every night. They hadn't seen a bear yet, but they didn't want to attract any if they could help it. The chickens were going to be enough of a headache.

Mammi stirred the coals while Dawdi

fetched some water from the hose to douse the fire.

"*Denki* for inviting us to your party. I know you didn't want to." How had Lois managed to slip into Jethro's chair without Mary Anne noticing?

"You're welcome," Mary Anne said. She wasn't going to deny that she hadn't wanted her in-laws to come to the party. She didn't want her in-laws in camp at all, but they had behaved themselves until now, so she couldn't really complain. She glanced in Willie Jay's direction. He sat on the edge of his seat, bouncing one knee up and down as if he couldn't contain his indignation much longer. Mary Anne sincerely hoped he wouldn't explode. Not on her birthday.

Lois glanced in the direction Jethro had gone, then snatched Mary Anne's hand and squeezed it like a lifeline. "Mary Anne, I would never say anything to upset you, but I'm begging you to move back home. Your husband needs you. You must see how terribly he is suffering."

Mary Anne pressed her lips together. She didn't want to have this conversation, especially now, when her heart had softened toward Jethro. He *did* love her and he *was* suffering, but Lois had no call to bring it up tonight.

Mary Anne tried to stand up and escape, but Lois just squeezed tighter, like a dying woman grasping for air. "Mary Anne, I know life with Jethro has been hard. He's like his *fater,* and I know how hard that can be to live with. But you don't give up on someone just because it gets hard. You gave up too easy. You moved out instead of staying and doing the hard work you needed to do to save your marriage. It was the same with the *buplie.* After the doctor told you that you couldn't have another one, you gave up even trying. You could have at least given the doctors more of a chance before depriving Jethro of a child."

Mary Anne's tongue dried out as if she'd swallowed a bag of sand. Of course Lois blamed her for the *buplie.* Lois loved Jethro too much to ever believe it was his fault. "How . . . how can you say that? You know very well I didn't give up on a *buplie.* Chris told Jethro that you had discussed it and had decided it was a waste of money to keep trying. Chris said it was better not to spend the money on doctors and tests, especially when it wasn't likely we'd ever get pregnant anyway. Jethro gave up. Not me." Mary Anne shut her mouth before her voice betrayed her. She had to blink rapidly just to keep the tears from falling.

Her hopes for a *buplie* had been dashed because Jethro and his parents had agreed it would cost too much to try for one. Gruyère cheese was too much money. Paint was too much money. Flowers were too much money. A *buplie* was too much money. Was it any wonder Mary Anne hated the very word?

Jethro had put a price tag on her happiness and decided it was too expensive.

Lois's eyebrows inched closer and closer together. She loosened her grip around Mary Anne's fingers. "What are you talking about?"

"It's always about how much a thing costs." They had crushed every last hope Mary Anne had cherished.

Lois stood up as if she couldn't contain whatever emotion was bottled inside her. "I never said that."

"Never said what?" Jethro had come back from the barn, and he stood ten feet from the fire as stiff as a post, his gaze darting between his *mamm* and Mary Anne. For sure and certain he was on his guard — from his *mamm* or his *fraa*, Mary Anne couldn't tell. "Mamm," he said. "It's time for you to go back to the tent."

Lois jabbed a finger in her husband's direction. "What did you do in my name,

377

Chris Neuenschwander? What did you tell our son?"

Chris sat behind and to Mary Anne's left so she couldn't see his face, and she wasn't about to turn around to look.

"What are you so worked up about, woman?" Chris said. Mary Anne had always been grateful that Jethro had never talked to her that way. Chris sounded as if he didn't give Lois credit for a brain in her head.

Lois didn't back down, not an inch. Mary Anne had always admired her tenacity, except when Mary Anne was the recipient of her sharp tongue and stubborn persistence. "Did you advise Jethro not to spend the money on infertility treatments?"

Mary Anne heard Chris shift on his camp chair. "The doctors charge an arm and a leg and make impossible promises."

Lois's breathing became fast and labored. "Four years ago I told you to take the three thousand dollars out of our account and give it to Jethro for infertility treatments."

Mary Anne's heart pounded so hard she could feel her pulse in her teeth. Lois had wanted to give them three thousand dollars? Hadn't she thought trying to get pregnant was a waste of money?

"You wanted to give us money?" Jethro said.

Lois ignored Jethro. Her focus was squarely on Chris. "You told me Jethro refused it. You insisted that I never talk about it again. You said I'd hurt Mary Anne's feelings."

Lois had no doubt gotten the attention of everyone trying to sleep in a tent, all the nearby dogs, and the chickens roaming the woods. Mammi stopped stirring the smoldering coals and pointed her stick in Lois's direction. It was still smoking. "You tell him, Lois. It's time to get to the bottom of this."

"What did you do, Chris?" Lois asked again.

Chris muttered something Mary Anne couldn't understand.

"Can you speak up, Chris?" Lois said. It wasn't a request.

Chris hissed his annoyance. "One of us had to be sensible. We needed that money for emergencies."

Mary Anne wouldn't have been surprised to see daggers shooting out of Lois's eyes. She seemed to get closer to Chris even though she hadn't taken a step toward him. "You told Jethro treatments were a waste of money?"

Chris grunted. "He agreed with me. In

379

vitro, or whatever you call it, costs twenty thousand dollars."

Lois turned on Jethro, as if he was her worst enemy. "You agreed with him?"

Jethro's expression was a mixture of shame and horror. "*Jah.* I . . . I just thought . . ."

"You just thought what? That your *fraa* would forgive you for loving Mammon more than her?"

Jethro searched Mary Anne's face, but she wasn't sure what he was looking for. Compassion maybe? She pressed her fingers to her forehead, but there was no stopping the headache that had already started.

Jethro took a step back as if she had shoved him, even though she was a dozen feet away. "The miscarriage alone cost two thousand dollars. Dat and I agreed that the doctors would bleed us dry before we ever got a *buplie.*"

Lois folded her arms across her chest. "And what did Mary Anne want?"

Jethro lowered his eyes. "I didn't ask her."

Lois was like a tornado trapped in a canning jar. "You didn't ask her?"

It felt as if a shard of glass lodged right between Mary Anne's ribs. To Jethro, she was an inconvenience, someone who spent money they didn't have and couldn't even give him a *buplie*. At times, he hadn't even seen her as a person.

"I'm sorry," Jethro whispered.

"Sorry won't keep you warm on a cold night." Lois's tornado seemed to come to rest. She huffed out a breath and dropped her hands to her sides. "Felty, could you help me with my tent?"

"For sure and certain, Lois. Are you calling it quits?"

Lois shook her head. "I'm moving to Mary Anne's side of the camp. Chris, you'll have to sleep in Jethro's tent."

"Now, Lois," Chris said, his voice rising to a whine. "Don't be like that. If you're going to move, at least let me come with you. I can protect you from bears."

Lois shot him a red-hot glare. "Don't bother. I'd rather be eaten."

"But Lois, you said yourself it's wicked for a wife to leave her husband."

Lois nodded. "I did say that, and as soon as you take the beam out of your own eye, I'll see what I can do about moving back in. Until then, you can make your own breakfast."

Willie Jay uttered the first words Mary Anne had heard from him all night. "Don't make a rash decision just because you're angry, Mamm. You don't want to lose your

381

eternal reward. Mary Anne has poisoned enough of the family already."

"Shut your mouth, Willie Jay," Jethro snapped. Mary Anne held her breath. She had never heard Jethro talk to his *bruder* that way.

To his credit, Willie Jay shut up. Maybe he figured he couldn't chastise Mary Anne without dragging his *mamm* into it. And Willie Jay wasn't likely to take on his *mater.*

Without another word, Lois stormed away, no doubt wanting to get her tent moved before Chris or Willie Jay tried to stop her. Chris jumped to his feet and jogged after her. Willie Jay growled, took down their camp chairs, and lumbered back to his campsite.

Jethro hadn't moved for a good three minutes. She wished he'd stop staring at her. "Mary Anne, I want to explain . . ."

"Ach," Mammi said, waving the smoldering stick in his direction. "It's too late for explanations, Jethro. Go back to your tent and think on your sins. Everything will look better in the morning."

"But . . ."

"Don't you worry. Felty and I will put out the fire and see that Mary Anne gets to bed at a decent time. Dennis is going to teach us how to do landscapes tomorrow. Mary

382

Anne has been looking forward to it."

Vell, she *had* been looking forward to painting tomorrow, but right now, she couldn't even muster enough enthusiasm to stand up.

Jethro hesitated, seemingly a bit surprised at how quickly Mammi had dismissed him. "But . . ."

"You've always been a little thick, Jethro," Mammi said, making her voice louder, as if hoping he'd understand her better. "I tell you, it's time to go to bed. Things always look better in the morning, and you've got to find your *dat* a place to sleep."

Jethro looked at Mary Anne as if he wanted her to save him, but she couldn't bear the thought of trying to come up with one more pleasant thing to say to him tonight. Something painful flickered in his eyes, but he seemed to give up whatever he was struggling against. He walked toward his campsite, passing within three feet of her, but she wouldn't look at him. Her *mammi* was wonderful wise, but Mary Anne couldn't imagine how things would look better in the morning. Even with Mammi and Dawdi standing there, she felt more alone than she had ever felt in her life.

Dawdi handed Mammi a bucket of water, and she poured it over the fire. The coals hissed, and a cloud of smoke rose into the air. "Well, now, what an exciting birthday party," Mammi said. "All things considered, I think that went very well. I hope you had a *gute* time, Mary Anne."

Mary Anne smiled as best she could. Lord willing, it was too dark for Mammi to notice the tears glistening in her eyes or her hands gripping the armrests for dear life.

Mandy would say Lois had ruined the party, but Mary Anne couldn't be anything but grateful. Just as Mary Anne had been wavering, Lois had reminded Mary Anne why she would never go back.

It was the best gift anyone could have given her.

CHAPTER FIFTEEN

Mary Anne woke with a start and sat straight up from her pillow. Had she heard something? She rubbed her hand across her forehead and tried to calm her racing heart. She'd been dreaming that Willie Jay had locked her in the Porta-Potty and was singing "Das Loblied" to her at the top of his lungs. She couldn't decide if she considered it a nightmare or just an irritation. Irritation was often the emotion she felt for Willie Jay.

She pulled her feet from the sleeping bag and swung them onto the ground. It was pitch black inside her tent — no doubt pitch black outside as well. She had slept lighter than ever since the RV incident, and something had for sure and certain woken her up. At least this time she hoped she wouldn't need to risk her life chasing whatever it was down the lane.

She stilled herself and let the noises of the night envelop her. A light rain pitter-pattered against the tent, but she didn't think that had woken her up. She could also hear Dawdi snoring softly under his canopy in his nice, comfy bed, but his snoring had become a part of the night sounds, like crickets chirping or the buzzy little song of the sparrow. She heard nothing out of the ordinary. It must have been the dream.

Trying to still her breathing, she listened carefully one more time. There it was, softer and coming from the direction of the barn, and it sounded suspiciously like a bear eating chickens. Jethro had closed the barn up for the night. There wasn't any possible way a bear could have gotten in, was there? Maybe it wasn't a bear. It sort of sounded like Jethro trying to imitate a bear.

Oy, anyhow.

She knew exactly what she was hearing.

With a sigh, she laid her head back onto her pillow. She should just ignore it. It would pass soon enough.

Probably.

But it sounded bad.

Growling, she sat up and turned on her lantern. Jethro would never suspect she had neglected him if she went back to sleep, but because this whole thing was her fault in the first place, she couldn't be so hard-hearted. She unzipped the tent flap and stuck the lantern out first to check for bears, foxes, or raccoons. Were there porcupines in these woods? There were definitely badgers that could sink their teeth into your ankle and never let go. All the badgers seemed to be elsewhere, and she didn't see so much as a bear track. She tiptoed across the clearing and up to the side door of the barn to the bathroom. She knocked softly.

"Uhhh," Jethro groaned. It sounded like he was on the floor, maybe with his head hovering over the toilet.

Mary Anne didn't wait to be invited in. She opened the door, stepped inside the small space, and closed the door behind her. No use waking the rest of the camp if she could help it. Jethro was indeed kneeling on the floor with his forearm draped across the toilet seat and his head resting on his forearm. "Did I wake you?"

His whole body convulsed, and he pointed his face toward the toilet. Mary Anne knelt down, braced his forehead with her right hand, and laid her left hand on the back of his neck as he retched into the toilet. It was something she'd done for him a handful of times over the years, like her *dat* had done for her when she was a little girl. She'd always found it comforting when someone held her forehead when she threw up.

She waited for him to finish, then handed him a piece of toilet paper to wipe his mouth. *"Denki,"* he said, panting and swiping his sleeve across his forehead. "I think I ate too much Cake in a Rind."

"I don't wonder that you did." She smiled at him. "I hope you know I'm very grateful."

"I saw your face turn a slight shade of green when you unwrapped your special treat. I knew you didn't want to hurt your *mammi*'s feelings." His tongue lolled out of his mouth, and he lunged for the toilet just in time. She placed her palm on his forehead again to give him some support. He coughed and spit, then sat down with his back against the wall and his legs splayed out in front of him. "I hope you don't mind that I'm using the wrong bathroom. The thought of using the Porta-Potty to throw up is enough to make me throw up."

"You're welcome to use this bathroom any time you want for throwing up. I wouldn't set foot inside that potty thing."

The thought of a Porta-Potty must have hit him hard. He threw up again, this time with a loud heave. Jethro had always been a loud thrower-upper. No wonder she'd heard him over the Willie Jay dream.

He finished, flushed the toilet, and sat

back. "*Denki* for holding my forehead. It can't be pleasant for you, but I always liked it when you did."

"I *should* be holding your forehead. It would have been me getting sick if you hadn't eaten the whole grapefruit cake."

He pressed his fingers into his shoulder muscles. "I think it was the eggs Anna put in the batter. There's no telling what those chickens have gotten into since your grandparents have been camping."

"I don't wonder but that those chickens won't be with us much longer."

Jethro leaned his head against the wall behind him. "There was a trail of black and white feathers between the Porta-Potty and Mandy's tent. I think Chester has a taste for Plymouth Rock hens."

"Oh dear."

"And one of them laid an egg directly under your quilting frames. I put it in the fridge in the house."

"I don't know if we dare eat it." It looked as if maybe Jethro was finished throwing up for a few minutes. Mary Anne got off her knees and sat down on the bathroom floor, resting her back against the door so she was facing Jethro. She sat cross-legged, while he had his legs stretched out in front of him.

He pushed himself up so he sat taller and

more firmly against the wall, then studied her face. She didn't like it when he looked at her that way, as if every hope and dream he had could be found in her eyes if he just looked hard enough. "I wanted to protect you."

"From Mammi's grapefruit cake?"

He gave her a wane smile. "*Nae . . .* well, *jah,* but I mean before. After you lost the *buplie.* I didn't ask you about doing more treatments because I thought I was protecting you."

Mary Anne did her best to breathe past the dark patch of mold that had been growing in her chest for almost four years. "Maybe, Jethro. Maybe you talked yourself into believing that." She paused to keep her emotions in check. "But I never did believe. It wasn't about anything more than money." She pressed her lips together. The words tasted that much more bitter because she'd chewed on them for a long time, but at least she had finally spit them out. Jethro was going to hear the hard and unpleasant truth.

He pressed his hand to his forehead, as if he were trying to knead the memories from his brain. "I've been so blind, Mary Anne. My regrets feel like a pile of stones pressing down on my head. They've very nearly buried me. Believe me, I know how deep my sins are and how far I need to go to get back to you." He scrubbed his fingers through his hair. "I *have* used money as a way to control you. It was easier to tell you that we couldn't afford something than to beg you not to try so hard. I couldn't bear to see you wear yourself out with all your grief. After you lost the baby, for weeks you stayed up all night long scrubbing floors and repainting walls and making quilts. You tiled our bathroom because I didn't like the linoleum. You spent entire days cooking gourmet meals. You wore yourself out."

"I knew how disappointed you were. I was trying to make it up to you."

He heaved a sigh. "I know that now. You were trying to be the perfect *fraa*. But I just wanted the woman I'd fallen in love with."

"You told me not to cry."

He winced, as if she'd poked a stick into his chest. "It was selfish, but I hated to see you cry. I hated the thought that you were in pain. I talked myself into believing that if you weren't crying, you must be okay. Looking back, I see how wonderful stupid I was. I didn't want both of us to suffer. I thought I was bearing your pain as well as mine just by wishing it was so. As long as you weren't crying, I told myself that you were okay."

"But it wasn't about my pain or your pain.

391

We could have kept trying for a baby, Jethro."

"I told myself I was protecting you, but maybe it was more about my selfishness than anything else. Dat said that those treatments hardly ever worked and would only give us false hope. I didn't want to see you crumble every time we got bad news from the doctor. I wanted to protect you from that horrible roller coaster. I was afraid it would destroy you, so I told you that we couldn't afford infertility treatments and that was that. I thought it would be like ripping off a Band-Aid instead of prolonging the pain."

She wanted to throw something at him, but the toilet paper was out of her reach. "How could you?" she whispered. If she tried for anything louder, she'd probably end up yelling her lungs out. Mammi and Dawdi were bound to wake up.

"I should have consulted you. I should have trusted our love for each other. I should have trusted you. The Mary Anne I married was feisty and determined. I forgot that, because I was so afraid you'd break."

"I did. I moved out."

"*Nae*, you knew you would break if you didn't move out. It was the bravest thing I've ever seen anyone do."

She dared to look into his eyes. He wasn't trying to soften her with flattery or say something he didn't really believe. For some strange reason, his praise made her feel as light as a chicken feather. He didn't hate her for moving out. Maybe she wasn't such a disappointment to him after all. "I was suffocating."

His face was as pale as a frost-covered sidewalk. "I'm sorry, Mary Anne. I did everything wrong because I loved myself more than I loved you. When you first moved out, you took the blame for everything — said that you were the wicked one. It irritated me so much because deep down I knew I was the one who did this to you. It's no one's fault but my own."

She'd been waiting to hear those words for weeks. He didn't blame her anymore. It felt like shrugging off a winter coat in the summertime. *"Denki,"* she said, her voice cracking in a dozen different places.

He must have realized she wasn't inclined to say anything else. "I love you, Mary Anne. Do you know that I love you?"

Unable to trust her voice, she nodded. She didn't have the heart to tell him that his love didn't change anything. She wasn't going back to him. He thought he loved her now, but she would never believe that he'd had a permanent change of heart. How long would it take for him to fall back into his old ways? How long before she disappointed him again? How long before he told her to stop buying artichokes and hummus? She didn't have the strength to leave him twice. This was it. This was the end.

Her heart pounded in open rebellion. *Ach!* Despite all her resistance, she couldn't deny that she loved Jethro. She had tried to talk herself out of it, but he had bought thirty-one bags of Cheetos for her sake, and he was sitting on the floor befriending a toilet because he'd eaten the cake meant for her. She could picture her *mamm* shaking a finger in her direction. *For goodness sake, Mary Anne. Are you too stubborn to offer your own husband some forgiveness?*

Mamm always said that was what marriage was. Day-by-day, minute-by-minute forgiveness. And a lot of hard work. The trick for Mary Anne was in deciding if all the hard work was worth the trouble.

She slumped her shoulders. "What does it matter, Jethro?" she said, a part of her longing for him to talk her into it. She was so lonely and so confused. And so tired of camping.

Concern flooded his expression as he lunged forward, and she thought he might try to grab her hand until he reached for the toilet, making it just in time before he threw up again.

His sudden nausea couldn't have come at a better time. It saved her from having to look into those dark eyes and reject him yet again, or maybe saved her from having to make a decision she wasn't ready to make.

She wanted to be sure, and tonight she was unsure of everything. She needed more time. Praise the Lord, Jethro was in no condition to persuade her. Every decision had to be on her terms and no one else's.

She'd never been more grateful for disorderly chickens, raw eggs, or Mammi's Cake in a Rind.

Things would look better in the morning. Mammi had said so herself.

CHAPTER SIXTEEN

Jethro's whistling had stopped. It wasn't necessarily because he was in the depths of despair, but he wasn't deliriously happy either. Like as not, he was too busy thinking deep, deep thoughts to give any time to whistling. Since his unpleasant night spent on the floor of the bathroom, Mary Anne had pulled away from him. He couldn't blame her. She'd found out some things about him that she didn't like, and she was even more convinced that all he cared about was money.

He'd made some serious mistakes, and Mary Anne knew everything now. Had he lost her for good?

Jethro forced a puff of air from his lungs. Thoughts like that were why he wasn't whistling anymore. He waved good-bye as the van pulled away from the house, unable to remember if he'd spoken a word to anybody on the drive home from work.

He didn't want to believe that things between them were getting worse. It had been the best and the worst of birthday parties. She had liked his gift, even though she hadn't actually seen it. She had smiled as if she really liked him, maybe even loved him. When he'd eaten her cake, her smile had gotten wider. But then Mamm had said too much, and Mary Anne had retreated into a place he couldn't reach her.

Jethro trudged around to the back of the house. No matter how things turned out, it was *gute* for Mary Anne to know his reasons, even if she didn't understand them or forgive him for them. He'd told her the truth. He'd apologized. Mary Anne was the kindest woman he knew. She would forgive him with all her heart and love him if she could.

Mandy and three of Mary Anne's cousins sat under the canopy with Mamm, Anna, and Felty working on Mary Anne's latest quilt. Jethro had grown accustomed to a herd of dogs and little children running about his backyard. An occasional chicken darted in and out of the pack of *kinner.* Jethro counted at least six of Anna's seventeen chickens that had survived a week in the woods. Lord willing, Anna would still have a few birds by the end of June.

Jethro headed straight for the quilt. Mary Anne could usually be found where the quilters were, and he needed to see her like a starving man needed a chocolate peanut butter pie. Mamm was engrossed in her quilting, but she looked up long enough to smile at him. "*Gute* day at work, Jethro?"

Lia also smiled, and he might have detected a pleasant look from Mandy, as if she didn't mind that he'd come around. Sarah Beachy ignored him completely. She was in the middle of telling a story.

"He and Pine sneaked out of the house in the middle of the night to go swimming."

"*Hallo,*" Jethro said. "I'm looking for Mary Anne."

Sarah rolled her eyes. "You're always looking for Mary Anne. You're like a lovesick teenager."

Mamm paused her stitching. "Why did they sneak out to go swimming? It seems more sensible to go during the day."

Sarah grunted. "They wanted to swim naked. It's called skinny-dipping."

Lily clapped her hand over her mouth. "Oh dear."

"They got their fill of naked swimming and walked home in the pitch dark. But they couldn't hardly see a thing. Pine stepped smack-dab on a skunk, and all three of them got sprayed something wonderful. I burned all their clothes and wouldn't let them in the house for two weeks. I filled that metal washtub with tomato juice, and they all bathed in it."

"That doesn't work," Felty said, threading a needle for Anna.

Sarah shook her head. *"Nae,* it doesn't. Baking soda, hydrogen peroxide, and dish soap. They still had to bathe in that three times. But they learned their lesson. There's no hiding the stench of sin — especially from your *mater."*

Jethro tried again. "Have you seen Mary Anne?"

Lia finally took pity on him. "She has been at this quilt all day, so we made her take a break to paint with Dennis."

Jethro tried not to frown. "She's painting with Dennis?" It wasn't proper for an Amish woman to go somewhere alone with a man, but Mary Anne hadn't done much of anything lately that would be considered proper, so Jethro didn't know why it mattered. Except that it did. "Do you know where they went?"

Anna inclined her head in the direction of Jethro's campsite. "They headed that way." She drew her brows together. "I hope they're not thinking of drawing that Porta-

Potty. Dennis has strange ideas about what is pretty and what isn't. He showed me one of his drawings of a man with a hand growing out of his forehead. I hope he doesn't teach Mary Anne to draw that."

With some sense of urgency, Jethro thanked Anna and started jogging in the direction of the Porta-Potty. He didn't want to appear too eager, but he didn't like the idea of his *fraa* being alone with another man, even if Dennis was seventy years old.

Jethro's campsite was empty. Adam Wengerd had gone home. Mamm had moved to the other campsite and was happily quilting with the Helmuths. For sure and certain everyone else was working their fields so they would have something to harvest come autumn time. The guilt settled in Jethro's gut. Willie Jay wanted an opportunity to call Mary Anne to repentance, but he needed to go home. It wasn't fair to let Naoma take care of the farm by herself.

Jethro ambled around the camp in no direction in particular until something bright yellow caught his eye in the thicket just beyond the campsite. It had to be Mary Anne's canary yellow dress that Jethro loved so much. It always made her hair seem extra golden.

Mary Anne, Dennis, and — to Jethro's

relief — Judy and Alice sat in a small clearing in a semicircle around an elderberry bush in full bloom. Dennis and Mary Anne each had an easel and a blank canvas in front of them, and Mary Anne was intently studying a stem of tiny white flowers in her hand.

Jethro took gentle steps in her direction so he had a perfect view of her profile, stopping before she caught sight of him. He adored the way her nose turned up slightly, and how the freckles played like carefree *kinner* across her cheeks. A look of pure contentment rested on her face as if she hadn't a care in the world except the lovely stem of white elderberry blooms she held in her hand.

Suddenly she looked up toward the sky and laughed at something Dennis said, stealing Jethro's breath in the process. This was how he wanted to see Mary Anne forever. Untroubled, eager, and perfectly happy.

An icy hand wrapped itself around Jethro's throat. He loved Mary Anne clear down to the marrow of his bones. He wanted her to come home so badly, he could taste the desire like strong *kaffee* on his tongue.

But with the desire came the realization that as much as he wanted her to come home, he wanted even more for her to be happy.

Not only did he want it but, at that moment, he ached for it.

Mary Anne deserved to be happy, and it was clear to anyone with eyes to see that Mary Anne would be happier without him. She didn't deserve to be saddled to someone like Jethro for the rest of her life. Jethro stumbled backward as the weight of his sins finally overtook him. He was so full of error, so riddled with scars and flaws, that to make Mary Anne sacrifice her happiness for him seemed almost cruel. He wouldn't ask her to do that, no matter how much he loved her.

He staggered back to his campsite and grabbed a corner of the Porta-Potty for support. He'd always known this day would come, no matter how much he wished otherwise.

It was time to let her go.

It wasn't easy for Jethro to put his life in *Gotte*'s hands. He had always wanted things to go his way, and he'd worked very hard to see that they had. Up until a few weeks ago, Jethro had thought he'd been doing a fine job running his own life — and Mary Anne's. He had gone fishing whenever he wanted to. His wife had kept his house clean and made him delicious meals every day. Mary Anne had stopped crying and had quit experimenting with new recipes. She had stretched their grocery budget as tight as a rubber band. He'd been proud he'd taught her to be frugal and content. Except for not having children, his life had been exactly as he'd thought he wanted it. That was usually the time *Gotte* reminded people who was really in charge.

After seeing Mary Anne sitting by the elderberry bush, Jethro had driven the buggy into town as if he'd been going to a fire. He'd made a few calls at the library, and then Mary Anne's friend Pammy had helped him on the computer. He'd sworn Pammy to secrecy, glad that *Englischers* didn't seem to have a problem with that swear-not-at-all rule.

He'd just finished taking down the last of the tents except his own when Dat and Willie Jay came into camp. They stopped short and stared at the indentation in the ground where the Porta-Potty used to be.

Willie Jay seemed more confused than angry, but the anger would no doubt come. "Jethro, what is going on? Where's my tent? Where's the bathroom?"

Jethro stuffed David Eicher's tent into its

403

bag and tossed it onto the pile. Maybe Willie Jay wouldn't be angry. Everyone was sick and tired of living in tents, and the *fraaen,* even the long-suffering ones like Naoma — for sure and certain wanted their husbands home. Of course, Jethro couldn't be certain that the other *fraaen* weren't like Adam Wengerd's wife. Maybe they were all enjoying the break from their husbands. Be that as it may, Willie Jay and the others would be sleeping at home tonight. "I'm taking down the camp."

Dat's brows inched together. He might have wanted to go home, but his *fraa* was staying in a tent on the other side of the camp. Jethro didn't know how either of his parents would take it, but he was going to send Mamm home too. She and Dat would either work things out between them or they wouldn't, but Jethro couldn't help them. He had enough on his own plate, and his stomach wasn't all that strong right now.

Willie Jay hooked his thumbs under his suspenders. "You're giving up?"

"I'm letting go," Jethro said, because he didn't know how else to explain it. Letting go and letting *Gotte* take over.

"But what about Mary Anne? You're just going to let her leave you like that when you haven't done anything wrong?"

"*Ach,* I've done plenty wrong. Mary Anne was kind enough to let everyone think she was the sinner even though the fault was mine."

Willie Jay exploded like a geyser. "Your fault? Mary Anne says it was your fault, but I never thought I'd see the day when my own *bruder* believed such lies. She's the one who left her husband. She's the one who sinned against *Gotte* and the church. That has always been your problem, Jethro. You make excuses for her because you love her too much."

There wasn't anything Jethro could say that would change Willie Jay's mind. A few weeks ago, no one could have convinced Jethro of a better way either. He had learned the hard and painful way. And that's how Willie Jay and Dat would have to learn. The Neuenschwander men were stubborn like that. Jethro laid a hand on Willie Jay's shoulder. "I appreciate your support and your righteous indignation. I really do. But your family needs you. This has been a great sacrifice for you and Naoma and *die kinner.* Go home and take care of your family, and I will take care of mine."

Willie Jay spread his arms and motioned around the camp. "You call this 'taking care of your family'? Mary Anne left you, and you're acting as if you're the one who needs to repent. Any more repentance from you, and Mary Anne will kick you out of your own house by September."

Jethro flinched. Mary Anne was going to be out of his life much sooner than that. His heart ached just thinking about it. "I called a driver to take you home. He'll be here in half an hour." Willie Jay looked as if he might want to argue for another three hours, but Jethro held up his hand to stop any objection. "I'm not listening."

"You never did." Willie Jay scowled, then seemed to give up whatever fight was still in him.

"But you're not sending me home," Dat said. "Your tent is still up, and your *mamm* is here."

Jethro frowned. "I *am* sending you home, Dat. And Mamm too."

"She won't go."

"She'll go. She might not go home with you, but she'll go."

"But we're your parents. We love you. We love you more than Mary Anne ever could. We want to help."

Jethro took off his hat and scrubbed his fingers through his hair. "I'm sorry if you're hurt by this, but I shouldn't have let you come in the first place. Mary Anne never wanted you here, and I was being selfish when I let you stay."

"There you go again," Willie Jay said, "apologizing for your *fraa.*"

Jethro gave the bag of David's tent stakes a little extra force when he tossed them in the pile. "Have you ever loved someone so much you would give your life for them, Willie Jay?"

Willie Jay's nostrils flared. "Of course. My *fraa. Die kinner. Mein bruder.*"

Jethro crossed his arms over his chest and ignored Willie Jay's reference to *his brother.* "Do you love them enough to *live* your life for them?"

"What does that mean?"

"I love Mary Anne. I would give my live for her, but she doesn't want it. All I have left is to live my life for her. And I won't let my *bruder* tell me how to live my life, even if he is a minister."

Willie Jay turned red as a sugar beet. "Doesn't my sacrifice mean anything to you? I've been camping because I wanted to help you get your *fraa* back. Don't you care that my family has had to get by without their *fater*? Naoma had to get her *onkel* to help her sow the alfalfa. But do I get any thanks for what I've done for you?"

"I am grateful, Willie Jay, even if I was

wrong to let you stay. I shouldn't have let you upset my *fraa* or make her uncomfortable. I don't blame you. I know where the fault lies. I appreciate you, Willie Jay, but I want you to go."

Willie Jay quickly rummaged through the pile of tents and sleeping bags until he found his things. Jethro tried to help him with his duffel bag, but Willie Jay pushed him away and picked it up himself. He slung the tent bag over one shoulder and the duffel bag over the other and carried his pillow and sleeping bag in his arms. "Where will the driver be?" he said, spitting the words out of his mouth like an insult.

"He'll pull up in front. I've already paid for it."

Willie Jay nodded curtly. "*Gute.* I wouldn't want to spend one more dime or one more minute on such an ungrateful *bruder.* Don't expect a Christmas card." He turned and marched away as fast as he could laden with all that gear.

Jethro pressed his lips together. He probably hadn't handled that well, but when had he ever done anything right? When things were finally settled with Mary Anne, he'd write to Willie Jay and apologize. Better yet, he'd go to Appleton for a visit and ask for forgiveness in person. Willie Jay loved being right. Jethro could gain his forgiveness with five minutes of groveling.

Not that he'd ever say he was wrong about this. Though it hurt with every breath, he was doing the right thing by Mary Anne.

Jethro shoved his hands in his pockets. "Why don't you load your things in the wagon, Dat? I'll go help Mamm take down her tent."

Dat didn't like that idea. "If anyone is going to help Lois take down her tent, it should be her husband."

"Do you really want to have an argument in front of Mary Anne's cousins? And her grandparents?"

"Her grandparents are having marriage troubles. They won't care."

"It's going to be hard enough for me to convince Mamm that she needs to leave. Maybe you should just hitch up the buggy and wait."

Dat huffed his displeasure, but he seemed willing to do what Jethro asked. It was bad enough kicking his own *bruder* out of camp. It was going to be nearly impossible to get rid of his *mater.*

Dat retrieved his sleeping bag, pillow, and the large canvas bag he'd used as a suitcase. "I'll hitch up the buggy and pull it to the front of the barn. Tell your *mamm* I'll be waiting."

Jethro nodded and held out his hand. Dat hesitated for a second before shaking it. "I'm sorry, but a man must leave his *mater* and *fater* and cleave unto his wife. I'm doing the best I know how."

"I know, son. Like as not, we'll refuse to talk to you for a couple of weeks, then we'll get over our anger and invite you to dinner. We'll be fine."

Jethro truly hoped so. He did love his parents. It would be a mighty blow if he lost them too. "*Denki,* Dat. I'll go see about Mamm."

Dat smiled, but there was disquiet in his eyes. Jethro knew the feeling. He had never seen Mamm so angry or so determined as she was the night of Mary Anne's birthday party. If Dat was humble and owned up to his faults, Mamm might be willing to go home with him.

Jethro's steps were slow in the direction of Mamm's tent. She was going to be hurt, but Jethro didn't know a way around it. Mary Anne's side of the camp had just finished dinner, and Mamm sat next to the fire with one of Lily's twins on her lap. Mamm was bouncing the little one on her knee and humming a tune. *Die kinner* seemed to be able to tell if a *mammi* or an impostor was holding them. Lily's baby sucked happily on her fingers and let Mamm play with her golden hair.

About a dozen cousins greeted Jethro as he made his way to Mamm's chair. Mary Anne was standing at the washtub with her back to him, washing dishes and laughing at something Mandy had said. The sight of her so happy twisted his heart like someone wringing out a dishrag. He wanted to be the one to make her smile. He wanted to be the person she was happiest being with. It was pure torture to know he wasn't.

"Mamm," he said, sitting in the empty chair next to her. "I need to talk to you."

Mamm gave him a brilliant smile. It was nice to know he could at least make somebody happy. "How are you, Jethro? Have you eaten? I think we have some leftovers."

Jethro glanced around to make sure no one was listening. He didn't want to embarrass Mamm in front of the Helmuths. "Mamm, I appreciate all the support you've given me."

Mamm's lips twitched. "I haven't been much of a support lately. I hope you aren't upset. I'm protesting your *fater*, not you, though you deserve it almost as much as he does. Do you need me to cook? I'll do it for you, but no one else over there."

"Mamm, I'm sending everyone home. Willie Jay is waiting for a driver to take him back to Appleton. Dat is waiting at the buggy to take you home." He said the last words slowly, just to make sure they sank in.

The lines bunched like freshly plowed rows on Mamm's forehead. "You want me to go home?"

"*Jah,* for Mary Anne's sake."

"What do you mean, for Mary Anne's sake?"

Jethro swallowed hard. "She'd be happier if her mother-in-law wasn't hovering over her, finding fault with everything she does."

Mamm lifted the baby off her lap. "Lily? Would you mind?"

Lily took her baby from Mamm's arms. "*Denki* for entertaining her. She's less squirmy if someone else holds her."

"I would love to hold her any time," Mamm said, with a tone that told Lily she wasn't in the mood to visit. Lily moved away with the baby, and Mamm turned her body and her full attention on Jethro. "First of all, young man, while I am prone to find fault with those who deserve it, I would never find fault with Mary Anne. She is my daughter-in-law, and I love her."

"Mamm, you know that's not true."

412

"It is so. I love her like my own daughter."

Jethro sighed. "You know it's not true that you don't find fault."

"I may have been angry with her for upsetting my son, but I have never said a word against her, and that's the honest truth."

"She thinks you hate her."

"Well, I don't. Secondly, if you think I'm going home with your *fater,* you don't know me very well. I'm mad at him, and Mary Anne has shown me that I don't have to put up with it."

It felt as if his cow kicked him in the shin. Jethro didn't know if he felt worse about how he'd treated Mary Anne or about how devastated Dat was going to be to find out Mamm wouldn't go home with him. He couldn't very well scold his *mamm* for being unreasonable and stubborn, or tell her she needed to work out her problems instead of running from them. He'd tried that on Mary Anne, and it had only made things worse. Much worse. Besides, that wasn't even true. He was the one who had been unreasonable and stubborn. Mary Anne was working out the problem the only way she knew how. It was a wonderful brave thing to do. Jethro understood that now.

Mary Anne walked by them, drying her

hands on a towel. Mamm reached out and grabbed her wrist. "Mary Anne, I need to talk to you."

Mary Anne glanced at Jethro as if she wanted to pretend he wasn't sitting there. She couldn't very well just walk on by with Mamm holding on to her like that. "Is everything all right?" she said, her voice betraying her uneasiness.

Jethro jumped to his feet and offered Mary Anne his chair. She raised her eyebrows as a tiny smile played at her lips. "*Denki,* Jethro." She sat down, and Jethro stationed himself behind his *mater.*

Mamm leaned back in her chair and folded her arms across her chest as if she would not be moved. "Jethro has asked me to leave the camp."

Mary Anne's eyes narrowed in confusion. "Does he want you to go back and cook for him?"

Any shred of assurance Jethro possessed blew away with the breeze. Did Mary Anne still think he was that selfish?

"Of course not," Mamm said, the scold evident in her voice. "You know my Jethro better than that."

Mary Anne pressed her lips together.

Mamm motioned toward Jethro's camp. "Jethro told everyone on that side to go home. He didn't want Willie Jay or any of the others to make you feel uncomfortable."

Mary Anne formed her mouth into an *O,* and she lowered her eyes and stared at her hands.

"Willie Jay preaches a *gute* sermon," Mamm said, "but sometimes he doesn't know when to quit. It's best if he goes home. Naoma doesn't mind listening to him talk." She reached out and gave Mary Anne's leg a firm pat. "I am humble enough to admit that I have said and done things that hurt your feelings, but I hope that I have behaved better in the last few days. I love you, Mary Anne, even though Jethro says you think I hate you."

Jethro nearly groaned out loud. He should have known better than to tell Mamm what Mary Anne had said. Mamm always spoke her mind, and she thought being honest and being blunt were the same thing.

Mary Anne drew her brows together. "I thought you hated me, but I'm not so sure anymore. I know you're wonderful angry with me." For sure and certain Mary Anne had become more plainspoken since she'd been living in a tent. She'd told Jethro what was what more than a few times.

He didn't know whether to be proud of her or sorry for himself.

"I was very angry with you," Mamm said. "But that's no way for a Christian to behave, and I'm sorry. My only excuse is that I'm a mother bear. I don't like to see my cubs get hurt."

Mary Anne nodded. "I understand."

Mamm reached back and touched Jethro's hand. "I learned a *gute* lesson. You can't know anything about anyone else until you know yourself. I'm sorry for judging you." She clapped her hands together. "Now. Do I make you uncomfortable? Because if I do, I'll pack up and head to my sister's place in Wautoma. She keeps goats and her house stinks to high heaven, but I'll do it if you don't want me here."

Mary Anne swallowed as if she had something stuck in her throat. "I would like you to stay. But if you want to get back to sleeping in a real bed, I won't begrudge it."

"Stuff and nonsense," Mamm said. "I need more time to cool off, and Chris needs to think on his sins."

"Okay, then." Mary Anne got to her feet and nearly knocked Jethro over with a brilliant smile. *"Denki,"* she said, her voice cracking like cold glass on a hot day. "I know how much your *bruder*'s approval means to you."

Jethro had to tell himself to breathe.

"Willie Jay will be fine. He's a minister. He has to forgive me or be a hypocrite. It's your cousin Norman I worry about. He'll probably never speak to me again."

Mamm huffed. "That man makes me appreciate the peace and quiet all that much more."

Mary Anne stifled a smile. "Norman likes to share his opinion."

Jethro shrugged. "We were always taught that it's *gute* to share."

"What about Lily's *dat*?" Mary Anne said. "Was he mad yet?"

"At first he wasn't going to leave without Lily." Jethro stuffed his hands in his pockets. "But he isn't as young as he used to be, and it's plain he's tired of camping. He gave in when I suggested he go home and take a nice, hot shower."

Mary Anne giggled. "His *fraa* will thank you."

Jethro glanced in the direction of the barn and the driveway. "I suppose I should tell Dat to go on without you."

Mamm stood and sighed like a goose. "*Nae*, Jethro. I'll do it. I haven't spoken a word to him for a week, and he needs a *gute* talking-to. I'll be back in an hour."

CHAPTER SEVENTEEN

" 'The little puppy looked up the lane. He looked down the lane. But his *mater* and *bruderen* and *schwesteren* were nowhere to be seen.' " Mary Anne paused and held out the book to let *die kinner* get a *gute* look at the pictures. " 'He was sad because he had disobeyed his *mamm* and now he was lost. The little puppy sat down in the middle of the road and cried.' "

"Run up that hill. They're on the other side." Beth and Tyler Yoder's little boy, Toby, was one of the few in Mary Anne's audience old enough to make much sense of the story. He was four, and as jumpy and twitchy as Mary Anne would have expected any four-year-old to be.

"I don't know," Mary Anne said. "Let's find out."

She turned the page. " 'A little girl found the puppy, took him home, and gave him something to eat.' "

Little Sarah, Ben and Emma's *dochder,* took her finger out of her mouth and pointed to the page. "Cow."

"*Jah.* The puppy meets a new friend." Mary Anne's gaze flicked to the ceiling of her tent as she heard a distant rumble. The storm was moving away from them, but it was still raining wonderful hard.

Lily, Lia, and Beth were outside standing under umbrellas trying to get dinner going. Mary Anne had volunteered to entertain *die kinner* while their *maters* cooked. It was a special occasion because Beth and Tyler Yoder had come for dinner. They weren't regular campers because neither Beth nor Tyler thought it would be wise to camp with Beth's new baby, a toddler, and a four-year-old.

Mary Anne had wholeheartedly agreed that they shouldn't be camping. She liked having the support of her relatives, but camping was a hardship her cousins had borne for her, and she felt the burden of their sacrifice every day.

Four little ones sat in a semicircle on the floor of her tent while Mary Anne faced them with the book propped on her leg, trying to make her voice heard over the rat-a-tat of fat raindrops against the canvas. Pine, Sarah Beachy's boy who liked Cheetos, sat behind little Sarah, just as engrossed in the story as any of *die kinner. Ach, vell,* he was probably even more interested. His eyes danced with every new puppy adventure, and a wide grin spread across his face as if he couldn't help himself.

Mary Anne had taken some of her non-toxic paints and painted a black nose and whiskers on each of *die kinner.* Pine had wanted a dog nose along with the rest of them.

" 'Can you help me find my *mater?*' " Mary Anne said in her whiniest, saddest puppy voice. There weren't many picture books written in *Dietsch,* so she translated the words from *English* as she read them. " 'The chicken didn't say a word. Chickens were like that sometimes.' "

"*Hallo,* Mary Anne?" It was Jethro, right on time from work.

"*Cum reu,*" she said.

Every head turned as Jethro unzipped the tent, stepped inside, and quickly zipped it back up again. Water dripped from his hat, and he took it off and hung it on the hat stand Mary Anne had stolen from the house. His smile could barely be contained as his gaze traveled around the tent. "What is this? A dog party?"

Toby giggled. "*Nae,* Cousin Jethro. Mary

Anne is telling us about a puppy."

"A puppy? That's the best kind of story. Can I listen too?"

Toby and Sarah nodded, and all four of them scooted to the left so Jethro could sit next to them. He turned and smiled at Pine. "Do you mind if I join the party?"

Pine blushed under his whiskers, no doubt embarrassed to be caught at storytime with the little kids, but he seemed to relax when Jethro reached into Mary Anne's cup of paint on the table by her cot and smeared black paint across his own nose. Aden Jr. giggled, and Sarah wasted no time in crawling onto Jethro's lap. Jethro gave Sarah's little shoulders a squeeze, and she settled in as if Jethro was her favorite person in the world.

Mary Anne grew warm from the inside out. Jethro didn't spend a lot of time around children, but he really was a natural *fater*. He didn't have a temper like so many men, and he was good-natured when he had a mind to be. If only she could have given him a child . . .

She immediately turned her thoughts in a different direction. It would do no good to cry just as the puppy found his family. " 'I'll never wander off again,' the puppy said. 'Hush,' said his *mater*. 'Drink your milk and go to bed and dream a happy dream. You are safe and all is well.' "

Mary Anne showed *die kinner* and Jethro the last picture, which was the mommy dog kissing her four puppies good night.

"Read another one," Toby said.

Mary Anne closed the book. "This is the only one I have. Go and find your *mamm.* It's time to wash for dinner."

Pine took a handkerchief out of his pocket, licked it, and scrubbed at the paint on his nose.

Mary Anne snapped a wet wipe from the container on her table and handed it to Pine. "Here, this will do a better job." She gave Jethro a wet wipe, and he started on Sarah's face while Mary Anne wiped up Toby and Crist.

Aden Jr. turned his face away from Jethro's wet wipe. "*Nae.* I a puppy."

"*Cum,* Aden," Jethro said. "You'll want a clean face. What if your *mamm* thinks you're a dog and won't let you have any noodles?"

The thought of no noodles for dinner did the trick. Aden Jr. let Jethro wash his face.

Pine took little Sarah's hand and led her out of the tent. Aden Jr., Toby, and Crist followed. Mary Anne smiled and handed a wet wipe to Jethro for his own face, then wiped her hands clean. While wiping down his nose, Jethro bent over and retrieved the puppy book from the floor. Out of the corner of her eye, she saw him turn it over in his hand and look at it as if he didn't know quite what to make of it.

Surely he recognized it, unless he had put anything having to do with the baby out of his mind. Maybe Mary Anne was the only one who still mourned the loss.

"You took this out of the storage chest." He said it so gently that Mary Anne turned and studied his face. It wasn't an accusation or a scold, and he didn't seem to be irritated about the tears that suddenly pooled in her eyes.

She sniffed them back and turned her face away. "I needed a book. The rain made *die kinner* restless, and their *mamms* got cross."

He slowly sank to her cot and leafed through the pages. "I bought this the week before you lost the *buplie*. His first book."

"And then it went into the chest with every other memory." She kept her back to him so he wouldn't see the pain in her eyes. She would never share the deepest parts of her heart with him again.

She sensed him close behind her even before he touched her. Standing behind her, he wrapped both arms around her shoulders and pulled her into the warmth of his chest.

Ach, how she had missed his smell. The sharp, clean scent of pine with a hint of earthy cedar. Surrendering to his embrace, she relaxed and rested her head back against his shoulder.

"I didn't know what to do, Mary Anne," he whispered. "There was so much blood, so much pain when it happened. I told *Gotte* I would do anything, anything if He would spare your life. I promised I wouldn't ask for another thing ever. 'Just save my wife. Spare my wife, Lord.' "

A tear dropped onto her face and slid down her cheek. It wasn't hers.

"And then the horrible news of no more babies. I told myself I had done it by making promises to *Gotte* that no man had a right to make. It was like falling into a dark hole with no bottom — just falling and falling with nothing to hold on to. I was afraid to grab on to you for fear of taking you down with me. We lost touch, and I didn't know how to help myself, let alone my *fraa.* I'm so sorry, Mary Anne."

"It doesn't matter anymore."

His arms tightened around her. "It matters very much to me, and I think it matters to you too. I tried to pretend our grief didn't exist. I asked you to stop crying. I bought a fishing pole and told myself I was happy."

Mary Anne hooked her fingers around Jethro's forearm. "We stopped talking."

"Because it hurt too much."

"I shut you out because I couldn't bear to disappoint you one more time."

"I thought I had fixed you — that you weren't broken or sad anymore." He nuzzled his cheek against her *kapp*. "I wanted to believe you were better because you packed away the baby blankets and stopped crying." He ran his hands up and down her arms. She stiffened to keep from trembling. "I was devastated we couldn't have a *buplie*, but *heartzly*, I was never disappointed in you one day in my life." He lay a feather-soft kiss on her forehead. "Don't you see? You are enough. I couldn't love you any more than if you had a dozen babies." He took her shoulders and turned her around. "You are enough, Mary Anne. You always have been."

A sob she'd been valiantly trying to suppress slipped past her lips. Jethro tugged her to him and clamped his strong arms all the way around her, as if she belonged to him and he belonged to her. Some sort of dam broke, and it was impossible to keep the tears back. She wept as she hadn't wept in almost four years. Jethro didn't make a sound, but she could feel his pain in the great shuddering breaths he took in time with hers.

He didn't tell her to hush, and she didn't care if he was disappointed or not. He held on to her as if she might run away. She held on to him as if he might disappear. "I wanted a baby so bad."

He smoothed an errant hair from her cheek. "You would make the best *mater* in the world."

"I begged *Gotte* for a baby, but He stopped listening a long time ago, and I stopped praying. I have to make my own happiness. You have to know that I'm not waiting for *Gotte* or you or anybody else."

He didn't pull back, and he didn't chastise her like she expected him to. He gave her a tender, I-love-you-no-matter-what smile and teased the edge of her bottom lip with his callused thumb. If she'd been trembling before, now her body was practically vibrating. "All I care about is your happiness."

A part of her wanted him to argue with her, to tell her how wicked she was, so it would be easier to leave him, to cut him out of her life. Another part of her — bigger or smaller, she couldn't tell — wanted him to convince her that he was the one who could and would make her happy if she'd let him.

She held perfectly still as he traced his

thumb down the valleys of her throat. She should definitely pull away right about now. They were alone together in her tent, and this kind of thing would definitely come to no good.

He winced as if she'd poked him with a pin, took a deep breath, and dropped his hand to his side. "And right now, you'd probably be happier if I got out of your tent."

Not really, but she didn't contradict him. She couldn't think straight when he was that close.

He stepped back, coming up against the cot in his effort to put some distance between them. "But I want to show you something first. Can I bring it in? It's a little wet."

She gathered her thoughts in time to be able to give him a fairly reasonable reply. "What is it?"

"I brought you a present." He grinned. "*Ach, vell,* it's not really a present because I don't think you'll want to keep it for yourself."

With that puzzling answer, he unzipped her tent and disappeared into the rain. The storm had petered out to a sprinkle.

Jethro ducked back inside carrying the old bench that used to sit in one corner of the barn. It was rickety and gray with age.

He set it next to the cot and smoothed his hand over the top. He should have come up with at least three splinters. "I braced the legs and put in about a dozen screws. A cow could sit on this thing." To prove himself, he sat down and patted the space next to him. "Try it out."

Mary Anne hesitantly sat. She'd rather not get a sliver in her *hinnerdale.* The bench didn't make one noise and didn't sway so much as a quarter of an inch. "It's wonderful solid."

He smiled as if she'd given him the moon. "I used one thousand-grit silicon carbide sandpaper. You could dance barefoot on this thing and never get a sliver."

"It's too bad I don't dance." She stood and ran her hand across the seat, then knelt and fingered the legs and the underside. Soft as a *buplie*'s bottom. "This is beautiful. It must have taken you hours."

His face practically glowed. "Do you think you can sell it?"

"You want me to sell it?"

"After you paint a farm scene on it, or flowers or a quilt design. Whatever you want. Do you think someone would buy it on your friend's Etsy page?"

"*Jah,* of course. *Englischers* like Amish

furniture. I sold another chair three days ago. And my quilt. Not an hour after Pammy put it up for sale, someone bought it for five hundred dollars."

Jethro seemed genuinely happy and interested that she'd sold a quilt. "They'll probably buy them as fast as you can make them."

"Yesterday someone put in a custom order for a quilt."

"Is that *gute*?"

She tried not to smile too wide. "*Jah.* They want a queen size with butterflies on it."

He gave her a half smile. "Your favorite thing."

"I've never done anything like it before. Pammy helped me find a pattern. It will be beautiful."

"For sure and certain. You're going to be rich."

"Not rich, but maybe have enough to move out of the woods." Her smile faded as she realized what that meant for Jethro. And for her. Would she be happy living by herself, or would the loneliness overwhelm her on cold winter nights? Would she find herself longing for Jethro's warmth or be content to cuddle in a fuzzy blanket with a *gute* book?

Living alone meant she would be able to do whatever she wanted to do, buy whatever she wanted to buy, paint and quilt to her heart's content, but maybe it would get tiresome without Jethro there. She'd miss that *gute* smell he brought home with him every day and the ready smile he was starting to show more often. If she left him for good, Jethro would be devastated. When she had first moved out, she had wanted to believe he didn't love her and would barely miss her except for the chores that wouldn't get done. But it wasn't so easy now that she knew the truth.

Jethro adored her.

How would she live with herself, knowing she'd done something so unfeeling to someone she loved?

Jah. She could admit it. She loved Jethro. He was a *gute* man, and not all that bad to look at. But maybe love wasn't enough. She had been every which way in love with him on their wedding day. That hadn't kept bad things from happening, and it hadn't kept her from falling out of love with him in the end.

Still, the thought of Jethro unhappy made her miserable.

Jethro gave her a sad smile and stood, as if every bone in his body ached. "Lord willing, you won't have to camp much longer." He swiped his hand across his mouth. "I . . . I want you to be happy, Mary Anne."

"*Denki,*" she said, frustrated that the tears sprang to her eyes so easily. She blinked them away. "I think I'll paint a whole flock of butterflies on this bench. I love butterflies."

"I know you do."

Mary Anne counted the money again as she ambled toward Jethro's tent. One hundred and fifty dollars for Jethro's old bench. She could hardly believe it. What a *gute* sanding job that had been.

Jethro had brought her two more chairs from a secondhand store in Shawano. He'd sanded them to buttery smoothness and told her she could sell them on Etsy. She had painted cows and horses and an old barn on the seats, and Pammy had sold them for fifty dollars each. Jethro was going to be so happy when he got his money.

It had been two weeks since Jethro had brought her that bench, and the camp seemed to change in some way every day. Mandy and Noah had gone home. Mandy was close to having her *buplie,* and Noah was anxious to have her in a more comfortable place to sleep. Emma and Ben had also pulled up their tent, with many apologies and regrets from Emma. Ben's MS was acting up, and she didn't want to risk his health.

Lia and Moses's family were still there. Lily and Aden seemed to enjoy living in a tent more than they liked their house. Mary Anne was concerned that they might camp here forever. Sarah Beachy and her boys were still camping, even though Sarah assured them she was going to get scoliosis or sciatica or some other back ailment before the summer was out. Sarah wasn't actually in camp much except to quilt and sleep. She spent her days at home, doing chores or visiting one of the expectant *maters* she cared for. Sometimes Mary Anne would hear someone come and fetch Sarah in the middle of the night for a delivery. Sarah must be exhausted all the time.

Their pile of firewood and kindling grew higher every day because Jethro had caught Mary Anne hauling sticks from the woods and absolutely refused to let her do it again.

Because Jethro was the only one on his side of the camp, he ate with them every morning and every night. He was always so appreciative of Mary Anne's *kaffee* that his smile made her giddy whenever he came for breakfast.

Jethro was chopping wood when Mary Anne arrived at his campsite. He exploded into a smile when he saw her, and she tried not to stare at his arms as he raised the ax over his head. His whole upper body looked as if it had been chiseled from a *gute* piece of cherrywood. He brought the ax down hard on the log, splitting it with one blow and sending wood chips skipping every which way.

After throwing the split logs onto his growing pile, he buried his ax into the chopping block and wiped his forearm across his forehead, never losing that smile that made her a little dizzy. He took out his handkerchief and wiped the sweat from his neck. "When I don't see you for a while, I forget how pretty you are."

She turned her face away to hide the blush. "You saw me this morning."

"It seems like an eternity when I'm away from you."

Even though she knew he was teasing, she couldn't help the way her heart thumped inside her chest. "Pammy sold that bench you sanded. And the chairs."

"Did she?"

She pinched the money between her fingers and held it out to him. "One hundred and fifty dollars for the bench plus a hundred for the chairs." She grinned. "Don't spend it all in one place."

He drew his brows together, stiffening as if she'd just delivered some very bad news. Not exactly the reaction she'd been expecting. "What do you mean?" he said.

"That bench you fixed up. I painted it, and Pammy sold it on Etsy. Didn't you . . . isn't that what you wanted me to do?"

He slowly nodded. *"Jah."*

"Vell, I'm paying you the money Pammy got for it."

Jethro took off his hat and gloves, bowed his head, and slowly combed his fingers through his hair. "This is . . . this is what you think of me?" It was a question, but she had no idea how to answer him. "I hoped that after all I've tried . . ."

Mary Anne eyed him in confusion. It was plain enough he wasn't angry, but he was hurt — deeply, profoundly hurt — as if she'd slapped him across the face. Had he wanted her to keep the bench as a gift? Was he upset she'd sold it? She tried to remember the conversation. She was sure he had asked her to paint it and sell it on Etsy. "What . . . what did I do wrong, Jethro? I don't understand."

With his hat and gloves in one hand, he turned his back on her and stood perfectly still, staring off to the west as if waiting for the sun to set. She held her breath. Was he going to explain? Give her a reason to apologize? "You didn't do anything wrong, *heartzly.*"

"Then why won't you look at me?"

He glanced in her direction and smiled as best he could, but the pain she saw in his eyes was almost unbearable. "Some things just can't be fixed."

Was he talking about her? Was he finally giving up on them because of something that happened with an old bench? Her legs wobbled like jelly. She didn't want him to give up. Not now. Not when she'd just discovered that his gaze made her weak and his touch made her breathless.

He seemed to remember she was there. Squaring his shoulders, he turned and gave her a warm, soft look like melted chocolate on a graham cracker. "Will you tell your *mammi* I won't be coming to dinner tonight? I think she was making her famous meatballs just for me."

Mary Anne forced a smile. "For sure and certain they're famous. One fell off Moses's plate and burned a hole in the tablecloth." Not a single line changed on his face, even at the mention of Mammi's cooking. "Lily got some corn on the cob, and I'm making blueberry cobbler." She tilted her head to coax him to meet her eye, but he was determined to look at anything but her. His avoidance drove a sliver of glass right through her heart. "Aren't you hungry?"

"*Ach,* I've got other plans, that's all."

He was lying. Normally, he would have traded his eyeteeth to be with her. Tonight, it seemed he wanted to be anywhere else.

She cleared her throat to remove the lump that had settled there. "*Ach, vell,* then. Take your money. That way I won't be worried that a bear is going to steal it from my tent."

He finally looked at her. "The money is yours, not mine."

"But didn't you want Pammy to sell it in the Etsy shop?"

"The bench was meant for you. I hoped you'd make some money from it. And you did. I'm wonderful happy for you." If this was Jethro's happy, she didn't want to see miserable.

"Oh. I just assumed." That was . . . that was too nice. He'd done more work on that bench than she had, and it had been his to begin with. "Are you sure? I don't wonder but you spent hours sanding it. And the chairs too." She held it out to him. "Take it, and consider it payment for the two hundred dollars I still owe you."

He made a valiant effort to smile, but there was so much unhappiness behind it she wanted to cry. "*Nae,* I want you to have it. For sure and certain the bench sold for so much because of your painting."

She glanced at the bills in her hand. Two hundred and fifty dollars. *Ach,* three whole months' worth of groceries, even if she bought sundried tomatoes and pine nuts. "That is very kind of you, Jethro."

He nodded, as if he found it impossible to speak.

She stood there staring at him, trying to figure out what had made him so unhappy — hoping he'd say something to explain the disquiet that had suddenly taken him. He paused for half a minute, looking at her like he was memorizing her face.

He obviously wasn't going to say anything else, and she couldn't stand there forever. "Will we . . . we'll see you for breakfast in the morning yet?"

He might have shaken his head, but it was so slight she couldn't have been sure. Without another word, he tapped his hat onto his head, slid on his gloves, and jerked the ax from the stump. Another log went onto the chopping block. Another swing of the ax. More firewood for Mary Anne's campfire.

He'd said all he was going to say.

With a heavy heart, Mary Anne walked away, her money balled tightly in her fist.

It wasn't until she was tucked tightly into her sleeping bag that night that she realized what she had done.

Shame kept her awake the rest of the night.

CHAPTER EIGHTEEN

Jethro smoothed his hand along the back of the last of the kitchen chairs. He'd sanded it down and painted it bright white, just like he had done with the other seven chairs. Mary Anne hadn't even noticed they were the chairs from their own kitchen, just assuming Jethro had gotten them from the secondhand store in town. He *had* bought three or four chairs secondhand, just so she wouldn't get suspicious, but most of what she'd painted and sold was from her own kitchen — the kitchen she would probably never set foot in again.

What did it matter if there was no place to sit?

Jethro took a deep breath, hoping to ease the weight on his chest that seemed to get heavier and heavier every day. He'd never felt so low, not even when he'd taken down Mary Anne's tent and she had told him she wanted a divorce.

For weeks he'd held on to a shred of hope that maybe she still loved him, that maybe she would consider being his *fraa* again. She'd smiled at him. She'd invited him to dinner and made him *kaffee — wunderbarr, wunderbarr kaffee.*

And then, like a baseball bat right to the chest, she'd tried to pay him for that bench.

He'd sanded that bench for her, finished those chairs because all he wanted was to make her happy, and her first thought was that he wanted to make a profit. Her opinion of him hadn't changed, despite all the changes he'd made, and it stung like a thousand wasps.

She didn't love him. She didn't want to love him. He'd truly lost her, and the only thing he could do now was help her get on with her life as soon as possible. The sooner she'd saved enough money, the happier she'd be, even if for Jethro it felt like he was planning his own funeral.

Eight chairs at fifty dollars apiece was four hundred dollars. With another quilt or two and a few more chairs, she'd have enough money to rent a small apartment in Shawano. It was a start. And the end.

He was devastated.

A hard knock on his back door made Jethro jump like a grasshopper in a frying pan. Felty stood on the other side of the door, smiling that kindly smile that meant he knew all about you and loved you anyway. Felty and Anna had been living under the canopy for over a month, and they were quite comfortable. Felty had lost his limp, and he took a nap on his own bed every day. One of their chickens roosted under their bed, but the other sixteen had disappeared. Anna held out hope they were exploring in the woods and would return any day. Jethro had seen too many feather trails to think Anna would ever get her chickens back.

"*Cum reu,* Felty," Jethro said. "But you didn't have to knock. Cousins come in and out of here all the time to use the bathroom."

Felty shuffled into the kitchen and eyed the table. "What happened to all your chairs? The last time I was here, you had a full set."

Jethro wrapped his fingers around the back of the one chair he still had left. "I . . . only need one," he said with a sheepish twist of his lips.

Felty narrowed his eyes as if he was trying to get a better look at Jethro. "Let's go sit down. That is, if you have any chairs left in the living room."

Jethro nodded. He had enough for Felty to sit on. Felty led the way, and Jethro brought the newly painted kitchen chair with him. The only thing left in the living room was Jethro's easy chair. Felty could sit there, and Jethro would sit on the kitchen chair. Might as well sit on it one more time before he gave it to Mary Anne.

"Sit here," Jethro said, motioning to his easy chair.

Felty paused and did a full turn as he gazed around the room. "I was certain you had a sofa in here."

Another sheepish look from Jethro. "I sold it."

Felty furrowed his brow. "I'm sorry to hear that. It was a wonderful lumpy sofa. Very soft."

Jethro didn't have anything to say to that. He'd sold it because he needed the money, but he didn't have to burden Felty with his troubles.

"I'll sit here," Felty said, sinking into the easy chair, "but you'll have to help me get out when it's time to go."

Jethro put the kitchen chair next to Felty and sat down. "Can I get you a drink of water or something?"

Felty waved away any suggestion of water. "*Denki.* I came to talk to you."

"Okay," Jethro said, drawing out the syllables. For sure and certain he had done everything wrong, but he didn't think he could bear any kind of scolding from Felty. Then again, he didn't know that anything could make him feel worse than he already did.

Felty pulled the lever on Jethro's easy chair and pushed himself back a bit. "Aw, that's better. Now, Jethro. I don't want you to think I'm complaining. Annie-Banannie and I have a comfortable bed and a roof over our heads, and Anna seems perfectly content, but I have to confess I'm a little bit tired of camping. The food is wonderful *gute,* but I miss my bathroom. It gets a little hard to hike to the barn three times a night." He held up his hand to stop Jethro from saying anything. "Now, I'm willing to stay as long as it takes, and I know these things take time. You can't rush love, especially true love, but it seems to me that you're not even trying anymore."

What could Jethro say to that? He *wasn't* trying anymore. Mary Anne had made it very clear she didn't want him. "I just want Mary Anne to be happy."

Felty gave Jethro's arm a friendly pat. "I know you do, but what I really want to know is what happened on Monday."

"Monday?"

"The day you stopped coming to dinner. And breakfast. We only see you when you come over to bring Mary Anne a chair or a can of paint. And that smile you paste on your face is so fake, it could be made out of plastic. So, what happened on Monday?"

Jethro shifted in his chair. Did he really want Felty to know how badly he'd failed where Mary Anne was concerned? "I realized she doesn't love me, that she would be happier without me, and I truly do want her happiness more than anything. I'm trying to stay away so I don't irritate her." He stood up and paced around the empty room. "I'm sorry, Felty. I'm working as fast as I can. By the end of August, Mary Anne should have enough money to move into an apartment. Then you and Anna can move back home."

"That's not good, Jethro."

"I'm sorry it can't be sooner, but it's the best I can do."

Felty shook his head. "*Ach,* Jethro. You are a little thick sometimes. We want Mary Anne to move home. You can't give up so easy."

"Maybe I'm not giving up as much as I'm facing the truth about how she feels about me. She'd be happier without me, and I

444

have to accept that and let her move on with her life."

Felty stroked his beard. "You're even thicker than I thought if you can't see how much she loves you."

Jethro couldn't let himself believe that for one minute. "*Nae*. I don't think she does."

"She lights up like a candle every time you come within spitting distance, and she makes a special pot of *kaffee* just for you every morning. I've never seen anybody take so much care with a cup of *kaffee*. It's like she's making it special for the king of Florida every morning."

Jethro scrubbed his hand down the side of his face. "She knows how much I love *kaffee*. She's thoughtful like that. It's not because she feels anything for me, except maybe pity."

Felty reached down and pulled the handle of the easy chair so he was sitting up straight. "Don't talk yourself out of it, Jethro. She had to dig her heels in wonderful hard because she didn't want anybody to move her. You've got to help her see she doesn't have to be so strong anymore."

"I've tried, Felty, but I'm not what she needs or wants. She wants freedom and happiness. She wants me to leave her alone."

"And so you're giving her all your kitchen

chairs," Felty said.

"I want her to earn enough money so she can do whatever she wants."

Felty raised his eyebrows. "She's not so sure what she wants anymore."

"She's sure. And I'm going to help her."

Felty shook his head as if in surrender. "Anna will never forgive you, you know."

"I'll never forgive myself."

Mary Anne lay on top of her sleeping bag, listening to the noise of her own breathing. She'd already given up trying to sleep. When she'd first moved out to the woods, she had feared she'd freeze to death every night or at least come down with a severe case of frostbite. Now she was so hot she could barely breathe. The air was so moist she could have wrung it out into a cup. She sat up and punched her pillow a few times to fluff it up. It was probably cooler in her tent than it would be inside the house, and she'd slept fine on hotter nights than this.

The weather wasn't the problem, and she knew it perfectly well.

She hadn't slept well in weeks, and tonight her thoughts felt like heavy stones on her chest. She should have been wildly happy. Wildly, wildly happy. She'd finished the butterfly quilt, it had been sent to the person who ordered it, and Pammy had paid Mary Anne this morning.

The quilt was probably the most beautiful thing Mary Anne had ever made. Butterflies of all colors flew up from flowers at the bottom of the quilt into a white background that Mammi and Lois and her cousins had quilted with spirals and curlicues. It was so *wunderbarr,* Mary Anne hadn't wanted to part with it.

But the buyer had paid nine hundred dollars! More than enough to rent a small apartment in Shawano. More than three months' rent if she decided to rent the room in Charlene's basement. Charlene had offered it to her weeks ago when she found out Mary Anne was living in the woods. In some ways, it was a very attractive offer. The rent was cheap, and Charlene wouldn't have to drive to Bonduel to pick Mary Anne up for work three days a week. But Mary Anne still dreamed of having a place to call her own with no one to answer to but herself. Mostly.

Mostly that was what she wanted.

But not really.

Jethro had all but ignored her for three weeks, talking to her only when he brought another chair for her to paint or when he wanted to see if she needed the buggy hitched. She'd made a lot of money from those chairs Jethro so thoughtfully found for her.

Everything in their lives had been about the money for so long, she had just assumed Jethro had wanted to make some money on Etsy too. He had done something amazingly unselfish for her, and she had immediately jumped to the conclusion that he wanted to be compensated. She was thoroughly ashamed. Jethro had been nothing but kind, and she had repaid him by assuming the worst. No wonder he'd reacted as if she'd turned out the sun on his life.

She had tried to apologize about the bench, but every time she mentioned it, he would get that strange, resigned smile on his face and tell her that he only wanted her to be happy — as if that made up for how badly she had treated him. He certainly wasn't mad at her or giving her the cold shoulder. Jethro wasn't like that. She had wounded him, and the hurt had gone straight to his heart.

Mammi had dropped little hints about Jethro every day since. "Isn't Jethro coming to dinner, dear? I know he loves my Indonesian beef stew." "Why don't you go over to Jethro's side and give him a cup of *kaffee*? He loves your *kaffee.*" Or things Mary Anne didn't really understand like, "That boy is thicker than a piece of rhubarb pie. You're going to have to go the rest of the way, Mary Anne."

Mary Anne had made Jethro a special pot of *kaffee* every morning for a week until she realized he wasn't planning to share breakfast with her and the cousins ever again. She'd stopped cooking altogether, and Mammi and the cousins had taken over. What was the fun of it if Jethro wasn't there to tell her he loved it or to smile and ask for seconds or thirds?

Mammi and Lois had finally gotten fed up with Jethro not showing up for meals and had marched over there this afternoon and practically ordered Jethro to a special party in celebration of Mary Anne's finishing her nine-hundred-dollar butterfly quilt. Mary Anne had heard the whole side of Mammi and Lois's conversation from her tent because neither Mammi nor Lois talked very softly when they had their minds set on something. Jethro, on the other hand, must have whispered the entire conversation. She hadn't heard a word he'd said to Lois and Mammi, but he had shown up for the party.

That was something.

But not enough.

Dawdi had built an extra big fire, and they'd roasted marshmallows and made banana boats. Jethro hadn't said a word to Mary Anne during dinner and barely spoke to anyone else either. He was plain miserable, and it was all her doing. If he was anywhere near as miserable as she was, there would never be happiness in the world again.

It didn't matter how many times she punched her pillow, Mary Anne could not get comfortable. She rolled onto her side and decided to add up in her head how much she'd earned from the quilts and furniture. Surely it was as *gute* as counting sheep. The problem was that every chair she counted had Jethro's touch upon it, and every quilt came with the thought that he had given her the quilting frames in the first place.

She punched her pillow again and rolled over to her other side. Who counted money to help them sleep anyway? Maybe she could count the things she liked about Jethro. Maybe she should come up with ideas for convincing him to come around and share a cup of *kaffee* with her again. She would love that more than he could ever know.

"Mary Anne! Mary Anne!"

Had she finally fallen asleep? Was she dreaming? One problem with camping was that she was never sure if she was awake or if those noises she heard were just sharing her dreams — except her throat was burning and the smell of smoke had to be real. She couldn't imagine anything like that in her dreams.

She opened her eyes, sat up, and gasped for air. There was a gaping hole in one side of her tent, and the bookshelf was on fire — horrifying, scorching fire. The hole in the tent grew as if the edges were melting like frost on a windowpane. The bookshelf was fully aflame, and the heat felt so intense, it scorched her bare skin.

A cough tore up her throat like a piece of broken glass, and thick black smoke hung in the air like a curtain. She had to get out, but her eyes burned, and she couldn't open them wide enough to see her way to the door.

First a shadow, and then something solid clamped violently and painfully around her wrist. She instinctively tried to pull away until she realized that someone wanted to help her. But did he have to be so rough about it? He pulled so forcefully that he wrenched her shoulder dragging her off the cot and across the tent. She gasped in pain, but the sound was swallowed up in the chaos of flames and smoke and sharp smells. They were both coughing as he dragged her out the tent door. He released her wrist and lifted her into his arms without even so much as asking permission. *Ach, vell,* he didn't really need it. Right now, she wanted the safety of his embrace more than anything in the world.

She wrapped her arms around his neck and buried her face into his shoulder as he carried her twenty feet from the fire. "Talk to me, *heartzly.* Are you okay?"

She lifted her head and coughed into his neck. "I'm going to have a very big bruise on my wrist."

She was kind of hoping he'd laugh, but it was too much to ask at the moment. "*Ach, heartzly,* you shaved twenty years off my life."

"Is she okay, Jethro?"

Mary Anne looked around her. Moses and Lia each had a fire extinguisher pointed at Mary Anne's tent. Foam dripped from what was left of Mary Anne's butterfly painting on the side of the tent, and the bookshelf wasn't burning anymore, but it was mostly a pile of rubble. Aden Jr. and Crist sat on the ground with their backs against the barn and stared at her tent as if they were two

Englisch children watching TV in their pajamas.

Lois held both of Lily's twins, and Dennis and Judy stood next to her surveying the damage.

Jethro didn't seem inclined to set her down. She didn't mind. He nudged her forehead with his. "Are you all right? What can I do? Do you need a drink?" She could feel his heart banging against his chest and his breath escaping in ragged spurts. Was he more shaken up than she was?

She clamped her arms more tightly around his neck. Shaken or not, he was her pillar. Strong, solid, and immovable. And safe. Forever safe. Why did she think she could live without him? Why did she think she wanted to? She was so confused she didn't even know which way was up anymore. "What happened?"

"I couldn't sleep." It was plain they both needed something better to count than money. "I don't know what I heard exactly, but I got out of my tent to investigate and your grandparents started yelling."

"I must have been sleeping hard. The sound of Mammi and Dawdi yelling usually wakes me up."

"They built the campfire too close to the canopy. It must not have been put out

453

completely. The canopy started on fire and set your tent on fire too."

Mary Anne caught her breath and snapped her head around to look for Mammi and Dawdi's makeshift bedroom. The canopy was gone. "Where are they? Are they okay?"

"They're okay. Judy and I pulled them out, and Aden, Dennis, and Moses put out the fire. I bought three fire extinguishers after the space heater exploded and stored them in the barn. There weren't really any flames. It just sort of melted, like your tent."

She nudged herself away from Jethro, and he set her on her feet. Taking her hand, he led her to where the canopy used to be. Nothing was left but the metal poles that held it up and the charred remains of the vinyl still smoking on the ground. Miraculously, Mammi and Dawdi's dresser, end tables, and bed sat right where they had been, seemingly untouched by the heat. The hat stand was covered with fire extinguisher foam, and it looked like a flocked Christmas tree, but other than that, it appeared Mammi and Dawdi had come out all right. Alice, in shorts and a T-shirt, was spraying the hot spots down with the hose, being careful not to get the bed wet, while Mammi and Dawdi stood to the side and stared glassy-eyed at the ashes. Mammi held

Sparky in one arm and her last surviving chicken in the other. She wore a fluorescent pink knitted nightcap with her baby blue flannel nightgown. Dawdi was in his night-shirt and socks.

Mary Anne ran around the burned edges of the canopy toward her grandparents. As best she could, she wrapped her arms around her *mammi,* Sparky, and the chicken. "Mammi, I'm so sorry. I should have checked the fire pit before I went to bed."

Mammi handed the chicken to Mary Anne. The chicken obviously knew who its mommy was, because the poor bird didn't want anything to do with Mary Anne. She squawked and fussed until Mary Anne dropped her on the ground, and she half-ran, half-flew through the ashes and hid under the bed. Mammi rubbed Sparky's head. "She's so happy under there. We're never going to get her back in that coop."

"Are you all right, Mammi?"

Mammi reached up and patted Mary Anne on the cheek. "It's a camping miracle, that's what it is, and I should know. I've seen my share."

How many camping miracles had Mammi seen? Mary Anne had been camping for almost three months, and she'd never seen one, unless she could count finding that rock that looked exactly like Willie Jay.

"We woke up, and the whole tent was on fire. But look. Our bed doesn't have a speck of dust on it, and Sparky and Sharon are safe."

"Sharon?"

Mammi pointed to the bed. "My chicken. It's a sign that *Gotte* approves of our solidarity. As soon as the fabric stops smoking, we can go back to bed as if nothing ever happened."

Mary Anne was very *froh* to hear that *Gotte* approved of solidarity, but she'd feel better if her grandparents didn't sleep out here tonight. *Gotte* might approve of solidarity, but that didn't mean they wouldn't get wet if it rained.

Jethro came up behind her. He must have had the same thought. "You should sleep in the house tonight. I'd feel better if we got everything cleaned up before you got back into that bed. And you need a roof."

Mammi sighed as if she were trying to be very patient. "Now, Jethro. *Gotte* just gave me a sign that He approves of our solidarity. How ungrateful would I be if I moved back into your house?"

"It's just for one night, Mammi," Mary Anne said. "And it looks to make down hard."

Mammi looked up at the sky. There was a little bit of a moon and a thick blanket of clouds. "Maybe rain is *Gotte*'s way of testing us."

"*Jah,*" Dawdi said. "He's testing to see how smart we are, and a smart man would go in the house."

Mammi shrugged and smiled in surrender. "Now, Felty." She set Sparky on the ground and held out her hand. "Jethro, would you be kind enough to get me my toothbrush? It's in the top drawer."

Jethro waded through the canopy ashes and pulled a toothbrush and toothpaste from the top dresser drawer. He handed them to Mammi and picked up the dog. "I'll carry Sparky. She likes me."

Moses and Lia were standing with their heads together, each holding a fire extinguisher. "Lia," Mary Anne said, "we're taking Mammi and Dawdi into the house to sleep."

Lia nodded. "We'll make sure everything is good and doused. I'm *froh* you're safe."

"Praise *Gotte* Jethro was there."

"Indeed," Lia said, smiling a weary smile.

They went in the back door and through the kitchen. It was too dark to see much, but were the chairs missing? Her exhausted mind must be playing tricks on her. They went into the bedroom, and Jethro lit both lanterns while Mary Anne turned down the covers. Mammi took one lantern to the bathroom to brush her teeth.

Dawdi sat on the end of the bed and took off his stockings. "I like this bed. It's only ten steps to the bathroom."

Jethro was still breathing as if he'd run a race. "I'll go help the others get things cleaned up out there. Will you be okay to see your grandparents to bed?"

Dawdi gave him a wry smile. "We're perfectly able to tuck ourselves in, thank you very much."

"I just meant that Mary Anne can help you find anything you need, like dental floss or toenail clippers."

Dawdi chuckled. "If I need to floss my teeth at midnight, I'll know who to ask."

Jethro didn't seem to find anything amusing tonight. "*Jah,* whatever you need, Mary Anne can help." He reached out and took Mary Anne's hand, intertwining his fingers with hers, his expression a mixture of fear and determination. Her heart skipped three beats. "Come find me when you're done."

His measured footsteps echoed down the hall, and before Mammi had finished brushing her teeth, Mary Anne heard Jethro close the back door behind him.

Mary Anne met Mammi in the hall when she came out of the bathroom. Mammi smiled as if she'd already had a very *gute* night's sleep. "*Ach,* Mary Anne. There is no one who will ever love you like that boy does. What a treasure."

Mary Anne knew it as sure as the sun would rise in the morning. She felt his love with every breath she took. She lowered her eyes. "I know."

"I know he ate almost all your birthday cake and bought a four-hundred-dollar fishing pole, but there are worse things a man can do. And if he has a *gute fraa* to love him and teach him and stand by him even when he deserves to sleep in the barn, he'll be a better man. Jethro loves you something wonderful. He'll never stop trying to be a better man for you."

Mary Anne wrung her hands. "I'm afraid, Mammi. Things might be very *gute* for a while, but Jethro's affection is bound to cool. Maybe he wasn't ever in love with me. Maybe he just misses my *kaffee* or the way I do the laundry."

Mammi cupped Mary Anne's chin in her hand. "Perfect love casteth out fear, Mary Anne. You can't let fear rule your life. That's no way to live. You have to trust somebody sometime. Like *Gotte,* maybe?"

Mary Anne hadn't trusted *Gotte* for a very long time, but Mammi didn't need any bad news to keep her awake tonight. "Maybe I'm the only one I can count on."

Mammi nodded with that wise look in her eyes. "You can always depend on *Gotte.* He'll take care of you, but He's not usually obvious about it."

"God moves in a mysterious way," Mary Anne said, trying to appease Mammi, even though she was pretty sure *Gotte* didn't notice her at all.

"*Ach,*" Mammi said. "People say that because they can't see it. His ways aren't all that mysterious if you're looking for them. He was obvious tonight when He saved our bed and our dresser, but usually *Gotte* works when we're not paying attention. Think about how you and Jethro got together. You met at a wedding in Ohio. Jethro had never gone to Ohio, but *Gotte* got him there so you could meet. What about when you lost the baby? An *Englischer* with a car just happened to be at your house so she could drive you to the hospital. And *Gotte* saved your life that day. I'll never forget how we prayed. Miracles haven't stopped. We just don't look for them anymore."

"But I've asked *Gotte* again and again for a baby, and He doesn't care."

"Oh, my dear, *Gotte* hears our prayers, but He answers them in His way and His time. He's not our personal wish granter."

Mary Anne had never looked at it that way. Did she think she was entitled to anything she asked for? *Vell,* what about all those other women who had babies whenever they wanted?

Mammi leaned closer. "I may be old, but I have a *gute* enough memory to know how babies are made, and you won't ever get a baby while you and Jethro are sleeping in separate tents. *Gotte* is a *Gotte* of miracles, but He's not likely to help if you and Jethro don't do your part."

Mary Anne ignored the heat that traveled up her neck. Sometimes Mammi said the most outrageous things — true, but outrageous. "That still doesn't solve the problem of Jethro. If I moved back in with him, how do I know he won't lose interest again?"

Mammi nodded. "*Ach,* people will let you down. It might even be Jethro who does it. But you can't stop loving him just because you're afraid he'll disappoint you. You forgive, you work it out, and you pull each other along. Sometimes you'll have to carry Jethro, and other times he'll have to carry you."

"I was doing all the carrying." Mary Anne

461

slumped her shoulders. "And I was so tired."

Mammi patted Mary Anne's arm. "Of course you were. Moving out was a wonderful *gute* idea."

"You think it was?"

"Jethro's problem was that he got stuck and you got stuck, and you had to do something dire to make him see it. If anybody knows how to be brave, it's you. You moved out because you wanted a better life. Maybe you've found it again, right where you left it."

Her heart swelled until she almost couldn't breathe. Was that what her journey had been about — three months of camping only to find what she'd been looking for just inside these walls? "I . . . I don't know," she said.

Mammi gave Mary Anne a swift kiss on the cheek. "*Ach,* Mary Anne, you're one of my favorite granddaughters, but it wonders me when you're going to stop punishing Jethro for his mistakes."

It was a horrible thing to say, but Mammi said it with a grandmotherly smile, so Mary Anne tried not to take offense. Punish Jethro? She'd never wanted to punish him. She had simply wanted to live her life her own way, without Jethro telling her what she could and couldn't do. She had been so angry at him for not caring, for being so unfeeling and taking her for granted, for not loving her the way she deserved to be loved. So angry and so hurt.

Ach.

Her cheeks suddenly got hot, as if she was still in that tent with her face to the burning bookshelf. At the time she never would have admitted to such resentment, but buried deep inside her had been the desire to see Jethro suffer, to make him sorry for what he'd done to her.

And he had suffered. The most terrible thing an Amish *fraa* could do to her husband was to move out. It embarrassed him in the *gmayna* and made him a laughingstock among the men. They no doubt questioned his righteousness and gossiped about him as if he were a sinner himself. She had known what would happen, and she secretly had rejoiced when it did.

This terrible truth about herself nearly knocked her over, and she reached out to the wall for support. Hopefully, Mammi didn't notice. "Do you need anything else, Mammi?" she said, trying to appear undisturbed at what she had just discovered about herself.

"Do you have an extra pillow for my feet?"

Dawdi called from the bedroom.

Mary Anne pushed herself from the wall, glad for a reason to turn away from her *mammi*'s searching eye. "There's one in here." She turned the knob on the spare bedroom door, but it wouldn't budge. Had Jethro put a lock on this door too? Was he trying to keep her from stealing more furniture? That couldn't be it. Even though she hadn't set foot in here for weeks, Jethro had told her she was welcome to get anything she wanted from the house.

"Is it stuck?" Mammi said.

Mary Anne jiggled the knob again. It was definitely new and there was definitely a lock on the other side. "Maybe somebody locked it accidentally."

Mammi yawned. "Felty will be all right without an extra pillow this once."

"*Nae*, I won't."

Mary Anne's curiosity got the better of her. She *had* to open the door just to discover why Jethro had locked it. "Let me see if I can open it."

"*Ach, vell.* I'm going to lie down before I fall over. I hope you find what you're looking for."

Mary Anne took Mammi's lantern and went to the kitchen to search the cupboards. Many of her pots and pans and pitchers and spoons had been taken outside. Except for her stoneware, her cupboards were mostly bare. But there was a small box of toothpicks on the top shelf. She got a toothpick out of the box and took it down the hall to the spare bedroom. She didn't often have cause to pick a lock, but when she was growing up, her *mamm* had a small room off the kitchen where she kept all the goodies. She locked it every night, but Mary Anne and Mandy had figured out how to open it with a bobby pin.

After setting the lantern on the floor, Mary Anne inserted the toothpick into the hole and felt around for the little mechanism that would unlock the door. She heard a satisfying click, and the door popped open. Raising the lantern, she shined it into the spare bedroom where Jethro kept his fishing pole. She took a tentative step into the room and gasped.

Eight white chairs surrounded the bed, each with a different scene painted on the seat. She didn't need to look closely to know exactly what was on each chair. She had painted them herself and sold them on Etsy for fifty dollars apiece. The bench Jethro had repaired and sanded sat below the window where the curtains were drawn so no one would be able to look in and spy what was in this room.

Mary Anne moved a chair aside and stepped closer to the bed. Folded neatly on top of the bedspread was a beautiful nine-hundred-dollar quilt with appliquéd butterflies rising into a white sky. Even by the light of the lantern, it was breathtaking.

Unable to support her own weight, Mary Anne sat down in one of her chairs — one of her own kitchen chairs — and stared numbly at the expensive quilt sitting on the bed where Jethro's fishing pole used to be. She thought she might burst with pride and love, shame and confusion.

What had he done, and why had he done it?

Mary Anne knew the answer even though her mind almost couldn't comprehend it. Jethro had sacrificed the kitchen chairs for her painting projects. He'd fixed and sanded a bench he already owned so he could buy it back from her. He'd special-ordered a quilt because he knew how much joy she'd get from sewing butterflies on it. All this time she'd been telling herself that Jethro didn't deserve her, but now she knew the truth. She didn't deserve him, even if she lived to be a thousand years old.

She hung her head, buried her face in her hands, and wept.

CHAPTER NINETEEN

Jethro closed the door behind him and looked into the woods without really seeing. Moses and Lia and Alice and some of the others were still cleaning up from the fire, but he barely paid them any heed as he stumbled in the darkness and felt his way around the side of the house where no one would notice him.

With his back to the wall, he doubled over and squeezed his eyes closed, burying his face in his hands as if he could shut out the world if he just pressed hard enough. His hands trembled, and he balled them into fists. It didn't do any good. Every muscle in his body was taut with energy. With every breath, he felt like he might disintegrate into a pile of sand.

He trembled as the memories washed over him. He'd almost lost Mary Anne once before, and every one of those terrifying emotions came rushing back to him. He had just helped Anna up from her bed and out and away from the burning canopy when he noticed Mary Anne's tent was on fire too. The panic had gripped him so tightly, he nearly lost the ability to move. But move he did, almost knocking Moses over in his desperation to get to Mary Anne in time. He hadn't cared about anything but saving his *fraa,* getting out of that fire, and holding her in his arms.

How could he bear to let her go? How could he possibly hope to survive her leaving him?

Jethro scrubbed a shaking hand down the side of his face. He'd have to find a way, because he couldn't stand the thought of Mary Anne camping in the woods for one more day. It wasn't safe. She had nearly caught fire and barely missed being run over by a runaway motor home. It was only a matter of time before she caught pneumonia or was attacked by a bear. He shuddered at the thought.

No matter how desperately he wanted to keep her close or how devastated he'd be by her leaving, he needed to get her out of the woods, and she needed to go now. He'd have all the arrangements made by morning, and Mary Anne could be somewhere safe by tomorrow night.

The despair weighed so heavily on him that he could barely put one foot in front of the other. Still, he hiked across the back lawn and into the woods, where he draped a tarp over the hole in her tent. It could all be sorted out in the morning.

Most everyone had gone back to bed, but for sure and certain no one would get much sleep. With a small light attached to his suspenders, Aden was helping Moses cover Anna and Felty's bedroom furniture with a tarp and some strips of plastic just in case it rained. "Is Mary Anne okay?" Aden asked when Jethro walked past him.

Jethro nodded. "She didn't breathe in much smoke."

"You got her out fast yet," Aden said. "Is she going to sleep in the house with Mammi and Dawdi?"

"I don't think so." He couldn't offer her the spare bedroom, and she wouldn't agree to stay there even if he could. But she needed a place to sleep, and he wasn't about to let her sleep under the stars. There weren't any stars tonight anyway, and she'd get soaked for sure and certain.

He had to brace himself against a tree to keep from running to her side when she finally came out of the house. She carried a lantern and walked slowly across the lawn.

If her legs felt as unsteady as his, it probably took all her concentration just to put one foot in front of the other without crumpling to the ground.

He couldn't bear to watch her struggle. Meeting her halfway across the lawn, he took the lantern, laced his fingers with hers, and tucked her arm to his side. She hesitated. "How are your grandparents?" he said, because *I'm desperately, madly, achingly in love with you* probably wasn't what she wanted to hear.

She nodded, and he recognized some sort of struggle on her face, though it was dark and hard to tell for sure.

He lifted the lantern and studied her face. She'd been crying. His heart sank even further. It was probably in Wautoma by now. Tears still glistened in her eyes, and their residue smeared over the light dusting of soot that covered her cheeks. He pressed her arm to his side. "*Ach, heartzly,* it's been a rough night."

She nodded again, as if she found it impossible to force a word past her lips.

"Do you want to try to go back to sleep? Your tent is ruined, but if you don't mind coming to the Neuenschwander side of the camp, you can sleep in my tent. I'll roll out a sleeping bag and watch over you while you sleep. If so much as a firefly gets within ten feet, I'll snuff it out."

She might have cracked a smile, even though it faded before he had a chance to enjoy it. "I can't take your tent."

"I want you to, Mary Anne. I won't sleep unless I know you're safe and dry, and the only way to be sure of that is to put you in my tent and guard it from sparks and fireflies." He stopped walking and turned to face her. "Will you . . . will you let me do this for you?" One last gift he could give her before she left him for good. Only the sheer force of his will kept his knees from buckling. How would he live without his Mary Anne?

She searched his face for an answer he couldn't give her. "Okay. But just for tonight. You can't camp out here without a tent. Tomorrow we will have to figure out something else."

"For sure and certain."

They stopped at Mary Anne's charred tent, where Jethro retrieved her sleeping bag, pillow, and a tarp. Then they took the fifty-yard walk to Jethro's tent. The distance between their camps had never seemed so wide.

Jethro's tent was much smaller than Mary Anne's, and she had to get down on her hands and knees to get inside. Jethro spread the tarp, and then Mary Anne's sleeping bag on the ground in front of the tent door. If any creature with sharp teeth and claws wanted to get in, they'd have to go through Jethro first.

He tried to ignore the soft movements on the other side of the tent as Mary Anne got into his sleeping bag and lay her head on his pillow. His longing would drive him crazy if he let it. He slipped into his sleeping bag and rolled onto his back, propping his hands under his head and staring up at the pitch-black sky. A flash of light traveled between two clouds, and the sky rumbled like a sleeping giant. Rain was only a few minutes away. When it came, he'd wrap himself up like a sandwich with the tarp on the top and bottom. He'd be dry enough. At least there wouldn't be any more fires tonight.

Mary Anne's soft voice floated from behind the tent flap. "Your pillow smells like you."

"Is that okay? Do you want to trade?"

"*Nae.* I . . . I like it."

"Oh."

She made a slight movement. Her arm, a hand, or maybe she'd rolled over. He probably should move far enough away not to hear her, or he'd never get to sleep. "Jethro?"

He loved the smooth timbre of her voice, like melted butter sliding across a stack of pancakes. *"Jah?"*

"Can I tell you something?"

"Anything, *heartzly.*"

"I'm sorry about how I've treated you."

Jethro hadn't expected that, especially because it was so unnecessary and so untrue. "You have nothing, *nothing,* to apologize for."

Her voice sounded so close, as if her face was right up against the canvas. "I understand why the bishop said, 'Is it I?' Because it was me. It was all my fault."

Jethro didn't know where this had come from, but he couldn't let her go on believing it. "You took the blame for everything, *heartzly.* You aren't the one who needed the bishop's lesson."

"I blamed you in my heart."

"As you should have. If I had been a better husband, you wouldn't have moved out." His voice faltered. If he had been a better husband, he wouldn't be losing his best reason for living. It had been his fault, and it was a bitter pill to swallow.

"I blamed you and *Gotte* for the baby, and I couldn't very well move out on *Gotte.* Mammi says He's always with me no matter where I go."

Jethro shook his head, even though she couldn't see it. "Mary Anne, you were brave enough to do what you had to do. I was thoughtless for not even asking you how you felt about infertility treatments. I should have found a way to pay for them. I should have talked instead of shutting you out. I should have loved you better."

"I should have put up more of a fight."

"You thought I was disappointed in you. You wouldn't have dared."

She was silent for so long he thought she had fallen asleep. "That's true." Another long pause. "I was angry, Jethro. I confess I wanted to hurt you."

"What did you do that I didn't deserve? Nobody likes to hear their sins shouted from the rooftops, but sometimes it's the only way to make a person understand. You forced me to see the kind of husband I was."

"At least you were willing to change. Another husband would have been too stubborn to admit he was wrong," she said.

Jethro wanted to draw hope from that small concession, but he couldn't be so careless with his heart. "I was stubborn at first. I told you we were stuck with each other and that we might as well make the best of it."

"I'm sorry you got stuck with me, Jethro." There was so much sorrow in her voice.

"I was angry, Mary Anne. Don't believe for one minute I think I'm stuck."

"But I'm useless to you."

"Useless?" He propped his elbow on the sleeping bag and rested his head on his hand. "Mary Anne, your most fertile part isn't your womb. It's your heart. That's where you dream and plan and imagine. That's where you nurture the seed of creation. Look what you've created since you've been in the woods."

"A few quilts and a couple of chairs to sell."

"It's more than a quilt and some chairs, though those are beautiful. You underestimate the joy they bring to people. But you've created so much more than that. Before you moved out, you had created a home with order and beauty. A place where everyone wanted to be, where I wanted to be. The place where my heart was. Then you brought all your cousins together to camp."

"That wasn't my doing," she whispered.

"It *was* your doing. They came together because they love you. And look what you've created in me. I have a new heart. For sure and certain you never thought that would happen."

"*Nae.*" She must be close to sleep now. He could barely hear her. "I never did."

I never did. It was like the final nail in his coffin. She didn't believe him. Did she feel anything for him at all? Friendship? Pity? Disdain? He couldn't be sure, and he didn't dare ask. If she told him she still despised him, he didn't think he'd have the strength to get up in the morning. Better to imagine she didn't hate him than to hear the sharp and devastating truth.

He couldn't tell her he loved her, though the words were trying to pry his lips open and leap out of his mouth. If she knew how much he wanted her, ached for her, loved her, she would only feel guiltier about leaving him.

His heart broke completely, and there wasn't even a night bird to witness it.

He rolled over on his side facing away from the tent. *I love you, Mary Anne,* he mouthed, though not a sound came from his lips.

His silence was the only thing he had left to give her.

CHAPTER TWENTY

Maybe Jethro didn't love her anymore.

If she hadn't been so completely exhausted, that thought would have kept her awake all night. As it was, it woke her up at about four a.m. and made it impossible to go back to sleep.

She desperately wanted to believe Jethro had bought those chairs and that quilt because he loved her, because he wanted to make her happy. But the realistic, brokenhearted part of her couldn't let herself consider such a possibility. Jethro wanted her gone. He was just trying to help her earn the money faster, so he could move back into the house before autumn.

Who could blame him? From the first, she had wanted to hurt him, and she had done a fine job of it. How could he love her when she'd been so cruel? Still, something whispered to her heart that Jethro had spent all that money for her and only her, though she couldn't understand why he would do such a thing when he knew she was planning on leaving. It didn't make sense. What could Jethro possibly gain from buying her chairs?

No wonder she had woken up so early. No wonder her heart hurt like an open wound.

After two hours of trying to toss and turn quietly so she wouldn't wake Jethro, Mary Anne gave up. It had to be almost six a.m. Surely Jethro would be awake. Maybe she could tell him how much his buying her furniture meant to her. Maybe she could confess that she loved him and that despite everything, she wanted to try their marriage again. Maybe she should just go stick her head in a bucket of cold water for all the good it would do her.

She slowly unzipped her tent. Had it rained last night? She hadn't heard a thing. The tarp lay in front of the tent door, but the sleeping bag was gone, as was the pillow. She hadn't heard Jethro get up, but she also hadn't heard the rain, even though there were puddles everywhere and the fresh smell of clean earth filled the air. Maybe he'd moved into the barn to get out of the rain.

Another twinge of guilt stung her like a

rubber band flipped at the back of her head. She shouldn't have taken his tent and left him out in the rain. But he'd asked her to let him do it. Her heart galloped around her chest. Jethro had wanted her to stay dry. That sounded like love to her. Maybe there was hope.

In the half light of the coming sunrise, she crawled out of her tent, which wasn't really her tent — just one more thing she had taken from Jethro, one more thing he'd been more than happy to give up for her. She could hardly bear the shame of her own behavior.

No one else was awake or at least out of their tents yet. Lord willing, Mammi and Dawdi would sleep until noon. They needed the rest more than anybody. At least they were in the house, warm and dry and safe.

Mary Anne tiptoed to her charred tent to inspect the damage. Her sewing machine and all her fabrics and paints hadn't been touched. Everything was safe and dry, even the new quilt top she was working on. The actual tent was where all the damage had been done. Someone had draped a tarp over the burned side of the tent. Her cot was right where she'd left it. It smelled like smoke but had been untouched by the rainstorm. The bookshelf was a pile of ashes, though some of her dishes and pots and pans had survived, but they would need to be thoroughly scrubbed before she could use them again. All things considered, she'd come out okay. She hadn't been planning on buying Jethro a new tent until she'd moved into a place of her own, but now she'd have to dip into her savings or she'd have nowhere to live for the rest of the summer.

Until she'd moved into a place of her own.

The thought hit her with a wave of nausea. She didn't want a place of her own. She wanted to be with Jethro, just when he wanted to get rid of her. All this time she thought she was being strong and stubborn. Now strength felt a lot like pride. Her precious freedom seemed like nothing but loneliness. She couldn't imagine any kind of life without Jethro. What had she done?

She sank to her cot as a quiet sob escaped her lips. Had she learned her lesson too late?

Suddenly, unexpectedly, Jethro was there, gathering her into his arms and holding her close. She melted into his embrace and let him stroke her back and whisper comforting words into her ear. "*Ach, heartzly,* I'm sorry. I know it looks bad now, but we'll find you a new home. I'll build you a new bookshelf. You can repaint the butterflies."

It took Mary Anne a few seconds to realize he was referring to the butterflies in the tent. They had burned away. *Ach,* if only he knew how little she cared about those butterflies now.

Just as she was about to ask him to never let go, he drew away from her. "Mary Anne, I don't want you to camp here anymore, even for one more night."

Ach! Her chest tightened, and she couldn't even draw a breath to beg him to take her back.

He slid his hand into his pocket and pulled out a paper. Pressing his lips together, he studied her face, for sure and certain looking for something, though she didn't know what. "I should have done this weeks ago, but I just couldn't bear to." He took her hand. "Ron Barker is a friend of mine at work. He has a cabin near the lake that he's willing to rent. It's wonderful small, but he'll let you have it for cheap if I'll do some repairs on it. It's not much, but at least it will get you out of the woods."

"You want me out of the woods?" She could barely form the words.

"I want you to be safe." He lowered his head. "You make the final decision. I won't force you to do anything, but I just . . ." He ran the back of his hand down the beard on his chin. "I can't stand it, Mary Anne. Last night, the terror almost buried me. Either you have to move out of the woods or I sleep at your tent door every night with my hunting rifle and a bucket of water."

Did he want her gone because he didn't love her anymore or because that was what he thought would make her happy? Her throat was so tight, it was like forcing air from a tiny straw. "Jethro, do you love me?"

It was almost as if he hadn't heard her. He unfolded the paper in his hand. It was a check. A check with lots of zeros on it. "I went to my *dat* this morning, and he gave me the three thousand dollars he was going to offer me four years ago. I've saved another seven thousand. I want you to have it. I want you to have the life you've always dreamed of."

With trembling hands, she took the check from him. Ten thousand dollars! She'd never seen that much money in her whole life. It made her a little dizzy and a little ill. Jethro was willing to give her everything he had. If that wasn't love, she didn't know what was. Her heart pounded against her ribs as if it wanted to get out of her chest. "Jethro," she said, her voice trembling like a newly hatched chick. "Do you love me?"

He folded his arms and looked away.

"Mary Anne . . . I don't want to . . ." He took a deep breath, pain flashing like lightning in his eyes. "I don't want to make you sad or uncomfortable, but I love you more than any man has ever loved his wife, and I want to be with you more than I want to breathe."

He could probably hear her heart beating but was too polite to mention it. Would he catch her if she happened to faint? Of course. Jethro would always be there for her, no matter what.

"But I would feel terrible if you felt guilty about it," he said. "One of us was bound to get hurt, and it's only fitting that it should be me after all the pain I put you through. I want you to be happy. And if that means I'm not a part of your life, I'll accept it. If you're happy, I'll be happy."

She nearly tackled him with her unbridled joy. Surprise popped all over his face as she threw herself into his arms. He may have been surprised, but Jethro was always ready to catch her. He lifted her off the ground, and she smashed her lips into his — not the most graceful kiss she'd ever given him but definitely the most eager. He tightened his arms around her.

Ach. She had forgotten the heat and power of his touch — the passion that welled inside her with a mere kiss. Of course, the feeling was almost overpowering because this was no mere kiss. The memories surged through her like a flash flood, leaving her gasping for air.

She felt the tears on her cheeks before she even realized she was crying. She had never been this happy or this troubled before. She loved Jethro with all her heart, but how could they ever fix the damage they'd both done?

He must have sensed her tears. Keeping one arm around her, he set her on her feet and cupped his hand around her cheek. "I love you, *heartzly,* but that doesn't mean you're obligated to love me back."

"But I do," she said, unable to control the sobs that wracked her body. "I love you, Jethro."

His face lit up like the sun before he lowered his head. She could feel his deep, quivering breaths. "I've waited to hear that for so long."

She kissed his cheek and lay her head on his shoulder. He enfolded her into an embrace as if he'd never consider letting her go. "I'm afraid, Jethro. Do you think we can ever make it back to where we were?"

He shook his head. "We've come too far to ever go back. As *gute* as our first years were, the next years will only be better. We have learned so many painful lessons. With *Gotte*'s help, we'll only grow more and more in love. Look at your grandparents. I want to be like them and grow old together. There will be more love and more joy than we ever could have imagined. I want to try. Will you try with me?"

She nodded. What else could she do? The thought of being without him broke her heart.

"You can keep the money in case I ever disappoint you again. I don't think camping is the answer to any of our problems."

"Nae," Mary Anne said. "This isn't my money, and it isn't your money, Jethro. It's our money, and it always has been."

"I know," he said. "I can't believe I accused you of stealing that two hundred dollars. It was just as much yours as it was mine, as is the house and the barn and this expensive tent. Everything is ours together. I'm sorry I didn't see it before."

Mary Anne ran her finger along the numbers on the check. "What would you say to using our money to try for a baby?"

His eyes glistened, and his look made her feel mushy inside. "I'd like that very much." He tugged one of her *kapp* strings. "But remember, you will always be enough. If you're with me, I will never want for another thing in my life. Do you understand?"

"Jah," she said. "I know that now." That knowledge was what freedom truly meant.

He brought his lips down on hers, and they shared a gentle, desperate kiss that was both an ending and a beginning. Right that minute was the start of their new lives together.

And the end of her days in a tent.

Praise the Lord.

"I see you two have finally come to your senses."

Mary Anne snapped her head around. Sarah Beachy stood outside the open door of the tent with her hands propped on her hips and her lips puckered in disgust. Jethro kissed Mary Anne again and faced Sarah with an unashamed look on his face. Mary Anne giggled. "I suppose we have."

"It's about time. My canopy is ruined, Johnny has started eating the bark off trees, and Pine has adopted a flock of wild chickens." Sarah kneaded a spot on her lower back. "And I'm sure I've developed a bulging disc and maybe polio. I'll be bedridden until Christmas. I hope you're happy."

Jethro squeezed Mary Anne's hands. "We are. Very happy."

Sarah shook her head. "Mammi always

said you were thick as a slab of strawberry pie, Jethro, but I had no idea it would take you this long to learn your lesson." She twisted her lips in what might have passed for a smile. "I suppose nothing important is ever easy. And my boys have gained a great appreciation for their beds and their *mamm*'s cooking. It wasn't all bad."

"I hope you know how much I appreciate your support."

Sarah waved away any talk of gratitude. "We're family, and family sticks together."

"Denki."

"And my Aaron has missed me something wonderful. I have you to thank for that, Mary Anne. It's *gute* for a husband to cherish his *fraa*. That's worth a whole year in the woods."

Jethro took Mary Anne's hand and led her out of the stinky tent. He kept holding her hand in plain view of Sarah. "Should we tell the others they can break camp?"

Mary Anne smiled. "They'll be so happy."

Mammi and Dawdi came trudging across the lawn, looking as if they'd had a rough time of it last night. Of course they'd had a rough time of it. Their canopy had burned down around their heads. Mammi's *kapp* was askew on her head, and her hair stuck out in directions that shouldn't have been possible. Dawdi's limp was back, and the dark circles under his eyes looked to be in the shape of two of the Great Lakes.

Mary Anne didn't want any delay in the *gute* news. She ran to Mammi's side and took her hand. Sarah and Jethro followed close behind. "Mammi, Jethro and I have decided to get back together. I'm moving back into the house, and you and Dawdi can go home."

Mammi frowned. "Now, Mary Anne, you don't have to pretend for my sake. I don't care that my tent has burned down. I'm determined to stay here until the bitter end and die with solidarity on my lips."

Sarah blew out a huge puff of air. "Mammi, you're even more stubborn than I am."

"*Nae,* Mammi, it's true." Mary Anne grabbed Jethro's hand and pulled him close to her. "I love Jethro, and he loves me. We want to try again."

Mammi eyed Jethro as if he might have a dread disease. "But Mary Anne, Jethro came to your birthday party and hogged all your cake in a grapefruit. He tried to kidnap us in the RV. He got rid of all your kitchen chairs. Are you sure you want to forgive him?"

Mary Anne laughed. "I'm sure, Mammi.

And he's not as bad as all that. He saved you from the fire and always brought fresh towels out to the barn bathroom. Once, he gave me a maple bacon doughnut."

Mammi's mouth fell open. "Maple bacon? Whoever heard of such a thing?"

Mary Anne had to smile to herself. The thought of a maple bacon doughnut was appalling to the woman who made oyster spinach salad for special occasions. "I'm serious, Mammi. I love Jethro. I never want to be without him again."

Mammi thought about it for a few seconds. She must have been counting Jethro's faults in her head. Then she bloomed into a smile and clapped her hands with as much enthusiasm as a weary eighty-five-year-old woman could muster. "I told Felty how it would be, didn't I, Felty?"

"*Jah.* You're smarter than a whole roomful of scholars, Banannie."

Mammi patted Mary Anne's cheek. "If you can stand to live with him, I won't stand in your way. Solidarity is over. We're moving home, Felty."

Was Mary Anne seeing things, or did Dawdi kick up his heels? She was probably imagining it. Dawdi was eighty-seven. Kicking up anything would for sure and certain put him in the hospital.

Mammi looked at Sarah. "Do you think your boys could help us move our bed back to our house?"

"*Jah.* It won't take but two hours."

"But what about my chickens? It will take all of us to round up my chickens."

Jethro glanced doubtfully at Mary Anne. Nobody but Mammi held out hope for the chickens. "We'll do what we can. I think there's still one under your bed."

Mammi smiled and nodded. "Sharon. She's always been the most loyal."

Sarah looked to the east side of the house and narrowed her eyes. "Is that a goat?"

They heard it — or rather them — before they saw it. A whole herd of goats bounded around the side of the house, making all sorts of noise and running in every direction. Most of them headed straight for Jethro's beautiful patch of green lawn, where they wasted no time in eating as much as they could. Cousin Titus followed behind them with a shepherd's crook in his hand, a toothpick between his teeth, and his wife Katie by his side. Katie was the sweetest, quietest girl Mary Anne had ever met, but she was the perfect *fraa* for Titus, who was as simple and guileless as a child.

Titus grinned when he laid eyes on their little group standing in the middle of the lawn with the unruly goats. "*Hallo*, Mammi and Dawdi! Jethro and Mary Anne! I heard there was a protest or something. Katie Rose and I decided to come and help, but we couldn't leave our goats at home. I hope it's okay that we brought them. They just need a little grass and a tub of water and they'll be fine."

"*Ach*, Titus," Mammi said. "You were always so thoughtful that way. No wonder you're one of my favorites."

Sarah looked up to the sky. "The Lord works in mysterious ways, and not a minute too soon."

Mary Anne reached out for Katie's hand. "It's so kind of you to come, but Jethro and I have decided to try to work things out. I'm moving back into the house, and everyone is taking down their tents and going home."

Katie gave Mary Anne a half smile. "*Ach.* I'm *froh* you've worked it out but disappointed we won't be able to camp. Titus and I love camping."

Titus smiled at Katie Rose as if she were the sun, the moon, and the stars — the best part of his life. It warmed Mary Anne's heart. That was how marriage should be. "Maybe we could camp here anyway. You wouldn't mind camping a few extra days,

491

would you, Sarah, just to keep us company?"

Sarah's glare could have peeled all the paint off those chairs Mary Anne had painted. "Titus Helmuth, you're going to take those goats back to your farm right this minute, and you won't breathe another word about camping. Is that clear?"

Titus's jaw dropped, and his toothpick dangled from his bottom lip. "I suppose so."

Sarah nodded. "*Gute.* I'll go pack." She made a beeline for her tent. No doubt she'd be ready to go in less than an hour.

CHAPTER TWENTY-ONE

Mary Anne had never seen anything quite like it. Mammi had assured her that people would come, but surely even Mammi couldn't have expected this crowd. There had to be at least fifty *Englischers* plus that many more Amish folks lined up at the starting line. Many of the *Englischers* were dressed in colorful clothes with fancy running shoes. Some of the Amish also wore fancy shoes. Others had on their plain black work shoes.

All these people had come to the First Annual Mary Anne and Jethro Neuenschwander Fund-Raiser 5K. Mary Anne hadn't been completely comfortable that Mammi had named a race after her, but Mammi had been insistent.

"We can't call it the First Annual Mary-Anne-and-Jethro-Want-to-Have-a-Baby Race, or the Dash for Infertility," Mammi had said. "That would be completely inappropriate."

Mammi had also liked "First Annual" attached to the title. "Then people can have something to look forward to next year."

A 5K had been Alice Swanson's idea. "It doesn't cost much, and people love to run — even the Amish. I've seen them."

Alice, Judy, and Dennis had helped Mammi make flyers and post the race on Facebook and other sites on the Internet. They charged twenty dollars to enter the race and another ten dollars for a T-shirt. Lia, Lily, and Mandy had organized a bake sale at the top of Huckleberry Hill, right on Mammi and Dawdi's wide front porch, and Dawdi had offered to give tours of the house and barn for ten dollars apiece, with a special treat baked by Mammi at the end of the tour. The *Englischers* loved anything Amish — even Mammi's baked goods. Dawdi had already given three tours and the race hadn't even started yet.

Dennis had mapped out a circular route so the 5K started and ended on Huckleberry Hill. Several of Mary Anne's cousins plus her in-laws stood along the route to direct people where to run, and Sarah and her boys had set up three water stations along the way, just in case a runner got thirsty.

It was a rare October day, not cold or rainy at all, as if Heaven was smiling down on their effort to raise money for the treatments ahead. Mary Anne pressed her hand against her heart. *Gotte* was so *gute.* How could she bear so much happiness?

Jethro had been working at the registration table, collecting money and handing out T-shirts. He climbed the porch steps and sidled next to Mary Anne as she gazed at the crowd of runners waiting for the race to start. "We were only missing one T-shirt, but Alice found it." He scooted closer so his arm brushed against hers. "I . . . I can't believe it, Mary Anne."

"I know," she whispered to keep her voice from cracking. "All these people. They don't even know us." Maybe she shouldn't touch him in public like this, but Mary Anne slipped her arm around Jethro's elbow. She craved the comfort of his steady and dependable touch. He kept her grounded, and the way she felt right now, she thought she just might float off the ground. "Should we tell her?" she said, watching Mammi as she bustled among the runners, making sure everyone's shoes were tied correctly and checking to see if they had applied enough sunscreen.

Jethro placed his hand over hers and

smiled. "Not yet. We don't want to spoil her fun, and we only found out ourselves this morning." He tugged her backward, past the busy bake sale and into the house, where all was quiet. Dawdi had suspended all tours until the race was over. Jethro wrapped his arms around her and kissed her like he was trying to make up for lost time. They parted, both of them breathless and wildly happy. "Mary Anne, my precious ruby. I've been wanting to do that all morning. I only have so much willpower."

She grinned. "Me too." She moved in for another kiss, confident that they had at least five minutes before someone came to find them. She held on to Jethro as tightly as she could.

Even though she knew she had many hard miles and long years ahead of her, Mary Anne's heart was filled to overflowing. She was learning to trust *Gotte* and Jethro, learning to let go of her fears, learning to speak her mind and let Jethro speak his. Learning to truly give her heart to someone who might break it, willing to be Jethro's rock and to let him be hers.

They needed each other now more than ever.

There was a baby coming in the spring.

ABOUT THE AUTHOR

Jennifer Beckstrand is the RITA nominated and award-winning author of the Matchmakers of Huckleberry Hill and The Honeybee Sisters series, as well as a number of novellas. Novels in her Matchmakers of Huckleberry Hill series have been RITA® Award and *RT Book Reviews* Reviewer's Choice Award finalists. *Huckleberry Hill* won the 2014 LIME Award for inspirational fiction and *Huckleberry Hearts* was named a *Booklist* Top 10 Inspirational Fiction Book of the Year. Jennifer has always been drawn to the strong faith and the enduring family ties of the Plain people. She and her husband have been married for thirty-three years, and she has four daughters, two sons, and four adorable grandchildren, whom she spoils rotten. Please visit her online at www .JenniferBeckstrand.com.